John Sandford is the pseudonym for the Pulitzer Prize-winning journalist John Camp. He is the author of *Rules of Prey*, *Shadow Prey*, *Eyes of Prey*, *Silent Prey*, *The Iceman*, *Night Prey*, *Mind Prey* and *Sudden Prey*.

The
Night Crew

John Sandford

HEADLINE
FEATURE

First published in Great Britain in 1997
by HEADLINE BOOK PUBLISHING

First published in paperback in 1998
by HEADLINE BOOK PUBLISHING

A HEADLINE FEATURE paperback

10 9 8 7 6 5 4 3 2 1

ISBN 0 7472 5621 7

Typeset by CBS, Felixstowe, Suffolk

Printed and bound in Great Britain by
Mackays of Chatham PLC, Chatham, Kent

HEADLINE BOOK PUBLISHING
A division of Hodder Headline PLC
338 Euston Road
London NW1 3BH

For Susan again

Chapter 1

The corner of Gayley and Le Conte, at the edge of the campus:

Frat boys cruised in their impeccably clean racing-green Miatas and cherry-red Camaro ragtops, with their impeccably blonde dates, all square shoulders, frothy dresses and big white teeth.

Two skinny kids, one of each sex, smelling of three-day sweat and dressed all in black, unwrapped Ding-Dongs and talked loud about Jesus and the Joy to Come; celebrating Him – and vanilla-creme filling.

At the Shell station, a tanker truck pumped Premium down a hole in the concrete pad, under the eye of a big-bellied driver.

And above them all, a quarter-million miles out, a buttery new moon smiled down as it slid toward the Pacific.

The Bee was impatient, checking her watch, bouncing on her toes. She was waiting at the corner, a Jansport backpack at her feet. Her face was a pale crescent in the headlights of passing cars, in the Los Angeles never-dark.

The Shell tanker driver stood in a puddle of gasoline

fumes, chewed a toothpick and watched her in a casual, looking-at-women way. The Bee was dressed by Banana Republic, in khaki wash pants, a T-shirt with a queen bee on the chest, a photographer's vest with fifteen pockets, hiking boots and a preppy black-silk ski mask rolled up and worn as a watch cap.

When she saw the truck with the dish on the roof, she pulled the mask down over her face, picked up the backpack, and stepped out to the curb. The Bee had small opaque-green eyes, like turquoise thumbtacks on the black mask.

Anna Batory, riding without her seatbelt, her feet braced on the truck's plastic dashboard, saw the Bee step out to the curb and pointed: 'There she is.'

Creek grunted and eased the truck to the curb. Anna rolled down the passenger-side window and spoke to the mask: 'You're the Bee?'

'You're late,' the Bee snapped.

Anna glanced at the dashboard clock, then back out the window: 'Jason said ten-thirty.'

Jason was sitting in the back of the truck on a gray metal folding chair, next to Louis. He looked up from his Sony chip-cam and said, 'That's what they told me. Ten-thirty.'

'It's *now* ten-thirty-*three*,' the Bee said. She turned her wrist to show the blue face on a stainless-steel Rolex.

'Sorry,' Anna said.

'I don't think that's good enough,' the Bee said. 'We might be too late, and it's all wasted.'

Behind the Bee, the Shell gas-delivery man was taking

2

an interest: a lot of people in a TV truck and a blonde in a ski mask, arguing.

'You better get in,' Anna said. She could smell the fumes from the gas as she turned and pushed back the truck's side door. Louis caught it and pulled it the rest of the way. The Bee looked at the two men in the back, nodded and said, 'Jason,' to Jason, said nothing to Louis and climbed aboard.

'Around the corner to Westwood, then Westwood to Circle,' the Bee said. 'You know where Circle is?'

'Yeah, we know where everything is,' Creek said. They'd been everywhere. 'Hold on.'

Creek took the truck around the corner, humming to himself, which he did when he was tightening up. Anna turned back to the Bee, found the other woman gaping at Creek, and grinned.

Creek looked vaguely like the Wookiee in *Star Wars*: six-seven, overmuscled and hairy. He was wearing a USMC sweatshirt with the sleeves and neck torn out. Tattoos covered his arms: just visible through the reddish-blond hair on his biceps was an American flag in red, blue and Appalachia-white, skin deeply tanned, with the scrolled sentiment, 'These colors don't run'.

'Hello?' Anna lifted a hand to break the stare. The Bee tore her eyes away from Creek. 'We need some facts and figures,' Anna said. 'How many people on the raid, where you're based, what specifically you object to – like that.'

'We've got it all here, but we've got to hurry,' the Bee said. She dug into the backpack, came up with a plastic portfolio and took out a sheet of crisp white paper. Anna flicked on the overhead reading light.

The press release was tight, professional, laser-printed. A two-color pre-printed logo of a running mustang set off the words 'Free Hearts' at the top of the page.

'Are these quotes from you or from the collective?' Anna asked, ticking the paper with a fingernail.

'Anything that's in quotes, you can attribute to either me or the Rat. We wrote the statement jointly.'

'Will we meet the Rat?' Anna asked. She passed the press release to Louis, who slipped it in a spring clip on the side of the fax.

'He's in the building now,' the Bee said, leaning left to peer past Anna out the windshield. 'Turn left here,' she said. Creek slowed for the turn.

'We'd like to get an action quote when they come out, as they release the animals,' Anna said.

'No problem. We can accommodate that.' The Bee looked at her Rolex, then back out the window. They were right in the middle of the UCLA medical complex. 'I'm sorry I'm so . . . snappy . . . but when Jason agreed to ten-thirty, we specified *exactly* ten-thirty. The raid is already under way.'

Anna nodded and turned to Louis. 'How're the radios?'

Louis Martinez sat in an office swivel chair that was bolted to the floor of the truck. From the chair, he could reach the scanners and transmitters, the dual editing stations, the fax and phones, any of the screens in the steel racks.

He fiddled with the gear incessantly, trying to capture a mental picture of after-dark Los Angeles, in terms of accidents, shootings, car chases, fires, riots.

'All clear,' he said. 'We've got that shooting down in

Inglewood, but that ain't much. There's a chase down south, Long Beach, but it's heading the other way.'

'Track it,' Anna said. Cop chases had produced at least two famous video clips in the past couple of years. If you could get out in front of one, and catch it coming by, it was a sure sale.

'I got it,' Louis said. He pushed his glasses up his nose and grinned at the Bee with his screwy nerd-charm. 'Why'd you choose Bee?' he asked.

'I didn't want a warm and fuzzy animal. That's not the point of animal rescue,' the Bee said. Her response was remote, canned, and Louis' grin slipped a fraction of an inch.

'And that's why Steve picked Rat,' Jason suggested.

The Bee frowned at the use of Rat's real name, but nodded. 'Yes. And because we feel a spiritual affinity with our choices.'

In the driver's seat, Creek grunted again, shook his head once, quick. Anna was watching him, taking his temperature: He didn't like these people and he didn't like the professional PR points – the press release, the theatrical ski mask. Too much like a setup, and Creek was pure.

A smile curled one corner of Anna's mouth. She could read Creek's mind if she could see his eyes. Creek knew that. He glanced at her, then deliberately pulled his eyes away and said, quickly: 'There's a guy on the corner.'

Ahead and to the right, a woman in a ski mask was standing on the corner, making a *hurry-up* windmilling motion with one arm.

'That's Otter,' she said. 'And that's the corner of Circle. They must be out – turn right.'

Creek took the corner, past the waving woman. The street tilted uphill, and a hundred yards up, a cluster of women spilled down a driveway to the street, two of them struggling with a blue plastic municipal garbage can. A security guard was running down from the top of the hill, another one trailing behind.

'Got them coming out,' Anna said, over her shoulder. A quick pulse ran through her: not quite excitement, but some combination of pleasure and apprehension.

Nobody ever knew for sure what would happen at these things. Nothing much, probably, but any time you had guards with guns . . . Did the guards have guns? She took a half-second to look, but couldn't tell.

As she looked, she reached behind her, lifted the lid on the steel box bolted on the back of her seat, pulled the Nagra tape recorder from its foam nest. Jason was looking past her, through the windshield at the action, and she snapped: 'Get ready.'

'Yes, Mom,' he said. He fitted a headset over the crown of his head, plugged in the earphone. Creek was driving with one hand, pulling on his own headset.

'Everybody hear me?' Anna asked, speaking into her face mike. The radios were one-way: Anna talked, everyone else listened.

Creek said, 'Yeah,' and took the truck over the curb, one big bounce and a nose-down, squealing, full stop. Jason had braced himself, and Louis had swiveled to let the chair take the jolt. The Bee toppled over and yelped, 'Shit.'

Ahead of them, the women carrying the garbage can were jerking and twisting down the driveway, doing the media polka – looking for the cameras, running for the lights, trying to stay away from the guards.

The raiders had gone into the back of the building, over a loading dock; the dock was contained inside a fence, with a concrete patio big enough for fifteen or twenty cars. At least a dozen women, all masked, milled around the patio; then a man ran out of the medical building, carrying a small, squealing, black-and-white pig. Then another woman, carrying boxes, or maybe cages.

As the truck settled, as Bee yelped, Anna was out and running, the Nagra banging against her leg. Jason was two steps behind her with the backup Sony, and Creek was out the driver's door, his camera up on his shoulder, off to Anna's left. Bee, a little out of shape, sputtered in their wake.

Then Creek lit up and Anna yelled at the man with the pig, 'Bring the pig. Bring the pig this way . . . Bring the pig.' The man saw them coming and walked toward them, and she had the Nagra's mike pointed at the squealing pig and Jason lit up.

The security guards saw the camera lights and the first one turned to the man trailing, yelled something to the other, who ran back up the hill. The first one continued down, and shouted at Creek, 'Hey, no cameras here, no cameras.'

A group of masked women headed toward him, walled him off from the rest of the milling crowd, pushed him toward the ramp. Frustrated, he climbed up the loading dock and hurried to the open door. Just as he was about to go through the door, he jumped back, and a young man in a blue oxford cloth shirt and jeans ran out of the building and headed toward the lights.

Anna said to the microphone, her voice calm, even, 'Creek, there's a kid coming in, watch him. Jason, stay with the pig.'

Creek backpedaled. When Anna spoke into his ear, he'd looked up from his eyepiece and spotted the kid in the blue shirt: trouble, maybe. Trouble made good movies. The kid was striding toward them, a dark smear under his nose, one hand cupping his jaw. He seemed to be crying.

'They were gonna kill this pig, for nothing – for soap tests or something, shampoo,' the masked pig-man shouted at Jason's camera. The pig was freaking out, long shrieking bleats, like a woman being stabbed. 'She's gonna live now,' pig-man shouted, as the pig struggled against him. 'She's gonna live.'

The patio was chaos, with the cameras and the Pig-man, the women with cages, all swirling around. Blue shirt arrived and Anna saw that he *was* crying, tears running down his cheeks as Creek tracked him with the lens. The dark smear was blood, which streamed from his nose and across his lips and chin.

'Give me that pig,' he screamed, and he ran at the pig-man. 'Gimme that.' The animal women blocked him out, not hitting him, just body blocking. Both Creek and Jason tracked the twirling scrum while Anna tried to stay out of their line; she kept the Nagra pointed, picking up the overall noise, which could be laid back into the tape later, if needed.

The Bee caught Anna's arm: 'He's just a flunky, forget him,' she shouted, over the screams and grunting of the struggle. 'But we're gonna do the mice now. Get the mice, in the garbage cans.'

The women with the blue garbage can were waiting their turn with the lights, and Anna spoke into the mike again: 'Jason, get out of there. Go over to that blue garbage can, it's full of mice, they're gonna turn them loose.' Jason took a step back, lifted his head, spotted the garbage can. 'Creek, stay with the kid,' Anna said. 'Stay with the kid.'

As Jason came up, the women with the garbage can, who'd been waiting, popped the lid and tipped it, and two hundred or three hundred mice, some black, some white, some tan, scurried down the sides and ran out onto the patio, looked around and headed for the nearest piece of cover.

Jason hung close and then the kid in the blue shirt went that way, screaming, 'Gimme those,' and, sobbing, tried to corral the mice. They were everywhere, running over his feet, over his hands, avoiding him, making the break. He finally gave up and slumped on the ground, his head in his hands, the mice all around.

Jeez: this is almost too good, Anna thought.

As Creek tracked him, the Bee came back with her nagging voice: 'Do you want an on-camera statement?'

And Anna thought, *Who's running this thing?* But she had to smile at the other woman's effective management: 'Yeah, but we'd better hurry,' Anna said. 'The cops'll be coming.'

Anna said into the mike, 'Jason, get on the Bee, she'll make a statement.' She pushed the mike up, raised her voice, shouted, 'Rat, where are you?'

The man with the pig turned toward her: 'I'm the Rat,' he said. His teeth were bared, his face spotted with what looked like mud, but could be pig shit.

'We're gonna need you over here: we need a comment,' Anna said.

'No problem,' he said. He handed the struggling pig to a woman. 'What exactly do you want?' The Rat had a deep, smooth voice, a singer's baritone. His eyes were pale blue behind the black mask.

'Just tell us why you did it,' Anna said, nodding at Jason's camera.

He leaned forward and stage-whispered, 'For the publicity.'

Anna grinned back and said, 'Tell that to the camera.'

Jason yelled, 'Hey, Rat: You wanna do this, or what?'

As the Rat and the Bee talked to Jason's camera, Anna pulled the mike down in front of her face and said, 'Creek, let's talk to the kid. Let me in there first.'

Creek hung back a couple of steps, so the camera wouldn't be right in the kid's face. Anna squatted next to him, and patted him on the shoulder. 'Are you okay?'

The kid looked up, dazed, a pale teenage child with brown eyes behind his gold-rimmed glasses. 'What?'

'Are you okay?' Anna asked again.

'They're gonna fire me,' he said. He looked back at the building. 'I was supposed to watch them. They were my responsibility, the animals. I was supposed to keep everybody out, but they came in so fast . . .'

'How'd you get the bloody nose?' Anna asked.

'I tried to hold the door, but they kicked through. Then about four of them held me and I couldn't get to the phone, and they tipped everything over in the lab, all the animal cages, everything.' He touched his face. 'I think the door hit me . . .'

'Look, there's gonna be two sides to this,' Anna said. She looked back at Creek, and said, 'Creek.'

Creek stepped away, spotted a mouse looking at him from the top of the loading dock and closed in on it. Behind him, the Bee and the Rat were still talking to Jason's camera; the pig was still struggling with the woman who'd taken it, but the squealing had stopped, and the scene was almost quiet.

Anna turned back to the kid and continued, 'The animal rights guys will be heroes to some people. And some people will be heroes to the scientific community.'

She patted his thigh. 'Now, go like this. From your nose.'

She made an upward rubbing gesture with her hand, on her own face.

The kid gulped. 'Why?'

'Want to keep your job?' Anna grinned at him. She was a small woman, dark-haired, with an oval face and cornflower-blue eyes behind gold-rimmed glasses: she had an effect on young males. 'Be a hero. Smear a little blood around your face and we'll put you on camera, telling your side. Believe me, they won't fire you.'

'I need the job,' the kid said tentatively.

'Smear a little blood and stand up . . . what's your name?'

The kid was no dummy: He'd been born in front of a TV set. He wiped blood up his cheek and said, 'Charles McKinley . . . How do I look?' His cheek looked like a raw sirloin.

'Great. That's McKinley, M-c-K-i-n-l-e-y, Charles, regular spelling.'

'Yeah.' He touched his face again: the blood was brilliant red.

'What's your job up there, Charles?' Anna got a few more details about the job, his age, where he lived.

'That's really great,' she said. 'Now what . . .'

The pig screamed, and Anna turned.

The woman who'd been holding it had carried it toward Jason's camera, where Jason was interviewing the Rat. As it screamed, the animal kicked free, and ran.

The Rat stooped and tried to scoop it up, like a bouncing football; but the pig went through, smacked into his ankle, and the Rat fell squarely on his butt: 'Shit,' he shouted. 'Get the pig . . .'

Jason was still on him, lights in his face: He rolled and the pig, now panicked, ran behind the woman who'd originally held him, did another quick turn, and as the Rat tried to get to his feet, ran squarely into the Rat's chest, knocking him flat on his butt again.

Jason stayed with it as the Rat scrambled to his feet.

Anna grinned and turned back to the kid: '. . . Tell us what happened, talk to this camera,' Anna said, pointing at Creek. 'Creek come on back.'

Creek lit up and the kid told his story, breaking into tears again as he got caught up with it.

Anna stepped away to watch Jason, and when the Rat got tangled in a long complicated explanation of animal rights, she broke in: 'How come all the women in the group?'

'There are some guys – they just didn't make it tonight,' Rat said. He started to say more, when Anna's cell phone rang.

She unclipped it and stepped away, glanced at Creek, who was still with the kid. 'Yeah.'

Louis, calling from the truck seventy-five feet away, excited: 'Jesus, Anna, we got a jumper on Wilshire, he's on a ledge.'

'Where?' A basic rule: everything happened at once. Anna looked back at the two interviewers, calculating.

'I don't know, somewhere on Wilshire, close, I think. I'm getting the address up.'

'Get it now,' Anna rapped. Very tense: a jumper would make everything. The networks, CNN, everything – if they got the jump. She could hear Louis tapping on the laptop keys, where he kept the address database. 'C'mon, c'mon.'

'I'm getting it . . .'

'How're we doing on the cops here?'

'You got a couple-three minutes, I just heard the call.'

'Get the address, Louis.'

'I'm hurrying.'

Anna turned to Creek: 'Get ready to wrap it up.'

And to the kid, 'Cops'll be here to help, minute or two.'

Louis came back on the phone: 'Jesus, Anna, it's just down the street, we're a half-mile out. And he's still up there.'

Anna spoke into the mike, her voice urgent. 'Jason, Creek. Back in the truck. Now! Kill the lights. Move it!'

'Hey, what, what?' Jason kept shooting.

'Close down! Get in the truck. Now.'

Creek's light went down and he was moving, no questions, but the Rat shouted at her, 'Wait a minute, wait, what're . . . Hey, Anna, we didn't talk.' And the Rat started toward her.

Anna, the phone pressed to her ear, walking back toward the truck, fumbled a card out of her shirt pocket and thrust it back at the Rat: 'Call me. We gotta go.'

Creek yelled at her: 'What?'

'We got a jumper,' she shouted back. 'Let's go, Jason . . .'

They ran toward the truck: Louis had climbed into the driver's seat and was backing off the sidewalk.

As Anna and Creek came up, he jammed it into park and climbed over the seat into the back, and Jason came through the side. Creek slipped into the driver's seat and Louis shouted, 'Down Westwood, then left on Wilshire, it's three blocks, it's a place called the Shamrock.'

Creek: 'I know the place: Jesus, it's two minutes from here.'

'Gotta hustle,' Anna said. 'Gotta hustle, gotta hustle.'

Creek spun the truck in a U-turn, paused at Le Conte long enough to make sure he wouldn't hit anything, then swept through.

'Louis, whatever happens with the jumper, this animal thing is an A-tape,' Anna said over her shoulder. 'We want the bloody-nosed kid to be a hero . . .'

Jason said, 'That pig really pissed off the Rat; I think it's heading for a barbeque.'

'I got a great shot of this little mouse, Louis, really cute,' Creek shouted over his shoulder.

'Shut up, shut up,' Louis said to them all. He had an earphone clamped over one ear. Then, 'The guy's still out there. On a ledge. There's hotel people talking to him. He's from a party, high-school kids.'

Creek had the gas pedal on the floor and they just caught the light at Wilshire. As they swept through the intersection, Anna said to Jason, 'Give yourself some space on your tape. You gotta be ready, but the first tape is good, too.'

'I'm ready,' Jason said.

'Creek?'

Creek nodded. Creek was always ready.

'Louis, talk to me,' Anna said.

Louis' eyes were closed, and he was leaning away from them, listening hard. 'There're cars on the way, we got maybe a minute by ourselves. Maybe two minutes.'

Anna said, 'Where's that Three truck? Weren't they still out?'

'They were drifting down south after that chase,' Louis said. 'They're way the hell down by Huntington Beach. They're out of it.'

Anna said, 'Jason, I want you tight on the guy. Creek will pull back a bit, get the full jump, if he goes. But I wanna see his face . . .'

'You got it, sugarbun,' Jason said.

Creek showed his teeth: 'Sugarbun?'

Jason grinned at him. 'Me'n Anna getting intimate.'

'Yeah?' Creek glanced at Anna, who rolled her eyes.

'Me'n Anna doing the thing,' Jason said. He was almost talking to himself, looked as though he might giggle. He was wound, his eyes big. He liked the movement, maybe too much. He was talented: might go big in Hollywood someday, Anna thought, if he didn't blow his brains out through his nose. 'Doin' the thing,' he muttered.

'Shamrock,' Anna said, and pointed. Ahead, a twenty-story green-glass-and-steel building showed a bright green neon shamrock at the top. And Jason, who'd crawled between the seats, spotted the jumper: 'There he is! He's toward the bottom, like five or six stories up, you can see him . . .'

15

He pointed, and Anna noticed that his hand had a tremor: not the trembling of excitement, but the jerk of a nerve breakdown. She glanced at his stark, underfed face: Christ, she thought, he's back on the crank.

She turned away from his straining face, and looked where he was looking. Five stories, Anna counted: And there he was. The would-be jumper wore dark pants and a white shirt. From a block away, in the lights that bathed the outside of the building, he looked like a fly stuck to a sheet of glass. 'Get us there, Creek,' Anna said, breathlessly.

They were doing seventy-five, the wheels screaming, right up to the hotel, then Creek hammered the brake and cut sideways and they went over the curb again and Jason spilled out, running toward the hotel with his camera.

The man on the ledge had his back to a sheet of plate glass, his arms spread. The ledge, Anna thought, wasn't more than a foot wide – she could see the tips of his shoes.

'Guys, I'm gonna try to get up there,' Anna said into her mike as she dropped from the truck. 'You're gonna be on your own for a minute: Jason, I want *face*.' She sprinted toward the hotel's front entrance, the Nagra flapping under her arm.

Hotels didn't want to know about media. As far as hotels were concerned, no media was good media. Anna had two options. She could try to sneak in, but that took time. Or she could run. She ran forty miles a week on the beach and if the stairs were placed right, no hotel security man in California could catch her.

She hit the glass doors and went through the lobby like she was on a motorcycle. Two bellmen huddled at the reception desk with a couple of clerks, and one of the bellmen saw her and just had time to turn, to open his mouth and shout, 'Hey,' when she was past him. The elevators were straight ahead, and a brass plaque with an arrow pointing to the right said *Stairs*.

She took the stairs. Ran up one flight, two, then a man shouting again, from the bottom, 'Hey . . .' Third floor, not even breathing hard. Anna got off at the fourth: There'd be security on the fifth floor, and the desk people might have called them. She ran into the hall on the fourth floor, looked right and left, decided that the right end would be the far end of the hotel. There should be another flight of stairs that way.

She ran down the hall, now aware of her heart pounding in her chest, turned a corner past a niche with Coke, ice and candy machines, to another stairway. She pulled open the door, looked up and down, heard nothing and ran up to Five. She took three seconds, two long breaths, pulled off her headset, shoved it with the Nagra up under her jacket in back, held it with one hand and sauntered into the hallway. Halfway down, three older men – security, probably – stood outside an open doorway. A dozen kids were scattered up and down the hall, a few of them talking, most just looking down at the open door. All the kids were dressed up, the boys in suits and ties, the girls in pink-and-blue party dresses, all with the stark white look of fear on their faces.

One of the security men looked toward Anna, and even leaned her way – but as he did, a woman shrieked, and the men in suits turned and ran through the open door.

My God, Anna thought, *he jumped.*

The girls in pastel dresses were looking at the door, the boys were looking at each other, all were frozen. Anna knew that this was one of the moments she'd remember: they were like sculpture in some modern wise-cracking installation called *California Kids*.

Then Anna moved, and when she did, a couple of the girls began sobbing, and one of the boys yelled, 'Oh, no. No, Jacob . . .'

Anna ran lightly down the hall, found another open door a few rooms closer than the one where the security men had been. She looked inside: a man and woman, both gray-haired, horrified, were standing at their window, looking out. Anna stepped inside:

'Did he jump?'

The woman, white-faced, looked at her, her mouth working, nothing coming out, then: 'Oh my God.'

Anna stepped around an open suitcase, walked across the room and looked out the window. The jumper was facedown, a black-and-white silhouette on the yellow stone, six feet from the pool. Ten feet from the body, Jason was moving in with his camera. From across the pool, Creek also focused on the body.

Anna took out the recorder, hit the record switch, held it by her side: didn't hide it, just held it like a purse.

'What happened?' she asked.

'I don't know . . . I think it was just kids, having a party. They were making noise, we could hear them running in the hallway. The next thing we know people were screaming and the hotel people came.'

Anna could feel the recorder taking up tape: 'Did you see

18

him go?' she asked the gray-haired man.

'I think he was coming in,' the man said. 'He turned and it was like he lost his balance and all of a sudden he jumped, like he was trying to make the pool . . .'

The woman turned to her husband. 'Jim, let's get out of here.'

Anna stepped back, looked at the luggage tag on the suitcase: James Madson, Tilly, OK. 'Are you Mr and Mrs Madson?'

The woman turned toward her. 'Yes, yes . . . Are you with the hotel? We'd like to check out.'

'You'd have to talk with the people downstairs. Are you all right, ma'am? What is your name?'

'Lucille . . . I'm all right, but the man, the boy, he . . . Jim, I think I'm going to throw up.'

She started toward the bathroom with her husband behind her, one hand in the middle of her back, patting her, and Anna stepped to the door and looked out.

Hotel security was there in force, along with four or five uniformed cops. She stepped back, said, 'Madson, M-A-D-S-O-N, Tilly, Oklahoma, T-I-L-L-Y,' to the Nagra, then popped the recording tape and slipped it inside the waistband of her pants. She had two spare tapes in a black pouch on the carrying strap: she took out a spare, slipped it into the recorder. Hotel security usually didn't ask if they could have the tape, they simply took it, destroyed it, and apologized later.

Anna stepped into the hall. Two of the men who'd been in the room were just coming back out. Hotel security and a manager-type. Before either could say anything, Anna said,

'Could somebody help my mother? I think she's gonna be sick.'

The manager-type asked, 'What's wrong?'

'She saw the man jump, she's in the bathroom . . .'

The manager went by, into the Madsons' room, while the security man ran down the hall toward the elevators. Anna turned the other way and walked back down the hall to the steps.

Into the stairwell, down and around, and around, to the first floor. Pause, listen. Nothing. She stepped into the hallway, saw a sign that said *Parking Ramp*, and went that way.

Creek was standing fifty feet from the body. No blood, no movement, nothing but a hotel clerk and three cops walking reluctantly toward it. Creek saw her coming and made his open-handed 'Got anything?' gesture.

She'd pulled the headset back on. 'Quick quotes from a witness,' she said into the mike. 'They said there was some kind of party before he jumped, or fell, or whatever.' Anna spotted Jason, headed toward them. 'Creek, look up there, fifth floor, about one, two, three, four, five windows to the right of the jumper's window . . . See where the curtain comes through?'

Creek nodded.

'I'm gonna see if I can get the Madsons to come over there.'

Jason came up and Anna asked, 'How'd you do?'

'I got his face all the way to the ground,' Jason said, with trembling satisfaction. 'He hit twenty feet away.'

'That's great,' Anna said. 'Look up there, to the left of where he was. I want you to yell, "Jim and Lucille Madson, come to the window".'

'What?'

'"Jim and Lucille" – I don't have the lungs for it.'

'You got nice lungs,' Jason said; and his eyes seemed to loop. Stoned, or coming down. Too much of this lately; the last time she'd gone to pick him up, he'd been wrecked.

'Just yell the names, huh?' she said.

'Yes, Mom.'

Jason yelled, and after a minute, the Madsons came to the window and peered out.

'Get them?' Anna asked.

Creek had the camera on the window. 'Yes.'

The Madsons went inside and Jason dropped the camera off his shoulder, his face suddenly somber.

'You know what?'

'What? Look, we gotta get . . .'

'I think I'm gonna hurl . . .'

Anna leaned closer to him: 'What the heck are you doing, Jase? Are you stoned?'

'No, no, no . . . I'm just having a little trouble dealing with this,' Jason said. He looked at the body.

'At what?' Anna cocked her head, puzzled.

'I'm just . . . my head's fucked up,' he said. Then: 'Anna, I'm sorry, but I gotta go,' he said. He pulled off the headset and handed it to her, shamefaced. 'I'm sorry, but I've never seen this before. I've seen bodies, but this was . . . He was smiling at me.'

He turned his knees in, so he was standing on the edges

of his tennis shoes, head down, like an embarrassed little boy. 'I gotta go. You gotta couple of bucks I could borrow until we sell this shit? Take it out of my cut?'

Anna stared at him for a second. Concerned, not angry. 'Jase, how bad is it?'

'It's nothing,' Jason insisted. 'You're probably done for tonight, anyway. You gotta couple of bucks?'

'Yeah, sure,' Anna said. She dug in her pants pocket, came up with a short roll of twenties, gave him two.

'Thanks.'

And he went, hurrying away across the stone patio, Creek peering after him. In the background, they could hear sirens: fire rescue, too late.

'What was that all about?' Anna asked, watching as Jason went out of the street.

Creek shook his head. 'I don't know.'

'Well . . .' Anna hoisted the camera, looked through the eyepiece, focused on the group of cops around the body and ran off fifteen seconds of tape. Then she ran it back, forty-five seconds, and replayed.

The jump was there, in and out of focus, but undeniably real, taking her breath away: and at the last second, the man's arms flailing, his face passing through the rectangle of the lens display, then the unyielding stone patio.

'Jeez,' she said. She looked at Creek. 'This is . . .' She groped for a concept, and found one: 'This is *Hollywood*.'

Creek muttered, 'Better go. The pigs are about to fly.' She nodded and they headed for the truck, walking fast, but not too fast. The cops were disorganized at the moment, but five minutes from now they wouldn't be. This would not be a good time to be noticed.

Louis had backed the truck into the street, jockeyed it into a no-parking zone.

'Where's Jason?' he asked, as Anna and Creek unloaded the cameras.

'Took off,' Anna shrugged.

'How come? Did he shoot it?'

'Yeah, he got some great stuff,' Anna said. 'I don't know what his problem is: he freaked.'

'Don't sound like the Jason we know and love,' Louis said, puzzled.

An ambulance went by, and Creek turned the truck in another U and they headed through light traffic back west down Wilshire.

'We get it all?' Louis asked.

'We got it all,' Anna said. 'The jump is an A-plus-plus. Probably the best thing we've ever had, exclusive. I'm gonna sell it with the pig as a package.'

'As a poke,' Louis said.

'Yeah. Let's find a spot where we can see the mountain.' Anna pushed a speed-dial button on the cell phone, waited a moment, then said, 'Let me speak to Jack Hatton. Anna Batory. Tell him I'm on Wilshire at the Shamrock Hotel.'

Creek looked at her curiously, and Louis said, 'Hatton? Why're you calling Hatton?'

'Revenge,' Anna said, and grinned at him . . .

Jack Hatton came on ten seconds later, his voice the perfect pitch of good cheer: 'Anna, how you doing?'

'Don't "how you doing" me,' Anna shouted into the phone. 'Remember the swimming cats? I hope you got lots more cat tape, you jerk, because we got the jumper coming off the ledge, all the way down. Two cameras, in focus, twenty feet, and there was nobody else here. So go watch channel Five, Seven, Nine, Eleven, Thirteen, Seventeen and Nineteen and then tell the Witch why you don't have it, you cheap piece of cheese.'

'Anna . . .'

'Don't *Anna* me, pal. And I'll tell you something else. We got there quick 'cause we'd just been up to UCLA for the animal raid, which you probably heard about by now, too late, as usual. We got a mile of tape on that, too, we got animals screaming, we got a riot. We got a kid beat up and bleeding. And when you see it on Five, Seven, Nine, Eleven, Thirteen, Seventeen and Nineteen tomorrow, you can explain that, too, dickweed.'

'Anna . . .' A pleading note now.

'Go away.' And she clicked off.

Beside her, Creek grinned. 'I'm proud a ya,' he said.

From the back, Louis said, 'Such language . . . we really gonna blow off Three?'

'No,' Anna said. 'But they'll be sweating blood. I'm gonna jack them up for every nickel in their freelance budget.'

'Most excellent,' Louis said, with great satisfaction. 'Get me a place where I can see the mountain and I will crank this puppy out.'

Anna punched the next speed-dial button: 'I'll start selling.'

Chapter 2

All done.

Anna sat in comfort and quiet at her kitchen table, a cup of steaming chicken-noodle soup in front of her, pricking up her nose with its oily saltiness. She yawned, rubbed the back of her neck. Her eyes were scratchy from the long night.

At moments like this, coming down in the pre-dawn cool, Creek and Louis already headed home, she thought of cigarettes; and of younger days, sitting in all-night joints – a Denny's, maybe – eating blueberry pie with a cardboard crust, drinking coffee, talking, smoking. Chesterfields. Some old name. Luckies. Gauloises or Players, when you were posing. She didn't do that any more. Now she went home. Sometimes she cried: a little weep didn't make her feel much better, but did help her sleep.

Anna Batory was a small woman, going on five-three, with black hair cut close, skater-style, or fencer-style. And she might have been a fencer, with her thin, rail-hard body. The toughness was camouflaged by her oval face and white California smile – but she ran six miles every afternoon, on the sand along the ocean, and spent three hours a week working with weights at a serious gym.

Anna wasn't pretty, but she wasn't plain. She was handsome, or striking, a woman who'd wear well into old age, if that ever came. She thought her nose should have been shorter and her shoulders just a bit narrower. Her hands were as large as a man's – she could span a ninth on the Steinway upright in the hall, and fake a tenth. She had pale blue killer eyes. One of her ancestors had ruled Poland and had fought the Russians.

Anna pushed herself away from the table and, carrying her cup of soup, prowled her house, making sure that everything was right. Looking out windows. Touching her stuff. Talking to it: 'Now what happened to you, old pot? Has Creek been messing with you? You're over here by the picture, not way out at the edge.'

Sometimes she thought she was going crazy, but it was a happy kind of craziness.

Anna lived on the Linnie Canal in the heart of Venice, a half-mile from the Pacific, in an old-fashioned white clapboard house with a blue-shingled roof. The house made a sideways 'L'. The right half of the house, including the tiny front porch, was set back from the street. The single-car garage, on the left side, went right out to the street. The small yard created by the L was wrapped in a white picket fence, and inside the fence, Anna grew a jungle.

Venice was coming back – was even fashionable – but she'd lived on Linnie since the bad old days. Anyone vaulting the fence would find himself knee deep in dagger-like Spanish bayonet, combat-ready cactus and the thorniest desert brush. If he made it through, he'd fall facedown, bloody and bruised, in a soft bed of perennials and aromatic herbs.

The interior of Anna's house was as carefully cultivated as the yard.

The walls were of real plaster, would hold a nail, and were layered with a half-century's worth of paint. Hardwood floors glistened where the sun broke through the windows, polished by feet and beach sand. They squeaked when she walked on them, and were cool on the soles of her feet.

The lower floor included a comfortable living room and spare bedroom, both filled with craftsman furniture. A bathroom, a small den that she used as an office and the kitchen took up the rest of the floor. The kitchen was barely functional: Anna had no interest in cooking.

'The fact is,' Creek told her once, 'your main cooking appliance is a toaster.' Creek liked to cook. He considered himself an expert on stews.

On the second floor of Anna's house, under the steep roof, were her bedroom and an oversized bathroom. Creek and four of his larger friends had helped her bring in the tub, hoisting it from outside with an illegal assist from a power company cherry-picker.

The tub was a rectangular monstrosity in which she could float freely, touching neither bottom nor sides nor ends; in which she could get her *wa* as smooth and round as a river pebble.

In the adjoining bedroom, the queen-sized bed was covered with a quilt made by her mother, the material taken from clothes her parents had worn out when they were young.

Under the canal-side window, the quilt looked like rags of pure light.

Creek and Louis had dropped her at the corner of Dell and Linnie just after dawn. The truck couldn't conveniently turn around on Linnie, a dead-end street no wider than most city alleys.

'Sorry about the Witch,' Louis said. The Witch would be calling her. Anna hated to bring work back to her house.

'That's okay,' Anna said. 'For this one time, anyway.' She waved good-bye with the cell phone, and walked down the narrow street to her house. A neighbor in his pajamas, out to pick up the paper, said, 'Hey, Anna. Anything interesting?'

'Guy jumped off a building,' Anna said.

'Nasty.' He smiled, though, as he shook his head, and said, 'I'll watch for it,' and padded back inside.

Anna had sold thirteen packages of the jumper wrapped with the animal rights raid. At fifteen hundred dollars for local transmission, she'd sold to nine stations, and at three thousand for the networks – Southern California stations out – she'd sold four. Hatton at Channel Three had called back twice, pushing. They wanted it, had to have it. Finally said the Witch would call.

She did, five minutes after Anna got home. The cell phone buzzed, and Anna went to the kitchen table and picked it up.

'Screw us on this, we'll never use your stuff again.' The Witch opened as she usually did, with a direct threat.

'We can live with that,' Anna said. She looked out the

kitchen window, at the dark line of the canal. In a couple of hours, the reflected ball of the morning sun would start crawling down its length, steaming the water, bringing up the rich smell of algae soup. She'd been asleep in bed, this whole conversation no more than a pleasant memory. 'We already told Hatton that. I only agreed to talk to you as a courtesy.'

'Courtesy my large white Lithuanian butt,' the Witch snapped. Anna could hear the pause as she hit on a cigarette. 'If we don't buy, you lose a big source of your income. Gone,' she said. Exhaling. 'Outa here. I promise you, we won't buy again.'

'You take a bigger hit than we do,' Anna said. 'You never know when we're gonna come up with something like this jumper . . .'

'You're not *that* good . . .'

'Yeah, we are: we're the best crew on the street. And your career life at Three is what? Four or five years? And you've been there three? You'll be gone in a year or two, and we'll sell to your replacement. And we'll make our point: You don't steal from us. Even if it's swimming cats.'

'I apologized for that,' the Witch shrilled.

'What?' Anna shouted. She banged the cell phone three times on the table top, then yelled into the mouthpiece. 'Did I hear that right? You *laughed* at us.'

'So I'm sorry now,' the Witch shouted back. 'Name the price.'

'Network price,' Anna said. She sipped at the soup. 'Three thousand for the package. Plus two grand for the cats.'

'Fuck that,' the Witch said. 'Network for the package,

okay, but the cats we did, we did with our own crew.'

'C'mon, c'mon,' Anna shouted. 'I'm making a point here.'

'So'm I . . . Five hundred for the cats.'

'I'm serious, we don't need you. Network plus a thousand for the cats.'

'Deal,' the Witch said. 'I want to see the fuckin' pictures in ten fuckin' minutes.' She slammed down the receiver.

Anna called the truck, and spoke to Louis. 'Send it to Three.'

'How much you get?'

'Four thousand – I got a thousand for the cats.'

Louis said, 'Examonte, dude,' and repeated the price to Creek, whose laughter filled the background. Anna grinned and said, 'We're dropping thirty-five thousand bucks in the pot – that's three times the record.'

Creek shouted at the phone, 'We might as well quit, we'll never do this again.'

'How're the radios, Louis?' Anna asked.

'Good. Nothing happening.'

'Call me.'

Anna hung up with Creek still laughing about the money. She'd wait until Creek had dropped Louis, and there was no chance of recovering for a quick run. Good stuff sometimes broke just at dawn, although the regular station trucks would be out prowling around fairly soon.

Waiting for bed, Anna trailed by the Steinway, touched a few keys, yawned, flipped through the sheets for Liszt's Sonata in B Minor. She'd been trying to clarify the fingerwork in the fast passages.

She didn't sit down – her head wasn't quite right yet. She put the music on the piano, said hello to a couple of plants, enjoyed the quiet. Went into the utility room and got a plastic watering can and filled it.

Barefoot, humming to herself – something stupid from *Les Misérables* that she couldn't get out of her mind – Anna took the watering can out to the porch, and started watering the potted plants. Geraniums, and some daisies: plants with an old-fashioned feel, bright touches in the shade of the jungle.

Back inside, she refilled the can and walked through the house, checking with two fingers the soil in a hundred more plants: some of them were named after movie stars or singers, like Paul, Robert, Faye, Susan, Julia, Jack. Most were small, from a desert somewhere.

On a broken-down Salvation Army table, the first piece of furniture she'd bought in California, she kept a piece of Wisconsin: a clump of birdsfoot violets, dug from the banks of the Whitewater River, and a flat of lilies-of-the-valley. Just now, the lilies-of-the-valley were blooming, their tiny white bell flowers producing a delicate perfume that reminded her of the smell of dooryard lilacs in the Midwestern spring.

Behind the California tan, Anna was a Midwestern farm kid, born and raised on a corn farm in Wisconsin.

The farm was part of her toughness: She had a farm kid's lack of fear when it came to physical confrontation. She'd even been in a couple of fights, in her twenties, in the good old days of music school and late-night prowls down Sunset. As she climbed into her thirties, the adrenaline charge diminished, though her reputation hadn't: The big guys still waved to her from the muscle pen on the beach, and told people, 'You don't fuck with Anna, if you wanna keep your face on straight.'

The toughness extended to the psychological. Farm kids knew how the world worked, right from the start. She'd taken the fuzzy-coated big-eyed lambs to the locker, and brought them back in little white packages.

That's the way it was.

Anna finished watering the plants, yawned again, and stopped at the piano. Liszt was hard. Deliberately hard. Her home phone rang, and she turned away from the piano and stepped into the small kitchen and picked it up. This would be the sign-off from Louis and Creek: 'Hello?'

'Anna: Louis.'

'All done?'

'Yeah, but I was talking to a guy at Seventeen about the animal rescue tape. I don't know what they did, but it sounds a little weird.'

'Like how, weird?' Anna asked.

'Like they're making some kind of cartoon out of it.'

'What?' She was annoyed, but only mildly. Strange things happened in the world of broadcast television.

'He said they'll be running it on the Worm,' Louis said. Channel Seventeen called it the Early Bird News; everybody else called it the Worm.

Anna glanced at the kitchen clock: the broadcast was just a few minutes away. 'I'll take a look at it,' she said.

She went back to the piano and worked on the Liszt until

five o'clock in the morning, then pointed the remote at the TV and punched in seventeen. A carefully-coiffed blonde, dressed like it was midafternoon on Rodeo, looked out and said, 'If you have any small children watching this show, the film we are about to show you . . .'

And there was the jumper, up on the wall like a fly.

Anna held her breath, fearing for him, though she'd been there, and knew what was about to happen. But seeing it this way, with the TV, was like looking out a window and seeing it all over again. The man seemed unsure of where he was, of what to do; he might have been trying, at the last moment, to get inside.

Then he lost it: Anna felt her own fingers tightening, looking for purchase, felt her own muscles involuntarily trying to balance. He hung there, but with nothing to hold on to, out over the air, until with a convulsive effort, he jumped.

And he screamed – Anna hadn't seen the scream, hadn't picked it up. Maybe he *had* been trying for the pool.

Anna and the night crew had been there for the pictures, not as reporters: Anna had gotten only enough basic information to identify the main characters. She left it to the TV news staff to pull it together. At Channel Seventeen, the job went to an intense young woman in a spiffy green suit that precisely matched her spiffy green eyes:

'. . . identified as Jacob Harper, Junior, a high-school senior from San Dimas who was attending a spring dance at the Shamrock, and who'd rented the room with a half-dozen other seniors. Police are investigating the possibility of a drug involvement.'

As she spoke, the tape ran again, in slow motion, then again, freezing on the boy's face – not a man, Anna thought, just a child. He hung there in midair, screaming forever on Jason's tape. The Madsons, from Tilly, Oklahoma, were also shown, but their faces at the window were cut into the jump, so it appeared that the Madsons were watching – as they had been, though not when the tape was shot.

At the end of the report, the tape was run again, and Anna recognized the symptoms: They had a hit on their hands.

Too bad about the kid, but . . . she'd learned to separate herself from the things she covered. If she didn't, she'd go crazy. And she hadn't seen the jump, only the aftermath, the heap of crumpled clothing near the pool. Less than she would have seen sitting at her TV, eating her breakfast, like a few million Angelenos were about to do.

Anna drifted away from the television, sat at the piano and started running scales. Scales were a form of meditation, demanding, but also a way to free herself from the tension of the night.

And she could keep an eye on the television while she worked through them. Five minutes after the report on the jump, the blonde anchor, now idiotically cheerful, said something about animal commandos, and a version of the animal rights tape came up.

The tape had been cut up and given a jittery, silent-movie jerkiness, a Laurel-and-Hardy quality, as the masked animal rights raiders apparently danced with the squealing pig, and dumped the garbage can full of mice. Then the Rat was bowled over by the pig – they ran him falling, crawling, knocked down again; and falling, crawling and knocked down *again*: they had him going up and down like a yo-yo.

The guards, who'd come and gone so quickly, had been caught briefly by both Creek and Jason. Now they were repeatedly shown across the concrete ramp and up the loading dock; and then the tape was run backward, so they seemed to run backward . . . Keystone Kops.

The tape was funny, and Anna grinned as she watched. No sign of the bloodied kid, though. No matter: he'd get his fifteen seconds on another channel.

'Good night,' Anna said, pointed the remote at the television and killed it.

She worked on scales for another ten minutes, then closed the lid of the piano, quickly checked on the back to see that the yellow dehumidifier light wasn't blinking and headed up to the bedroom.

In the world of the night crew, roaming Los Angeles from ten o'clock until dawn, Anna was tough.

In more subtle relationships, in friendly talk from men she didn't know, at parties, she felt awkward, uneasy, and walked away alone. This shyness had come late: she hadn't always been like that.

The one big affair of her life – almost four years long, now seven years past – had taken her heart, and she hadn't yet gotten it back.

She was asleep within minutes of her head touching her pillow. She didn't dream of anyone: no old lovers, no old times.

But she did feel the space around herself, in her dreams. Full of friends, and still, somehow . . . empty.

Chapter 3

The two-faced man hurried down the darkened pier, saw the light in the side window, in the back. He carried an eighteen-inch Craftsman box-end wrench, the kind used in changing trailer-hitch balls. The heft was right: just the thing. No noise.

He stopped briefly at the store window, looked in past the *Closed* sign. All dark in the sales area – but he could see light coming from under a closed door that led to the back.

He beat on the door, a rough, frantic *bam-bam-bam-bam-bam*.

'Hey, take an aspirin.' The two-faced man nearly jumped out of his shoes. A black man was walking by, carrying a bait bucket, a tackle box and a long spinning rod.

'What?' Was this trouble? But the fisherman was walking on, out toward the end of the pier, shaking his head. 'Oh, okay.'

He must've been beating on the door too hard. That's what it was. The man forced a smile, nodded his head. Had to be careful. He balled his hand into a fist and bit hard on the knuckles, bit until he bled, the pain clearing his mind.

Back to business; he couldn't allow himself to blow up like this. If there were a mistake, a chance encounter, a random cop – he shuddered at the thought. They'd lock him in a cage like a rat. He'd driven over here at ninety miles an hour: if he'd been stopped, it all would have ended before he had her.

Couldn't allow that.

He tried again with the door, knocking sedately, as though he were sane.

Light flooded into the interior of the store, through the door at the back. The man knocked again. Noticed the blood trickling down the back of his hand. When did that happen? How did he . . .?

The door opened. 'Yeah?'

The boy's eyes were dulled with dope. But not so dulled, not so far gone that they didn't drop to his shirt, to the deep red patina that crusted the shirt from neckline to navel, not so far gone that the doper couldn't say, 'Jesus Christ, what happened to you?'

The two-faced man didn't answer. He was already swinging the wrench: the box end caught the boy on the bridge of the nose, and he went down as though he'd been struck by lightning.

The two-faced man turned and looked up the pier toward the street, then down toward the ocean end. Nobody around. Good. He stepped inside, closed the door. The boy had rolled to his knees, was trying to get up. The man grabbed him by the hair and dragged him into the back.

* * *

The doper was *wrecked*. As in train wreck. As in broken. As in dying.

Even through the layers of acid and speed, he could feel the pain. But he wasn't sure about it. He might wake up. He might still say, 'Fuck me; what a trip.' He had done that in the past.

This stuff he'd peeled off the slick white paper, this was some *bad shit*. A bad batch of chemicals, must've got some glue in there, or something.

He wasn't sure if the pain was the real thing, or just another artifact of his own imagination, an imagination that had grown up behind the counter in a video store, renting horror stories. The horror stories had planted snakes in his minds, dream-memories of bitten-off heads, chainsaw massacres, cut throats, women bricked into walls.

So Jason suffered and groaned and tried to cover himself, and frothed, and somewhere in the remnant of his working brain he wondered: *Is this real?*

It was real, all right.

The two-faced man kicked him in the chest, and ribs broke away from Jason's breastbone. Jason choked on a scream, made bubbles instead. The man was sweating and unbelieving: Jason sat on the floor of the shack, his eyes open, blood running from his mouth and ears, and still he said nothing but, 'Aw, man.'

The man had been hoping for more: he'd hoped that the doper would plead with him, beg, whimper. That would excite him, would give him the taste of victory. That hadn't happened, and the heavy work – kicking the boy to death –

had grown boring. The boy didn't plead, didn't argue: he just groaned and said, 'Aw, man,' or sometimes, 'Dude.'

'Tell me what it's like when you fuck her,' the man crooned. 'Tell me about her tits again. C'mon, tell me. Tell me again what it's like when you *do the thing*.' He kicked him again, and Jason groaned, rocked with the blow, and one arm jerked spasmodically. 'Tell me what it's like to fuck her . . .'

No response: maybe a moan.

'Tell me about Creek: he looks like a monster. He looks like Bigfoot. Tell me about Creek. Was he with you two? Were all three of you fucking her? All three at once?'

But the doper wasn't talking. He was in never-never land.

'Fuck you,' the two-faced man said, finally. He was tired of this. He could hear the ocean pounding against the pilings below them, a rhythmic roar. He took a long-barreled Smith & Wesson .22 revolver from his coat pocket and showed it to the bubbling wreck on the floor.

'See this? I'm gonna shoot you, man.'

'Dude.' Jason was long past recognizing anything, even his own imminent death, the killer realized.

He squatted: 'Gonna shoot you.'

He pointed the pistol at the forehead, and when the roar of the surf started to build again, fired it once.

The boy's head bumped back. That was all.

The two-faced man waited for some sensation: nothing came.

'Well, shit,' he said. He'd been having more fun when the doper was alive. Had he really fucked her? Anna? He had all the details. So maybe he had.

He stood up, pulled open the window on the ocean-side wall, and looked down. Deep water. Everything dark, but he could hear the water hissing and boiling.

Just like it should be, he thought, looking out, for this kind of scene.

Chapter 4

At a little after one o'clock, Anna stirred, then woke all at once, aware first of her pillow, then the room, then the faint whine of a jumbo jet blowing out of LAX. She lay in bed for a few minutes, rolled over, looked at the clock, yawned, sat up and stretched.

Showered, washed her hair.

Anna liked dresses, a little on the hippie side, small flowers and low necklines, when she wasn't working, or working out.

For work, she had a carefully thought-out uniform, designed to make her fit in as many social slots as possible. The uniform consisted of cream-colored silk or white cotton blouses with black slacks, expensive black boots, and one of several linen or light woolen jackets, depending on the season. She had three Hermès silk scarves, and always carried one or another in a buttoned inside pocket, along with a pair of gold earrings. If she dumped the jacket in the truck and rolled the sleeves on the blouse, she was hanging out. If she wore the coat, she was all business, still casual, but working. If she added the scarf and earrings, she could get by at anything short of a formal affair. Even at a formal affair, she could pass as a caterer.

Any of the looks might be necessary in a night's work, doing reconnaissance before the cameras lit up, especially if the work scene involved cops or security people allergic to publicity.

She also needed a more formal look if she'd be on-camera herself. She didn't like going on-camera – anonymity made everything easier – but sometimes an interviewer was necessary. When there was no choice, she needed the right look.

For the camera guys, appearance didn't matter: there was no way to camouflage the video lights.

Now, out of the shower, she dried her hair, pulled on a pair of shorts and a T-shirt, and laced her running shoes. Stopped in the kitchen for a glass of orange juice, bracing against the wall to loosen her calves as she drank it.

The day was fine, cool, with blue skies and a light breeze from the ocean. The beach was a half-mile away, and she loosened up as she walked over on Venice Boulevard, then took a finger street down to the beach.

A very large black man, who'd once been a second-string linebacker for the L.A. Raiders, was doing pull-ups on a rack set into the sand. He lifted a hand to Anna, continuing the pull-up with only one hand. Anna waved back and continued on to the water's edge, turned right and started running. Six miles: three miles up, three miles back. She ran along the surf, through the shore birds, a quarter mile behind another runner, feeling the sun.

When she started running, her brain was empty. The

further along the beach she got, the more it filled up: Maybe go south tonight, haven't been south for a while. Wonder what happened to that burned kid, at that house fire, the last time we went south? Kid was trying to save a cat, wasn't he? Could be a feature on his recovery? It'd have to be the first item on the run. Louis could get a phone number . . . On the other hand, it might be a bone to throw to Channel Seventeen . . .

Six miles, a little over forty-two minutes. When she got back, the linebacker was sitting on the bottom bench of the basketball bleachers, putting braces on his knees.

'Hey, Dick,' Anna said. 'How're the knees?'

'Snap-crackle-pop, just like cornflakes,' he said.

'Rice Krispies,' Anna said.

'Yeah, whatever; ain't been gettin' nothing but worse.'

'Gonna have to decide,' Anna said.

'I know.' He pushed himself up, hobbled around the edge of the court. 'So stiff I couldn't walk down to the water.'

'Take the knife, man,' Anna said. 'Anything's better than this.'

'Scared of the knife. They put me to sleep, I don't think I'll wake up. I'll die in there.'

'Oh, come on, Dick . . .'

They talked for another five minutes, then Anna headed home. As she left, the sad linebacker said, 'If I could run half as good as you, I'd still be playing.'

The cell phone was chirping when she got home. Louis again, ready to set up for the new night? A little early for that. 'Hello?'

Not Louis.

'This is Sergeant Hardesty with the Santa Monica police.' He sounded a little surprised to be talking with someone. 'Is this Anna Batory?' He pronounced her name 'battery'.

'Ba-Tory,' she said. She spread her business cards around, and often got tips on the cell phone. 'What's happening?'

'Ma'am, I'm sorry, but there's been an accident. One of the persons involved carried a card in his billfold that said you should be contacted in case of trouble.'

She didn't track for a second, and then the smile died on her face: 'Oh my God, Creek,' Anna said. 'Is his name Creek?'

'I don't know, ma'am,' the voice said, shading toward professional sorrow. 'I don't have an identification on the person. Could you go down there?'

The body was on the beach, just at the waterline. If she'd run another five or six miles that morning, she would have tripped over it.

A line of three cop cars, two with light bars and a plain white institutional Chevy, marked the spot; a medical examiner's van sat ten feet above the water, the longest fingers of surf running up between its tires. At the back of the van, a cluster of civil servants gathered around what looked like a pile of seaweed: a body covered with a wet green blanket. Two uniformed cops kept a semicircle of gawkers on the far side of the cop cars.

Out on the ocean, two jet skis chased each other in endless wave-hopping circles, their motors like distant chain saws; beyond them, a badly-handled sloop pushed south toward

Marina Del Rey, it's jib flogging in the stiffening breeze.

Anna trudged across the sand toward the cop cars with a growing dread. She'd tried to call Creek at home, but there'd been no answer. Creek was always out on the water. She'd thought, any number of times, that he would someday die there.

One of the uniformed cops sidled along the line of cars, cutting off her line: 'They called me,' she said, pointing toward the group on the waterline. 'They think that's a friend of mine.'

'If you could just wait here . . .'

She waited by the cars while the cop walked down to the group by the water and said something to a plainclothesman, who looked briefly at Anna and nodded. The cop waved her over, and passed her on his way back to the car. 'Hot,' he said as he passed. And he added, 'Hope it's not your friend.'

Anna jerked her head in a nod, but the kind words did nothing to help the growing sourness in the back of her throat.

At the water, a balding man in jeans and a T-shirt squatted beside the body, probing it. Two more men sat on the bumper of a medical examiner's truck, chatting, one with a set of Walkman headphones around his neck. Two plainclothes cops, one male, one female, were watching the man at the body. As Anna came up, they both turned to her.

The woman cop wore designer jeans with a crisp white blouse, and carried a blue blazer folded over one arm. Her round retro-chic sunglasses might have been stolen from one of the three blind mice. She was dark-haired and dark-complected, a little taller than Anna, with a square chin and square white teeth. She carried an automatic pistol in a shoulder rig.

Her partner was a large man, balding, gray-haired, a little too heavy, with deep crowsfeet at the corners of his eyes. His clothes were straight from JCPenney, and his black wingtips and pant cuffs would be filled with sand.

Like the woman, he'd taken his jacket off, and carried what appeared to be an antique Smith & Wesson revolver on his belt. There was an odd body language between them, Anna noticed. When they moved, even a foot or two, the guy tracked her, but the woman was unaware of it.

The man smiled, and the woman wrinkled her nose, as though Anna were a smudge on an antique table.

'I'm Jim Wyatt,' the cop said. 'This is my partner, Pam Glass.' The woman nodded, cool behind her glasses. Wyatt frowned, then said, 'Do I know you? I've met you . . .'

'I do TV news, cop stuff,' Anna said. 'You've probably seen me around.'

Wyatt nodded, grinned again, the openness of a good interrogator: 'That's it. You were at that raid on the burglary ring, God, couple of years ago. They thought the guys had killed that woman on Marguerita . . .'

Anna pointed a finger at him, felt as though she was babbling. She didn't want to look at the body; she'd do anything to delay it. 'You were the guy who kicked the door.'

A good piece of tape: the cops filtering across a yard to the target house while a neighbor's dog went crazy, barking; Wyatt drawing his gun, waiting for others to get in position, but not waiting too long, because of the dog. Then he turned the corner of the house with two guys in body armor and they took down the door.

Creek had gotten the good shots and the cops'd taken three men, a woman, and two hundred pieces of stolen electronic equipment out of the place, everything from home blood pressure kits to cell phones and bread machines. There really hadn't been much danger, but the tape was nice.

Stalling: *Don't be Creek, don't be Creek . . .*

'That was me,' Wyatt said, flattered that she remembered, pleased to meet her again. He'd been a hero for several hours. 'Are you still doing the TV stuff?'

Anna nodded: 'Yeah, same stuff, cops, fires, fights, accidents, movie stars.'

'A lot of police officers don't like to be called cops,' Glass said, breaking in.

'I know,' Anna said. She glanced toward the blanket – an army blanket, olive drab. The man squatting next to it was doing something to an exposed paper-white ankle. Looked too small to be Creek, and too white. No shoe or sock. The skin wrinkled by the water. The victim's face was still covered by the blanket. To Wyatt, she said, 'I hope to God this isn't my friend.'

'His ID said Jason O'Brien . . .'

She almost fell down. Jason? She'd never thought of Jason. A sense of relief flooded through her, followed instantly by a sense of shame, that she should be so relieved.

Wyatt said, 'Are you all right?'

She caught herself. 'Aw, jeez . . . Jason?'

'He had a card that said to call you,' Glass said.

Wyatt, looking down at the blanket, said, 'So you're pretty close?'

'Not close, but he's a friend. He was our backup camera, our second camera when we needed one. He used to call me Mom,' Anna said. 'He's a kid – was a kid.'

'Did you see him yesterday?'

'Yeah. He was shooting with us last night. He split around eleven.'

'You didn't see him after that?' Glass asked.

'No.' Anna explained about the animal rights protest and the jumper, and Glass and Wyatt nodded. They'd seen the stories. 'So what do you think?' Anna asked. 'Drugs?'

Wyatt shook his head. 'Wasn't drugs: why'd you think it was?'

Anna shrugged. 'Jason did a lot of dope, I think. He got weird.'

'All your friends do dope?' Glass asked.

'A couple,' Anna said. She wasn't intimidated: there was no crime in knowing dopers. 'Jason did some crank, a little crack when he could get it. He liked cocaine, but he couldn't afford it most of the time. Some weed.'

'Why'd he leave last night?' Wyatt asked.

Anna shook her head. 'I don't know. He said he was gonna ride all night, but then, after the jumper . . . I don't know.' She thought about it for a second: now that he was dead – if he was dead, she thought, if that was Jason under the blanket – his hasty departure seemed even odder. 'He said the jumper made him feel bad and he was gonna take off. We all figured that was bullshit – the rest of the crew and me. Maybe something was going on.'

'Why was it bullshit?' Glass asked.

''Cause I've seen him crawl inside a car with a decapitated woman to get a better shot, and the head was laying on the front seat with the eyes still open and a smile on the face,' Anna said. 'How's a jumper gonna bother him? There wasn't even any blood.'

'Huh.' Wyatt nodded, and stared north up the beach, toward the mountains hanging over Malibu, like the hills might have the answer. When it didn't come, he sighed and said, 'Will you take a look? Just to make sure we've got the right guy?'

Anna nodded, swallowed, found she had no saliva in her mouth. She saw dead bodies all the time, but not dead friends.

Wyatt said, 'Frank, lift the corner of the blanket, huh?'

Frank stopped whatever he was doing with the leg and picked up the corner of the blanket – Wyatt was watching her face – and there was Jason.

No drugs, this one.

He was lying on his stomach, his head slightly downhill toward the water, his face turned toward her. He didn't look like he was asleep: he looked like he'd been changed to wax. The visible eye was cracked open, and his tongue hung out, like the limp end of a too-long suede belt.

His head looked wrong, misshapen, and something had happened to his cheeks. There was no blood, so the outlines weren't clear, but he seemed to have been slashed by a knife or razor. But that hadn't killed him: a bullet had. In his forehead, just above the visible eye, was a clean dark bullet hole.

'Aw, God,' Anna said, turning away. She felt like she ought to spit. 'That's him.'

'All right,' Wyatt said. Frank dropped the blanket.

'When did you find him?'

'He washed up about, mmm, two hours ago. People saw his body in the surf, thought he was drowning. One of the lifeguards went in after him, pulled him out.'

As he spoke, a tear rolled down Anna's cheek, and she frowned, and brushed it away. No tears. She didn't cry. Then another one started.

'He involved with any gangs? Buying dope, causing them trouble?'

'No . . . I don't think so. But I don't know him well enough to say for sure. Why?'

Wyatt shrugged: 'Those cuts on his face. They looked like they might be gang signs. They look the same on both sides, both cheeks.'

'I don't know,' Anna said.

'Okay. Listen, we're gonna need a complete statement from you,' Wyatt said. 'When you last saw him, where he lives, who he knows, any troubles he might have had. Family. That kind of stuff. The address on his ID isn't any good.'

Anna nodded. 'He moved around a lot – he was living down in Inglewood, I think, an apartment. I've never been to his place, but I've got a phone number. We'd usually pick him up at the pier, he worked at the ShotShop photo place.'

Glass looked down at the pier, a mile south. 'Right here?'

'Yeah.' They all turned to look down at the Santa Monica pier, a gray line of buildings thrusting into the water a mile to the south.

'Has he been having trouble with anyone? Buying the crank or something?' Wyatt asked.

'He was pretty cheerful last night: he was riding with us because he heard about the raid, and set up our contact – he only rides with us once or twice a month, when we've got something complicated going on. He just seemed like . . . Jason. Nothing special.'

'And you don't know about the crank. Who his supplier might have been.'

'No. I don't,' Anna said.

'You don't know much about anything, do you?' Glass said.

'Get off my case,' Anna snapped. 'I got a goddamned friend dead on the beach and I don't need any bullshit from cops.'

Glass took a step toward her, Anna stood her ground, but Wyatt took a half-step himself, between them. 'Pam, take it easy.' And to Anna: 'You too.'

Anna spent another ten minutes with them, picking up their weird body-dance again, and agreed to drive herself back to the station to make a statement. Wyatt walked part of the way back to her car with her.

'Sorry about Pam,' he said. 'She hasn't been doing homicide all that long. She's still kind of *street*.'

'She like to fight?' Anna asked.

'She's not afraid of it,' Wyatt said, glancing back at the woman, who was peering down at the body.

'Listen, last night,' Anna said, 'Jason might have been high. I don't know, I can't always tell, because he was so hyper. But when we got up to the hotel, for the jumper, he was shaking like a leaf. He was okay when he was shooting, but when we were riding up, he was . . . shaking. Jerking, almost, like spasms in his arms.'

'All right, we'll tell the doc. You're gonna be around, right?'

'Yeah. Wait.' Anna dug in a pocket, took out a business card, borrowed a pen from Wyatt and said, 'Turn around, let me use your back.' Using his back as a writing surface – he seemed to like it – she scribbled two phone numbers on her card, and handed it to him. 'The first number is my home phone, it's unlisted with an answering machine. The next one is the cell phone I carry around with me. And on the front is the phone in the truck. I'm always around one or two of them.'

'Thanks. Make the statement.' He looked back at his partner, sighed and started that way.

'Makes your teeth hurt, doesn't it?' Anna said after him.

He stopped and half-turned. 'What does?'

'Wanting to sleep with her so bad.'

Wyatt regarded her gloomily, then broke down in a self-conscious grin. 'I don't think a woman could ever know how bad it gets,' he said. He started walking back, then turned, and in a tone that said, *This is important*, he added: 'And it's not just that I want to sleep with her, you know. That's only ... the start of it.'

Chapter 5

Anna made the statement, and headed south. Creek lived in a town house in Marina Del Rey with two Egyptian Mau cats, seven hundred sailing books and a billiards table he claimed had been stolen from the set of a James Cagney movie. He still wasn't answering the phone, and Anna suspected that he'd be on his boat.

Lost Dog was a centerboard S-2/7.9 with a little Honda outboard hanging off the stern, and Creek had sailed it to Honolulu and back. On his return, Anna had presented him with a Certificate of Stupidity, which hung proudly in the main cabin, over the only berth big enough for Creek to sleep on.

Anna dumped her car in a parking lot, walked across the tarmac to the basin, down the long white ramp, through the clutching, pleasant odors of algae and gasoline. She spotted the *Lost Dog*'s kelly-green sail covers, so at least he wasn't out sailing.

He was, in fact, down below, installing a marine head where he'd once carried a Porta Potti.

'Creek,' she called, 'come out of there.'

Creek poked his head up the companionway. He was

shirtless, had a hacksaw in his hand, and his hair was sodden with sweat. He read Anna's face and said, 'What happened?'

'Jason's dead,' Anna said bluntly.

Creek stared at her for a moment, then shook his head wearily, and, 'Aw, shit.' He ducked down the companionway and the hacksaw clanged into a toolbox. A moment later, he emerged again, wearing gym shorts, his body as hairy as a seventies shag carpet. 'Fuckin' crank, I bet,' he said.

'He was shot,' Anna said.

'Shot?' Creek thought about it for a moment, then shrugged, an Italian shrug with hands. 'Still, probably dope.'

'Yeah, maybe,' Anna said.

'What else would it be?'

'I don't know,' Anna said. She filled him in on the details: where the body was found, how. 'I was afraid it was you.'

'Naw; I won't float.'

She let some of it out, now: 'His face looked like notebook paper: it was white, it was like . . .' She happened to look into the harbor water, where a small dead fish floated belly-up. '. . . Like that fish. He didn't look like he'd ever been alive.'

'You know who he hung out with,' Creek said. 'You give those kids enough time, they'll kill you. Fuckin' crazy Hollywood junkie crackheads.'

Anna looked up at him, nibbled her lip. She didn't want to tell him that she'd given his name to the cops, but she had to. He had to be ready. 'Listen, I had to make a statement to the cops. We might have been the last people who saw Jason alive, except for the killer. I told them about Jason using the crank and the other stuff, 'cause it might be relevant.'

Creek exhaled, threw his head back and looked at the Windex at the top of the mast. 'Wind is shit today,' he said. And: 'They'll be coming to see me.'

Anna nodded. 'That's why I stopped by. They wanted the names of everybody on the crew with Jason,' she said. 'I think we ought to bag it tonight, maybe for a couple of days.'

'Fine with me. I've got work to do on the boat,' Creek said. He flopped his arms, a gesture of resignation. In the bad old days, Creek had run boatloads of grass up from Mexico. He'd never been caught with a load, but at the end, the cops had known all about him, and when he'd been tripped up with a dime bag, they'd used it to put him in Chino for three hard years. He considered himself lucky.

'If this was Alabama, I'd still be inside,' he said. He hadn't smuggled or used drugs in a decade, but if the cops ran his name as a member of the night crew, they'd get a hit when his name came up: and they'd be around. 'You better get in touch with Louis.'

'Already did, on the phone,' Anna said. 'But I wanted you to know they'll probably be coming around. I woulda lied to them . . .'

'Nah, they would of caught you, and then they woulda wondered why you were lying.' He grinned at her: 'You want to go out and sit in the sun?'

On the afternoons when Creek wasn't working, he'd crank up the Honda outboard, motor out of the marina into the Pacific, raise just enough sail to carry him out a bit further, then back the jib, ease the main, lash the tiller to leeward and drift, sometimes all night, listening to the ocean.

Anna shook her head at the invitation: 'I don't think so,'

she said. 'I want to get back home, take a bath. I smell like a
. . . dead guy. I've got it in my nose.'

Jason had worked with them on and off for two years – they'd
probably been out with him once a month, perhaps a little
more often. Say, thirty times, Anna thought, a few hours each
time. He was good at it: he had an artistic eye, knew how to
frame a shot and wasn't afraid to stick his face into trouble.

His main shortcoming was a lack of focus: he would get
caught by something that interested him – might be a face,
or visually tricky shot, and lose track of the story.

Anna cleaned up the house for a half-hour, bored, on edge
and depressed all at once, and finally dragged two old
Mission chairs into the back and began sanding the paint
off. She'd found them in a yard sale, in reasonable condition,
and figured she'd make about nine million percent profit on
them, if she could ever get the turquoise paint off them.

The work was fiddly, dull, but let her think about Jason:
not puzzling out the murder, not looking for connections,
just remembering the nights he'd spent in the back of the
truck – the decapitated woman on Olympic; the crazy Navajo
with the baseball bat in the sex-toy joint, the pink plastic
penis-shaped dildos hurtling through the videotape like
Babylonian arrows coming down on Jerusalem.

She grinned at that memory: stopped grinning when
she remembered the fight at the Black Tulip, when the
horse-players had gone after the TV lights. Or the time they
taped the two young runaways, sisters, looking for protection
on Sunset, the fifty-year-old wolves already closing in . . .

At seven o'clock, with the daylight fading, she quit on

the sanding, went inside, made a gin and tonic. The TV was running in the background, as it always was, and as she turned to go back outdoors, she saw the tape of the guy being hit by the pig. He was getting more than his money's worth, she thought, and grinned at the sight. Then: *Jason got that shot*. She stopped smiling and, still smelling of the paint-stripper, carried the drink out to the canal-side deck and dropped into a canvas chair.

'Anna.' Her name came out of the sky.

She looked up, and saw Hobart Page looking down from his second-story sundeck next door. 'We're having margaritas. Come on up.'

'Thanks, Hobie, but, uh, I had a friend die. I just want to sit and think for a while.'

Another voice: Jim McMillan, Hobie's live-in. She could see his outline against the eastern sky. 'Jeez. You okay?'

'Yeah, yeah. Bums me out, though,' she said.

'Well, come over if you need company.'

She'd just finished the drink when the phone rang – the home phone, the unlisted number. Creek or Louis, maybe her father, or one of a half-dozen other people, she thought.

But it was the cops: 'Ms Batory . . . Lieutenant Wyatt.'

'You're working late,' Anna said.

'We're just wrapping up here,' he said.

'Wrapping up? Did you find out who did it?'

'Afraid not. We did locate his apartment, not much there. Unless we get a break, we're not gonna be able to do much with it . . . it looks like dope, or just random.'

'So you're giving up?'

'No – but right now, we've got nothing,' Wyatt said. 'We checked out the ShotShop and I think he might have been killed there. He could've been dropped right out the back window into the water, and the window was unlocked, which it wasn't supposed to be.'

'Was there any blood? He was pretty beat up . . .'

'Not visible blood, but there was a roll of photo paper in the back – you know, one of those printed scene things?'

'Yeah . . .'

'Anyway, the owner said it was back there, half unrolled, and now it's gone. Maybe he was killed on the paper, and the paper was thrown out the window. It would've sunk . . . So we've got crime scene guys looking for blood, and checking around to see if the paper's under the pier, but even if we find it, it won't be much. We're looking for anyone who saw anything, but we haven't found anyone so far.'

'Did you talk to the fishermen out there? There are always a few . . .'

'Yeah, yeah, and we'll talk to more of them tonight. But listen – I didn't call to update you. We found O'Brien's next of kin, an aunt and uncle out in Peru, Indiana. I don't think they're too well off, but, uh . . . They'd like to talk to you.'

'Me? What for?'

'I think they'd like you to make the arrangements for a funeral and so on . . .'

She rubbed the back of her neck: 'Aw, jeez . . .'

'Well, you're the only friend we can find,' Wyatt said. 'There was nothing of value in his apartment – some electronic gear and an old bike, clothes. Anyway, I didn't want to give them your unlisted phone number, but told them I'd ask you to call back.'

'All right, give me the number.'

Nancy Odum answered the phone in Peru and passed it off to her husband, Martin. Martin Odum said, 'We don't fly, and it's a long way to come to get a stereo set. If you could handle the arrangements, we'd be happy to pay you somethin' for your time.'

'No, that's okay,' Anna said, thinking, *No it's not.* She'd never arranged a funeral, and hoped she'd never have to.

Martin Odum continued in the same glum tone: 'His mother and father are buried here in Peru, we thought maybe . . . cremation? We could sprinkle the ashes on their graves. If that'd be okay with you?'

'I'll take care of it,' Anna said. 'He had a few hundred dollars coming from my company, I'll use that for the cremation and to ship the remains. Uh, his stuff, do you want me to sell it? I don't know how much I'd get, but I could send you whatever it is.'

'That'd be nice of you, ma'am.'

They worked out the rest of the melancholy details, the phones making funny satellite sounds; and the Odums sounded as morose as Anna felt. When they were done, she hung up, mixed another drink, thought about making it a double and did.

Back outside, sitting in the canvas chair, she let her mind drift: and it drifted, under the influence of the alcohol, to the last funeral she'd been to, so long ago . . .

Anna had grown up on a farm in south-central Wisconsin, a 480-acre corn operation that lay in the crook of the Whitewater River, not far from Madison.

Her mother was a piano teacher, and she'd died in an automobile accident when Anna was six. She could still remember the melancholy, almost gothic circumstances of the funeral at the small Baptist church, and the slow procession to the tiny graveyard down the dusty gravel road: how bright and warm the day had been, the red-winged blackbirds just beginning to flock, one particular bird perched on a cattail, looking her in the eye as the procession passed . . .

Death and music . . .

Anna was the best pianist at the University of Wisconsin-Milwaukee, the year she graduated. She moved to UCLA, and the year she took her MFA, she was one of the best two or three in the graduate school. Not good enough. To make it as a concert pianist, she would have had to have been the best in the world, in her year and a year or two before and after. As it was – one of the best at UCLA – she got session gigs movie music.

She still played the hard stuff, out of habit, and, really, out of a kind of trained-in love. But in her one last semiregular gig, Sunday nights at the Kingsborough Hotel, she played a dusty, romantic, out-of-date jazz.

Her mother's music: they'd played a piece of it at her funeral, and all those Wisconsin farm folks had thought it was a wonderful thing.

Too early, half-drunk, Anna went to bed.

Alcohol never brought sleep.

Instead, it released unhappy images from some mental cage, and they prowled through her dreams, kicking old memories back to life. From time to time, half-awake, she'd imagine that she'd just groaned or moaned. At three in the morning, she woke up, looked at the clock, felt herself sweating into the sheets.

At three-fifteen, she heard a noise, and was instantly awake. The noise had a solid reality to it.

Not a dream noise.

Anna slept in a pair of Jockey underpants. She slipped out of bed, groped around for a T-shirt that she'd tossed at a chair, but hadn't found it when she heard the noise again. She moved silently to the head of the stairs, listened.

Tik-tik . . . scrape.

Back door, she thought. Definitely real. She was getting oriented now, stepped to the nightstand, found the phone. When she picked up the receiver, the dial lighted and she pushed a speed-dial button. Two rings and a man answered on the other end: Jim McMillan, from next door, groggy with sleep. 'What?'

'Jim, this is Anna. We got one: he's right outside my back door.'

'Holy cow.' Then she heard him speak to Hobie: 'It's Anna, she's got one outside her back door,' and Hobie: 'Okay.'

Jim said to Anna, 'We'll call the cops and start the web. You lay low.' A little excitement in his voice now.

'Yeah. Be careful.'

Life in Venice was getting better, but there'd been some

tough times; still were. Their version of the Neighborhood Watch was a little heavier-duty than most, knowing that the cops would always take a while to get there. Jim would start a calling tree, which would branch out over the surrounding two blocks, and in five minutes there'd be people all over the street.

But she had to get through the five minutes.

Anna had both a handgun and a fish-whacker in the bedroom. There'd be people around, so she went for the whacker, which she kept against the back side of the chest of drawers. On the way, in the dark, she stepped on the T-shirt, picked it up, pulled it over her head. She found the whacker . . . and heard a windowpane break.

Quietly. Like somebody had put pressure against it to crack it, and then tried to pick out the pieces – but at least one piece had fallen onto the kitchen floor.

Damn them. They'd hurt her house.

Anna went to the stairs, began to creep down. The whacker was made of hickory, looked like a dwarf baseball bat, and was meant to put ocean game fish out of their misery. Creek had drilled out the business end, melted a few ounces of lead sinker on his barbeque grill and poured the lead into the bat. If anyone was hit hard with it, surgery would follow.

At the bottom of the stairs, Anna heard another piece of glass crack. She moved to the open arch between the living room and the kitchen, risked a quick peek. The obscure figure of a man hovered outside the back window, three feet to the right of the door. He'd done something to the window, and had then broken out a piece. As she watched, a hand came through the broken pane, and a needle-thin ray of light played across the inside of the door. He was trying to see the lock.

Even if the posse arrived in the next couple of minutes, she didn't want to be trapped inside the house with some crack-smoked goof. She bunched herself in the arch, eight feet from the door. The hand with the light disappeared, and then, in the near darkness, she saw another movement. He was reaching far inside, trying to get to the deadbolt. She waited until the hand was at the door, then launched herself across the room, one big step with the whacker already swinging, and *Whack*!

Hit too high, and caught the window frame and the arm at the same time. And as she swung, she screamed, 'Get out!' and raised the whacker again, but the man outside groaned and jerked his arm back through the window, tearing out more glass.

She heard him stop once heavily on the porch, a running step, and then a heavy-duty spotlight caught him from a neighbor's yard across the canal, and someone yelled, 'There he is.'

Anna stepped to the door and flipped on the porch light, and at the same time, someone yelled, 'He's going west,' and someone, from the front of the house, 'There he is, Larry, there he is.'

Anna ran through the house to the front door and out, down the short sidewalk to the street – ten yards away, a man in jeans and a black jacket was running away from her, along the edge of the street. He was hurt, she thought: something funny in the jerky way he held his left arm.

Pak Hee Chung, the Korean businessman from across

the street, ran out of the front of his house carrying a shotgun, saw Anna and shouted, 'Get back inside,' and then fired the shotgun in the air, a three-foot flame erupting from the gun as the muzzle blast shook the street.

The man in black, now thirty yards away, spun, crouched. Anna shouted, 'Pak, he's got a gun,' just as the man fired, four quick *pok-pok-pok-pok* shots, and Pak fumbled the shotgun and went down on his stomach.

'Gun,' Anna screamed. 'He's got a gun.'

Hobie ran out of the house behind her and shouted, 'Get out of the way.'

Anna ran back a few steps and turned to look at the man in black, now running again, forty yards, and Hobie opened up with a handgun, five fast shots into the night. The man kept going, turned the corner. There was a flash of lights, another searchlight, somebody screamed, 'Stop or I'll shoot,' and again she heard the *pok-pok-pok* and a louder *bang-bang*.

Pak was on his feet again, running down the narrow street, apparently unhurt, and for no apparent reason, fired the shotgun into the air again. Again the lightning flash and the muzzle blast rattling the neighborhood.

Like her dad's twelve-gauge, Anna thought in an instant of abstraction. She found herself on her knees, looking up the street.

Then Hobie was there, next to her in his pajamas, fumbling shells into a revolver. 'Goddamn,' he said excitedly, 'I just shot the shit out of Logan's garage. Don't tell them it was me, huh? Let them think it was the asshole, Logan'd like that anyway.'

'Yeah . . .'

Pak ran back, still carrying the shotgun: 'Everybody okay?'

'What happened to the guy?' Anna asked.

'I don't know. Everybody was shooting, nobody got hit. Bet we scared the shit out of him, huh?' He looked back up the street and suddenly laughed wildly, a long scary cackle, and Hobie and Anna looked at each other. This was something new . . .

Then three more men were running around the corner at the end of the street, one of them carrying a rifle; they stopped when they saw Pak, Hobie and Anna.

'Who's that?' the rifleman shouted.

'Pak and Hobie and Anna,' Hobie yelled back.

'Everybody okay?'

'Yeah . . .'

'He came back that way – you see him? He's stuck down Linnie.'

'Didn't see him this way.'

'Get the guys up here, get the guys up here . . .'

'Better get off the street,' Pak said. 'Anna, lock yourself inside. We'll get a line set up and dig him out of here.'

'Be careful,' Anna said. She looked down at her bare legs. 'I better go put some pants on.'

Pak said, 'You're okay with me,' and jacked another shell into the shot gun and grinned.

Hobie was standing behind Pak and he winked at Anna, while Anna blushed and said, 'I'll be back in a second,' and Pak yelled, 'Get those guys going . . . we need a skirmish line . . .'

By the time Anna was dressed, fifteen neighborhood men, a half-dozen women and two cops had walked the street, and found nothing at all. Anna walked with them as they checked again, knocking at every door.

'Like smoke,' Pak said. 'Must've swum the canal.'

When the last house was checked, they gathered at Pak's, wallowing in the scent of testosterone. Pak started a stream of instant coffee coming out of the microwave, and Pop-Tarts from the toaster; Logan, the old Vietnam vet, was saying, 'Like this night in fuckin' Dong Ha, man, pop-pop-pop a fuckin' firefight in the front yard, my garage is all shot to shit . . .'

He *did* seem pleased, Anna thought.

The debriefing – party – at Pak's lasted an hour, and everybody went to look at the broken glass on Anna's back porch. The intruder had used masking tape to tape off one pane in the multi-pane window, then used pressure to punch out a hole. Anna made a brief report to the two cops, who seemed more interested in Pak's coffee and Pop-Tarts. Larry Staberg brought his jigsaw and a piece of plywood over, cut out a shape to fill the small broken windowpane, and nailed it in place.

'Pretty much good as new,' he said, as his wife rolled her eyes at Anna.

'Good until I get it fixed,' Anna said. 'Thanks, everyone.'

As the party broke up, Logan said to someone else, as he walked away from Anna, 'When I heard him firing, it sounded like a twenty-two, but the holes in my garage are bigger than that, maybe thirty-eights . . .' When she heard 'twenty-two,' a small bell dinged in the back of Anna's mind, but she forgot about it on the way upstairs. She wouldn't sleep much during the rest of the night, but as much as she turned the whole episode over in her head, she never put the .22 used by the dark man together with the .22 used on Jason.

Not then.

Chapter 6

L ate afternoon.

The day felt like it had gone on forever. Anna was a night person. A full day in the sun left her feeling burned, dried out, and the midday traffic magnified the feeling. At night, Los Angeles traffic was manageable. If she had to drive during the day all the time, she'd move to Oregon. Or Nevada. Or anywhere else. In the small red Corolla, half a car length ahead of a cannibalistic Chevy Suburban, walled in by a daredevil in a brown UPS truck, she felt like she was trapped in a clamshell, and she was the clam.

After the excitement of the prowler, she'd tried to go back to bed; not because she was sleepy, but because she felt she ought to. She never got up until noon, at the earliest.

But she hadn't been able to sleep. She'd gone to bed too early, under the influence of the booze, and the chase had gotten her cranked up.

So after lying awake for an hour, she got up, showered, went downstairs, ate breakfast – and got sleepy. She fought it for a while, and finally, at eight o'clock, crashed on the couch. When she got up, three hours later, she felt like her mouth was full of fungus. Off to a cranky start: and trying to figure out the funeral made her even more cranky.

Since the case involved murder, and was believed to involve drugs, the medical examiner wanted to get tissue tests back before releasing the body for cremation. She should call back, she was told, every day or two.

For how long?

'Well, you know . . . whatever it takes,' the clerk said.

The cops had no similar problems with Jason's apartment. They had taken out two cardboard cartons of paper, and that was it. A sleepy Inglewood police sergeant, a fax from the Odums in his hand, gave her the keys.

'We're all done with it,' he said.

'Are you really working hard on this?'

He yawned and rubbed his eyes, causing her to yawn in sympathy. 'Yeah, yeah,' he said. 'We are, but it's basically a Santa Monica case. Nothing happened down here.'

She borrowed the cop's phone to call Wyatt, at Santa Monica, and as she waited for the transfer, frowned at the fax from the Odums. They had a fax? Did everybody have a fax?

'Yeah, Wyatt . . .'

'I'm down in Inglewood. Are you doing anything up there?'

Wyatt talked for a couple of minutes, and Anna decided that he wasn't doing much.

'There's nothing to go on,' Wyatt said. 'Nobody saw anything, nobody heard anything – we had a guy out on the pier all last night, talking to the fishermen, and he came up with exactly zero. We don't have anything back from the lab yet, so we're not even sure that's where he was killed. And the most likely motive involves the worst anonymous ratshit dopers in the whole goddamn country. So I don't know what more to do. Keep talking to his friends. Like your pal, Creek.'

'Creek's okay,' Anna said.

'He did time for dope,' Wyatt said. 'He was dealing bigtime, is the word.'

'He was smuggling, not dealing. And he quit cold. He hasn't had anything stronger than Jack Daniel's since he got out.' She could hear him yawn, and it irritated her: 'Maybe you need a nap,' she suggested.

Wyatt ignored the sarcasm. 'Yeah, I could. And Pam backs you up on Creek, by the way. She went out to talk to him.'

'Pam? Your partner?'

'Yeah.' Anna half-smiled, and even on the phone, Wyatt picked up the vibration.

'Why? He's a Romeo or something?'

'Not exactly. He does have an effect on . . . a certain kind of woman.'

'What kind?'

'The anal, blazer-wearing, Hermès-scarf owning, power-sunglasses type, with no kids.'

'Huh. Like you.'

Anna almost started, then grinned into the phone: she'd deserved it. Wyatt continued, 'Pam's got a collection of Hermès, but no kids.'

'Big surprise,' Anna said. 'Good-bye.'

'Hey, wait . . .'

73

He wanted to talk more about Pamela Glass; Anna wasn't in the mood.

From the Inglewood police station, Anna headed over to Jason's apartment. The apartment was a neat, four-building complex surrounded by an eight-foot chain-link fence. She took the car through a narrow access gate, which a sign said would be locked at midnight; the sign had been over-painted with graffiti. She glanced at her watch: already three o'clock. She had to move. Creek and Louis would be at her house in two hours, ready to roll.

She left the car in a guest parking slot, and headed into the complex. A dozen people sat in lawn chairs around a swimming pool, drinking beer, talking in the fading sunlight. Old Paul Simon tinkled from a boom box, 'Still Crazy After All These Years'.

Get it over.

Jason's apartment was routine California stucco, tan, concrete steps going up to external walkways, rust stains running down from roof-edge gutters. The weather had been dry, but the walkways smelled like rain. Green, red, yellow and blue doors alternated down the walkways, an uninterested attempt at decor. Anna looked at the keys – 237 – found the door, a red one, looked around, waiting for somebody to object. Nobody did; she was alone on the walk. She had a little trouble with the key, finally got it to go and pushed inside.

Smelled carpet cleaner. He hadn't been here long.

The apartment was nearly dark, the only illumination coming through the open door and a back window. The room

74

she was in, the front room, was littered with empty pizza cartons, comic books, Big Gulp plastic cups. A *Playboy* and a *Penthouse* lay in the middle of the carpet. The cops had dumped everything, and left the litter where they dumped it. She left the door open, groped for the light switch, found it, flicked it. Nothing happened. Lights out.

'Jeez,' she said. Her voice didn't quite fill the room, and she paused, and thought, *What*? She stepped back and looked out along the walkway, heard voices, a woman's, then the deeper rumbling from a man.

Coming up the stairs. Still worried about being taken for an intruder, she pushed the door shut, stood for a moment in the gloom, waiting for her eyes to adjust. There'd be a circuit breaker somewhere, she thought. Probably in a closet or back in the kitchen.

The apartment was almost *too* quiet: like the ghost of Jason had muted all the little normal sounds, the creeping subliminal pitter-patter of cockroaches, warping of wood, flaking of paint. She pushed the feeling away and headed toward the small kitchen nook: *Find the light*.

He got her as she stepped into the kitchen.

He was off to the right, next to a small dinette table.

Anna was looking the other way, sensed him a fraction of a second before he was on her, started to turn, started to say something, to cry out . . .

He threw a large hand over her mouth, wrapped a heavy arm around her chest, tripped her with a sweeping leg, and they lurched back into the living room and hit the floor, Anna on the bottom. The impact took her breath away for a second, and she thrashed frantically, trying to get an arm loose, trying to get her feet working, trying to kick, but he was very strong, very professional: he'd done this before.

The arm around her chest tightened and he pulled her head back and said, close by her ear, 'If you scream, I'll punch your lights out. If you stop kicking, I'll let you breathe. C'mon . . .' They thrashed for another moment, but he'd wrapped a leg around her legs and she felt as though she were fighting an anaconda.

And he said, 'C'mon, goddammit, I don't want to hurt you, I just want you to shut up. If you'll shut up, nod.'

Exhausted, sweating, scared, she relaxed, involuntarily, and nodded and he said, 'I swear to God, if you scream, I'm gonna bust you in the mouth.'

And he took his hand away from her mouth.

She drew a breath to scream, reconsidered: 'Let me go,' she said, trying to look at him. She started thrashing again, trying to turn, but he held her. All she could see was his chin.

'We're gonna go like this over to the couch, and I'm gonna sit you down. I'll be right in front of you and if you yell I'll hit you. I want to be clear about that.'

'All right, all right.' Not hurt yet.

'Here we go.' He rolled, and pried one arm around behind her, caught her fingers in a hold, and she thought, *Cop*, and said, aloud, 'That hurts.'

'Not much,' he said. 'Not yet, but it will if you put a move on me.'

'Are you a cop? You sound like a cop.'

'No.' He'd released her legs, got his knees under himself,

and slowly pushed up to his feet, pulling Anna along, past a cable reel that Jason was using as a coffee table. Then he pushed her and twirled her at the same time, she found herself staggering uncontrollably backward, until the couch hit her calves and she fell back onto it. He was right there, his face obscured in the gloom, a fist an inch from her chest.

'What's your name?' he asked.

'Let me out of here.'

'What's your fuckin' name?'

'Fuck you.' He didn't seem frightening, somehow. 'Let me out of here.'

'In a minute. Gimme your arms.'

'What?'

'Gimme . . .' He grabbed one hand, and she tried to jerk free, but he put a hand on her forehead and said, 'Sit still, goddammit.'

'What do you want?'

'Needle tracks.'

What? She stopped fighting, and a penlight clicked on. He turned her arm wrist up, and played the beam down her forearm.

'Other arm.'

She turned her other arm up, and he looked it over, then shined the light into her eyes, dazzling her.

'What's your name?' he asked again.

'Fuck you. Who are you? What the hell are you doing here?'

'You oughta watch your mouth,' he said. 'And it's none of your business. You sit right there. If you start to get up . . .'

'Yeah, I know, you'll beat me up.'

He sounded embarrassed: 'Yeah.'

He was groping around on the floor, keeping his eyes on her, but not until he moved back to her did she see that he'd picked up her purse. He popped it open and dumped it on the wire-reel table, shined the penlight on it and stirred through it.

Anna's purse was small, and there wasn't much: a billfold, a comb, a lipstick, a roll of Clorets, a handful of change, a couple of ripped-in-half movie tickets. He opened the billfold and looked at her driver's license. She still couldn't see his face, and the light, held chest high, made it more difficult.

'Anna Batory,' he said. He looked up from the license. 'You were with the TV crew.'

She wasn't going to be raped, she decided; probably not beaten up. The guy had a hard force about him, but not the hyped energy that produced an attack. And he knew about her: 'Yeah, I'm with the video crew.'

'You shot the video on Jacob Harper.'

'Who?' Now she was confused.

'Jacob Harper – the kid who tried to fly off the Shamrock.'

'Oh. Yeah, we were there.' What did the jumper have to do with Jason's apartment?

'Where'd Jason O'Brien get his dope?'

'I don't know . . .'

'C'mon, he worked for you, you've got a key to his apartment.'

'He didn't work for me; he was a part-time guy, like once a month. And the cops gave me the key.'

'The cops.' After a moment's silence, he asked, 'Why would they do that?'

'Because nobody wants his body. I'm supposed to take care of funeral arrangements and there's nothing more here that the cops want.'

'Huh.' He stood up, looked around in the gloom and said, 'Damn it.'

'You hurt me,' Anna said. She was getting a feel for him. He hadn't wanted to hurt her. 'You could have broken my arm.'

'Ah, shut up,' he said. 'You're not hurt and we both know it.' Then: 'Your boyfriend's a doper.'

'What?'

'This guy Creek.'

'He's not my boyfriend, he's my partner. He hasn't done any dope for ten years.'

'Bullshit. He's got no job, he lives in a nice apartment at the Marina and he's got a yacht.'

'No job? I'll tell you what, pal, we're out there two hundred and fifty nights a year . . .'

'Yeah, some Tinkertoy fuckin' movie wannabees with cameras, for Christ's sake.'

Now she was getting hot. 'Yeah? We grossed better than three hundred and fifty thousand last year. Me'n Creek and Louis took home better than ninety apiece, after expenses. How much'd you make?'

'That much? Ninety?' Surprise.

'Yeah.' She would have sulked, if she thought she could have afforded to. But she had to stay on top of him.

Another moment of silence, then he was moving away from her. Over his shoulder he said, 'Fucking L.A., you goddamn people are a bunch of ghouls, you know that?

Making a buck off snuff films.'

She kept her mouth shut: she was about to get out of this, and didn't want to argue. A step or two later, he added, 'Don't scream after me. It'd just piss me off and I'd have to run and I'm probably gonna come back and see you again.'

Anna was on her feet: 'About what?'

'I need to know about O'Brien. I'm not done with him yet, and you're the only connection I've got.'

'Listen, if you think Jason had anything to do with the jumper, you're wrong.'

'No. You're wrong,' he said. He hesitated, then said, 'I came down on you a little hard, when we went to the floor. You oughta take a couple ibuprofen. Hot bath, or something. You could have pulled something.'

'You're so thoughtful.'

'I bit my lip when we hit.'

'Well, that's just too bad.' She couldn't believe the gall: he seemed to be looking for sympathy. She crossed her arms over her chest.

'Well, it stings like hell,' he said. Then he was out the door, slamming it behind him. As he went through, she got a better look at him in the late afternoon: an impression of sandy-brown hair, very white teeth. Probably blue eyes, she thought. Athletic, but not stripped down to muscle and bone: maybe a few extra pounds, in fact. Big shoulders. And gone.

She went to the door after him, thought about screaming, jerked the door open and stepped outside . . . and saw the top of his head disappearing down the stairwell. Opened her mouth, shut it again. She was safe enough, unhurt and still alone – maybe she *didn't* want to piss him off.

* * *

The circuit-breaker box was in the kitchen, the door open. She threw the switch and two lights came up. She went back through the living room, shut the door, and then took out the cell phone, found Wyatt's card in the pile of purse litter and dialed him. A clerk answered the phone, and she asked that Wyatt be called at home and that he call her back; he called back two minutes later.

'What?' he asked without preamble, when Anna picked up the phone.

'I just got to Jason's apartment and there was somebody here. He jumped me.'

'You hurt?' He sounded cautious, nervous. Why?

'No, he just tripped me and held me down and then he pushed me on the couch and then he left. I thought he might be a cop, but he said he wasn't.'

'White guy?' The odd tone still in his voice.

'Yeah . . . Hey, you know him?'

'Probably another doper.' But he was lying; and he wasn't good at it. 'As long as you're not hurt . . .'

'The door was locked and he was inside. How'd he do that?'

'He's probably a friend of O'Brien,' Wyatt said. 'Look, do you want a car to come around? I can call Inglewood.'

She thought about it for a moment. 'No, I guess not. I mean, unless you wanted to look for fingerprints. You know, detect something.'

Wyatt sighed and said, 'We got thirty sets of fingerprints out of the ShotShop, and we could probably get thirty more.'

Anna said, 'Tell me the truth about something. You know, instead of lying.'

'Sure.'

'Do you think Jason might be connected to the jumper we filmed?'

Wyatt hesitated before he answered, and Anna read it: 'You do!' she said. 'So'd the guy here. Tell me why.'

'Look Miss – Anna – goddammit, you're not a police officer, okay? Just clean up the apartment, pack up his stuff and get out of there.'

'Maybe you better call Inglewood,' she said. 'I better file a complaint: the guy was trying to rape me.'

Silence.

'Okay, I'll do the call,' Anna said. 'I know where his prints are, too. They're all over my purse and billfold. I'll mention to the Inglewood cops that you might have some idea about who it is.'

'Jesus, you're a hardass. You're just like Pam, bustin' my balls all day, now I gotta deal with you. I'm tired of it.'

'Life sucks and then you die,' Anna said.

More silence. Then: 'The kid who jumped off the building was tripping on wizards.'

'I don't know that brand,' Anna said, breaking in.

'Acid and speed. Maybe a lick of PCP.'

'Okay. Like rattlers.'

'Rattlers were last year,' he said. 'But yeah – like that. A little heavier on the acid. Anyway, he popped a couple and decided the ledge was a runway and that he could fly.'

'So . . .'

'So the wizards are little pink extruded dots on strips of wax paper.'

'I've seen them,' Anna said.

'When you buy them, the dealer just rips off however many dots you can pay for,' Wyatt explained. 'So the kid had a strip of dots in his jacket pocket. When we rolled your friend over, so did he; what was left of them, anyway, coming out of the water.'

'Huh. That's weird.'

'*That's* not weird,' Wyatt said. 'That's just a coincidence: these fuckin' wizards are all over the place. But I get this wild idea, and put the two strips together, and guess what? The two papers matched up. Your friend's strip had been ripped off the jumper's.'

'What?'

'Yeah. Now *that's* weird.'

Anna made a quick connection: 'So how'd the guy here know about it?'

Wyatt sighed again, and said, 'Look, you seem like an okay . . . person. Huh?'

'Yeah, I'm an okay person.' *Okay* meant that a cop could trust her – *person* expressed a belief that she was some kind of wacko feminist to be doing what she was doing, and he didn't want to argue about it.

'He's an ex-cop,' Wyatt said. 'He's a decent guy.'

'He's a jerk, he scared my brains out,' Anna said, angry at Wyatt's defense. 'What'd he want?'

'He's interested in the case,' Wyatt said.

'Interested? Is that all it takes?'

Wyatt cut her off: 'His name is Jake Harper,' he said.

'The jumper was Jacob Harper, Junior. His son. His only kid.'

'Ah.' What had Harper said? *Ghouls making a buck off snuff films*.

She let it go. *I'm okay*, she thought, when Wyatt hung up.

Jason's apartment was a sad clutter of heavily used clothing, cheap film gear, books on directing and movie-making, portfolio tapes, cans of Campbell's soup: all the hopes a kid might have in Hollywood, California. Bundled up and sent back to Peru, Indiana, it wouldn't mean a thing.

Anna did a quick survey, separating the potentially salable stuff from the useless, stacked the salable stuff, and then found the apartment rental office and talked to the sleepy manager.

'. . . not worth much, but we'll be taking it out in the next few days. Until then, it's under police seal,' Anna said. 'They still need to process some fingerprints, so if you could keep your eye on the place, we'd all appreciate it.'

'If it ain't too torn up, he's got some deposit money coming back,' the manager said.

'Nice of you to mention it,' Anna said.

The manager was a chunky square-faced Iranian with a black beard and an accent that combined Detroit and Esfahan: 'Ain't my building. And the owner's an asshole. Why should he get the kid's cash?'

'Right on, brother,' Anna said.

Chapter 7

A long bad day, and still not over.

On the way home, Anna stopped at a traffic light on Santa Monica, and her eyes drifted to a Mobil station on the corner.

A man was washing the windshield on a Volvo station wagon, at a self-serve pump. He was wearing jeans and a loose, wide-sleeved white cotton shirt, such as might be advertised in *The New Yorker* – Sea Island cotton, like that.

The instant she saw him – his hair thinner, maybe lighter, maybe speckled with white, a few pounds heavier, but the way his hands connected to his body, something almost indefinable – the very instant she saw him, she thought: *Clark.*

She slid down in her seat, but couldn't tear her eyes from him. He finished with the squeegee, turned and deftly flipped the squeegee stick back toward a water can hung on the side of the gas pump. The sponge end of the stick hit and slipped perfectly through the hole in the water can: exactly as she'd seen him do it fifty times before.

'Oh my God,' she said aloud.

A car behind her honked, and her eyes snapped up to the

rearview mirror, then down to the traffic light. Green. She automatically sent the car through the intersection, then pulled over and turned.

The Volvo was still there, but Clark had gone inside. A moment later, he came back out, slipping his wallet into his pocket, climbed in the car, turned on the lights, eased into the cross street, then zipped across Santa Monica and headed the other way.

She thought about following him.

Thought too long, and he was gone.

Clark.

She drove home on autopilot, random thoughts, images and memories scrambling over each other like rats. She stuck the car in the narrow garage, slipped sideways past the front fender into the house and, without turning on the lights, went to the phone.

She had messages waiting on the answering service: she ignored them, and dialed Cheryl Burns in Eugene, Oregon. She mumbled the number to herself as she poked it into the handset, praying that Cheryl would be in her shop. She was: she answered on the first ring. 'Hello, Pacifica Pottery . . .'

'Cheryl? This is Anna.'

'Anna!' Pleasure at the other end. They got together every year or so, when Cheryl and her husband brought a load of their wood-fired pots from Oregon down to the L.A. basin. In between visits, they talked on the phone, once every two or three months. Anna and Cheryl shared one of the close connections that time and distance didn't seem to affect. 'How are you? How is everything?'

'Sort of messy right now,' Anna said, thinking about

Clark. 'A guy I work with . . . was murdered.'

'Not Creek!'

'No. A guy named Jason, he was a college kid we used part-time, you don't know him.' Awkward segue: 'Listen, what do you hear from Clark?'

There was an empty heartbeat there, then an almost masculine chuckle: 'Uh-oh. Are you seeing him again?'

'Not seeing him, but I just saw him,' Anna said. 'At a gas station. He's here in L.A. I saw him on Santa Monica.'

'I know. He called and asked for your phone number, last month sometime. I didn't give it to him.'

'He called! Why didn't you tell me?'

'Because you messed each other up so bad the first two times. I didn't want the responsibility.'

'Cheryl,' Anna said, pushing her hair up her forehead in exasperation. 'I can take care of myself.'

'No, you can't.' In her mind's eye, Anna could see her shaking her head. 'Not with Clark . . .'

'Damn it, Cheryl . . .'

'. . . But I saved his L.A. address and phone number in case you called and wanted it,' Cheryl said, with a teasing tone. 'I had the feeling you might hook up. Cosmic vibrations, I guess.'

A little jolt, there. Pleasure? 'What's he doing here?'

'He's got an artist-in-residence gig with UCLA. Composition. Two years, he said, so . . . he'll be around.' Another dead space, then Cheryl again. 'Well? You want his number?'

'I don't know.'

'I better go get it . . . then you can tell me about the murder.'

Cheryl read Clark's phone number; Anna noted it, doodled around it as they talked. At six-thirty, still chatting, Anna casually picked up the TV remote, aimed it at the set in the corner, hit the power and mute buttons and flicked through the channels.

At CNN, the Harper kid was flying off the ledge, followed by ten seconds of talking head, then a shot of the pig taking out the Rat. They'd picked the Keystone Kops version.

'Cheryl, have you seen the TV news thing about the guy who jumped off the ledge here in L.A.?'

'Well, sure, everybody's seen it. You can't get away from it.' Then, excitedly, 'Was that you guys?'

'Yeah. It's getting around. Have you see the animal rights thing, at the medical center?'

'Oh, the guy with the pig. Cracked me up. Was that you, too?'

'About two minutes apart, story to story. And you're getting them way up there in Oregon?'

'Hey, it's not like we're in Tibet . . .'

As they talked, the Blue Shirt kid came up – Anna had forgotten his name – but he'd been interviewed again, probably the day after the animal rights fight. The interviewer was not familiar. The kid was wearing a lab coat, had a fat lip, and a couple of grinning professor-types hung in the background of the interview. Louis had made him into the hero of the piece, and that had influenced the stations who'd picked it up: and it was still building.

What was his name? Like the mountain, right? Not Everest. McKinley. Charles McKinley. He was playing the role just right, Anna thought, watching the muted TV as Cheryl chattered in her ear, a sort of charming, little-boy bashfulness.

Anna and Cheryl were still on the phone when Creek arrived, doing his shave-and-a-haircut knock. Anna walked out to the end of the phone cord to let him in, said, 'Cheryl,' to him, and he called out, 'Hi, Cheryl,' and stuck his head in the refrigerator.

'Cheryl says she wants your body,' Anna said, as he emerged with a bottle of Leinenkugel Light.

'She can have it, as long as she gives it a good cleaning once in a while,' Creek said. As Anna repeated his answer, Creek popped the top on the beer and wandered down the hall. A moment later, Anna heard him tinkling on the piano.

When she got off the phone, she ripped Clark's number off the scratch pad where she'd written it, looked at it for a moment, then folded it in two and stuck it under a magnet on the refrigerator.

Clark. She got a Coke from the refrigerator and sat on the piano bench with Creek, facing away from the piano. Creek smelled pleasantly of sun-sweat and turpentine.

'You're early,' she said.

'Thought you might like to talk, running around after Jason like that.' He was chording his way through a fake-book rendition of 'Autumn Leaves'.

'Yeah.' She'd told him that morning about the prowler,

now she told him about the man in the apartment.

'Maybe I ought to look him up,' Creek growled, when she finished.

'I don't think so,' she said, reaching over to pat his back. His back felt like a boulder. 'He's got connections with the cops and the cops are talking drugs. You better stay low.'

'I don't want him fuckin' with you,' Creek said.

'I don't think he will,' Anna said. 'I talked to Wyatt about him – I was scared, and called Wyatt, and he knew who he was . . . Oh, and Wyatt told me that his partner was over to interview you.'

'Yeah, I . . . guess.'

She felt the sudden evasiveness in his voice: 'Look at me, Creek,' she said.

He shook his head. 'I ain't looking at you.'

'Oh my God, you jumped her,' Anna said, half-amused, half-horrified.

'Did not. Jump her,' Creek said. 'And that's a nasty phrase anyway. High school.' He segued to a couple of bars of 'Ain't Misbehavin'. 'But she is a *tasty* little thing.'

'Pretty hard edges for a cheesecake,' Anna said. Creek's adventures with women sometimes grew complex.

'Hey, you know, nobody really appreciates what a woman cop goes through every day,' Creek said tartly. 'Especially one with some decent looks.'

'Just how much of her did you look at?'

'None of your business.'

'Ah. And would I be right to suspect that this somehow leads to your getting the cabin painted on the boat? You smell like paint.'

'She wants to learn to race and she's gonna help me with the maintenance,' Creek said defensively. 'So shut up.'

'Help like Teri did.'

Creek shuddered: 'I asked you never to mention that name.'

'Sorry.'

'Now I have to find a priest,' Creek said. 'To cleanse me.'

She smiled now. 'Sorry again.'

'Easy to be sorry,' Creek said. 'You don't have to live with the pain.'

Anna snickered and Creek laughed and went to the 'Jelly Roll Blues', running down the chords.

And after a little while, Anna said, 'Clark is in town.'

The music stopped. Creek turned to her, suddenly pale, as though the tan had run out of his face, like blood. 'Aw, shit,' he said.

They left Anna's at nine-thirty, the long, brutal day dragging on. Creek was brooding, silent. Anna was annoyed by the silence, the annoyance layered atop her already general grumpiness. She'd wanted to talk about Clark, but Creek didn't want to hear it. 'That's *too* personal,' he said. 'I can't tell you what to do and I don't want to think about it. Go find a girlfriend to talk to.'

Louis was sitting outside his apartment, standing on the curb in his white shirt and plaid jacket, carrying the laptop. He'd updated the address database with GPS numbers, and claimed that with his new GPS receiver he should be able to put them within a few feet of their actual position, anywhere in L.A. County, southern Ventura or Santa Barbara.

'What's happening with Jason?' he asked, as he ducked his head and climbed aboard.

'I'm trying to figure out a funeral,' Anna said, as he sat down. Creek pulled away from the curb and Louis brought up the electronics. Anna asked, 'What's going on?'

Louis started monitoring the cops from his apartment, an hour or so before they went out. He had a scanner on an old trunk at the foot of his bed, and Creek claimed to have seen him adjust the volume dial with his toes, without opening his eyes. 'Nothing really heavy, but something's going on with the hookers up on Sunset,' he said, twiddling a dial. 'Hard to tell what's going on, but I think it might make a movie.'

'Boys or girls?' Anna asked.

'Girls. There was a call about ten minutes ago. The cops hit a club up there, cocaine thing, and I guess dumped a bunch of girls out on the street, lined them up, and a fight started. Somebody said it looked like a riot . . .'

'Everybody'll be there,' Creek said. He sounded as grumpy as Anna felt.

'I don't think so,' Louis said, not yet catching the crankiness in the front seat. 'There hasn't been much on the air. You sorta had to be following it.'

'So let's go,' Anna said.

The riot was a bust.

A few cop cars still lingered, a few girls strolled along the street, mostly looking at reflections in the store windows. There was the familiar air of trouble immediately past, but no action – like arriving ten minutes after a thunderstorm, with nothing but puddles to show for the violence.

They headed toward the valley, Anna thinking about cruising Ventura. Louis got some movement on the radio, but it was small stuff, and too far south. By the time they'd arrive, there wouldn't be anything to see, or other crews would already be working it.

'Wish the bitches had been doing something,' Louis said. 'Would've made the night simple.'

'Don't call them that,' Anna snapped.

'Why not?' Louis asked. 'That's what . . .'

'Shut the fuck up, Louis,' Anna said.

'Ooo, what's your problem?' He was smiling, trying for a bantering attitude, but he didn't understand.

'Best be quiet, Louis,' Creek said, and Louis shut up. A minute later, Anna, now in a sulk, said, 'Sorry, Louis. You can talk now.'

'Is there a problem I don't know about?' he asked tentatively.

'Yeah, but it's mine,' Anna said.

'Fatburger coming up,' Creek said. Creek knew every Fatburger in L.A. County.

'Stop, I need some caffeine,' Anna said. 'Louis?'

'Diet Coke.'

'Fatburger and a Coke,' Creek said.

Anna got the food, waited, paid, carried it out to the parking lot. Two valley guys, in their late teens or early twenties, both with buzz cuts, three-day-artist-hangout stubble and black jackets, were leaning against the hood of a beat-up

Buick, and one of them said, 'Hey, mama.'

Anna put the Fatburger sack and three cups of coffee on the hood of the truck and turned back to them: 'Hey, mama, what? Huh? What?'

One of the guys straightened up and said, 'Hey, mama, what'cha doing tonight?'

'I'll tell you what I'm doing. I'm working instead of leaning my lazy fat ass on a piece-of-shit junker outside a Fatburger.'

'Hey . . .' The second guy pushed away from the Buick.

Then Creek got out of the driver's side of the truck and the second guy leaned back against the Buick again, while the first one hitched up his jeans. Creek said, 'Anna, get in the truck.'

'This guy wanted to talk to me,' Anna said.

'Anna!' Creek wasn't talking bullshit. 'Get in the fuckin' truck.'

Anna, still fuming, picked up the food and got in the truck and Creek said, 'Sorry, guys.' Back in the truck, as they pulled out, Creek said, 'What was that all about, huh? You want to get in a fight outside a Fatburger and spend some more time talking to cops? Huh?'

'Bad day.'

'Bad day, my ass,' Creek said. 'Take your fuckin' bad day someplace else.'

'Jesus, you guys, go easy,' Louis said, nervous. Creek and Anna didn't fight.

'Yeah, yeah, gimme a Fatburger,' Creek snarled.

They rode in silence until Anna's cell phone rang.

'Anna Batory?' Male voice. Familiar. *Heavy stress*, she thought.

'Yeah.'

'This is the guy you met in O'Brien's apartment this afternoon.'

'Yeah, Harper,' Anna said. 'What do you want – where'd you get this number?'

He ignored the use of his name and the demand for an explanation of the number. 'I need to see you,' he said. 'Like *right now*. Actually, I need you to come to where I am.'

'Why should I?'

'Because it has something to do with you,' Harper said. 'I gotta call the cops pretty soon, but I need you over here first.'

'*What* has to do with me?'

'Look, you might be in serious trouble. If you want to know about it before the cops come banging on your door, come see me now. Otherwise . . . and hey, you might even make a few bucks.'

She thought for a second, then said, 'I'm bringing a friend.'

'It'll cause them trouble,' Harper said.

'I'm not gonna be alone with you. Not after you jumped me, like that, you . . . abuser.'

Creek looked at her oddly, and Harper, after a second, said, 'Whatever you want to do.'

Harper was waiting under a streetlight on Cumpston, a couple of blocks south of Burbank Boulevard, a neighborhood of stucco ranch homes. The yard behind him was bordered with an evergreen hedge, long untrimmed, and pierced by a picket gate that had curls of white paint peeling off.

Creek got out with Anna.

'I understand you had a problem with Anna,' Creek said, and Anna suddenly realized that she might have a problem with the two men.

Harper had turned toward Creek with a small crouching movement that suggested he'd just set his feet; and he wasn't backing up.

He was good-looking in a mildly beat-up way, Anna thought, a big man with broad shoulders, big hands, a nose that had been broken a couple of times. He carried a heavy tan, with sun-touched hair, like a beach bum, but he was too old for that: late thirties, she thought. He wore an expensive black sport coat, silk, she thought, over a pair of jeans.

And way down in the lizard part of her brain, something went, 'Hmm . . .'

Creek was gliding sideways and Harper was pivoting to cover him, and Anna said, 'I swear to God, the first one of you guys who throws a punch, I'll kick him in the balls.'

Creek stopped moving and Harper relaxed, spread his hands. He glanced quickly at Anna but spoke to Creek. 'If you had the same problem, you would've done the same thing, pal.'

Creek stared for a moment, then nodded abruptly: 'So what do you want?'

'I want you to come in here,' he said. He tipped his head back toward the house. 'But don't touch anything.'

'Whadda we got?' Creek asked, interested now.

'We got a dead dope dealer,' Harper said.

Anna stopped: 'Have you called the cops?'

'No. I will, soon as you've gone through.'

'The cops could put you in jail for not calling in right away,' Anna said.

'Yeah, maybe, but I've got bigger problems than that. Come on. Maybe you want to bring a camera?'

He said it in a cheap way, and Anna said, 'Shove it.'

While Louis waited with the radios, Harper led them up the walk. The door was just ajar, a light on inside, and Harper took a ballpoint pen out of his pocket and pushed the door open with the butt end of it. 'Don't touch the door, don't touch anything.'

'Was the door open when you got here?'

'Yeah, and the light was on,' he said as they stepped across the threshold. 'As soon as I got in, I knew . . .'

'Aw, jeez,' Anna said. The smell hit her, and she flinched away from it. Old blood and human waste, mixed up and curdling.

'Flies,' Harper said absently, tilting his head back. Anna looked up, saw hundreds of bluebottle flies clustering around the light. 'Back here.'

He led the way to a bedroom with mustard-covered walls and *Rolling Stones* covers thumbtacked to the walls. But the main attraction was a man who, at first glance, looked like a grotesque German Expressionist painting, muscles and blood exposed, everything gone black. He'd been handcuffed to the bed, his feet tied with ripped sheets. He was nude except for a pair of briefs, face up and gagged. He'd been cut to pieces with a knife.

And not quickly, Anna thought. The face looked as though

the skin had been peeled off. A halo of blood surrounded the head, as if it had been violently shaken back and forth. So he'd been alive for the peeling . . .

'Christ, what is this, what're we here for?' Creek asked. 'We've seen this shit . . .'

'Yeah, so've I,' Harper said. He looked at Anna. 'You know him?'

'Even if I did, I'm not sure I'd recognize him,' she said. 'But I don't think so.'

'Name is Sean MacAllister,' Harper said. 'Been busted three times on minor drug stuff, once with O'Brien in the car . . .'

Anna was nodding: 'Jesus, we do know him. Sean, oh my God . . .'

Harper was going on: '. . . The bust never got to trial because there was some problem with the stop. O'Brien lived here for a couple of weeks, between apartments.'

'I don't know – we never picked up Jason here. Are you sure that's him?' As she said it, she had to turn away.

'Pretty sure,' Harper said. 'His billfold was still in his pocket.'

'So what do you want from us? Why don't you just call the cops?' Creek asked.

'I wanted you to look at this,' Harper said. He was standing next to the bed, and he pointed to the man's bare chest. A knife rip crossed it from armpit to armpit.

'What?' Anna asked.

'Read it,' Harper said.

'Read it?'

She and Creek edged closer. She couldn't see it, but Creek

could: he looked at her suddenly and she said again, 'What?'

'Says "Anna",' Creek said, almost to himself.

And then she saw it: her name in carved flesh. 'My God.' She stood in shock for a moment, then turned to Harper: 'Why?'

'I don't know.' He was watching her closely. 'He was a small-time dealer, that's about all I know.'

'Your son's dealer?'

'I don't know. I hope not. I tracked him through your pal O'Brien.' He looked around the room. 'All I found was a little grass. Nothing else.'

'No dots,' Anna said, and he nodded. She looked at the grotesquerie again, the muscle mass that had once been human, the *Anna*, and she turned away from the bed, suddenly felt as though a hand had been clapped over her mouth, suffocating her: 'I gotta get out of here.'

Chapter 8

Harper and Creek followed her outside, and Anna held her head over the picket fence and gagged. Nothing came up but a stream of saliva. After a moment, she turned back to the two men: 'Sorry.'

'So you didn't know the guy,' Harper said, a statement, not a question.

'Not except to nod to. I never met Jason's friends, except on the job.'

Harper was looking at her skeptically, and Anna said, 'Look, Jason was a part-timer. He worked maybe once or twice a month, when he came up with something.'

'Dope stuff?'

'No. Usually UCLA stuff. The night your son died, that was the last time we saw him. He had the inside track on a college animal rights group that raided the medical labs at UCLA . . .'

'I saw it on TV, the pig thing,' Harper said. 'How'd that connect with my kid?'

Creek said, 'It didn't. The raid was college kids, and your son was at a high-school party. The only connection was that they were a few blocks apart about the same time, and we happened to catch them both.'

Harper rubbed his chin, looking at Creek. 'You're sure?'

'Work it out yourself.'

Harper looked away, into the middle distance, then back, and nodded. 'All right. But my kid's dead, your friend's dead, they shared a dealer, and now a dealer's dead – and Anna's name is carved on his chest. *Something's* going on.'

'Did you see any of these dot things in there – the wizards?' Anna asked.

'How'd you know about the wizards?' Harper asked sharply.

'Wyatt told me. He told me about you so I wouldn't report that I was mugged.'

'Okay.' He looked at his shoes. 'Sorry about the thing at the apartment. I didn't know who it was, I was in there illegally, sort of. Not a good place to be caught messing with an apartment . . .'

'So how'd you track this guy down?' Anna asked, looking at the house.

'Got Wyatt to check Jason on the computer, found the arrest, got MacAllister's name, checked with the phone company and got an address. No problem.'

'You keep stepping into shit like this, it's gonna be a problem,' Creek said. 'Leave it to the cops.'

'I can't.' Harper shook his head: 'I've got a slightly different agenda than the cops.'

'What? Revenge?' Anna asked.

'Nah.' Harper said. He looked back at the house, as Anna had. 'But I'd like a little justice.'

'Leave it to the cops,' Creek said again.

'You don't get justice from cops,' Harper said. 'You get procedure. Sometimes you get arrests. Occasionally you get convictions. You never get justice.'

'So what do we do here?' Creek asked.

Anna took out her phone. 'Make a call.'

They called Wyatt at home, hoping for a charitable referral to the local Burbank cops.

'What?' Wyatt grumbled into the mouthpiece. His voice was thickened by sleep.

Anna identified herself and told him about the man on the bed.

'Stay out of the house, don't touch anything,' Wyatt said. He was awake now, and unhappy. 'I'm gonna call L.A.'

'I think we're in Burbank,' she said.

'All right, I'll call Burbank. You wait.'

'We're in the street right outside the house,' Anna said, glancing at Harper. 'It's a little complicated. I'd better let you talk to your friend Jake.'

'Jake? What's he doing there?' Wyatt asked, even more unhappy.

'I'll let him tell you,' Anna said, and she handed the phone to Harper.

Louis stuck his head out of the truck: 'We've got a fire in Hollywood Hills, the girlfriend of somebody big, the way the fire guys are talking.'

'Forget it,' Anna said, cutting him off. 'We've got problems.'

The first cop car arrived five minutes after Harper got off

the phone: not Burbank, but North Hollywood. Burbank was two blocks away. The cops talked to Harper, briefly, a little chilly, and started the murder routine: cops around the house, neighbors on lawns, yellow crime scene tape, medical examiners, L.A. homicide detectives and, eventually, Wyatt. He nodded wordlessly as he passed them, flashed a badge at a cop outside the door and went in. Five minutes later, he was back out.

'What a mess,' he said.

'Yeah,' Anna said. 'And we had a prowler at my house this morning. He had a gun . . .'

'I hope you called someone,' Wyatt said.

'I live in Venice. The neighbors chased him off, the cops came over and had a Coke.'

'Might not be you,' Wyatt said. 'I mean, on the guy's chest.'

She got a quick mental flash of the body, and felt herself tighten up: whoever had done that was far gone. But she wouldn't fool herself, either: 'C'mon, how many Annas do you know?'

Wyatt said, 'All right. I don't want to scare you any more than you are, but – remember the cuts on O'Brien's face? I thought they looked like gang marks?'

'Yes?'

'They were like this, remember?' He made a quick slashing triangle design on the palm of his hand with the opposite index finger.

'Triangles,' Anna said.

'Or A's,' Wyatt said quietly. 'Upside-down A's.'

'Oh, no.' She put her hands to her cheeks. 'Can't be A's.'

'Could be,' Wyatt said. 'We gotta have a serious talk with the L.A. guys.'

'Are they upset?' She looked toward the house. 'About us going inside?'

Wyatt glanced toward Harper: 'Not as much as you might think.'

'Wasn't her fault anyway,' Harper said, stepping into the conversation. 'She didn't know what she was gonna see. I took her in. I thought she might say something – might know the guy.'

'Did she?'

Harper glanced at her, then suddenly grinned, the first time she'd seen him smile. *Nice smile*, she thought. 'No. She went outside and barfed.'

'Did not,' Anna said.

Creek, looking past them, said apprehensively, 'Uh-oh, here we go.'

An L.A. detective was headed their way, the languid, dangerous stroll affected by cops when they were being cool. He was carrying a rolled pamphlet. He glanced at Anna, nodded at Creek and said to Harper, 'How are you, Jake?'

A movie line: one that should have been followed by a cigarette flicked into the street. Harper shrugged: 'You heard about my kid.'

'Yeah. Brutal.' The detective looked back at the house, and then said, 'Listen, I know this is a really horseshit time to ask you this, but I got a problem . . . I gotta come see you. About Lucy.'

'Gonna do it this time?'

'I gotta. She's crazier than a shithouse mouse. If I don't

get out of there . . . but I can't leave the kids.'

'Call me,' Harper said.

'I'm hurtin' for cash . . .' The cop was embarrassed.

'We'll put it on your Sears card,' Harper said. He poked the cop in the ribs, and the cop nodded and said, 'I'll call you – thanks.' He nodded at Anna, glanced at Wyatt and strolled away.

'What was all that about?' Anna asked Wyatt.

'Jake's a lawyer,' Wyatt said. 'He has about half the cop business in the county.'

'I thought you said he *was* a cop.'

'*Was*. Ten years ago.'

The lead detective's name was Carrol Trippen, a tall, impatient, prematurely white-haired Anglo. He split them up, talked to each of them for a moment, compared their stories and finally sent them downtown to make statements.

'Are we in trouble? Should I get a lawyer?' Anna asked, as Trippen started back toward the house.

'Harper pisses me off, calling you guys,' Trippen said sourly. 'But it wasn't your fault, and I know where he's coming from. I got bigger things to worry about than hassling people who looked at a dead guy.'

The cops kept Anna, Harper, Creek and Louis apart until the statements were done. Anna was interviewed by a sleepy cop with bad breath and a yellow shirt with a new coffee stain.

When they finished, he peered at her over his coffee cup and said, 'Tell you what: You know this guy. The killer.'

'If it's me.' She'd been having second thoughts.

'C'mon. Even *you* think it's you.'

'So what do I do?'

'First thing is, with this prowler you had, I'd move out of your house. Stay at a motel for a few days, don't tell anybody where you are. When you've got to work, meet your friends somewhere. You got a cellular, anybody can get in touch if they need to.'

'I'll think about it,' Anna said, but she wouldn't leave her house.

'Do that. And I need you back this afternoon, if you can make it – we got a shrink and a serial killer profiler, they're gonna want to talk to you.'

'You're sure he did both Jason and Sean?'

'Trippen talked to Wyatt, and they think so. He says there's a level of violence there. You don't see it on the average murder. And this Sean was tied to the Jason guy, and Jason was tight with you.'

'All right.' And she knew him – but who was it?

Harper and Creek were waiting in the lobby when Anna got out. Louis was wandering around with the truck, waiting. When Creek saw Anna step out of the elevator, he dug out his cell phone, pushed a speed dial, got Louis: 'We're ready.'

'Are you headed home?' Harper asked, as the three of them walked down to the exit.

'I guess,' Anna said. She glanced at her watch. 'The night's shot.'

'Are you moving out of your house?' Harper asked.

'No.'

'Then I'd like to come by and look around,' he said.

'Bad idea,' said Creek.

Harper turned to him: 'Look, I used to do this for a living. I want to see where she lives – what the place is like. If the news is bad, I want you to help get her out of there. I'd just as soon she didn't get carved up until I find the guy who did my kid.'

'That's very sentimental,' Anna said.

Harper shrugged: 'I've got priorities.'

Creek was nodding: 'And you've got a point.' To Anna: 'Maybe I should stay over.'

'Good idea,' Harper said.

Anna shook her head, said to Creek: 'You'd drive me nuts.' And to Harper, 'When he lays around the house, he lays *around* the house.' Nobody smiled at the old vauderville line.

'This ain't a comedy routine,' Creek grumbled. Then: 'Maybe we could get the cops to send somebody over, protection.'

'Fat chance,' Harper said. 'You know how many serial killers are running around L.A. right now? Probably a half-dozen.'

Anna grunted, 'Huh,' and glanced at Creek. 'Half-dozen?'

'No,' Creek said, following her thought, shaking his head. 'We *ain't* doing no story on that.'

Anna sent Creek and Louis home in the truck. Louis was shook, having talked with the cops twice in two days, having had statements taken. Louis thrived in anonymity – sought it, treasured it. 'Everything's gonna be okay, right?' He was anxious, twisting a shredded copy of the *L.A. Reader* in his hands.

'Yeah, for us,' Anna told him. 'You guys take the truck, go home, get some sleep.'

'I just don't want anything to happen to us . . . to you,' Louis said, eyes large. 'I mean, if anything happened to you . . . what'd happen to me?'

'It'll be okay, Louis,' she said, giving him a quick smile and a pat on the back. 'I promise.'

When she told him she'd ride with Harper, Creek took her aside to whisper furiously: 'What the fuck is this? You don't even *know* him, he could be, you know, *the guy*.'

'Nah, we know what he's doing – his kid,' Anna said.

'Oh, horseshit,' Creek said in exasperation. He added: 'You started acting perky as soon as we met him outside the house, and now you're starting again.'

'Perky?' That made her mad. She put her hands on her hips and started, 'What are you . . .'

'Figure it out,' Creek said, and he stalked off to the truck. When he got there he turned and said, 'And what about Clark?'

Smack.

But he was in the truck and kicking it over before she could think of a proper reply.

Harper drove a black BMW 740IL. The cockpit showed as many ant-sized instrument lights as a jumbo jet. A half-dozen golf putters cluttered the passenger side. Harper popped the passenger door for Anna and tossed the putters in the back.

'Nice car,' she said, when he climbed in the driver's side.

Cars were about four-hundredth on her priority list of Important Things in Life.

'Freeway cruiser,' he said, indifferently.

'And you play a little golf, huh?'

He looked at her, cool, and said, 'I do two things: I practice law, and I play golf.'

'I mean, like . . . seriously?'

'I'm serious about both,' he said; and she thought he was a little grim. Good-looking, but tight.

'Chasing a little white ball around a pasture.'

He looked at her, still not smiling: 'If golf was about chasing a little white ball around a pasture, I wouldn't do it,' he said.

She turned toward him, her face serious, touched his arm. 'Would you promise me something?'

'What?' The sudden, apparent intimacy took him by surprise.

'Don't ever, ever, *ever* try to explain to me what golf is really about.'

This time he grinned and she thought: *Mmm. Harrison Ford.*

At her house, he took a flashlight out of the trunk and walked once around the outside, checked the bushes, said, 'Ouch, what the hell is that?' and a couple minutes later, 'Good.'

Inside, he looked at the windows, including the boarded-up back window, and said, 'Leave the board for the time being,' and, 'You need to get some empty beer cans or pop cans. Before you go to sleep at night, stack them up inside the door. If anybody tries to come through, it'll sound like the end of the world.'

'Okay.'

'Your bushes scratched the heck out of me.'

'That's what they're for.'

'Okay. You got a gun?' he asked.

'Yeah.'

'Let's get it.'

He followed her upstairs to the bedroom, and she took the gun from its clip behind the bed's headboard.

'Smith & Wesson,' she said, handing him the chromed revolver.

'Good old six-forty,' he said. He checked the ammo: 'With three-fifty-seven wadcutters. You're in good shape. Do you know how to shoot it?'

'I went through a combat class when that was the fad,' she said. 'I go up behind Malibu every year or so and shoot up a gully, like they showed us. Ten feet.'

'So keep it handy,' he said. He handed the gun back, glanced at the quilt on the bed, said, 'Old-fashioned girl, huh?'

She opened her mouth to say something when the doorbell rang. They both looked at the head of the stairs: 'Uh-oh.'

'Probably not Aunt Pansy with a fruit pie,' Harper said, glancing at his watch.

'You think a killer is gonna ring the doorbell at' – she glanced at her watch, too – 'five-oh-five in the morning?'

'Probably not,' he said. 'Let's go see . . . you go first.'

'Why me?'

''Cause you've got the gun.'

That seemed practical, if not particularly chivalrous. She led the way down, feeling slightly silly, gun in her hand, paused in the hallway, then whispered back, 'Now what?'

'Get away from the door and yell,' Harper suggested.

The doorbell rang again as they stepped into the kitchen and Anna shouted, 'Who is it?'

'Me. Creek.' Creek's voice, all right.

'Oh, boy,' Anna said. She went to the door, slipped the chain and pulled it open. Creek slouched on the porch, and his eyes stopped briefly on Anna and then flicked back to Harper.

'Just thought I'd check,' Creek said. To Harper, 'You all done?'

'Yeah, I'm done . . . I need to talk to Anna for a minute, alone. Then I'll be out of here.'

Creek nodded and stepped back on the porch, and pulled the door shut.

'Sorry about that,' Anna said. And she was thinking that Creek showed up at fairly inconvenient times.

'Yeah, no problem.' Harper took a slender leather wallet out of his jacket pocket, took out a thin gold pen, found a card and scribbled on it. 'My home phone. The office phone is on the front. Call me if anything comes up.'

'And you've got my card,' Anna said drily. He must've taken it from her purse.

'Yup.' Unembarrassed.

'I think we should let the police . . .'

She was talking over him, and only caught the last part: '. . . boyfriend stay over, it'd be another layer.'

She stopped: 'What?'

'Maybe you oughta have your boyfriend stay over,' he repeated. 'He'd be another layer between you and the killer. He's a big guy . . .'

'He's not my boyfriend. Creek's a friend.'

'Yeah? But you can trust him?'

'With my life.'

Harper bobbed his head, and said, 'Then you might think about it, even if he drives you nuts. I'll tell you what: This guy isn't gonna go away. This nut. He's thinking about you all the time. Sooner or later – he'll turn up.'

Chapter 9

The two-faced man sat in the dirt, a hedge brushing his right ear, a fender a foot from his left. The spot was guarded, out of sight, and had the feel of a den. He was comfortable in it; he put the pistol barrel beside his nose, drew a breath scented with gunpowder and oil.

He waited; and as he waited, he lapsed into a fantasy.

He was invisible, drifting through Anna's house, hanging a few inches above the floor, like a wisp, or a genie. She was in the bathroom, naked, doing her face, bending over a counter, looking in the mirror.

Could she feel him there, so close, coming up behind? He reached out to touch the smooth bumps made by her vertebrae.

Mmm . . . no. She had to be totally unknowing. Unknowing, he'd be witness to her most intimate moments. Perfect moments.

But it'd be kind of neat if he could materialize, too. Not just an ethereal eye, watching, but somebody who had the power to materialize right behind her.

He edited: now he could materialize.

And she'd be naked, there, bending over the bathroom counter, putting on lipstick.

No. Edit again.

She'd be wearing nylons, with a garter belt, but that's all, nylons and a garter belt, no underwear, putting on lipstick, and he'd come up behind her and the first thing she'd feel would be his fingers trailing down her spine like a cold draft.

All right, he liked that. Return. He drifted in the door, set down beside her. She was leaning over the sink, her breasts free, nipples pink, a dark shadow where her legs joined; he put out a hand, touched her spine.

When he was a child, years before, he'd been captured by the image of Humpty Dumpty. Not the fall, but the shell. Because that's how he knew himself to be.

He had two faces, not one. The outer face looked to the world – a somber face, even when he was a child, but pretty, and forthright. The inner face was something else: dark, moody, fetid, closed. The inner face contemplated only himself. He might have been whole, once. But the wholeness had been beaten out of him, shattered like Humpty Dumpty.

His father had sold cars. Thousands of cars.

His father had been on television every night, prime time, with his fake nose and white painted face, his oversized shoes and Raggedy-Ann hair.

He was the most famous clown in the world, reeling across the sales floor with a gallon-sized jug marked XXX: 'Hey, you think Big Bandy is jes' being funny when he sez you can get this like-new Camaro for the low-low price of $6,240? What'd I say? Did I say $5,740? Another Bandy slip-o-the-tongue, that's old Bandy getting into the old brandy again, makin' mistakes like saying this like-new Camaro only $5,240. Whoops. There I go again. Get down here quick and you could get this Camaro for . . . Whoo, that's good stuff. Old Bandy may be into the old brandy again, but I'm as good as my word, so whatever ridiculous price I just said, that's all you'll pay . . .'

He could take the ridicule at school, Old Bandy being his father, because everybody knew that Old Bandy was making millions. What he couldn't take was when Old Bandy got into the old brandy at home, and beat the shit out of him.

His mother was worse. His mother was a small, dark-haired devil who drank more old brandy than Old Bandy did, and she'd turn him in – 'You know what your son did today?' – as though he wasn't also her son.

And the things he did, that every kid did, would somehow boil in his father's brain, and he'd open the bedroom door in fear and find the old man standing there with a stick in his hands and a darkness around his eyes.

His parents' sex life was as bad as the beatings: they'd get drunk and screw on the couch, or the floor, or the stairs, and if everything wasn't going just right, his father might hit her with an open hand, bat her around. She seemed to approve of it, taunt him until he hit her. Their ravings were impossible to escape: a shattering scream would drag him into the hallway, and there they'd be, sweating, bleeding, drunk, naked.

Whatever happened at home, the family had an outer face for the world: Mom gave money to the symphony and the art museum and was something in the Junior League and every other goddamn silly group willing to ignore her character in return for her money.

The young boy created the two faces as a means of survival: the outer face was bland, careful, somber and never raised its voice to his parents; never commented on the sex or the beatings; not after the first few times with the stick.

But the inner face raged against them.

The inner face wanted to kill them.

His father had a .45 automatic, a big blue Colt. He kept it hidden in a leather holster fastened behind the headboard of his bed. His father took it out every once in a while, to look at it, hold it, aim it at the TV, dry-fire it. Then he'd go into the bedroom, reload it and hide it.

In the sixth grade, two-face dreamed of killing his parents with the .45. The dream had become part of his daily reality, the inner face pleading with the outer. The outer face prevailed, with logic: if he killed his parents, they'd lock him in a room somewhere, and that would be all for him. Even the inner face recognized the unacceptability of that outcome.

Still, the power of the killing mood was so strong that he took the shells out of the .45 and threw them down a sewer. Not because he didn't want to kill them; but because neither face wanted to go to jail.

But he would kill them, sooner or later; that was inevitable. He'd build an elaborate alibi – building the mechanisms of the alibi was one of his favourite fantasies – and then he'd do it. He'd kill his father outright. He thought about a shotgun, aiming it at the old man's chest, pulling the trigger. He'd do his mother with a knife. Very slowly . . .

He got a hard-on thinking about it.

Life with his parents turned him, twisted him. He knew too much from the very start, and the girls sensed it. They shied away from him. And when the hormones hit, everything got worse: he had the fire inside, but no outlet.

And with adolescence, the inner face grew stronger, to dominate the outer, although the outer continued to shield his real nature. And the inner face needed to be fed.

For years, the inner face was content with cruelties to animals and smaller children.

In eighth grade, he'd killed a cat he found crossing their back yard, beat it to death with a dowel rod. The first blow broke the cat's back, and a dozen more killed it. He buried it along their back fence line, carefully shoveling dirt over the body, smoothing the spot, even transplanting a chunk of sod to conceal the fresh dirt.

Nobody had suspected him: and in the next week, a half-dozen cardboard signs were nailed to phone poles, asking for help finding a red-black-gray tabby named Jimbo.

A small thrill; which the inner face contemplated, patiently, turning it over and over.

The next time he killed a cat, he killed it only after a protracted hunt. He had to know where it came from: so when he killed it, he could carry it up to the neighbor's porch, ring a doorbell, and with a real tear in his eye, say, 'A car hit your cat.'

The neighbor lady had broken down in tears, her daughter had been distraught and the outer face had cried with them, real agony. So much so, that the neighbor lady walked him home, to thank his parents for his concern.

In the eleventh grade, he took a major step, when the inner face noticed that Mrs Garner was never without her coffee.

Mrs Garner was thirty, a dark-haired, almost-pretty young science teacher, with long, slender legs. He was drawn to her from the start; a week into class, he'd stopped at the front of the room, and the outer face had ventured an awkward pleasantry.

Mrs Garner had frozen him, had said, 'Go to your chair, please.' Two or three of the girls in the class had exchanged quick, knowing glances, smirking, at the snub.

As quickly as that – snap – he hated the woman.

And noticed that she carried the coffee cup with her during chemistry class, and would, from time to time, duck into the teacher's work space at the back of the room to freshen the cup.

The inner face considered that for a time: that Mrs Garner never seemed to wash the cup after she started using it, but simply filled and refilled it. He got to class very early one day, while Mrs Garner was in the teachers' lounge for her hourly smoke, and tipped a small dose of chlordanc into the cup.

Mrs Garner never noticed when she drank it: but a half hour later, she suddenly declared herself to be ill, and on the way to the door, collapsed in convulsions. Two-face was a hero: he took charge, ran to the principal's office, got an ambulance on the way. Ran back, knelt by Mrs Garner as her convulsions nearly pulled her apart.

She was sprawled on her back, her dress hiked up her legs; from two-face's perspective, kneeling next to her, he could see far up her legs to the squared-off juncture, and a few random dark hairs outside her white cotton underpants.

He was ferociously aroused; and for years afterward, he pictured himself kneeling next to Mrs Garner's body.

He didn't think, until later that day, that for two hours after the poisoning, the poison bottle – an iodine bottle that he'd emptied to take the chlordane – was still in his pocket. If anyone had suspected poisoning, he would have convicted himself.

And it didn't occur to him until after he'd dumped the bottle in a trash barrel that he hadn't wiped it for fingerprints.

Nor did he consider for almost a month that the chlordane bottle where he'd gotten the poison was still in his parents' garage with the other pesticides.

Eventually, he thought of it all, and the two faces agreed: He'd been lucky to get away with it.

Mrs Garner lived, and returned to class, although her memory was never as good as it should have been. Her science was never as good. The other teachers were told that she might have accidentally poisoned herself with one of the compounds that sat around the science room, odd powders in small vials, not all identified; and they pitied her as her hands shook when she tried to grade papers or to write.

The two faces watched her for the rest of the year, and for all of his last year in high school. Proud of their handiwork. Tempted to finish it.

But too smart.

The inner face retracted, went back to the small cruelties. The other face matured, and learned even better how to mask the inside.

As two-face grew older, he had some women, but none that he really wanted. He got the leftovers, the losers. The ones he wanted sensed the wrongness about him, and turned away.

Then came Anna. The look of her, the sound of her.

She was his woman, always had been. He didn't know exactly why, didn't realize that his first view of her reminded him of his first glimpse of Mrs Garner, but there wasn't any doubt, never the slightest, from the first time he'd seen her amongst the others, heard them talk about her. She'd turned the key in him, and the inner face had gone outside. Had dealt with his rivals. One to go.

He still processed those images through his imagination: like Anna herself, the images excited him, turned him on, as did the memories of Mrs Garner. O'Brien and MacAllister, thrashing in their own blood. The inner face fed on the blood, swelled with it.

And Anna must feel it, somewhere in her soul. Or would feel it, when she was no longer surrounded by these others.

Two-face and Anna were fated to be together . . .

He fantasized: Anna bent over the bathroom counter, her buttocks thrust toward him, the sinewy structure of her spine and the soft sheets of her back muscles . . .

Then Anna turned and spoke to him.

He edited frantically: she couldn't see him, how could she speak to him? He edited, but she persisted, and she said:

'. . . talking to Les and he said the guys at Seventeen are

going to ditch their overnight monitoring guy and the guys in the truck are gonna have to do their own, like with one scanner.'

Another voice: 'Oh, that's horseshit.'

The editing broke down, snarled, crashed: and the two-faced man suddenly came back. He was sitting in the dirt with a fender next to one cheek and a hedge next to the other. He had a .22 pistol in his hand.

The voice was real. And so was Anna.

He pushed himself up, and stepped out.

'Anna?'

Chapter 10

Harper pushed and Anna weakened: he was having an effect on her. Creek could stay, she decided.

'But you've got to give me space,' she told Creek, when Harper had gone. 'You can't follow me around the house. You can't fix anything.'

'Maybe I could do some painting,' Creek suggested, peering around the front room.

'No painting,' Anna said. 'No fix-up, no clean-up, no hedge-trimming. You sleep, you watch TV. We eat, we got to work.'

He grumbled about it, but agreed. 'I'm gonna have to repark the truck . . .'

'You've got the truck? I thought Louis dropped you off.'

He shook his head: 'I put him in a cab – the truck's down the block.' The dead-end streets between the canals were too narrow for the truck to maneuver. When they had to stop momentarily at Anna's, they'd leave it at the intersection of Linnie and Dell, usually with Louis to watch it.

'If it's there when Linkhof gets up, he'll call the cops and get it towed.' Linkhof was the antisocial neighbor.

'Yeah. I can ditch it at Jerry's. The cook'll be there, he can see it out the window.'

Anna nodded. 'All right. I'll ride down with you.'

She got a jacket, and when Creek said, 'Gun,' self-consciously put the Smith in her jacket pocket, on the opposite side from her cell phone, which she carried by habit. 'If the cops see us walking back at this time of night, they'll stop us, and if they frisk us, I'll be downtown again,' Anna said.

'We'll stop at Jerry's, get a coffee. The sky'll be getting light in a half hour, we can walk back then,' Creek said. 'Besides,' he added, 'we're white.'

White.

The way things worked in L.A. Still, the pistol felt like a brick in her pocket as they walked in the dark toward the truck.

The truck represented a lot of heavy lifting. They'd started, five years earlier, with a rusty Dodge van, cast-off video gear and spanners, and a lot of metal shelving from Home Depot, which Louis and Creek had bolted to the floor. The floor on the Dodge leaked, both from rust-outs and the new bolt holes, and Louis sometimes emerged from the back suffering from advanced carbon monoxide poisoning.

After three years of street work, building their reputation and their contacts, walking tapes around to the TV stations, they'd ditched the van and bought the truck from a cable station that had decided to get out of the news business. The truck came with the dish and a compressed-air lift; Louis put in the electronics. The dish alone saved hours every night;

if they could use the relay antennas on the mountain – and they could from almost anywhere in the Los Angeles bowl – they could dump video and voice to everyone.

And the equipment was getting better: Creek's camera was almost new . . .

Anna felt a little thump every time she saw the truck: a lot of work. Something she was good at.

But she didn't see the man by the truck until they were almost on top of him, she and Creek talking away, and Creek said, 'Hey.'

The man turned – heavy shoulders, big hands, and she thought of Harper – but this guy was black. He said, 'Anna?'

The questioned slowed Creek: Creek had gone into his long-stride, somewhat-sideways combat approach, closing quickly. But now he hesitated, and Anna said, 'Who is that?' and the man lifted an arm toward Creek, and Creek said, 'No!' and went straight into him.

The shots were loud, the gun spitting short, sharp spikes of fire at Creek, three times, four, five. Creek twisted, still moving in, while Anna clawed at her pocket. Then Creek was on him, reaching, and the man turned to run.

His head snapped back and he screamed, and Anna gave up on the gun and started for Creek. The shooter snapped forward and began to run. *Creek let him go*, Anna thought . . . the man disappeared down the street as Anna turned to Creek.

And Creek fell down. Slumped, rolled, looked up at her.

'Gun,' he groaned. 'Get the gun.'

'He's gone . . .'

'Get gun, get gun,' he said, urgently, and Anna, not wanting to believe, dropped down next to him and said, 'You're okay?'

And in the dim light of the street, saw the black blood on his mouth, on his face and neck, the blood on his shirt.

Lights were coming on down the street and she screamed, 'Police, call the police, ambulance . . . man shot. This is Anna, call nine-one-one,' and someone shouted back, 'I'm calling . . .'

Creek grabbed her by the coat and said something urgent but unintelligible. His hand was wrapped in fabric, and Anna plucked it away. A woman's nylon stocking, a little darker than nude; maybe suntan. Creek had pulled it off the shooter's head, snapping his head back. The shooter wasn't black. He'd been wearing a mask.

That all ran through her head in an instant, and then she tossed the stocking away and shouted down at him, 'Are you okay? Goddamn, Creek . . .'

'Ahh . . .'

A man was running up the street toward her. 'Anna?'

'Yeah, it's me,' she shouted back, half-standing. 'My friend is shot, somebody help.'

The man arrived, a neighbor named Wilson, stood uncertainly over her in bluebird pajamas. 'Henry's called the cops,' he said.

'Gotta have an ambulance, he's hurt bad,' Anna said, looking up at Wilson, eyes big.

Another neighbor, Logan, was in the street, running toward them, a flashlight in one hand, a gun in the other. 'Somebody hit?'

'Ambulance on the way,' Wilson said.

'Let me take a look,' Logan said. He squatted next to Creek, shined the light on his face and neck: 'Three hits,' he said. 'No arteries . . .' He pulled up Creek's shirt. There were two small puckered blood entry wounds, one just outside Creek's left nipple, another two inches above that.

'Bad?' Creek mumbled.

'The face isn't bad, I don't think, I can't tell about the chest. The goddamn slugs can rattle around in there.' He pulled the shirt down. 'Nothin' to do but wait.' And to Anna, he said, 'What're you into, darlin'?'

Anna shook her head. 'Cops think it's a fruitcake guy, a nut.'

'Stalkin' ya?'

'Yeah, something like that.' She screamed back down the street. 'Where's the fuckin' ambulance?' And to Creek, 'Hold on, Creek, God . . .'

More lights were flicking on, and a man shouted back: 'On the way. Two minutes.'

Creek was flat on his back, his eyes half-hung, looking sleepy. She had him by the shirt, blood on her hands and jacket, Logan at his head, and she yelled at him, 'Creek, c'mon, c'mon, hold on.'

Chapter 11

Neighbors started leaking down the street, and built a ring around Creek and Anna. Then the cops arrived, two car lengths ahead of the ambulance, and the ambulance attendants dropped an oxygen mask on Creek's face and lifted him onto a gurney.

Anna, pushed away, stepped up next to the truck, felt the pistol against her leg. The cops were right there, the red rack lights banging off the houses, the neighbors gathering, everybody watching Creek.

If the cops found the gun on her, they'd take it, they'd ask questions: might hold her until they checked the gun against slugs taken from Creek. She didn't have that time. The truck door was right there, and she stepped up, and inside, toward the back. She opened the hideout box where they kept the Nagra, looked guiltily toward the open door, pulled the gun out and dropped it in the box.

When she stepped back to the door, Creek was going into the ambulance, his eyes staring up at the night sky. Logan stepped over: 'Blood pressure's not too bad, that's what they said.'

'Jesus, Logan.' She clutched his arm, let go.

'If he's not bleeding out, he'll be okay,' he said. Logan was watching his hands: he wanted to pat her somewhere, but wasn't sure exactly where, how she'd take the intimacy. 'Once he hits the OR, they'll handle it.'

The ambulance eased away from sight, carefully working through side-stepping neighbors, then the driver hit the siren button and the ambulance disappeared down the block and around the corner. A uniformed cop walked over to them, one hand resting casually on his pistol. 'Are you the lady who was with him?'

Anna nodded: 'Listen, there's a lot going on here. You've got to call the Santa Monica, or L.A. County.'

The cop put her in the back of his car, but left the door open while he and his partner worked the street, taking names and addresses of witnesses. Another cop car arrived, and two more cops began pushing people back toward their homes.

Anna slumped in the back seat, her mind filled with Creek. He was a big man, almost overmuscled, hardened by life . . . but on the ground, looking up at her, he'd seemed almost frail, baby-like, dependent. Helpless.

She turned to look out the back window and felt the cell phone in her pocket. The first two cops were down the block, and after a second's thought, she found Harper's card, took out the cell phone and punched in the number. Nobody home. She left a message and hung up, put the phone away.

And she thought of the masked shooter. He was Harper's size . . . but the voice? The voice hadn't been right for Harper, as far as she could tell. Of course, the shooter had been wearing the stocking. But she'd heard it before. The voice was familiar somehow: tickled something in the back of her brain.

Another cop car arrived, and after talking with the first arrivals, the two new cops came over to the car. 'You say the man ran that way . . .' They pointed down Dell.

'Yeah, and there's a stocking . . .'

She showed them the nylon, and one of the cops asked, 'You don't wear nylons like this, do you? Just curious . . .'

'No. I wear nylons sometimes, but not this color.'

'Okay.' A flat *okay*. Not skeptical, but not necessarily buying it, either. 'So you say he went that way . . .'

The new cops put her back in the squad car and started tracing the path of the shooter, walking down Dell with their flashlights. She watched until the phone rang. She snapped it open, and said, 'Yes?'

Harper: 'Couldn't wait to hear my voice again, huh?' He said it lightly.

'Creek's been shot.' Silence. She tried again. 'Creek's been . . .'

'Christ, the guy's going through a psychotic break, the shooter. How bad is he? Creek?'

'Pretty bad, I think. He couldn't talk when they put him in the ambulance.'

'Where are you?'

'In a cop car, by my house, on Linnie. We were walking up to the truck.'

'Fifteen minutes,' Harper said, and he was gone.

He was almost a half hour, not fifteen minutes, rolling up in the growing light of dawn. He spotted Anna in the cop car and started toward her, but the cops walled him away. They argued for a while, and she saw him show one of the cops a card: but this cop apparently didn't need legal advice, and shook his head.

'You've got to go back downtown,' one of the uniforms said a moment later. 'I understand you've already been there tonight.'

'Yes.' She looked past him at Harper, who was arguing with another cop, his hair flopping into his eyes as he talked. 'Why can't I talk to that man?'

'We want to get a statement from you before you talk to anyone else. You have a right to see your lawyer if you want, but they'll tell you about that downtown,' the cop said. He looked back at Harper: 'He used to be a cop.'

'Homicide,' Anna said.

'Used to be,' the cop said.

So she did it all over again: talked to cops, to a different shift, fresher, just up, three of them this time. Dictated a statement, impatient, worried about Creek. Demanded information about Creek: he was alive, they told her, should be okay. The detectives in the unit were beginning to gather around her.

'This guy is . . . this guy is berserk,' a detective named Samson told her.

'You remember that case down in Anaheim?' asked another cop. 'The guy would stalk these people for weeks, then slash them, then he started killing them? When was that? That was like this.'

'Guy's dead, though,' Samson said.

'Yeah? When did that happen?'

'I don't know – I heard it. He hung himself in prison.'

'Besides, it's more like that one over in Downey, the kid with the Taurus wagon,' said a third cop. 'Man, I couldn't believe he'd do them right in the wagon. Told his mother the blood was some kind of fertilizer for a greenhouse . . .'

'Yeah, I remember. Whatever happened to him? He used both a gun and a knife, didn't he?'

'Can I go?' Anna asked.

Harper was waiting in the same spot where he'd waited the night before, in the hall near the exit.

'Creek's in the OR at L.A. General,' he said. 'He's got three bullets still in him, twenty-twos. If it'd been almost anything else, he'd be dead.' They were walking at speed, heading for the door. They hit it with a bang and were into the street, side by side.

'The face isn't bad, just barely caught some skin, in and out. No nerve damage, nothing,' Harper said. 'The problem is with the chest. One tore a hole in his left lung and collapsed it; another one went between two ribs and rattled around behind his heart.'

'Oh, God.' Standing on the street, she started to cry, one hand to her face. Harper draped an arm around her shoulder and pulled her head into his chest: 'Listen, the docs down there are good.'

'I had the gun in my pocket, I couldn't get it out.'

'Well, you can't . . .'

'He was right there,' she said, pointing at a parking meter,

135

trying to make him see it. 'The guy was right there, he said my name. I had the gun, but I couldn't get it out . . .'

She started to cry again and he squeezed her head in tight: he smelled of clean sweat and deodorant, his arms felt like bricks. She let herself go for a moment, leaning into the comfort of the man, then pushed back, wiped tears with the back of her hand. 'Let's go see him.'

'You're his sister,' Harper muttered as they pushed through the emergency room door. The place smelled like all emergency rooms, a combination of alcohol and raw turkey.

Anna nodded, and five seconds later, at the desk, she said to a nurse, 'My brother was shot and they brought him here. Can you tell me where he is?'

Her distress came through: the nurse never questioned her. 'He's still in surgery,' he said, tipping his head down the hall. 'There's a waiting room . . .'

'Can anybody tell us how he is?'

The nurse shook his head: 'He should be all right, if he's in good shape, and they say he is. That's the best thing.'

'How . . . are they operating right now?'

The nurse glanced at the clock: 'They have been for almost two hours.'

'Oh, Jesus.' The tears started again and Harper steered her toward the waiting area.

Anna wasn't good at waiting, and Harper was worse.

While she sat, remembering the attack, and the days before it – all going back to Jacob's leap, and Jason's death – he read an aging copy of *Modern Maturity*, the sports section of a three-day-old *USA Today*, and a coverless *Time*.

A man with a bad hand cut came in, and Harper went over to talk about it, until a nurse shooed him away. He walked around and jingled change in his pocket, got coffee for the two of them. Three or four times, he went to the desk, came back with nothing new. He put his feet up, tried to sleep and failed.

An hour after they arrived, Pam Glass walked in, her face haggard. She was wearing one of her power suits, with an Hermès knotted at the throat, but the rims of her eyes were red with stress and tears.

'Why didn't anybody call me?' she asked Anna. 'How is he?'

Anna said, 'Where? We didn't know . . . he's still in surgery.'

'He was supposed to call me this morning and he didn't and I thought . . . I don't know what I thought.' She was not quite babbling: 'I didn't hear from him and I went in and Jim said he'd been shot, I was getting a cup of orange juice and Jim came over and said Creek was shot . . .'

'You better sit down,' Harper said. He introduced himself and said, 'I saw you a couple of days ago, I was in talking to Jim.'

'Oh, yeah . . .' she said vaguely. She looked back toward the operating suite: 'What have you heard?'

'Not much: he's hurting. And he's been in there a while.'

'Oh, my God . . .'

Anna was watching her; and watching her, knowing that Creek had made a connection with the woman. Nothing forced here, no sense that Creek was a fling for her. She liked him, a lot. And Anna liked her, for that.

Anna sat on a too-soft chair with her legs curled beneath her, and stared, running mental movies of her time with Creek. Glass tried to read a *Times*: Harper wandered.

'Look,' Harper finally said to Anna. 'We're not gonna do your pal any good sitting around.'

'I'm not leaving until I know how he is,' Anna said.

'Neither am I,' Glass said.

Harper pulled a chair out of the line beside Anna's, and faced it toward her. 'What have you been doing the last couple of days?'

The question had a rhetorical sound to it, and Anna shrugged and opened her mouth and Harper cut her off: 'I'll tell you what. You've been shuttling around from one bunch of cops to another. Santa Monica, L.A., Venice, these guys up in Burbank, whoever they were . . .'

'North Hollywood . . .'

'Whatever. And you know what? All those cops are hoping that somebody else'll get this guy, because they ain't got squat, and they don't have enough time to chase him with everything else they gotta do.'

'We're chasing him,' Glass said grimly.

'C'mon,' Harper said to her. 'How many hours will you put on it? The only reason L.A. tolerates me running around is because I used to work there, and they're hoping I might turn something up and call them. They just don't have the time.'

'They'll *make* the time,' Anna said grimly. 'The only reason this guy isn't a big story is that nobody's paid attention to him. If I want them to pay attention, they will.'

'Oh, bullshit,' Harper said. 'How're you gonna do that? You can't . . .'

'You don't know everything about television,' Anna said, interrupting. 'You look at anybody in this place' – she waved at the emergency room in general – 'and I could do a story on him – or her – and I could sell it. Anybody. You, me, the nurse guy, the guy with the cut. A serial killer? Everybody would take it, if it was done right. And I'll tell you what – the cops don't want to chase him, I'll put them on CNN tomorrow morning. *Then* they'll chase him.'

Harper was shaking his head: 'All right. Maybe you could do that, but . . .'

'You'd just start a cluster-fuck,' Glass said, interrupting him. 'They'd bring in the nine patrolmen with the flattest feet and put them in suits and have them go around with notepads, playing investigator, and nothing would get done. I mean, you'd just panic them – us – and piss 'em off.'

'I've dealt with a couple of these guys, the fruitcakes,' Harper said intently. 'They're crazy and screwed up but most of them are . . . sort of smart. Twisted, but not stupid. You sic the cops on him really heavy – you put him on TV – and he'll love it. And then he'll kill somebody else just to keep things going. One of your friends, maybe. And he'll be looking for you, too. He'll be out there – and if the cops don't get him, he'll get you, eventually.'

'Are you trying to scare me?' Anna asked coldly.

'Yes. 'Cause you should be scared. Now what I'm suggesting is, we get a little proactive . . .'

'Proactive? You sound like the Long Beach chamber of commerce.'

'What I'm saying is, you talk to me: about your friends, about Creek's friends, about the dopers you've known, about weird shit you've seen the last couple of months. Creek must know some dopers, living where he does, there's dope coming through the Marina all the time, and with your job . . .'

'You've been down to look at Creek's place?' Glass asked.

'Sure. Looked at his boat, looked at his house . . .' He turned back to Anna. 'But getting back to the point: talk to me. Let me debrief you. The shooter – you know him. We can work out a few ideas together, and I'll check them out.'

Anna said, 'Look, Jake, I don't know what's going on, but I really think you're wasting your time. This can't have anything to do with your son. If you think about it . . .'

He spread his hands, then touched her knee: 'So maybe it doesn't. I'd like to find out for sure, though. That's the only thing I've got – I want to know what the dope was about.'

'If you find the dealer, what're you gonna do?' Glass asked.

'I don't know,' he said.

'Kill him?' asked Anna.

He looked away from them, down the hall. 'I don't know. I doubt it. But I won't know for sure until I get there.'

They were still talking when a doctor came down the hall, surgery gown showing a half-dozen blood spots, his mask pulled down under his chin. He pulled off his cap as he came up, looked at Anna and asked, a little doubt in his voice, 'Are you Mr Creek's relatives?'

Anna and Glass were on their feet: 'How is he?'

'You don't look like sisters.'

'Different mom,' Anna said. 'Tell us . . .'

Again, their intensity banished doubt about the connection and the doc smiled gravely and said, 'Unless there's something we didn't find, he should be okay.'

'Oh, thank God,' Anna said, and Glass started to leak tears again.

'But he's hurt badly,' the surgeon continued. 'The lung will repair itself fairly quickly, but there's muscle damage in the chest wall and the back muscles, and that'll take a while.'

'When's he gonna be able to talk?' Harper asked.

'Tomorrow, probably. He's going to be pretty sleepy for a couple of days, at least. Then he's going to hurt – but I doubt he'll be in here a week.'

'Did the police tell you about the circumstances of the shooting?' Harper asked.

The doc nodded: 'Yes. We'll list him under an alias – we do it all the time in battering cases. If somebody doesn't know exactly where to find him, they won't.'

'Aw, that's great,' Anna said.

Glass started sniffing again, and then turned to Anna and said, 'I don't cry for anything. Ever.'

Anna nodded. 'Neither do I,' she said, another tear rolling down her cheek.

They stayed until Creek had gone to the recovery room, then Glass left in a hurry: 'I'm moving in here,' she declared. 'I've got to get some stuff together, and get some time off.'

'Moving in?' Anna asked.

'The guy may be stalking you, but he's killing the people around you,' Glass said. 'I'm gonna get a chair and sit in his room with a gun.'

When she was gone, Harper and Anna stood by the side of the street, the sun beating down. 'What're you gonna do?' Harper asked.

'Try to get some sleep,' Anna said. 'Try to think of some names.'

'Think of some names?'

'Yeah. I'm gonna talk to you. And something else.'

'What's that?'

'When you go looking for this guy,' Anna said, in a way that left no doubt, 'I'm coming with you.'

Chapter 12

A nna made lists.

She slept, exhausted, but her brain made lists, the crazies, the dopers, the men who'd come on to her in the past six months, anyone who might have fixated on her.

She dreamed, twisting in the percale sheets, of the man at the truck, the shooter: a big man, with something familiar to him, a way of holding his shoulders. And the voice: he'd said only one word, her name, but he'd spoken it before, in her hearing. She knew this man.

But who was it? She found herself paying attention to Harper, when he spoke her name. Was the voice the same? She didn't think so – but now she was confusing her memories of the shooting with other moments, with other people calling her name.

She made lists.

A thump – a human sound – from downstairs. She rose out of her sleep like a diver coming to the surface, breaking through, gasping, looking around, thinking, *gun*. But she had no gun, the gun was in the truck.

Then another thump, running water . . . and she recognized

the thump as a toilet seat going up, then coming down, the water in the downstairs toilet.

Harper. He'd been sleeping on the couch. He wouldn't go away. She pushed herself up, glanced at the bedroom door. Closed, not locked.

Harper? No. She knew why Harper was here.

When she came down from the bedroom, hair still wet from the shower, Harper was putting at a paper circle on the living room carpet. 'Your floor breaks about an inch toward the back wall, on a fifteen-foot putt,' he said.

'Do tell.' She went on past and picked up the phone in the kitchen.

'He was awake for an hour about noon, but he's sleeping again. He's doing fine and without complications, he could be out this week.' Harper said. He was squatting, looking over a ball at the paper circle.

She put the phone back on the hook: 'How is that possible? This week?'

'They push them out in a hurry,' Harper said. He stood up, and hovered over the ball, then looked at Anna. 'Are you going to say something before I putt?'

'No.'

'I'd hate to have you say something right in the middle of my backswing.'

'No, go ahead.'

He moved the putter head back an inch, and Anna said, 'Watch it.' The stroke came through, and the ball missed the paper circle by two inches. 'That's fuckin' hilarious,' he said.

'Are we gonna talk, or are you gonna spend the afternoon playing with your putter?'

They walked out to Jerry's, into the sun, Anna quiet, head down. Harper carrying the putter, swinging it, balancing it, turning it like a walking stick. The afternoon traffic was already building toward the rush, and they had to wait before crossing Pacific to the restaurant.

'You're not scared enough,' Harper said, as they walked.

'What?'

'Most people, if a madman was stalking them, they couldn't move,' he said.

She thought about it as they crossed the street, and said, 'Maybe I'm burned out on being scared. Going out every night, we see all kinds of stuff, people shot and stabbed and squashed in cars and burned to death. When you see enough of it, you've got to assume it won't happen to you. You must've felt like that when you were a cop.'

'Nope. Never did. I was scared shitless all the time.'

Logan had parked the truck in the restaurant lot after the shooting, and now Anna unlocked the door, knelt on the seat and fished in the hideout box for the .357, got it, turned, and caught Harper appreciating her ass. She hopped out of the truck and dropped the pistol in her jacket pocket.

'I thought you kept the gun at home,' Harper said, grinning. He knew he'd been caught, and he wasn't the least abashed by it; he twirled the putter like a baton.

'I do, but I had it last night when Creek got shot, and I didn't want the cops to take it.'

Jerry's was Anna's regular spot, with comfortable booths

and decent coffee, mostly empty in the late afternoon, the waiters bustling around, getting ready for the dinner rush. The owner, Donna Tow – Jerry's ex-wife – came over with coffee and said, 'Heard about Creek. I called the hospital and they said he'd be okay.'

'Looks like it,' Anna said. They talked for a few more minutes, Anna giving her a quick account of the shooting.

'Too goddamn many guns around,' Tow said, as she headed back toward the kitchen.

Anna and Harper slid into a booth, and a waitress brought a pot of coffee and two cups. 'So what are we doing?' Anna asked Harper.

'Having you along won't make it easier,' Harper said.

'It might; I'm probably smarter than you are,' Anna said.

'*That* could help,' he said. He grinned again: he wouldn't be goaded.

'So what . . .' The grin faded and he squared himself in the booth and said, 'Names. The whole thing is connected to O'Brien and Jacob: You shoot Jacob's . . . fall . . . and the next thing, the guy is coming after you and kills O'Brien and MacAllister, who also happen to be connected by drugs. Somewhere in there, we'll find his track.'

'But I didn't know that much about Jason,' Anna said. 'We'd done a few things over at UCLA, Creek and Louis and me, and he was taking film classes, and heard about us. He came up with a story – this was a year or so ago – and we shot it and sold it. So he started looking for stuff, and whenever he'd come up with something, he rode along, shot it, and got a cut, ten percent.'

'But you weren't social.'

'No. He'd get me by phone, or if I needed an extra guy, I'd call him up. He was good with a camera and he had a cool head when things were getting rough. He'd keep shooting no matter what . . .'

'I know.' A sudden deep sadness crossed his face, and Anna reached out and touched his hand on the coffee cup. 'I'm really sorry about your kid. I mean, I really am.'

'Yeah.' He looked out the window, at a woman skating by in the street, Walkman phones on her ears. 'Christ, I hardly knew him. I mean, I'd see him all the time – but I didn't know him. It was like, I could get to know him later. My ex-wife, I think she did a pretty good job with him, now this . . .' He shook himself and said, 'So do you have any ideas about O'Brien? Where we start?'

'I know one name and face – Bob – and I've heard about a couple of other people. But if we can find Bob, we might have something.'

Bob, she told Harper, was also in film at UCLA. A few months earlier, Jason had called about a possible story. They'd arranged to meet in Santa Monica, and when they did, Bob was with him. They were both high.

'They either shared the dope or shared the dealer,' she said. 'One way or another . . .'

'So let's go talk to Bob,' Harper said, pushing the coffee away.

'Hospital first,' Anna said.

Creek was in a third-floor critical care unit, sleeping, an IV dripping into his arm. Pam Glass was curled up on a chair next to the bed, reading a magazine, wearing the same clothes she'd been wearing that morning. When she saw them coming, she smiled, weakly, and stood up. 'He should sleep for another hour or two,' she whispered.

'Have you been home?' Anna asked.

'No, I just went down to the corner for a sandwich. I'm okay.'

'God, Pam . . .' They both turned and looked at Creek. His hair had been tamed, and was pulled back under his head. His face was pale under the sailor's tan, his cheekbones more prominent than Anna remembered. And he looked, she thought, almost . . . old.

'An hour or two?' Anna asked.

Pam nodded. 'What are you guys doing?'

'Looking around,' Harper said.

Glass hardened up: 'Look, I know you were a hotshot when you were with the sheriff's department, but I don't think we really need . . .'

Harper grinned at her and said, 'Shhh . . .'

'What?'

'Just a minute ago you were really worried about Creek. That's a very nice aspect of your personality.' He looked at Anna and tipped his head toward the door. 'Let's go. We can be back in two hours.'

On the way to UCLA, Harper said, 'I've got a question, but I don't know exactly how to phrase it.'

'Think real hard,' Anna said. 'Pretend the question is a putt.'

'Okay. The thing is, you're an interesting woman. We're just starting to know each other, and I figure we can go one of two ways – we can have a pure business relationship, or we can think about maybe, you know, doing something together. I mean, not for sure, but leave the possibility open, since you don't seem to be involved with anybody. You know what I mean?'

'No. I don't think I understood the last sentence at all; it was too complicated,' Anna said. She understood. She was also enjoying herself.

'I'm saying that I've been tempted to come on to you, just a little bit,' Harper said.

'A little bit tempted, or a little bit come on?'

He changed lanes with a lurch, cutting off a Mercedes that had been coming up from behind. 'A lot tempted to come on a little bit.'

'Okay, I've got that. Go ahead.' She put her feet on the dashboard.

'But if there's no point, I'll forget it,' he said. 'Give up. On the other hand, if there is a point, then I'll continue to be tolerant and charming and liberal and shit, in my own cowboy way.'

'Jesus,' Anna said, pinching the bridge of her nose. 'Cowboy. You were probably born in Reseda.'

'So is there a point, or not?'

'Well,' she said, letting her eyelids droop, 'I wouldn't *totally* give up.'

'Totally,' he said, satisfied.

Tracing Bob took time. The administration offices were closed, but they found a course guide in the library. Anna thought Bob and Jason had been taking an editing course together: they found a course description that might be right, located the classrooms on a map. They got into the building as a kid was coming out, then walked through the hallways, looking for someone who might be a teacher. They didn't find any, but after talking to a few students, scored with two pale-faced kids in an editing room.

'Red-haired guy, skinny, sorta hard-faced like a skater,' Harper said, giving them a description from Anna.

'Like from Arkansas, or somewhere? This hillbilly accent?' asked one of the kids.

Anna snapped her fingers: 'That's him: I forgot the accent.'

'Well, his name's Bob, all right. I don't know his last name, but he works at Kinko's, at night.'

Bob was already on the job, and recognized Anna as soon as they walked in. He lifted a hand, walked over: 'How's it going?'

'We need to talk,' Anna said. 'About Jason.'

'Jason? I haven't seen him for a couple of weeks.'

'We *do* need to talk,' she said. She looked around. 'Who's your supervisor?'

They took him out behind the Kinko's, into an overflow parking lot, where he lit a cigarette and said, 'Jesus, I can't believe he's dead. Dead?'

'We're gonna send his ashes back to Indiana,' Anna said.

Bob – his last name was Catwell – shuddered: 'When I die, I hope they don't send me back to Fort Smith. Nasty.'

'He was murdered,' Harper said. 'The guy who did it

took his time. Beat him to death. His skull was in about fifty pieces.'

'Aw, man,' he said. Then: 'What do you want? Why are you talking to me?'

'Whoever killed him may be coming after me. I don't know why, but that's the way it is,' Anna said. 'There's a possibility that whoever did it was somehow involved in dealing drugs to Jason. You know Jason got into it a little heavy – and the last time I saw you, you both were into it.'

'Oh, no,' Catwell said. He flicked the cigarette in a bush and took a step back toward the store.

Harper moved quickly – very quickly – between Catwell and the Kinko's back door. Anna remembered the ease with which he'd taken her at the apartment. He said, 'We really need to know where you got the crank, or whatever.'

'Fuck you,' Catwell said. 'You can get killed talking about shit like that.'

'Talk to us, or talk to the cops,' Anna said. 'The cops are crazy to get this guy. He's killed two people and shot a third one.'

'That sounds like a reason *not* to talk.'

'If you give us a name, we'll forget you,' Harper said, pressing him. 'If you don't, we'll feed you to the cops. They'll be on you like a hot sweat. And when they get the name, they won't hide where they got it. You'll be right down there identifying the guy.'

'I don't have to tell anybody any fuckin' thing.' He walked around Harper toward the door.

'You know better than that,' Anna said, talking to his back. 'Sometimes you do have to tell; you know they can squeeze you. If you don't help us, the cops'll be here in ten minutes. So help: please.'

'You won't be able to stay here if you don't,' Harper said. 'Your ass'll be back in Fort Smith.'

'*Please*,' Anna said.

Catwell got to the door before he stopped. He faced the door, unmoving, for a full ten seconds, then finally turned, and said to Anna, 'So you used to, like, party down with Jason and Sean.'

Anna, confused by the tone of his voice, said, 'What?'

Harper asked, 'Sean? MacAllister?'

Catwell shifted his gaze to Harper: 'You know him?'

'Yeah, I saw him last night,' Harper said. To Anna, he said, 'The late Sean MacAllister.'

Anna was closing in on Catwell. 'When you said I partied down with them, what'd you mean?'

Catwell's eyes slid away, and he made a 'you know' bob of his head: 'You know . . .'

'No, I don't; but I've a bad feeling about what you think.'

'Well, maybe it's not true,' Catwell said.

'That I was sleeping with them?'

'Yeah, I guess.'

'Where'd you hear that?'

'Listen, if it's not true . . .'

'I don't care about that, 'cause for one thing, they're both dead.'

'Sean?' Now Catwell was scared. 'They killed Sean, too?'

'Yes.' Anna nodded. 'Same guy, but with a knife. Now where'd you hear I was sleeping with them?'

'Uh, you came to a party one night, off Sunset? To get

Jason, but he was really wrecked? So you left without him?'

She remembered: 'At BJ's. Upstairs.'

'Yeah.'

'What's BJ's?' Harper asked.

'Club,' Anna said. To Catwell: 'So what'd they tell you?'

'That, uh, you know . . .'

'What?'

'Slept with them. At, uh, the same time . . . like in a pile.'

'Ah, jeez,' Anna said. 'They told everybody that?'

'Sure. I mean, like it wasn't any big secret.'

'I didn't even *know* MacAllister,' Anna said.

'He and Jason had an apartment together, over by BJ's, down the hill from there,' Catwell said.

Anna looked at Harper and walked in a circle around the parking lot, ran her hand back through her hair: 'Jeez.'

'What?'

She looked at him: 'He's not trying to kill me. I'm perfectly safe,' she said.

'Say that again.'

'I'm not in trouble – *you're* in trouble,' Anna said.

'What're you . . .'

'He's not gonna kill me. He's gonna kill you, Jake. Somebody already said it. Pam? I think Pam did – he's killing the guys he sees around me. Ah, God: he only shot Creek because Creek was with me. If we'd seen it . . .'

'Huh.' Harper thought it over. 'Like he's eliminating the competition.'

'Yeah. So I've got no problem.'

Now Harper shook his head: 'Don't think that. If he gets to you . . . I don't think you'd enjoy the date. And to Catwell:

'Who else was at that party? High-school kids?'

'I don't know. People coming and going. Street kids, for sure. I don't think they were in high school no more. But I was loaded, man. I can barely remember . . . but I remember the story about Anna.'

'Good memory,' Anna said.

Catwell said, 'No, man. I mean, it was like a *hot* story – what you guys done. They said they were gonna send it in to *Penthouse*.'

'Aw, man, that damn Jason,' Anna said. 'Uh, you didn't tell anybody you'd been sleeping with me?'

'No. Jesus.'

'So give us a name, Bob,' said Anna.

He was weakening. 'Goddammit, if I do, you can't tell anyone.'

'We're not interested in you,' Harper said. 'We just need a name. The guy who sold to Jason.'

'Tarpatkin,' Catwell said softly. 'He works out of the Philadelphia Grill on Westwood. He's a Russian, he'd be there by now, probably. Later, for sure.'

'Does he sell wizards?'

'What? Wizards?'

Harper described them and Catwell shook his head: 'Tarpatkin's been around a while. He only sells to people he knows and he only sells coke, heroin and high-priced hash. He doesn't fuck around with that other shit.'

They got a description: Tarpatkin was tall, gaunt, pale, with long frizzy black hair and a goatee. 'He looks like the devil,' Catwell said. 'And Jesus, please don't let him find out who you talked to.'

* * *

'Got time to swing by the hospital again,' Anna said, looking at her watch. 'He says the guy's at the grill all night.'

'All right.' Harper had a remote key entry for the car, unlocked her door from twenty feet, then opened it for her, touched her back as she got in. Almost courtly, she thought. Old-fashioned. Not unpleasant. 'Sorry about that sleeping-around thing . . . bunch of kids bullshitting. Nobody pays any attention to it.'

'Somebody did,' Anna said. 'Still: I'm a little shocked.'

'So we've got to check this BJ's place. Our guy must be hanging out there, if he heard that story.'

'Yeah, but that doesn't get going until late.'

'So we look up this Tarpatkin first,' Harper said. 'I'm looking forward to that.'

In the car, headed back, she asked casually, 'What kind of women do you go out with? Lawyers? Golfers? Country-clubbers?'

He thought for a long moment, guided the car through a knot of curb cruisers, and said, finally, 'I don't go out much any more.'

She looked at him curiously. 'You don't seem shy.'

'I'm not. I'm just . . . tired. I mostly want to work, play golf and mess around at my house. I used to go over to see Jacob a couple of times a week. Maybe we'd go out to eat.'

'You're gonna miss him.'

'I can't even believe he's gone,' Harper said, hunching down over the steering wheel, holding on with both hands.

'So maybe I'm being nosy.'

He grinned. 'Maybe you are.'

'Well. That's what I do,' she said.

Then she shut up, because sooner or later, she thought, he'd have a little more to say. He wasn't glib. He wasn't exactly taciturn, but he didn't have much of a line of bullshit.

And after a while he said, 'Going out with women . . . is just a lot of trouble. Most of them you meet, you know nothing's going to happen – but you've got to spend a few hours with them anyway, being nice. I guess I'm too busy for that. When it's obvious that nothing's going to happen, I'd like to say, "Well, that's that. I'll get you a cab and we can all go home".'

Anna pretended to be horrified: 'Have you ever done that?'

'Of course not. I'm too polite.'

'I'd think you've got a lot of women coming around. You look okay, you've got a lot of hair, guys like you make some money.'

'You'd be surprised how many women don't care about money,' he said. But then he shrugged and added, 'But, yeah. There were quite a few women around for a while. Now I'm getting a reputation as a nasty old curmudgeon, so it's not quite as intense as when I was . . . on the market.'

'No girlfriends at all?'

'Not right now not for a while, really. I'd like to . . .'

He stopped. 'What?' she pressed. 'Like to what?'

'We don't know each other well enough,' he said, 'for me to tell you what I'd like to do.'

A parking place appeared a half-block from the hospital's emergency entrance; Harper dove into it, chortling, fed the meter. But as they started down toward the hospital, a man in a suit in the dimly lit glassed-in entry half-turned toward them, saw them and then suddenly and hurriedly turned back to the hospital doors and disappeared inside.

'Did you see that?' Anna said.

'Yeah.' Harper broke into a trot, Anna running beside him. 'Somebody who doesn't want to talk to us. You know him?'

'Couldn't see his face,' she said.

'White hair,' Harper said. They were moving fast now, hit the doors to the entry, burst into the reception area. No white-haired men. A guard was looking at them, quizzically. Harper hurried toward him, Anna a half-step behind.

'A white-haired guy just came through here,' Harper said. 'Did you see where he went?'

The guard said, 'Yeah, he . . . hey, who are you guys?'

But he'd started to point, down the hall: the elevators were just around the corner.

'Elevators,' Anna said to Harper. And she said to the guard, 'Call the intensive care unit on the third floor. If a white-haired guy shows up, watch him . . . he may have a gun.'

Harper was already hurrying toward the elevators, Anna catching up as the guard said, 'Yes, ma'am,' and picked up a phone.

They turned the corner. Three elevators, one with the door open, waiting. Of the other two, one was on eight, coming down. The other was on two, stopping at three.

'Damn it,' Harper said. He looked around and Anna said, 'Stairs'd be faster,' and they went left and up the stairs, around two flights; as they got to the third floor, Anna heard a door shut below them, the hollow tunnel sound of metal on concrete. She stopped, looked down. 'You hear that?'

'Yeah,' Harper grunted, but he went on past, into the corridor on three. Two nurses were talking at a work station, one with a phone in her hand, and looked up at them.

'Did a white-haired man . . .'

'No. Nobody came here. The guard just called . . .'

'Is Pam Glass still down in intensive care, the police officer?'

'I think so . . .'

They went that way, and Anna blurted, 'Maybe he went down. You heard that door close, he couldn't have been too far ahead of us.'

'Yeah.' They turned the corner into the intensive care unit. Glass was standing next to Creek's bed; Creek's eyes were closed. No white-haired man.

'Nobody just came through here?' Anna asked.

Glass shook her head. 'No. What . . .?'

Harper said, 'Tell them,' and ran back toward the stairs. Anna asked Glass, 'You got your gun?'

'Yes.'

'Keep a hand on it, there's a guy,' and turned and ran after Harper. She caught him on the stairs and Harper glanced back at her, grunted, shook his head and kept circling down. They came out in a sub-basement, looked both ways, finally turned left, a shorter hall and an exit sign.

The exit led to an underground parking ramp: they hurried along the ramp, and Harper said, 'Get the gun out.'

Anna took the gun out of her jacket pocket, feeling a little silly – and a little dangerous – and held it by her pants leg as they turned up the ramp toward a pay booth. A Latino was running out an adding machine in the booth, and Harper said, 'Did a man just run by here?'

'Yes, *si*, he went that way, one minute.' He pointed up the ramp to the street. They ran up the ramp and found . . . traffic.

Harper looked both ways, down at Anna and said, 'He's gone.'

She shoved the gun back into her jacket and said, 'Yeah.'

Creek had been awake for a few minutes, had maybe recognized Glass, but maybe not: 'He was drifting,' Glass said. 'He thought he was on his boat.'

Anna told Glass about the white-haired man, and finished with, 'It's possible that it was nothing.'

'No.' Harper disagreed. 'That move he made – I saw that two hundred times when I was a cop. Especially working dope. Someone sees you, figures you for the cops and he turns and splits. Runs in the front door, runs out the back. Just like that: and that's what he was doing.'

'I see it all the time,' Glass said.

'That's what it felt like,' Anna admitted. She kept looking at Creek, then glancing away: his figure disturbed her. He looked hollow, tired. Old, with lines in his face that she hadn't noticed before. He'd always been the opposite of those things, a guy who'd go on forever.

Now he lay there, little of him visible other than his hair and oddly pale eyelids, breathing through a plastic mask, his breath so shallow, his life bumping along on the monitors overhead, like a slow day on a stock-market ticker.

Chapter 13

They left Glass and Creek – Glass said she'd try to get Creek moved again, in case the white-haired man was a real threat – and went back into the night, heading for the Philadelphia Grill.

'The guy was probably a doper,' Harper said, ''cause he moved so fast. Like a guy who's holding. He didn't stop to look us over, he didn't stop to see if we were coming after him – he just took off. And the way he went out, he must've already been in the hospital, because he knew about the parking ramp exit and how to get there in a hurry.'

'That worries me; he was scouting the place,' Anna said. 'What surprises me is, he was old. Or older.'

'Maybe not – could've been blond, could've been the light on his hair.'

'No. He was older. Fifties, anyway. The way he moved, I'm thinking . . .' She closed her eyes, letting the scene run through her mind. 'He saw us, he turned, he sort of groped for the door, he pulled it open, almost hit himself with it. He was a little creaky. Maybe even a little heavy. He wasn't a kid, though. He just moved like an older guy.'

'That doesn't fit the profile of any psycho I ever heard

of,' Harper said thoughtfully. 'Maybe the guy in Chicago – Gacey. He was sorta porky, and a little older than most of them. I think.'

'He's not what I expected,' Anna said. 'The prowler was fast, and the guy who shot Creek, *he* was fast. Really fast. He had to be a young guy.'

'So we've got *two* people giving us a hard time?' He looked at her with thin amusement. 'And we can't find either one of them?'

The Philadelphia Grill was a baked-meatloaf-and-powered-potatoes place on Westwood, jammed into the lower corner of a colored-concrete building; it had a wraparound glass window, but the window was blocked with blinds pulled nearly shut.

Inside, the clientele seemed to hover over their coffee, arms circling the cups, as though somebody might try to take the coffee away from them; and they tended to look up whenever the door opened. The blinds, which blocked the view in, were open just enough that, from the inside, they could see out.

'There he is,' Anna muttered.

Tarpatkin looked like her idea of a crazy killer: his pitch-black hair, six inches long, streamed away from his narrow face, as though an electric current were running through it. He had thin black eyebrows over a long, bony nose; his lips were narrow, tight, and too pink, the only color in his face. He was dressed all in black, and was reading a tabloid-sized real-estate newspaper. He had one hand on a cup of tea, showing a tea-bag string and tag under his hand. He was wearing a heavy gold wedding band, but on his middle finger. An empty cup sat across the table from him. 'What if he's the guy?'

'Do you know him? Ever met him?' Harper said.

'No. I'd remember the face.'

'Then he's not the guy, because you know the killer, at least a little bit,' Harper said. 'Slide into the booth across from him; I'll get a chair.'

Tarpatkin watched them coming, eyes just over the top of the paper. His expression didn't change when Anna slid into the booth: 'Hi,' she said, smiling. Harper hooked a chair from an empty table across from the booth, turned in backward and sat down, just blocking Tarpatkin's route out of the booth.

'Mr Tarpatkin – name's Harper, and my friend here is Anna.'

'Hello, Anna,' Tarpatkin said. 'Is that a gun in your pocket, or are you just happy to see me?'

'No, no, it's a gun,' Anna said pleasantly.

'We'd show it to you, but in here' – Harper looked around – 'somebody might get excited and we'd all start shooting.'

'What do you want?' Tarpatkin asked.

'Just need to talk,' Harper said.

'That's all you guys ever want,' Tarpatkin said. 'Talk. Then your ass winds up in jail.'

'What?' Anna's eyebrows went up and she glanced uncertainly at Harper.

Tarpatkin caught it, and clouded up: 'If you assholes ain't cops, you can get the fuck out of my booth.'

'We're not cops, but I used to be, and I still know a lot

of deputies,' Harper said. 'The thing is, you're caught right in the middle of a major murder case and the cops are freaking out. You can talk to us, off the record, or talk to them, on the record.'

'You're talking bullshit, man, I don't know any murder mysteries.' His language veered from formal, almost scholarly, to the street, and then back again; he might have been two people. Tarpatkin shook out the newspaper, as though he were about to resume reading.

'One of your clients, Jason O'Brien, got taken off in a really bad way a couple of days ago. Beat to death, carved up with a knife.' When Harper said it, Anna was watching Tarpatkin's eyes: they flickered when Jason's name was mentioned. 'And maybe you know a guy named Sean MacAllister?'

Another flicker: 'He knows them both,' Anna said to Harper, not taking her eyes off Tarpatkin.

Tarpatkin didn't deny it: this was news he could use. 'Carved up?'

'You know a guy who likes knives?' Harper asked.

Tarpatkin thought for a second, then said, 'I know a couple of them, but they don't know those two. When did this happen? I haven't seen anything about it in the paper.'

Anna told him, briefly, and then said, 'We're looking for a guy selling wizards. We understand you don't, but we're hoping that you might know who does. Right around here – the university neighborhood.'

Tarpatkin looked her over for a moment, then said, 'Honey, I don't know what kind of mission you're on, but you really don't want to mess around with those people.

They're amateurs – they're crazy and they'll kill you for a nickel.'

'Somebody might be trying to kill me for free,' Anna said. 'We're trying to get him to stop.'

'Huh.' He pulled at his goatee, then said, 'Let me give you fifteen seconds on how the smart part of this business works – and for the tape recorder, if you're wearing one, you'll notice that this is all hypothetical.'

He pulled a napkin out of a chrome napkin holder and smoothed it on the tabletop. Anna thought he was going to write on it, but then he started folding it as he talked: L.A.-diner origami. 'Suppose you got a small-time dealer,' Tarpatkin said. 'He's got maybe seventy-five, a hundred regular customers. He only takes new customers from recommendations, and only after looking them over.

'This guy is making, say, ten grand a week after expenses, no taxes. He flies over to the Bahamas a few times a year and makes a deposit, takes a little vacation. In ten years, with some careful investments, he's got eight or ten million in the bank, and he moves to the Bahamas full time. Or Mexico. Costa Rica. Somewhere . . .

'If he's smooth, he don't have to worry too much about the cops, because he's such a small-timer, and when they come around, he cooperates. The cops always want the big guys – Christ, if they busted everybody like this small-timer, they'd have to build twenty new jails. So, they don't. I mean, hey, he's a small businessman. A little better than insurance, maybe not so good as selling stocks and bonds.'

Anna broke in: 'But these other guys are different.'

Tarpatkin shook a finger at her, like a schoolmaster

making a point. 'I'm coming to that, honey – they're very different. They go into the dope business, and they think, "If I sell a pound of crank, I make ten thousand dollars. If I sell a ton of crank, I make twenty million dollars. So I'll sell a ton of crank. This year."

'And since they've been to the movies, they know the business is dangerous. So they buy a load of guns and knives and dynamite and chain saws and whatever else they can think of. Then to get their heads right, they get into the product themselves. The next thing you know, you've got these drug freaks with guns and dynamite and chain saws, and there's crank all over the street and everybody's going crazy looking for them – competitors, cops, DEA. They always find them. Go to jail, don't get your twenty million. Or wind up in a bush somewhere, with your head cut off.'

He shook his head sadly, and asked in his street patois: 'Is this any fuckin' way to run a fuckin' business?' And then back to the scholar: 'I think not. But these are the people who are selling your wizards.'

'So can you put us onto somebody?'

Tarpatkin shook his head. 'No, I can't. I stay away from those people. However, if one of you has a cell phone – or a regular phone, for that matter – I could ask around and call you.'

'So you wanna talk to the cops,' Harper said.

'No. But I don't know anything – not what you want. Why would I? I don't hang with those people. I stay as far away as I can.'

'That's bull,' Harper said. 'You guys have always got your ears to the ground . . .'

Tarpatkin shrugged: 'Well, you could drag me out into the street and beat the shit outa me until I tell you what you want . . . except that I don't know it.'

Anna and Harper looked at each other, and then Anna dug in her purse, found a pen and wrote her cell phone number on Tarpatkin's folded napkin. 'Call me anytime,' she said.

'I will. You're a little sweetie.'

'About your hypothetical dealer sending his hypothetical money to the Bahamas,' Anna said. 'How long has he been doing this, hypothetically?'

'Could be eight years,' Tarpatkin said. He bobbed his head and smiled; one of his canine teeth was solid gold, and it winked at her from beneath his ratty mustache.

Outside, Harper said, 'I don't know what we could do: all we got is threats of siccing the cops on him.'

'We could drag him out in the alley and beat the shit out of him,' Anna said wryly.

'In that place, we'd get about three steps,' Harper said. 'I have a feeling they sort of look out for each other . . . In fact . . . just a minute.' He walked back to the diner door, pulled it open, looked in, then walked back, shaking his head. 'He's gone. He'll be in the Bahamas by dawn.'

As they were getting into Harper's BMW, the phone in Anna's purse rang. She glanced at Harper, then took the phone out and clicked it on: 'Hello?'

A little girl's voice, oddly tinny, with an adult's vocabulary and intonations, said, 'The men you want to see are brothers named Ronnie and Tony and they live . . .'

'Just a minute, just a minute,' Anna said. And to Harper: 'Gimme a paper.'

She found the pen in her purse and Harper groped in a door bin and finally came up with a road map. 'Write on it,' he said. The tinny little girl's voice recited an address in Malibu, and finished, '. . . real modern, gray weathered wood, lots of black glass, right on the hill above the highway. You won't have any trouble finding it.'

And she – it, Tarpatkin? – was gone.

'Voice-altering phone deal,' Harper said, when Anna described the voice. 'Lot of dealers use them. You get like twenty choices of voice.'

'Why?'

'So in case we were recording it, he wouldn't be on the record.'

'Strange life.'

'Trying to make it to retirement,' Harper said. 'Two years.'

Anna glanced at her watch: 'We've got time to run out to Malibu. Or we could head down to BJ's.'

Harper glanced at her: 'The question about BJ's is this: you'll see some people you know, but so what? How do we pick out the guy?'

'If he talks to me, or comes on to me . . .'

'*Somebody's* gonna come on to you, you go to a party box. That's what it's for.'

Anna thought about it for a minute. Harper was not only right, but he was also on the track of the people who'd fed dope to his son. She'd go with that: 'Malibu,' she said.

Harper nodded. 'We spot the house, but we don't do anything. I want to check with some guys in the sheriff's department, run these names. Ronnie and Tony . . .'

Harper had a Thomas Brothers Guide stashed in the back seat. Anna turned on the car's reading lights as they dropped onto the PCH and made the right turn up toward Malibu, and began paging through the maps.

'If the address is right, it's just before the turnoff for Corral Canyon,' she said after a moment.

'Should be easy to pick out,' Harper said.

They sat in companionable silence for a while, not much traffic, just cruising. Then Harper said, 'How come you're not going out with anyone?'

'I don't know,' she said. She looked out her window, away from him: nothing to see but the dirt bluff rising away from the highway into the dark. 'I've just had other things.'

'Been a little lonely?'

'I've been busy,' she said. And after a few seconds, 'Yeah, I've been a little lonely. Then . . .'

'What?'

'Ah, there's this guy. I went out with him years ago; pretty intense. I thought we were gonna get married, but we didn't. I saw him the other day, at a gas station. He's out here on a fellowship, I guess – I called a mutual friend. Anyway, it all sorta came back on me . . .'

'What's he do?'

'He's a composer. Modern stuff – the New York Philharmonic debuted one of his poems, "Sketch of Malagá".'

'One of his *poems*?'

'Compositions; he calls them poems. He's not really that

arty, just knows . . . how to work the levers on the classical music machine.'

Harper glanced at her: 'Sounds like you might resent that, a little.'

'Oh, no. I guess it's necessary. But I wasn't good at it.'

'So you're a musician.'

'That's what I really am,' she said. Harper had a way of listening – maybe picked up when he was a cop – that seemed to pull the words out of her. He was attentive: *really* listened.

She told him about growing up in Wisconsin, about her mother's death. How she'd been the best pianist in her high school, the best they'd ever had. That she'd been the best at the University of Wisconsin-Milwaukee, the year she graduated. That she was one of the best two or three in graduate school.

'Not quite good enough,' she told him, staring out the window at the night. Clark had also been a pianist, not quite at her level, but he'd seen the writing on the wall much sooner than she had. He'd branched into direction and composition, started working the music machine.

'Couldn't you have gone that way?'

'Nah. Performance is one thing, composition is something else. Takes a different kind of mind.'

'Did you ever try it?'

'I was never really interested in it,' she said.

'So what happened?'

'We were living together, and he was the big intellectual and I was doing session gigs. Movie music. I don't know; it pulled us apart. I kept thinking that if you just played well enough, practised hard enough, you'd make it. And that wasn't the game at all . . . So I went to Burbank, and he went to Yale.'

'Ah, that's really excellent,' Harper said.

'What?' she asked, half-smiling.

'You *do* resent the mealy little poser.'

'No, I really don't,' she protested. Then, 'You'd like him. He even plays golf.'

'*Rock bands* play golf,' Harper said, not impressed. 'So . . . are you pining for him?'

'I don't know,' she said. 'Maybe.'

'Shit.'

'Yeah, it's sort of a problem. You know, if you're thinking about . . . it might be sorta awkward having you stay over.'

'I'm gonna stay over,' he said. 'But I won't be rattling your doorknob in the night. Staying over is business.'

'Okay.' Was she just the smallest bit disappointed? Maybe.

'Would you play something on the piano for me?' he asked.

'If you like.' The car seemed hushed; the outside world away from the two of them. 'What music do you listen to?'

'Mostly hard rock or hard classical; some old funky blues and jazz, but only for an hour or so at a time.'

'We like the same things,' she said, 'except I'm not so big on rock, and a little bigger on the jazz . . . what should I play for you?'

'Maybe something by, I dunno . . . Sousa, maybe.'

He turned quickly, saw her embarrassed: 'That was a joke, for Christ's sake,' he laughed. 'Loosen up, Batory.'

'So who do you like?'

'You could play me anything by Satie.'

'Satie? Really?'

'Really,' he said. 'I've been listening to him a lot; he's very delicate and funny, sometimes.' He glanced at her, interpreting her silence as skepticism. 'I'm a lawyer, not a fuckin' moron,' he said.

She ducked her head and pointed up the hill. 'Malibu,' she said.

The house was a half-block east of Corral, on a short, hooked turnoff with a circle at the end. There were two other homes on the circle, all three showing lights, and all with steel fences, darkened and turned to resemble wrought iron, facing the street. The driveways were blocked with decorative eight-foot-high electric gates between stone pillars.

'We'll just keep rolling through,' Harper said, looking out through the sweep of his headlights. 'Look for dogs, anything that might be a dog . . .'

'I can't see anything,' Anna said.

They were back out at Corral: Harper stopped, looked both ways, then said, 'We'd be crazy to try to get in the front.'

'Get in?' She looked back at the house, at the fence and the hedge behind it, the security sign next to the stone pillars beside the driveway. 'That place is a fort.'

'Let's go get an ice cream,' he said. 'Isn't there an ice cream place down at the shopping center?'

She got a Dutch chocolate and he took a raspberry and they

sat on a bench outside of a Ben & Jerry's and ate the ice cream, talking about nothing of importance. When they finished, Harper wiped his hands and face with the tiny napkin from the ice cream parlor, pitched it into a trash container and said, 'You drive.'

'Why?'

'I want to go back there and take one more look. Maybe get out.'

'Jake . . . this is a really bad idea.'

He nodded. 'I know, but I can't figure out what else to do. I just want to stand on one of those stone pillars, if I can, and take a look. See what's in there.'

'Jake . . .'

'What, you chicken?' he asked.

Never a chicken. Never.

One of the houses had gone dark, but the target house showed lights on all three floors. 'We'll roll right up, I'll hop out, do a quick step-up, look in and then get right back in the car and we're out of there,' he said.

'Aw, man . . .' But she felt a little thrill, a little of the roaming-through-the-night feel; she took the car into the hook and heard Harper's door pop.

She slowed and he said, 'Keep rolling, slow, I'll latch the door, don't want them to see headlights stopping . . .' He hopped out with the car still moving, pushed the door shut until it caught, looked around once as he approached the fence and then stepped on a horizontal brace-bar, pulled himself up and looked into the yard. Anna continued through the circle, headed out toward the street; she rolled her window down and looked over at his back and said, in a harsh whisper, 'Let's go.'

'Just a minute . . .'

And suddenly he was over the fence and out of sight.

'Oh, no . . .' She continued moving, but her mind was churning. Better to move than to stop, she thought; she'd go out to the street, do a U-turn out of sight, and come back in. What was he thinking, hopping over the fence? He *was* a moron. She was at the street, touched the brakes to show the red flash of a departing car, did the U-turn on Corral and started back in; rolled the window down on his side as she went, and tried to look back.

As she did, somebody behind the fence screamed: 'Get him . . . get him, over there.'

And Harper shouted, 'Anna, the highway.'

She couldn't see him, but his voice was clear enough: Anna rolled through the circle again, accelerating, the wheels squealing on the new blacktop. Down the short street, a finger of fear in her throat, left down the hill, the BMW tracking as though it were on rails.

BAK!

Was that a shot? Her face jerked to the right, but all she could see was hillside. She'd heard something, but what was it?

BAK!

A shot, that's what it was. She jammed her foot to the floor, powering through sixty-five, downhill, then hammered the brake as she got to the bottom, paused at the highway, then ran the light and headed around to the left . . .

She looked up the bluff, saw nothing but scrub brush and

weeds; the house was right there, fifty feet ahead . . .

And so was Harper. He was spilling down the hill, tumbling, hitting every ten feet, dirt flying, not quite out of control, but not quite under control, either. A car passed her going north, and as soon as it was clear, she swerved across the highway to the left, up onto the narrow weedy shoulder, powered through the dirt and rocks until she was directly below him. He landed in a cloud of dirt, struggled to get up, limped around the car as she popped the passenger door, fell inside and gasped, 'Go . . . go.'

'I can't . . .' She was looking into a stream of cars coming up from the south . . .

BAK!

'Go, that's a fuckin' gun.'

She jumped on the gas, still on the shoulder, blinked her lights a few times to intimidate a small white northbound car and swerved across the highway.

'Are you all right?'

'Yeah.' He was out of breath, and his shirt was ripped. 'Boy, was that stupid.' He was looking out the back window.

'No kidding,' she said, angrily. 'What did you . . .'

'Yell at me later.' He was looking out the back window. 'Right now, I think they're coming after us. A Cadillac just cleared the bottom of the hill coming this way, I heard them yelling about getting a car.'

'Oh, boy.' The highway was not particularly busy. The northbound cars arrived in short packs, with open stretches between the packs. In the rearview mirror, she saw headlights slewing left to pass a slow moving southbound car, taking advantage of a break in the oncoming traffic.

'You're gonna have to drive a little faster,' Harper said.

'Hold onto your socks.' She floored it. Anna always liked speed, and the big BMW accelerated like an unwinding spring, seventy, eighty, ninety, a hundred, all without hesitation. She blew past two cars, had five seconds of peace in the right-hand lane, then squeezed past an idling Jaguar in the face of an oncoming pickup.

Harper winced, then reached up to the overhead and found a handle to hang onto. 'Maybe not this fast,' he said.

'They're still back there,' she said. The Cadillac was cutting through the traffic like a shark through a school of tuna – but its lights seemed to be getting smaller.

They blazed through Malibu, past the shopping center, the garage doors of the beach houses blurring into one long gray line. 'Anna, for Christ's sake, you're doing a hundred and twelve. Slow down . . .'

She shook her head: she was mad, and she could drive. He deserved to be scared. She took another car, pushed a little harder on the gas, glanced down at the speedometer: a hundred and eighteen. 'This thing rolls.'

'Jesus,' Harper said. He turned to look behind them: 'Anna, they're out of sight. They're out of sight.'

'Keep watching for them,' she said. She let the car out for a few more seconds, feeling the speed, then eased off the gas, watched the speed drop below a hundred. Fifteen minutes later, they burned through the Sunset intersection; two minutes later, she turned up Temescal, dropped to a cruise and looked at Harper.

'You were limping.'

'I might've sprained my knee . . . I banged myself up coming down the hill.'

'And got shot at . . .'

'But nothing happened . . .'

'Jake . . .' she said in exasperation.

'I was standing there, and I could see some people moving inside a window and there was a crack in the drapes. And I just thought I could take a look . . . and I got in and there was another window down the side. And then everybody started yelling,' he said, talking fast. 'There must've been some kind of alarm, and I was stuck in the back and people were coming out the front. I ran right past the pool in back, there was a woman out there, she started yelling and I went over the edge and some asshole started shooting.'

'What do you expect, prowling a house? I used a fish-whacker on a guy who was doing that.'

'Yeah, well . . .' After a moment he said, 'It seemed like a good idea at the time.'

Anna laughed aloud, the first time since she'd heard that Jason was dead. She liked the speed.

Harper made her stop at a gas station pay phone, got a number for the Malibu cops, dialed it and said, 'There's been a shooting . . .' He gave them the address, and hung up. 'Stir up the bees' nest,' he said.

'What for?'

'See what happens.'

There was no point in even trying to go to BJ's; Harper was a mess from the fall down the hill. He looked, as he said, like he'd been whipped through hell with a soot-bag.

At Anna's house, Harper hobbled up the walk: 'It's not really damaged. It just hurts; but nothing's loose.'

'I've got some of that blue ice stuff you can put on it,' she said.

'That'd be good.'

She kept the ice packs in the refrigerator, and went to get one while Harper disappeared into the bathroom. She stood outside the door with the ice pack and said, 'Okay?'

Harper opened the door. He'd pulled his golf shirt over his head, and turned around to show her his back. He looked like he'd been scourged, long fiery rips running down his back. 'Not so good,' he said.

'You must've run into some thorn trees up there.' She walked around him to the medicine cabinet, found some antiseptic cream. 'C'mon, I'll put some of this stuff on.'

He sat shirtless in a kitchen chair, while she pulled a desk lamp around, focused it on his back. Some of the scratches were deep, but none were still bleeding; he also showed a scrape on his shoulder and a large red-blue bruise on his forearm.

She dabbed on the antiseptic cream and he flinched and said, 'Ow,' and 'Is there a sliver in there?'

She touched the spot again and he flinched and she said, 'Maybe. I'm gonna have to wipe this off.'

'Well, take it easy.'

'Hey, I'm doing the best I can.'

She wiped the cream away with a Kleenex, spotted a broken thorn – and then, further down his back, three more of them. 'Sit still,' she said. 'I need tweezers.'

The thorns took quite a while, but she got them all, and layered on the antiseptic cream. 'You'll make a mess out of a shirt,' she said.

'I've got a couple of old T-shirts,' he said. He stood up, turned around once in his tracks, stretched, flexed, testing his back, and said, 'I'm gonna be a little sore in the morning.'

Anna could suddenly smell him, sweat and some kind of musky deodorant and blood, maybe, a salty smell; and realized that she was standing very close to a large half-naked man in her kitchen, and that patching up his back might have broken down a wall a little before she'd intended.

Harper picked up the sudden change of atmosphere and laughed, lightly, and said, 'Suddenly got a little close in here.'

'Yeah.' She flushed.

She reached over to pick up the first-aid cream and he caught her arm and said, 'So . . . could you kiss me once to make it feel better?'

'Well . . .'

He kissed her very easily, and she kissed back, again, just a little out of her control, for that extra half-second that she hadn't intended. She pulled away and said, 'Oh, boy,' and Harper said, 'Maybe I better get that T-shirt.'

The T-shirt put a little distance between them, but not much: at least, she thought, there wasn't so much skin around. He brought a kitchen chair into the hallway, next to the piano, and said, 'You were gonna play a Satie for me.'

'It's late . . .'

'I can't lie down until my back dries up a little,' he said.

So she played for him: the delicate, familiar, simple little 'First Gymnopedie'. The final chords hung in the hall, and when they died, she said, 'There. Like it?'

He bobbed his head: 'Yeah.'

Sticky silence.

'I don't suppose you'd want to come sit on my lap for a minute, over on the couch,' he said.

'Maybe just for a minute,' she said.

So they necked, for a while, and he was careful with his hands; held on tight, but didn't presume; or not too much.

'You don't presume,' she said, after a while. 'Too much.'

'I'm a subtle guy; I've got you figured out, and not presuming is my way of worming myself into your confidence. Then, just when you're looking the other way, bang!'

'Could have picked a better word,' she said.

'Hmm . . .'

Harper's father had worked at a bank for forty years, he said, just high enough up to get a golf club membership back when that was done. His mother had been a housewife and a better golfer than her husband. Harper had taken the game up early, gone to college on a golf scholarship and was 'last man at UCLA'.

'Didn't get along with the coach,' he said. 'Got along with his wife, though.'

'Ah.'

'The coach and his pals convinced me I'd never make the tour,' he said. 'I was taking the law enforcement sequence because that was the easiest one to fit around the golf. The next thing I knew, I'm working for the L.A. sheriff's department. Nine years, never liked it much: I finally went off to law school because the police work was driving me nuts.'

'What happened with you and your wife?'

'Ah, you know . . . We just couldn't keep it together. First I was on the street all the time, then I got sent to vice and I was hanging out with dopers and hookers . . .'

'Mess around a little?'

'Never. But you start to reflect the culture. Sometimes I think I scared her. Or disgusted her,' he said. 'Then I started going to law school full time, and then I moved up to homicide, Christ, I was so busy I never saw either her or the kids . . .'

And he carefully opened up Anna, again, as he had in the car: he got her to talk about her mother, her brother, her father.

'Pretty normal family, until Mom died,' Anna said. 'After that: I don't know. It just seemed like everybody started to work themselves to death . . . We still had some good times, but overall, there was a pretty grim feeling to it. When I go back now . . . I don't want to stay.'

'Did your brother teach you to drive? Like tonight?'

Anna laughed: 'My dad used to fix Saabs as a sideline – we'd have six or seven Saabs sitting around the house at any one time. I started driving them when I was a kid – I mean, like really a kid, when I was seven or eight. My dad and my brother used to run them in the enduro races at the county fair, I'd pit crew . . .'

'Sexism,' Harper said.

'Severe sexism,' she agreed. 'Once . . . my dad always took me up to Madison for my music lesson, but one time, in the summer, he'd cut hay when it was supposed to be dry all week, and the next thing you know this big line of thunderstorms popped up over in Minnesota. You could see them coming on the TV radar, and he was running around baling and he just didn't have time to take me. So when he was out in the field – I was so mad – I jumped in this old Saab and drove in myself. I was ten, I had to look through the steering wheel to see out the windshield. My music teacher didn't see me coming, and I got through the lesson, but she saw me drive away and she freaked out and called the cops and called my dad . . .' She laughed at the memory: 'He never missed another lesson, though.'

'Ten?' he asked.

'Yup. I can drive a tractor, too. And a front-end loader.'

'If you could do plumbing and welding, I'd probably marry you,' he said.

And they necked a little more, until he shifted uncomfortably and said, 'We either stop now, or we . . . keep going.'

'Better stop,' Anna said. She hopped off his lap, leaving him a little tousled and forlorn. She laughed, and said, 'You look harassed.'

'A little,' he said, and again, some underlying source of amusement seemed to rise to the surface of his eyes.

She turned and headed for the stairs. 'No rattling of doorknobs, okay?'

'Okay,' he said, watching her go. She was on the stairs when he called after her, 'You weren't thinking about this other guy, were you? This Clark weasel-guy?'

'No . . . no, I wasn't, and he's not a weasel,' she said. And, in fact, the name 'Clark' had never touched her consciousness.

But it did that night.

Sitting on Harper's lap had aroused her – hadn't turned her into a blubbering idiot, but she'd liked it, a lot – and in her sleep, she relived a night with Clark, pizza and wine and a little grass. And Clark, talking, touching her, turning her on . . .

She rolled and twisted, and woke a half-dozen times, listening: but nobody touched a doorknob.

Chapter 14

The next morning they bumped around the kitchen, not talking much but jostling each other, eating toast, looking at the blue morning sky, touching; working up to something.

Then Wyatt called for Harper. Harper took the phone from Anna, listened a while, said quietly, 'Thanks, man . . . let me know.'

'What?' Anna said.

'The Malibu cops went over to Tony and Ronnie's place after the shooting and the woman up there – you could hear her screaming at me? – anyway, she ran out the back and threw a bag of dope over the hill.' He picked up his putter and twirled it like a baton.

'Over the hill? Down where you were?'

'Yeah. She was trying to get rid of it – she thought they were being busted. But a cop coming up from the next yard saw her, found the bag. They took five pounds of methedrine off the hill, got a warrant, took a half-pound of cocaine out of a bedroom and found receipts for a couple of rental storage places.'

'Almost big enough to make the papers,' Anna said.

'Almost . . . They took the rental places down this morning and found lots of interesting chemicals. There's a factory, somewhere – they're still going through the paper, looking for an address.'

'And they're all arrested.'

'All but Tony. Turns out Tony didn't live there – he lives up the hill – so they had to let him go.' He looked bleakly pleased with that.

'So what're we going to get out of this? Will they ask about your kid?'

'That's part of the agenda,' Harper said, putting on his grim face. 'As a favor. They owe me, now.'

Creek didn't seem to have changed much, although his doctor said he was improving: 'He was awake, asking about you,' the doc said. 'He was more worried about you than about himself.'

'So he's fine,' Anna said.

'No. He's still got one foot in the woods. He could still have a clot problem, the way his lung was damaged . . . but he's looking better. And that friend of his is a real morale boost.'

Glass was sitting by Creek's bed, reading a mystery, looking up every few minutes to see if he had wakened.

'I should have been here,' Anna said. A little finger of envy touched her. Glass had been here, she hadn't; she had been the one perceived as faithful. Of course, she hadn't been: she'd been running around Malibu getting shot at, and necking with a guy Creek didn't like . . .

'. . . blood work looks fine,' the doctor was saying. 'He

could be out walking around in a week, and you'd never know he'd been shot.'

But Creek's face still looked like it had been made of old parchment; Anna shivered, and turned away.

They were just leaving the hospital when the cell phone rang and Anna lifted it out of her jacket pocket and said, 'Yeah?'

'Let me talk to Harper.' A man's voice, not one that she knew.

She looked at Harper and said, 'Jake: It's for you.'

Harper took the phone and said, 'Yeah.'

He listened for a moment, then handed it back to Anna: 'I don't know how to hang it up.'

'What's happening?'

'I gotta drop you off.'

She looked at him, catching his eyes: she was beginning to get into him, like she could get into Creek. Harper's eyes shifted, but just a second too late. 'Something happened,' she said. 'I'm coming.'

'Anna . . .'

'Shut up. I bailed your butt out last night when you were falling off the cliff: that counts for something.'

'Something – but this is different.'

'I'm going,' she said.

Harper drove downtown, hard, jumping lights, busting traffic, ignoring the fingers from angry drivers, getting there. 'Gimme the phone,' he said, as they pulled into a no-parking zone outside the Parker Center. She handed it to him and he poked in a number, listened for a minute, then said, 'We're here,' and then, 'Okay.'

He handed the phone back to Anna and said, 'Wait here. If a cop tries to move you, tell him your boyfriend's a cop and he's inside talking to Lieutenant Austen.'

She nodded and said, 'Okay,' and he hopped out of the car and hurried away. Five minutes later, he was back. He jumped in the car, did a U-turn and they were gone, headed north.

'Where're we going?'

'Malibu,' he said.

'What for?'

'See a guy.'

'Jake, goddammit . . .'

'Look: I don't know what's going to happen.'

Ronnie's house – or Tony and Ronnie's, or whatever it was – looked abandoned behind its gate. Fluorescent-yellow crime-scene tape was wrapped around the stone posts, with a notice forbidding entry to anyone who wasn't a cop.

Harper pulled into the driveway, climbed out, stuck a key in a lock at the side of the gate. As the gate silently rolled back, Harper got into the car and drove up the driveway to the garage, where he parked. He walked around behind the car, pressed a button on his key and the trunk popped open. He took out a small brown-paper grocery sack, with a rolled top, like a kid's lunch bag.

'Let's go,' he said. Anna started toward the house, but he said, 'This way – we're just parking here.'

He was walking away from the house, up the hillside.

'Where're we going?'

'The next house up is Tony's. There's a pathway up here somewhere, through the plantings.'

'Your friends,' Anna said. 'Do they know what you're doing?'

'They think they do,' Harper said. He turned and looked down at her. 'Listen, I sorta wish you weren't here, but . . . I can use the help. My friends'll help me out from a distance, because they know I'd never talk about it. But they won't be here when the shit hits the fan and I might need somebody to be here.'

She shrugged: 'So I'm here. If this is the jerk who shot Creek, who's been chasing me around . . .'

'Probably not this guy,' Harper said. He started up the hill again, then pointed: 'There's the break in the brush, that's the path . . . This isn't our guy, but he knows our guy, I think.'

He took a few more steps up the hill, then stopped again. 'Whatever happens here, you do two things: you don't freak out, and you stand there with your gun and you watch everything and don't say shit, no matter what happens. No matter what happens. If we bump into somebody, you're this tough methedrine chick and you keep your mouth shut.'

They climbed through a hedge and up the hill, Harper still carrying the sack, then broke into a grassy slope below a pool patio. The house, a white concrete Mediterranean-modern, loomed over the patio. Harper never hesitated, but with Anna hurrying behind, climbed straight ahead, crossed the patio, took another key out of his pocket and pushed it into a back-door lock.

'Alarms are off,' he said, as he turned the key. 'No dogs.'

'Your friends tell you that?'

'Yeah. Don't touch anything.' He stuck his head inside and hollered, 'Hello? Anybody home? Anybody?' No answer. He took a few more steps into a red-tiled wet room: 'Hello? Anybody home?'

The house answered with the silence of emptiness. 'We're okay,' he said. He unrolled the sack, took out a pair of yellow plastic household gloves and handed them to her. 'Put these on.' She took the gloves and he took out a pair for himself, stuck the bag under an arm and pulled the gloves on, wiggling his fingers. 'Good,' he muttered. He opened the sack again, took out a brown fabric wad, shook it into the recognizable form of two dark nylons and said, 'For your head.' He pulled his on like a stocking cap, so that he'd pull it down over his face with one move.

Then he opened the sack a last time, and took out a gun, a black revolver.

'Jake?'

'Yeah. Now we both get one,' he said, and she felt the weight of the pistol in her pocket. 'These are bad people . . . C'mon.'

'What're we doing?'

'Look around the house. Probably won't be much, but you can't tell.'

The house might have been elegant, in a certain California-nouveau way, but it wasn't. The furniture looked like it had been rented, complete with the phony modern graphics on the walls; the pale green carpets were stained and the exposed hardwood near one row of windows was raw and warped, as though the windows had been left open for several weeks, and rain had come in; and the curtains stank with tobacco – cigars, Anna thought. The basement was empty except for a pile of cardboard appliance boxes at the bottom of the stairs – boxes for TVs, stereos, computers, Xerox machines, satellite dishes, VCRs, an electric piano. 'Haul the packing boxes to the top of the stairs and fire it down,' Harper said as he peered at the mess.

The master bedroom contained a circular bed with a circular headboard and custom rayon sheets; it faced a projection TV. Beside the TV was a rack of porno tapes, along with a few Westerns and music videos. The chest of drawers held perhaps two hundred sets of Jockey underwear and almost nothing else. A dozen suits hung in a closet, along with a pile of blue boxes full of dry-cleaned shirts and more underwear. The other four bedrooms had been slept in – the beds were unmade – but neither the bedrooms nor the adjoining baths showed much in the way of personal effects – nothing feminine – and only the most basic shaving and washing supplies.

They found nothing of special interest – no paper. The house was eerily devoid of records of any kind. 'He doesn't do business here,' Harper said.

'I don't think he really lives here,' Anna agreed. 'He must have a place somewhere else – this is like a motel room. You notice in the bathroom, his shaving stuff is still in a Dopp kit.'

'Yeah . . .'

Harper glanced at his watch: 'Let's go.'

'We're done?'

'Not exactly.'

He led the way downstairs, looked around once more, then pulled her into a book-lined office. All the books were in sets: none of them, as far as Anna could tell, had been opened. Harper started pulling them off the shelves, letting them drop to the floor. He did it almost idly.

'Jake?' Anna asked. 'What're we doing?'

'Waiting,' he said. 'Tony ought to be here any minute.'

'What?' She turned and looked out of the library; the front door was out of sight, but it was right around the corner.

'We'll hear the car,' he said. 'He'll either put it in the garage and come in through the kitchen, or he'll leave it in the drive and come through the front door.'

Anna was confused. 'What? We're gonna jump him?'

'More or less,' Harper said. He pushed a few more books on the floor. One of them was a fake: the cover fell open to reveal a hollowed-out interior packed with money. Harper turned and gazed at her for a moment, weighing her, and then said, 'That's why we're here.'

She thought she could talk him out of it: 'Jake, we can't do this – too much could go wrong. Somebody could get hurt, bad.'

But he wouldn't move. 'I've done stuff like this two hundred times. Tony oughta be paranoid enough that . . .' And then they felt, rather than heard, arrival sounds from outside. Harper said, 'Quiet now . . . just stick with this.'

He dropped to his hands and knees and crab-walked into the front room. From her angle in the office, she could see him easing up to a crack in the drapes.

Five seconds later he was back: 'Shit. He's with somebody. Another guy. Stay with me, Anna.'

'Aw . . .' She was trapped: a bad idea that she'd ridden too far, and now it was too late to get out. So she crouched, tense, and Harper pulled the nylon over his face, and waved a hand at her, and she pulled hers down. Then Harper took the gun out of his pocket and they waited.

Tony came through the door and he was shouting when he came through: 'You don't tell me that shit, you don't tell me, you just fuckin' well better . . .' He was a short, paunchy man in his late thirties, wearing a gray dress suit, a striped tie over a blue silk shirt; the man with him was tall, thin, with a mustache, a deep tan and a black leather briefcase; in good shape, like a serious tennis player. When Harper, with the mask and gun, stepped out of the office, his double-take spun Tony around in midsentence.

'If either one of you fuckin' move, I'm gonna blow your fuckin' heart right through your fuckin' spine,' Harper growled. His gun, held in both hands, was pointed at Tony's chest. 'Lay down on the floor, on your backs, heads toward each other, top of your head toward the top of his head, arms stretched out so they overlap.'

'What the fuck . . .'

'LAY ON THE FUCKIN' FLOOR,' Harper screamed, and the pistol began to shake and jerk, and Anna could see him chewing on the nylon mask; if he was acting, he was terrific. If he wasn't, he was crazy. 'LAY DOWN, YOU MOTHER FUCKERS, OR I'LL . . .' Saliva and anger seemed to choke him and he gnashed at the nylon, and suddenly his teeth broke through and he ran three steps toward Tony, the gun poking out at Tony's forehead, and Tony screamed back, 'No, no, no . . .' and the two men got shakily down on the floor, lying on their backs, arms stretched over their heads.

Harper, gun fixed on Tony's head, fished a pair of open handcuffs out of his pocket and dropped them on Tony's face. 'Put them on. I want to hear them snap shut.' Tony put them on. The tall man was next: 'Thread 'em through Tony's, then snap 'em.'

'I'm just a lawyer . . .'

'Yeah, yeah, yeah . . . you fuckin' scum, you fuckin' lawyers . . . You fuckin' lay there . . .' The language had been stolen from Tarpatkin, but had a drug-fired sound to it, a crazy emotional edge. Harper stepped to the door and pushed it shut – slammed it. Then he bent over the men, patted them down, found a cell phone in Tony's coat pocket, tossed it aside. To Tony: 'You got a dealer working the Westwood area. He was selling wizards down to the Shamrock Hotel last week . . .'

He was a street thug, Anna thought: he was doing it perfectly. Maybe too perfectly. He moved to one side, put his foot on the lawyer's chest.

'. . . I'm gonna give you the convincer. I'm gonna shoot your lawyer here, free of charge. Just to show you that I'm serious. Shoot him right in the fuckin' brain, so you're attached to a dead man, you can explain to the cops later, YOU FUCKIN' CREEP . . .' He was shouting again, and the lawyer was screaming, 'No, no, no,' trying to sit up, but pinned by his hands over his head and the weight of Tony on the cuffs.

Then Harper, looking down at the lawyer, stepped back far enough that Tony couldn't see him, looked at the frantic lawyer, put one finger over his lips, pointed the gun at the floor beside the lawyer's head and fired once.

The lawyer jerked forward, convulsing with the muzzle blast, then fell back, understood instantly: He went limp and silent.

'NOW YOU BELIEVE ME?' Harper screamed.

'You'll fuckin' kill me anyway,' Tony screamed back. 'So fuck you.'

'Not before I peel your fuckin' skin off with a potato peeler I seen in your kitchen,' Harper said. Tony twisted, and Harper kicked him in the chest and Tony shouted, 'Stan, goddamn, are you dead? Stan, goddammit . . .' And Harper kicked him again, and Anna, out of sight, tried to wave him off, but he ignored her. He had the gun pointing at Tony's head and he was shouting again, 'ALL RIGHT, MOTHER FUCKER, I DON'T HAVE THE PATIENCE TO SKIN YOU ALIVE, SO I'M GONNA KILL YOU NOW. GOOD FUCKIN' BYE . . .'

Tony was thrashing against Stan's dead weight and Harper pointed the gun and Tony screamed, 'John Maran at the Marshall Hotel on Pico, for Christ's sake . . .'

Harper's voice went suddenly soft, and somehow more threatening. 'You better be telling me the truth,' he said. 'If you're not, I won't be coming back.'

'What?' Tony was confused.

'Get on your feet, lawyer.' Harper kicked the lawyer once, and the tall man rolled over, started to blubber. Tony shouted, 'You asshole, whyn't you say something . . .'

The lawyer, stooping over him, pulled down by the short play of the cuffs, shouted back, 'You crazy fuck, they were gonna kill us, I saved our lives.'

'You bullshit . . .' Tony tried to get up, but Harper pushed him down. 'Stay down.' And to the lawyer, 'Drag him over to the basement stairs.'

As the lawyer dragged Tony toward the stairs, Anna noticed the cell phone, picked it up, put in her pocket. In the basement, Harper put them on either side of a steel support pole and threaded the cuffs through. 'Like I said, if there's no John Maran at the Marshall Hotel on Pico, I ain't coming back.'

The lawyer had followed this thought, but Tony hadn't: 'So fuck you,' Tony said.

'Tony . . .' the lawyer said.

'Fuck you, too, you fuckin' snotty Yale asshole . . .'

The lawyer took a deep breath, and said, 'Look, I'm trying not to wring your fat little neck, Tony.'

Tony was amazed: 'What'd you say?'

'I said, I'm trying not to wring your fat little neck, you dumb shit. What he's saying is, if he leaves us here, what're we gonna do? Chew our arms off, like rats? We won't break these handcuff chains or this pipe.'

Tony finally caught it, looked once around the blank walls of the basement, and turned to Harper, 'Hey, man . . .'

'Is Maran right?'

After a moment of judgment. 'No. Ask for Rik Maran. You ask for John Maran and . . . you won't get him.'

'Better be right,' Harper said.

* * *

They went up the stairs, Anna first, and at the top, they peeled off the stockings. When Harper started past her to the door, she set her feet and hit him in the solar plexus as hard as she could: Harper's abdomen wasn't his toughest part. He half caved in and took an involuntary step back, eyes wide, and wheezed, 'Jesus, Anna . . .'

'You sonofabitch, you scared my brains out,' Anna whispered harshly, not even knowing why she was whispering. 'I didn't know what you were gonna do. You should have told me ahead of time.'

'I was afraid you wouldn't go along.'

'Oh, bullshit – what haven't I gone along with?'

'Well, anyway, we got the name,' he said, trying to straighten up. He got going again, and led the way out the back, across the patio and down the hill. And when they got to the car, he avoided her eyes, but said again, 'We got the name.'

'Yeah, we've had four names. We've been on a name safari all week and we haven't gotten anything but a chain letter,' she snarled at him over the top of the car. 'We haven't found out anything.'

He got in the car and she climbed in, still furious, and pulled the safety belt down and snapped herself in, and sat with the palms of her hands flat on her thighs.

'You gotta pretty mean punch.'

'Don't patronize me,' she spat back. 'Don't try to humor me; just shut up.'

They eased out of the driveway, down the hill; the ocean looked as green and lazy as ever, as though it didn't know, she thought, that Creek was coughing up lung tissue.

* * *

Halfway into town, Harper broke the unpleasant silence to say, 'We've got to find a phone book somewhere, and figure out where this hotel is.'

Anna took out her cell phone, punched the speed dial for Louis. Louis was apparently sitting next to the phone: he snapped it up halfway through the first ring. He'd been to see Creek; he didn't want to think about it.

'I know,' Anna said. 'Is the laptop handy?'

'Yeah?'

'Punch up the Marshall Hotel on Pico and route us there from the PCH up in Malibu. And give me the number.'

'Just a sec.' He took more than a second, but less than a minute, and Anna repeated his directions to Harper. Then she dug in her pocket, pulled out Tony's cell phone. 'When you talk to this Rik Maran, tell him that a guy is bringing a box for him . . . that you're at the courthouse, waiting for Tony to get out, is the only reason you're answering the phone. Use the voice you used with Tony and the lawyer.'

'What?'

She repeated it as she punched the number for the Marshall Hotel into her own phone. When the clerk at the hotel answered, she said, 'You have a Mr Rik Maran as a guest. I'd like to speak to him.'

'Just a moment . . .'

Maran came on ten seconds later, his voice, dry, reedy, like he might have spent a childhood in Oklahoma, a long time ago: 'This is Rik . . .'

'Call Tony now, on his cellular,' Anna said, and punched off.

A minute later, Tony's phone rang, and Harper picked it up. 'He ain't here . . . who's this? Okay. We're at the courthouse, we got a big problem, but I ain't got time to talk about it. There's a guy coming over, he's got a box for ya . . . I can't talk, this fuckin' thing's a radio, man.'

Harper punched out without waiting for a reply.

Anna said, 'I don't know what I'm doing. If I had any brains, I'd bail out of this now. This whole thing is not right; we're running in the wrong direction.'

'We don't have any other direction,' Harper said. 'This is what we've got.' A few seconds later, he added, 'You're pretty smart, this phone thing. Thinking of it like that.'

The Marshall Hotel was one of the older buildings on Pico, a four-story hollow cube with a brick front and stucco sides, outdoor walkways on the inside of the cube, and windows that looked like holes in an IBM punch card. The bottom floor had a small diner, a check-in desk, and an open courtyard with an above-ground pool and a patio, with a scattering of tables on the patio.

Anna went in first, wearing her sunglasses and a scarf as a babushka, walked through to the courtyard and took an empty table where she could see the desk. A waiter came over and she said, 'A menu? And a white wine . . . Anything good.'

Harper followed a minute later, carrying a briefcase. He stopped at the desk, exchanged a few words with the deskman, shook his head and walked out to the patio and took a chair near the pool, on the other side of a clump of palm.

Maran came out a few seconds later, looked around, spotted Harper and his briefcase, and went that way. Anna watched him and dug into her memory: Maran was sandy-haired or blond, but the hair was cut so tightly to his head that she couldn't tell. His face was skeletal, his body wraith-like, his gestures tired, almost languid. He looked like one of the late, hard self-portraits of Vincent Van Gogh, and she thought: AIDS. Maybe. But he moved smoothly enough, he wasn't shaky, as she'd expect if he were dying.

She'd never seen him before, she was quite certain of that.

She took out her cell phone and called Tony's number, heard it ring thirty feet away. Harper answered, and she said, 'I don't know him – I've never seen him.'

'Okay. Stay where you are. We'll be right back.'

'Where're you going?' she asked, alarmed.

But he'd rung off. A moment later, on the other side of the patio, Maran and Harper headed toward the hotel.

She had only a moment to think about it, but something in the way Harper moved brought her out of her chair. She took just a second to drop a twenty on the table, to keep the waiter off her back, and followed them. They stepped inside an elevator and as the doors closed, Anna stopped, watched the indicator light. The light stopped on three . . .

She turned the corner, started down toward a gift shop, swerved into a stairwell and started running. Ten seconds later, she stood at the door on the third floor, pushed carefully through, listened . . . and heard a door shut down the hallway.

But where, exactly? The doors on the hall were identical, the hallway carpet unexpectedly thick, sound-deadening. She walked slowly down the hall, listening: took a small notebook out of her purse, and a pen; if somebody came along, she'd stop and write in it, as though she were making a note.

But there was nobody in the hall, nothing but silence and the smell of old tobacco smoke.

And then an impact.

Not a sound, exactly, more of a feel; then a sound, muffled, anguished, and another impact. Up ahead, somewhere . . . she hurried down the hall now, but as quietly as she could, listening. Where was it coming from . . .

She passed a door. A possibility. Listened. Another impact, a groan: No. Somewhere ahead, the next room.

Another impact, an animal sound, a wounded animal. Across the hall now. Another. She pressed her ear to the door: and with the next impact, she could feel it.

She tried the knob: locked. Hit the door with her fist. 'Jake! Jake! Jaaake!' Her voice rising. She'd scream it, if she had to.

The knob turned under her hand, and Jake was there, on the other side, a dazed, crazy look in his eyes. He held what appeared to be a broken chair leg. One hand was covered with blood, and there were spatters of blood on his golf shirt.

'Ah . . .' she said, involuntarily. She put a hand on his chest and pushed, and he stepped back, and she went into the room.

Maran was on the floor, face up, bleeding from the nose: he was conscious, but just barely. There was no blood at all on his upper body, but his legs looked wrong. He looked like a paraplegic whose legs had withered . . .

Anna shut the door and said, 'What'd you do?'

'Hit him,' Harper said. He seemed confused, uncertain of where he was.

'Is he gonna die?' She looked toward the phone.

'No, I just . . .' he drifted away, and she caught his arm and squeezed.

'What? Jake?'

'Broke his legs,' he said. He looked at the chair leg in his hand. 'A lot.'

'So let's get out of here,' Anna said. Maran was trying to roll, but there was no leverage in his hips and legs, and he flailed weakly, futilely. He tried to turn himself with his arms, and he moaned again.

'Call an ambulance,' Harper said.

'We can do that outside,' she said, and she pushed Harper toward the door. Harper dropped the chair leg. Anna said, 'God, wait a minute,' carried the leg to the bathroom and quickly, carefully rubbed it down with a towel, then dropped it in the bathtub and turned the hot water on it.

'Now,' she said.

Harper followed her dumbly through the door, down the stairs, out past the gift shop. She stopped him at a bank of phones, dialled 911, and said, 'There's a man hurt really bad in room three-thirty-three at the Marshall Hotel on Pico. Hurt really bad. Better get an ambulance here fast.'

On the street, she could taste the bile at the back of her throat: 'That the guy?' she asked. She looked up at him, his eyes clearing a bit, and then at the blood splatters on his shirt.

'He sold the stuff to Jacob and his friends. He didn't know Jacob, but he described the whole bunch of them.'

202

'Jason?'

'He had no idea who Jason was.'

'Maybe he was lying,' Anna said.

'No. Christ, he was bragging about it. I asked him if he'd seen the kid who tried to fly off the Shamrock, and he was laughing about it in the elevator. You know what he told me? He sold to the kids because "That's my market". That's what he said, like he was some kind of toy-company executive.'

'Ah, God.'

'"That's my market", for Christ's sake. That was in his room – that's when I hit him in the face. He was still smiling when he went down.'

'Jake . . .'

'I feel like I should have strangled the miserable little motherfucker,' Harper said bitterly, as they got to the car. He looked back up the street.

'I wish I'd killed him.'

'So why'd you want the ambulance?'

He looked at her, shook his head: 'Because I'm fucked up.'

Chapter 15

Back on the street, moving quickly, Harper still shaky: 'You drive,' he said, tossing her the keys. 'I'm not functioning too well.'

'All right.' She opened the car, climbed in, adjusted the seat. As she pulled away from the curb, she heard the siren: There was usually a siren somewhere in the L.A. background, but this one was closing in. As they pulled away, she saw the flashing lights a few blocks down Pico, headed toward the hotel.

'Ambulance,' Anna said. She looked at Harper. 'If that makes you any happier.'

'I dunno.' They spent the next five minutes in a ragged silence, Harper staring out the passenger window, away from her. She took the time to think, working over the logic of a connection between Harper's son, a high-school kid from the southeast burbs, and Jason, a street kid from Hollywood and UCLA. Where was the connection? And it would have to be a massive coincidence . . .

The lightbulb went on.

'I've given you a hard time about this connection between your son and Jason,' she said. Harper turned toward her; he was still off track, almost uninterested. 'I couldn't see how there could be a connection. But I let you do all the thinking about it. I had too much other stuff to worry about.'

'Has to be a connection,' he said. 'The paper was torn, and it matched – I saw the two ends, I put them together.'

'There *is* a connection,' she said. 'It's been staring us in the face.'

'What?' Now he turned to her.

'When your son jumped, Jason was right there, almost underneath him. I didn't see it, because I was in the hotel, but Jason was close. A few yards away. He was hanging out before your son jumped, he was planning to ride with us all night. But right afterwards, he couldn't wait to get away from us. Like something had happened in that few minutes. Like he got some drugs.'

Harper thought about it, then closed his eyes and said, 'Goddammit.' And then: 'We've got to look at the tape.'

'You've seen it?'

'I saw it a half-dozen times before Ellen called and said it was Jacob. The tape was all over the TV, I didn't know, just some jerk flying off a building.'

'I'm sorry,' Anna said, aware of the hollowness of the sentiment. *this was what she did.* 'Look, I'm gonna call Louis. I never really looked at the raw tape. I was busy selling while Louis did the editing. I looked at Jason's at the time, but didn't see anything unusual.'

'So where does Louis live?'

She slowed, looked at him carefully: 'You sure you want to look at this stuff?'

'I have to.'

'If there's something on the tape, it means . . . I mean, there'd be no *real* connection. So my problem wouldn't have any connection with yours. Or you.'

He smiled, just faintly, then leaned a little closer and patted her on the leg, just once: '*We've* got a connection now. Whatever's on the tape. You're not sliding away that easily.'

Louis' apartment was a nerd's nightmare – or maybe a dream – a jumble of Domino's pizza boxes, empty Fritos bags, a fat blue plastic garbage can marked 'Aluminum only' with a backboard behind it, half-full of Diet Coke cans.

A projection TV sat in the middle of the front room, showing a severed power cord sticking out from beneath it, like a rat's tail. The longest wall was dominated by industrial gray steel racks full of stereo, computer and telephone equipment, all of which seemed hooked together.

Louis met them at the door wearing a ketchup-stained T-shirt, gym shorts and a stunned look. He'd been up all night, he said, working, and had just gotten to sleep when Anna called.

'I got the tape set,' he said. He kicked through some litter in the front room. 'You guys want some Fritos? I got some somewhere. I got coffee going.'

'Coffee,' Anna said. 'Wash the cups.'

'I already did,' he said, unconvincingly. He was back a minute later with the coffee, saw the cut cord on the projection TV and said, 'Oh, shit. I forgot about that. I'll have to put it up on a monitor.'

'What happened to the cord?' Harper asked.

'I needed a plug last night,' Louis said. 'I mean, it was

207

convenient, and it's easy enough to put back on. If you'd
rather see it on the big screen . . .'

'Monitor's fine, probably better,' Anna said. To Harper:
'You're sure you want to watch?'

'I'm sure.'

Louis pulled the drapes to sharpen up the monitor, and started
the tape. He caught the last few minutes of the animal rights
hassle, the guy knocked over by the pig, then a few random
spacing shots inside the truck, then suddenly the bouncing
run across the patio of the hotel. Anna caught a glimpse of
herself running toward the entrance, and then the lens
steadied, swung up and fixed on Jacob. They could see his
face, a confused smile, the boy's head bobbing as the camera
tried to orient itself.

'Aw, Jesus,' Harper said, involuntarily turning away,
closing his eyes.

'Get out of here,' Anna said.

'Naw.' He turned back, transfixed, as Jason zoomed in
on Jacob's face. The camera hung there, staying with the
face, suddenly pulling back to get some perspective, then
closing in again, getting tight, catching expressions.
Professional, Anna thought: very, very good.

At one moment, Jacob looked as though he might be
dreaming. At the next moment, he seemed confused, or happy.
He reached out once and Anna thought, 'Here it comes,' but
he leaned back, seemed startled to find a wall behind him,
and Anna blurted, involuntarily, 'No, no . . .'

Harper stared. The kid started talking, maybe back to the
window he'd climbed out of. The camera view pulled back:

yes, he was talking to the window. He looked down at the pool, then back at the window. A pale schoolboy face appeared at the window, then a girl's face, then the boy again, and the kid looked at the pool again.

'He thinks he can make the pool,' Harper said.

The camera closed in on his face, and suddenly, Jacob shook his head, said something, and the first faint wrinkle of fear crossed his face. He turned to the window, and one hand went out, touching the wall behind him. He took a step back to the window, but his right leg had to pass his left, and there was nothing out there, and suddenly, he was leaning over empty space: he was falling, and at the last possible instant, he tried to jump, to propel himself out toward the pool . . .

Jason stayed tight, the face and the trailing body, so close, the feet almost behind the head as Jason stayed with it . . .

'Stop!' Anna shouted.

Louis cut the tape, looked at her.

'Back it up, rerun in slow motion. Look at his right hand.'

In slow motion, Jacob almost seemed to be swimming in the air. And at one point, a white, almost formless shadow seemed to pass out of his right hand. It stayed in view of the camera only for an instant, but it was coming at Jason, possibly passing over his head.

'That's the paper,' Anna said.

'You can hardly see anything,' Harper said shakily.

'There's something there,' Anna said positively. To Louis: 'Let's see Creek's stuff.'

Creek had been further away, going for a longer perspective – but the paper coming out was clearer. The paper itself was no longer than a dollar bill, and only half as wide, and it fluttered, twisted, and landed behind Jason's leg.

Jason stayed with the body for five seconds, zooming close; and Creek was still on the scene when Jason turned, almost stumbled, looked down, looked up and around, then stopped to pick something up.

'That's it,' Harper said. He stood and turned away from the television and said, 'There's no connection: none. We've been chasing a wild goose. Goddammit, I'm dumb. Goddammit.'

'God,' Louis said. 'We should've looked . . .'

'No connection. I didn't see how there could be no connection. I thought Jacob had to be part of something bigger, that it couldn't be that simple, that he just took some bad shit and flew off a ledge . . .' The words were coming in a bitter torrent. 'He was *my* son. If he was dead, it had to be *important*. Instead, it's just . . . this fucking everyday ratshit life. No reason, no plot, nothing important, he's just fucking dead.'

'Ah, God, Jake.'

'What can I do? I thought I wanted to kill the guys involved, and it turns out, nobody really even knew what they were doing. So I break a guy's legs . . . Fuck it,' he said. 'Let's go see Creek.'

Creek was dopey, but awake. He smiled, a lopsided smile, and mumbled something.

'He's much better,' Glass said, almost domestic. Anna thought he still looked caved-in. They sat for a while, Anna and Pam talking at Creek like he was a child. Harper sat with his elbows on his knees, staring at the floor. Anna wasn't sure how much Creek understood of what they were saying, and she was as worried about Harper as she was about Creek. When Creek drifted off to sleep, they left.

In the hall, Harper said, 'I'm sorta impressed by Pam. She's really taking care of him. How long had she known him? Couple of days?'

'Creek makes an impression,' Anna said grudgingly. She didn't want to, but she was starting to like Glass, brittle as she was.

Harper said, 'What next?'

Anna shrugged. 'Well . . . I don't know.'

He picked up her tone and said, 'Listen, I'm sticking with you. No way you're gonna get rid of me.'

'You really don't have any obligation . . .'

'Yes, I do.'

'No, you don't.'

'Look, if you don't know what I'm talking about, then you've really got your head up your ass,' he snarled at her.

She thought about that a minute and then said, 'We go to BJ's and start tracking the sex story. But that's later on – it doesn't get started until late. Until then, I don't know. I'm numb.'

'So am I.'

'The tape . . . God, Jake, I'm so sorry.'

'Yeah . . . I wonder, if you don't mind . . . could you drive me somewhere?'

'Anywhere,' she said.

'I want to hit some golf balls.'

'What?'

He didn't look at her, just bobbed his head: 'Yeah. That's what I want to do.'

Chapter 16

Anna drove to a range east of Pasadena, a dusty place on the side of a mountain where, Harper said, 'You can hit from real grass.'

'That's important?'

'Essential,' he said.

The parking lot was up the hillside from the range itself, and they walked down a flight of stairs to the small clubhouse. The owner was a high-school friend of Harper's, happy to see him.

'This is Larry,' Harper said to Anna. 'Larry, this is Anna.'

'Pleased to make your acquaintance,' Larry said, his eyes shifting from Anna to Jake with some private amusement. He wouldn't take money for the range balls: offered as many as Harper wanted to hit.

'Do you want to hit a few?' Harper asked Anna.

'No. I'll get a coffee and sit and watch . . .'

There were a dozen golfers at the range, banging luminescent yellow balls down three hundred yards of sorry grass and desert rut. A fifty-foot-wide strip of longer, slightly healthier turf made up the teeing area. Larry got a plastic chair and a cup of coffee for Anna, and she settled in as

Harper began hitting the balls. He hit a six iron for fifteen minutes, one ball after another, like an automaton, his swing seemingly slow, almost lazy. Easy as it seemed, the balls rocketed away in long, soft, left-curving parabolas.

As she watched him, she realized he was emptying his head, or trying to. When he failed, the golf balls, though their flight still looked perfect to her unknowing eye, were followed with muttered imprecations.

Anna got up once for a fresh coffee: Larry was leaning on the counter, watching Harper hit. He called her ma'am, and then said, 'He looks sorta sad. You two had some problems?'

Anna said, 'His son died last week.'

Larry seemed to contract: 'Aw, man.'

'He's pretty messed up.'

'I knew something was wrong.' He looked out toward Harper and said, 'He's got the prettiest swing I ever saw, outside the pros. But he looks tight today.'

Ten minutes after Harper started hitting, Larry turned on the lights. Harper stayed with the six iron for a while, then switched to a fairway wood. When he finished with that, he put it away, grinned quickly at Anna and said, 'Could you run an errand for me?'

'Sure.'

'In the trunk of my car – push this trunk button on the key – there's a shoe box with a pair of brown golf shoes.'

'Be right back,' Anna said.

She headed out to the parking lot, climbing the stairs, whistling tunelessly as she went. Harper was hitting balls again, a louder crack now, and she turned to look back, saw the balls bounding into the net at the end of the range. He was hitting them hard now, working at it.

She walked up to the car, punched the trunk key as she walked up and saw the lid pop open and the light come on.

There was no presentiment, no intuition, no sixth sense. She never saw the man or even suspected his presence. She was looking in the trunk of the car when he said 'Anna,' and the hair rose on the back of her neck.

He was ten feet away, moving toward her quickly, soundlessly, dressed all in black: she couldn't see his face, and again, for an instant, thought he was black.

Until she realized: nylon mask.

But even then, the softness and reasonableness of the voice lulled her, ever so slightly. She *knew*, but she didn't *believe*.

'Get away,' she said, stepping sideways.

'Anna, we need . . .'

'Get the fuck away,' she said, the fear rising in her voice. She lifted one hand, fingers spread in front of her face, to fend him off. With the other hand, she felt behind her, along the side of the car, as she moved backward.

'Anna, it's all right.'

She turned to run, got two steps, but he grabbed her arm and she twisted violently, and tried to scream. But he pulled her close, pulled hard, and the breath seemed to leave her: the scream died in her throat.

'Anna, we need some time.' His voice was harsher than it had been before, a huskiness that seemed plainly sexual. 'I've got my car . . .'

She could hear the words, but couldn't process them. She slashed at him with the fingernails of her right hand, caught him across his face, tried to kick at him . . .

And he hit her.

Hit her with an open hand, on the side of the head. The blow knocked her off her feet, in the narrow space between the two cars. Again she tried to scream, but nothing happened. The man was standing over her. 'Anna,' he said, 'Anna, Anna, come on, Anna . . .'

She scrambled to get away, but he was pushing her down into the gravel. She kicked straight out, caught an ankle, and he fell on top of her, swearing, catching his weight on one hand. She tried to get up, get free, but he was clinging to her shirt.

She was overwhelmed by her impressions of the man: He was strong, but his stomach was soft. He'd eaten onions, and not too long before. He'd perfumed himself with something, he was sweating.

And he had an erection: as she tried to crawl forward between the cars, he was pressing his hips into her butt, and she felt him, distinctly. She twisted, and hit him in the face with one fist. She could see the wet spot on the nylon stocking where his mouth was, and just the barest flash of eyes, but nothing else. He was like a dark psychotic snowman.

She was still struggling for air as she got her hands on the front tires of the two cars and pushed back and up, got her feet beneath her. He chanted, 'Anna, Anna,' trying to pin her over the car. He could have beaten her unconscious – she was afraid he'd do that – but for some reason, he'd only hit her once. He seemed to be making an effort not to hurt her badly, and that allowed her to resist, though never quite escape.

As they continued the violent scrum in the space between the cars – it seemed to have gone on forever, but actually couldn't have been more than a few seconds – and her breath began to come and she tried again to scream, but the sound came out as a groan, or a cry; not loud enough to be heard below.

'Oh, no, Anna, you don't do that, oh, no . . .'

He was right on top of her, his face riding up over her right shoulder. She turned quickly, almost as though to kiss him, but instead, she bit: and caught a fifty-cent-sized circle of flesh below his cheekbones and bit down *hard*.

He shrieked, and pulled back, but she was hooked in like a leech, and her head came up with his, and she bit harder, felt her teeth cutting through tissue.

And suddenly she was gone. She felt odd, floating, and realized that she was lying on the ground. She could smell the gravel and the dry earth beneath it, feel the gravel chips pressing into her cheeks . . . but she didn't know how she'd gotten there.

His voice seemed far away, and she pumped her legs once, trying to get under a car, but he was riding her again, one hand pulling at the zipper on her pants, and she could again feel his erection grinding into her.

'You goddamn bitch . . .' He hit her on the head. 'You bitch, you bit me . . .'

'Don't,' she groaned. 'Don't do that . . .' He was thrusting at her now, a hard, heavy pumping, and she could feel his breath coming harshly into her neck as he continued to grope for the zipper. She bore down on his hand, trying to grind it into the gravel, and he tried to turn her. As he did, she snapped at him with her teeth again. He pulled back, and when he lifted away his face, lifted his chest high enough to get a full breath, she finally . . .

Screamed.

High, piercing, loud.

Her attacker froze, then clouted her again, and again, then half stood.

Dizzy, hurt, she tried to crawl, thought she heard somebody shout from below, 'Hey . . .' and they were coming, running.

She crawled away from him, trying to stand, and screamed again, and he said, 'See you later.' He kicked her in the back and she pitched forward onto her face, catching herself with her hands, gravel biting into her.

When he did that, kicked her, he turned, but she rolled and the anger had her by the throat now, and she went after him, as he ran across the parking lot toward the hillside. He saw her coming and said, 'Get away,' and slowed to hit her. She dove under his arm and grabbed his leg in a football tackle. But he didn't go down, like football players on TV. Instead, he took the impact, then hit her again, kicked her free and ran.

There were more people coming now, men running up the hill. Her attacker was headed toward the hillside brush, and she was on her hands and knees and then on her feet, running, blind with the anger, no fear at all. She caught him again as he tried to climb and he said, 'Jesus Christ,' and hit her again, clumsily. She was faster than he was, but couldn't fight the longer reach and heavier weight. But if she could just hold on until Harper got there . . .

She tried for his eyes and he hit her one last time, this time catching the side of her nose, and she fell back down the hill, too stunned to get up. But she tried, hearing him above her, tried to get her feet going . . .

She was still trying when Harper arrived, three or four men with him, two of them carrying golf irons. 'Oh, my God, Anna.' She felt no fear at all, barely heard him: but there was fear in his voice. He picked her up and said, 'Oh, my God, she's bleeding bad. Larry, we gotta get her to a hospital.'

But she was waving him off. She wasn't hurt, though she had an odd stinging or burning sensation just above her hairline, and her face was numb, and part of her back. 'No, no, no . . . let me go.'

She tried to tell them: they had to get him, get up the hill.

'We're going to the hospital . . . Where'd he go? It was the guy? Did you get his number?'

He confused her for a minute, then she understood: they thought there'd been a car. She shook her head and pointed at the hill. 'He ran . . . that way.'

'Larry, call the cops, we got him on foot.'

Larry started back toward the stairway, but said, 'Not for long. Basket Drive's over there, and there's an overlook. Bet that's where he's parked.'

Harper shouted at him, 'Larry! Call the fuckin' cops! Tell *them* . . .' And as he put her in the passenger seat and pulled the buckle over her, he asked, 'Where's the hospital, somebody?'

One of the other golfers, an older man with a short steel-colored crewcut and aviator glasses, said, 'I'll ride along, I can point you.'

'Get in.'

'I'm all right,' Anna protested feebly.

'Bullshit.' Harper had piled in the driver's side, the steel-haired man in the back, and she realized that Harper was frantic: 'Hang on.'

The hospital was two minutes away. Harper insisted on carrying her inside, and as they came through the emergency room doors, a nurse behind the counter took one look and ran around and grabbed a gurney and pushed it toward them. Harper put her on it, the sheets stiff and starched beneath her, and the woman started asking questions and then . . .

She drifted away. She could hear them talking, a noisy hash of words. Then another woman was there, in a suit, looking down at her face. She closed her eyes – couldn't seem to help herself – and then she was rolling along a corridor, around a turn to the left. More voices, all women now, and something cool touched her face, wet.

'Anna?' Woman's voice.

She opened her eyes. She was looking at a light on the ceiling. She tried to pull herself back together.

'Yeah. I'm here,' she said.

'How do you feel?'

'Not so bad.' She actually grinned. 'I think I could walk out of here. But I'm tired.'

'I'll bet.' Anna turned her head and saw the woman: she had an absorbent gauze pad in her hand, and it was soaked with blood. 'Is that from me?'

The woman looked down at the pad and said, 'Yes – you've got a scalp cut. Not bad, but they bleed like crazy. You'll need some stitches. And you've got some smaller cuts on one of your arms.'

The doctor shined a light in her eyes, gently moved her head, her neck, compressed her ribs. Had her remove her blouse and jeans, found small cuts, scuffs and bruises on her arms, her side, one leg.

'I think you're okay,' the doctor said, conversationally. 'I better put a few stitches on that scalp cut, though.'

'Go ahead.'

The doctor used a topical anesthetic, but the stitches still hurt. 'Nice that you've got dark hair – they'll be completely invisible,' the doctor said. 'Your face was covered with blood when you came in, like a mask. Your friend thought you were dying.'

'He was pretty freaked out,' Anna said. Despite the stitching, she yawned, apologized, and said, 'I don't know what's wrong with me.'

'Your system is closing down. You'll need some sleep. With the adrenaline and the wrestling around, the blows . . . you had about two weeks' wear and tear in two minutes. You'll sleep for a while.'

Then she asked, 'The gentleman who brought you in . . . he wasn't involved in any way, was he?'

Anna was startled. 'No, no, he was actually hitting golf balls, and I went out to the parking lot to get something. Some shoes, actually, and this other guy was waiting.'

'You're sure? You can tell me.'

'I know what you're getting at,' Anna said. 'This guy . . . he's okay.'

'All right.' The doctor dropped her hands to her lap. 'All done – except the part where you pay.'

They were at the hospital for two hours: when it appeared that Anna would be all right, Harper sent the elderly golfer back to the range in a cab, then sat next to the bed where they put her.

Two uniformed cops came by, spoke to her for a few moments, then an L.A. County detective showed up. The detective took her through the attack, then said, 'Uh, could you, uh, stand up . . .'

She stood up and he turned her by the shoulder and said, 'Yeah.'

'What?' She tried to look over her shoulder.

'We're going to have to take your jeans,' he said; he seemed embarrassed. 'The guy, uh . . . ejaculated on you . . .'

'Ah, God,' Anna said. The doctor said, 'I'll get you some scrubs.'

'I'm sorry,' the detective said, 'but we can get a DNA trace – we might even get lucky and get a cold ID.'

'Fat chance,' Harper said.

The detective shrugged: 'It's been done.'

The doctor got her some green scrub pants, and Anna gave her jeans to the detective, who put them in a plastic bag. 'Pasadena's got some guys going over the parking lot,' he said. 'If we could get you back there for just a few minutes, we'd appreciate it.'

'Can I go?' Anna asked the doctor.

'Yes – but you'll be sore tomorrow,' the doctor warned.

'Take some ibuprofen tonight and as soon as you get up in the morning.'

The owner of the driving range met them in the lot, where he'd been talking to a half-dozen cops. Things were happening now, Anna thought: the story was getting larger. But the range owner was thinking *lawsuit*. He was a worried man. Anna showed him a small smile: 'Don't worry about it,' she said. 'We brought the trouble to you.'

'I'm sorry, I'm sorry,' he said.

'Yeah, yeah.' Anna walked the cops through the lot, showed them where the struggle took place, where the guy ran. The scrub pants flapped around her ankles as she walked. The cops traced the flight path in the dark, up the hill through brush and shrubs, found a few scuff marks near the scenic overlook.

'We'll check the houses around, see if anybody saw a car,' one of the cops said. 'I wouldn't be too hopeful.'

'You're lucky,' said another one. 'If he'd just wanted to take you home, he could've hit you with a sap, dumped you in the trunk of his car and nobody would've known what happened. But he tried to talk to you.'

'It's love,' said the first cop. 'Saved by love.'

Anna slept on the way home, drifting in and out. When they pulled up outside her house, Harper got out, his gun at his side. He looked around the yard, then came back and opened the car door, led her to the house, waited while she unlocked the door, then led the way inside. He checked the ground floor, the doors, the windows, then the second floor.

'Should be okay,' he said. 'But the guy's tracking us. He picked us up somewhere along the way, and followed us right out to the range. If we stay here, we'll be sitting ducks.'

'Unless it was just the Pasadena neighborhood pervert.'

'You don't believe that,' he said.

'No. He knew my name.'

She left Harper downstairs, moving furniture, the better to repel boarders, and went upstairs and looked at herself in the big bathroom mirror. Scuffed up, she thought. Beat up. She shivered, thinking about it: and about the man's sweat on her, about the semen on her pants.

She pulled off her blouse and bra, slipped out of the scrub pants, wadded them, threw them toward the waste basket and then growled after them. She surprised herself with the growl, a harsh, guttural snarl. The guy had been controlling her life for a week. Had gone after people she'd known, people she loved, had come after her.

She looked at herself again in the mirror, a slender dark-haired, beat-up elf in a pair of blue Jockeys for Her . . .

The guy was just trying to corner her, control her, possess her . . .

She stretched, stuck out an arm, twisted: hurt a little bit, but not that much. Looked at herself in the mirror again, and suddenly the anger came back, and she tottered with it, put her hands on the counter and closed her eyes, trying to keep her balance. She snarled again: she wanted to kill something . . .

Let the feeling ebb . . . Brushed her teeth, stood in the

shower for ten minutes, steaming out, then pulled on a robe and went back down the stairs.

Harper was sprawled on the couch, looking at the TV, which he hadn't bothered to turn on. He was barefoot, tired.

'Hey, Jake,' she said.

'Yeah?'

'We were gonna go to BJ's tonight.'

'We're never gonna get there,' he said, shaking his head. 'We're cursed.'

'Tomorrow,' she said.

He nodded: 'How're you feeling?'

'I gotta get some sleep: I'm wrecked.'

'So go to bed: I got it covered down here.'

'I wanted to tell you . . . When you told me this afternoon that if I didn't know why you were hanging around, I must have my head up my ass . . .'

'Yeah?'

'Maybe I do, sometimes,' she said. 'I'm nervous about relationship stuff. But before the driving range thing . . . I was sort of planning to take you upstairs tonight.'

He thought about that for a second, and a *pleased* look crossed his face. 'That would have been nice.'

'I'm still gonna do it, if you're around,' she said. 'But today – today was a little too much.'

'I know. I *will* be around.'

Back upstairs, she crawled under the quilt her mother made, and before she drifted away, thought about Jake: she liked him, a lot. She even liked watching him hit golf balls.

On the darker side, she thought about the scene in Louis'

living room, when they looked at the tape.

What did she do for a living? What was she becoming? And why wasn't she more frightened? She *was* frightened – but above that, she was angry, and in some dark way, interested. *My God*, she thought: *this is a good story. Gotta get right on it.*

She was supposed to be a musician, a classical pianist – but whatever anyone might think about the night crew, it was apparent from the Jacob tapes that they were very, very good at what they did. Watched a man dying, never lost the frame.

And she ran the crew. She was better on the street, she thought, than she was at the piano.

Then she was gone, asleep, a killer back in the dark drapes of her dreams; and with it, a hard little diamond of anger.

She was gonna get him.

Chapter 17

The two-faced man was covered with blood – his own blood – running down his face and arms. He licked at it, and the blood was both sweet and salty on his tongue; but his face was on fire.

The wounds hurt, but didn't really matter: what mattered was the failure. The explosion of his dreams.

Anna didn't want him.

And he'd run like a chicken.

He'd felt real fear: Anna had come after him like a madwoman, and he thought for a moment that she'd pull him down. If the others had gotten there, they would have lynched him.

The humiliation hurt worse than the bite – although the bite hurt badly enough. He gagged in pain, pressed the palm of his hand to his cheek.

Still. He would heal. But the memory of thrashing up the hill, being chased by this small woman . . . that memory wouldn't go away. He'd remember that forever.

He'd gone to her expecting recognition. He'd eliminated the others. Hadn't that proven something? Didn't that give him some rights? He'd expected resistance, but then, he thought, she'd see the fire, feel the steel, and she'd come with him.

She'd slept with other men. He didn't like it, but he accepted it. He also knew that the others didn't love her: they simply used her. Jason O'Brien, Sean MacAllister, her driver, Creek. Users. Takers.

He'd *gone* to her; virtually begged her . . .

He flashed back to the sex: he'd bent her over the car, had been plucking at her pants, and suddenly, from the friction of the contact, the excitement, he'd ejaculated.

He remembered that without pleasure; because he also remembered running frantically across the parking lot, his penis protruding from his pants, wobbling around like a crazed-comic compass pointer, leading him into the brush.

He'd managed to tuck himself back inside before he hit the thorn trees, or he'd really have been hurt.

Had she seen that? Were she and her bodyguard off somewhere, laughing about it?

He closed his eyes: Of course they were. He could feel it.

And quick as that, love turned to hate; as it had with his teacher, Mrs Garner. As it had with a kitten that scratched . . .

He'd have to get her, now. He'd have to erase her.

The inner and outer faces agreed.

She didn't want him? Okay.

First, he'd show her what fear was. He'd frighten her worse than she had frightened him.

He licked at the blood on his arm.
Then he'd cut her to pieces.
Anna Batory was a dead woman walking.

Chapter 18

One of the dreams, something unpleasant, woke her; the diamond of anger was there, like a pebble in her shoe. Unlike a pebble, she cherished it, nurtured it, willed it to grow . . .

The clock glowed at her in the near-dark: six in the morning. She rolled over, tried to sleep, failed. Giving up, she swiveled to drop her feet on the floor – and needles of pain shot through her shoulders and ribs. She said, 'Ooo,' silently, rolled her arms, then cautiously stood up. Her legs hurt, especially along the inside of her thighs; and she could feel the strain in her butt, where the big muscles connected to her pelvis, in her shoulders, and in her ribs. Her head itched: not thinking, she reached up to scratch, and felt the stitches.

Jeez. The guy had done a number on her.

She went to the bathroom, read the label on an ibuprofen that warned against taking more than two, took four, steamed herself out in the shower again, and, as an afterthought – a Harper thought? – shaved her legs. The hot water felt good, and as it poured down on her neck and back, she thought about what had happened so far.

Jacob was connected to Jason only through coincidence: Jason's dealer hadn't sold to Jacob Harper, and was apparently hostile to the people who had. So what did that leave?

The white-haired man? The white-haired man who'd run from them at the hospital was out of keeping with last night's attack, and the attack on Creek – so much so that she nearly dismissed him as part of the problem: she didn't know what was going on there, but the white-haired man simply did not fit.

Last night's attacker had been young and strong. Younger than she was, she thought. He liked cologne, and though he was stronger than she was, he wasn't nearly as strong Jake. What else? He'd been coming to court her? Could that be right? He'd tried to talk to her . . .

She finished showering, tiptoed around the bedroom getting dressed, found her running shoes and a pair of socks and carried them downstairs. She wouldn't be running, but the shoes were quiet. She went to the front door and saw that Harper had piled Coke cans next to it. She unstacked them quietly, unlocked the door, looked out, spotted the paper, reached out and grabbed it. Relocked the door, feeling virtuous.

She ate cold cereal with milk, read comics, pulled on a pair of socks, got a yellow legal pad and a No.2 pencil from her office, sat at the kitchen table and tried to untangle the maze . . .

White-haired guy. Dead end.

Courting her. He must've met her; he expected her to know him – but maybe not by name or face; maybe he expected only a kind of cosmic connection. Something he said hinted at that; that they were fated together.

And that fit with the killings, and the attack on Creek: if Anna was at the center of a sex triangle, a three-way, or even four-way, maybe he'd conclude that he had to eliminate his competitors.

He must've heard the story – which meant that anyone who knew all of them – Jason, Sean, Creek and herself – was a possibility. And that was not many people. On the other hand, anyone who knew them at all knew that she wasn't sleeping with either Jason or Sean: the idea was ludicrous. They might suspect Creek, because they worked so closely together . . . but Creek was the last one attacked. Why? Because he was the most dangerous? The hardest to get at?

Huh. They really needed to get to BJ's.

She was still struggling with the list when Harper bumbled out of the guest room, unshaven, wearing last night's pants and a T-shirt.

'How are you?' he asked.

'Creaky,' she said.

'I'm gonna get cleaned up, then we gotta run up to my place so I can get some clothes.'

'All right, and I want to get up in the hills and try out the gun. It's been a while.'

He looked at her for a moment, then said, 'Best thing you could do is go back to your dad's place for a visit. This guy is freaking out: he'll be dead meat in two weeks, whether you're here or not.'

'If I believed that, I might go, but I'm looking at the cops and I'm not seeing much. So . . . I'm gonna stay.'

He sighed, scratched his prickly face: 'All right. You can shoot out back of my place.'

'Really?' Didn't sound like the valley.

And it wasn't. He lived on a dirt road off Mulholland Highway, halfway down a hill a few miles west of Topanga. Anna laughed when she saw the place, a rambling collection of white-stucco blocks with deep green eaves and red-tiled roof, something that a skilled hippie might have put together in the sixties.

'What?' he asked, when she laughed. His eyes crinkled, amused, at the sound of her.

'It's great,' she said. 'How much land?'

'Twenty acres.'

She was amazed: 'How can you afford it?'

'Bought it fifteen years ago,' he said. 'Built a few pieces at a time.'

'You built it?' Amazed again.

'Yup. Took some classes at the vo-tech on block-work; made friends with a guy who had some heavy equipment, helped him build his place.'

He stopped in a gravel patch in front of the garage. As they got out, a car passed on the road at the bottom of the hill, honked twice, and Harper waved. 'Widow-lady neighbor,' he said.

'Hmm,' Anna said. 'Attractive, rich . . .'

'Blonde, and got the big, you know . . .'

'Ears . . .'

'Exactly the word I was groping for.'

'Yeah, grope,' she said.

The house was cool inside, and a little dim after the glare of the sun on the semi-desert; it was bachelor-neat, the neatness of a man who'd lived alone for a long time, and learned to take care of a house; not precise, not tidy, but most things in their own places, less a couple of socks next to the couch, a couple of beer cans on a table next to a couch that faced an oversized television.

'Gotta get some clothes.' He fished a half-dozen golf shirts out of a drier, plugged in an iron. 'There's a gully out back, if you want to take a look,' he said. 'Take some beer cans out . . . watch out for snakes.'

She'd brought a box of cartridges with her; and with the pistol in her jacket pocket, and a half-dozen empty beer cans in a sack, crunched through the short dry weeds behind the house, fifty yards out to the mouth of the gully. She found a spot where she could prop the cans against the dirt gully-wall, put them down, and backed off about eight paces.

'All right,' she said. She had the gun out, barrel down, and she said, 'One,' and the gun was up, the heel of her right hand cupped in her left, and she fired a single shot.

The gun bucked, and the muzzle blast was like a slap on the side of the head; her ears rang like a distant phone. Damn; forgot her earmuffs. But the slug had bitten into the dirt four inches from the target can. Not too bad.

She looked around, finally walked back to the house and got some Kleenex, ripped off enough to make marble-sized wads, and pushed them into her ears as she walked back out.

The Kleenex helped, and now she started running through the routine she'd been taught in her gun classes: two shots, one-two. Then three, one-two-three. At twenty feet, she'd hit the target can with one shot out of every four or five. That was fine, the cans were just aiming points: hearts. While she missed with the other shots, she was always close – inside a man's chest. She moved closer, and the number of hits went up. Eventually, she was shooting from six feet, hitting the cans almost every time.

She didn't see Harper coming, but she felt him, turned, took one of the Kleenex wads out of her ears and said, ''Bout done.'

'You're not bad,' he said. He was wearing a fresh blue golf shirt and faded jeans.

'Always had guns around,' she said. 'Out in the country. Want to try?'

'Nope. But let me see a quick two-tap.'

She nodded, put the wad of paper back in her ear, and did a quick two, one of the cans spinning away up the gully.

'But it's much easier when you're shooting at a target, nothing's moving, you're not frightened, you've got no handicaps . . .'

'Yeah, yeah, they told us all that – and they also said, you gotta do what you can.'

'Go ahead and do another double-tap,' he said, moving up behind her. He put his hand flat against her shoulder blade.

'Don't push, I might shoot myself in the foot,' she said. 'And I've only got one round left.'

'So shoot the one round, and don't worry – I'm a highly

trained veteran of police combat,' he said. 'I know what I'm doing.'

'All right,' she said, doubtfully. 'Say when.'

'Take it slow, make an aimed shot . . . whenever you're ready.'

'Okay.' She squared herself to the target. 'Ready?'

'Yeah.'

She focused on the cans, then lifted the gun. As she did, she tightened her legs, expecting a push, or a pull. Instead, he slipped both hands around her, catching her with a lifting motion just under her breasts, and at the same time, kissed her on the neck.

Anna felt like she was coming out of her shoes – liked it – and at the same time, focused on the target and squeezed off the shot.

'Jesus,' Harper groaned, reeling back, hands over his ears. 'I think you blew my eardrums out.'

'That's what you get,' she said, primly. She dumped the spent shells.

'How much longer are you going to do this?'

'I'm done,' she said. 'I could use a beer.'

As they walked back to the house, he said, 'I don't want to seem impolite, you know, but hanging around you for the last couple of days . . .'

'Yeah?'

'Anna . . . I'm getting fairly desperate.' His voice was convincing.

'I think we can fix that,' she said. And she looked around, at the hillside, the house, the perfect blue sky. 'And it's such a nice day for it.'

* * *

And they did fix it, and more than once; but the second time they made love, as Harper began to lose himself in her . . . Anna looked up at the ceiling and saw the holes the bullets had punched on the gully-wall, and instead of thinking of the man with her then, she thought of the man last night.

And she thought again, *Gonna get you.*

Chapter 19

Harper was driving down the narrow canyon road, through the night, occasional snapshots of the L.A. lights ahead of them. He was not happy with the trip: he wanted to spend the evening at his house, but Anna was going hunting, with or without him.

'BJ's: that was the only time Jason and MacAllister were hooked into me, so the guy must've been at the party.'

'No,' Harper said, shaking his head. 'You don't know how many times they told that story.'

'What's the point of telling it if nobody sees the woman? It's no big deal being in a three-way anymore, you can get one for fifty bucks down on the strip.'

'Really?' he pretended to perk up.

She ignored it: '. . . so I figure what happened is, I show up at the party, ask around for him, he's a little unhappy when I blow him off – he was really a mess, but he thought he could still do it, he needed the money – and so he starts spreading the story with his pal. Whoever it is saw me, and heard the story. Had to be.'

'Doesn't have to be.'

She sighed: 'Okay. Not technically: but that's all I've got, and I'm going with it.'

The party box was running hard. Anna led the way up the narrow, smoke-filled stairway, the buzz-cut hulk at the door looking past her at Harper. When Harper looked up at him, he stepped out of sight into the party room, and a moment later stepped back out; Anna realized that a warning was now rippling through the room – Harper had been taken for a cop.

The hulk was a redneck, a southern kid with a layer of hard fat in his face and under his *Eat More Spam* T-shirt. He nodded vaguely at Anna and said to Harper with a thin, sarcastic edge, 'We're checking IDs, officer.'

Harper smiled a cop smile at him and said, 'I'm proud of you.'

'Have you got a warrant?'

Harper opened his mouth, but Anna cut in: 'He's not a cop. Not anymore.'

The hulk was doubtful: 'So what's he want? He don't fit here.'

'He's taking care of me,' Anna said. 'Do you know Jason O'Brien and Sean MacAllister?'

A spark of interest lit in the hulk's eyes: 'I heard they're dead.'

'That's right. Now the guy who killed them is coming after me. We're trying to find out who it is.'

The hulk's forehead wrinkled as he thought about it, and then he said, 'You know who'd know? Trip what's-his-face. He hung with the guy . . . hang on one second.'

He stepped out of sight again, and a moment later was back: 'Come on,' he said.

Harper looked at Anna and showed a quarter-inch of a smile: he'd caught the warning move, and now the cancellation.

The party room was actually four rooms: a bar area, a large tiled dance room, and two smaller rooms at the sides, with rickety plastic lawn tables and chairs. All four rooms stank of tobacco smoke, and an edge of something sharper: crack, Anna thought. No grass; this club was a little harder than a pothead might want.

The population dressed in black, both male and female. Harper, with his blue shirt and sport coat, looked like he'd just arrived from Iowa. The hulk led them to the second room, spotted a thin man in a black mock turtle, with oval gold-rimmed glasses, and held up a finger. The man tipped his head and the hulk led them over.

'This is a TV lady, used to work with Jason O'Brien.'

'Anna,' the man said. He smiled quickly, a click on-and-off, showing a couple of pointy canine teeth. He looked at Harper: 'Who's your attractive friend?'

'Jake Harper,' Harper said, and stuck out his hand. The man took it, warily, but Jake shook cheerfully and said, 'Is it Trip?'

'Yes, Trip.' He had a drawl, a very faint cultured hint of New Orleans. 'I heard about Jason and Sean. Not the details.'

'You don't seem surprised,' Anna said. 'Do your friends get killed a lot?'

'From time to time,' Trip said, with faint amusement.

Anna nodded: 'Okay. I came up here one night, about

three weeks ago, to pick Jason up, but he was too messed up to work,' she said. 'But that night, he started a rumor that he and MacAllister and I were in a three-way. We think whoever killed them heard the rumor. We're wondering who was here that I might know, or might know me.'

Trip pursed his lips, then said, 'Well, I suppose ninety percent of the people here are in film, one way or another. Writers or actors or directors, or trying to be. And you're actually doing some media, so . . . I don't know; maybe several people knew you, or *of* you.'

Anna shook her head: 'I didn't see anybody I knew.'

'Let me think . . .' Trip turned slightly away and closed his eyes, and then waited; and after a few seconds, opened them and turned slightly back to her and said, 'Were you? In a three-way?'

'No.'

Trip let his eyes drift to Harper: 'Too bad; they're kinda fun.'

'I keep telling her,' Harper said. 'I even got the other woman.'

'Shut up,' Anna snapped. To Trip: 'Somebody who must've been tight with MacAllister and Jason both.'

'MacAllister did some work in porno: acting work. Jason might've taken the pictures, I don't know – but both were friends with the guy who produces them. Dick Harnett, Bunny Films, they're out in Burbank.'

'That's it?'

'Actually, no. You know who else used to hang with them? China Lake.'

'Who?'

'China Lake, the actress. She played a junkie girl on "90210" one week. She was up here with them a couple of times.'

'Bunny Films, in Burbank, and China Lake – you know where we can find her?'

'Probably practising for her role as a junkie girl,' Trip drawled, letting the New Orleans out again. 'Look downstairs in the ladies' restroom. Dark-haired girl, shaved around the ears.'

The women's restroom was a sewer, four metal booths on an uneven concrete floor, everything a little damp, the stink of urine and vomit in the air: China was alone, staring at herself in a cracked mirror, her eyes underlined with gray rings of exhaustion, her shoulders not much more than bare bone. Anna thought she might be nineteen.

'China?'

She turned her head and looked first at Anna, then at Harper, with little interest: that Harper should be in a woman's restroom didn't seem worthy of comment, or even notice. 'Yeah?'

'My name is Anna Batory. I used to work with Jason O'Brien, before he got killed.'

'I heard he was dead, and Sean,' she said. She turned back to the mirror. 'You got anything good on you?' Without waiting for an answer, to Harper, 'Are you a cop?'

'No.' He shook his head: 'We're looking for whoever killed Jason; they're coming after Anna here.'

'Really? You got anything good on you?'

Anna shook her head: 'We're looking for a guy who might

have hung out with Jason and MacAllister. Pretty big guy, about like Jake.' She nodded at Jake. 'And a little out of shape. Not real fat, just sort of fleshy. Could be pretty weird.'

'That's everybody I know,' China said. 'Except . . .'

'What?'

'Most of them are skinny. You sure you don't have anything good on you? You look like you do, like you got money.'

They talked for another two minutes: a woman came in, glanced at Harper, said nothing, just went on to a booth and closed the door. Harper looked at Anna, faintly embarrassed, looked at China, who'd gone back to her mirror, and shook his head. Nothing here.

'All right,' Anna said. She held a card out to China, and when the woman didn't take it, slipped it into a pocket in China's small leather purse. 'If you hear anything, or think of anybody, call me. There might be . . . something good in it.'

China brightened. 'You got something good?'

'Great lead,' Harper said, as they left the club. 'Now what?'

'Bunny films.'

'Anna, it's ten o'clock at night.'

'So, we bang on a door – maybe there'll be somebody around. What else are we gonna do?'

'I could come up with something.'

Behind them, in the club, a man leaned in the door of the women's restroom and said, 'Aren't you China Lake?'

China turned and said, 'Hey: You got anything good on you?'

The man shrugged, and unconsciously reached up to touch his cheekbone. 'Probably,' he said. 'I got a little of everything.'

'You do?' China brightened, the circles seeming to fade from beneath her eyes. She looked almost young enough to be her age. 'I've been waiting for you.'

Chapter 20

On the way out Sunset toward Burbank, Anna spotted a red-haired woman in a leather biker jacket and skinny jeans, leaning on a window, hands in her jeans pocket, smoking a cigarette: 'Stop, pull over,' Anna said. 'By that woman.'

Harper pulled over: 'What's going on?'

'How do you roll the window?' The window rolled down and Anna yelled, 'Hey, Jenny . . . It's Anna.'

The woman had been watching the car as it slowed, and now she smiled, flipped her cigarette up the street and said, 'Anna. Where've you been?'

'Working. Come on, get in.' Anna turned around in the front seat, popped the lock on the back door. 'We'll get something to eat or something.'

The woman nodded and said, 'Nice wheels,' as she slipped into the back seat. And Anna said, 'Jenny Norden, Jake Harper. Jake's a lawyer, Jenny's with Lutheran Social Services.'

Harper's eyebrows went up: 'You're pulling my leg.'

Norden grinned at him and said, 'Nope. I'm a born-againer.'

'Anna's friends,' Harper said, as he pulled away from the curb.

'I can't believe you're sleeping with a lawyer,' Norden said, tongue-in-cheek.

'Who says I am?' Anna asked.

'I do,' Norden said. 'You've got that really clear-skin look.'

'What's wrong with lawyers?' Harper asked the rearview mirror.

'Nothing. I am one,' Norden said.

'Yeah? You know the difference between a lawyer and a trampoline?'

'You take off your shoes to jump on a trampoline,' Norden said. 'You know what the lawyer said when he stepped in a cow pie?'

'Oh my God, I'm melting,' Harper said. 'You know the difference between a rooster and a lawyer?'

'A rooster clucks defiance,' Norden said, and Harper said, 'All right, she's a lawyer.'

'I told you that,' said Anna. Then she laughed, and her laugh made Harper laugh, and he asked, 'What?' and Anna said, 'I just got the clucks joke.'

'If you loved me, you wouldn't laugh,' Harper said.

Then Anna turned in her seat again and said, 'Hey, Jenny! Do you know a guy named Dick Harnett, supposed to be in porno?'

'Sure – you're doing a story that'll ruin his life, I hope,' Norden said.

'We don't even know him – but we need to talk to him. I've got a problem.' And she explained it.

Norden listened carefully and then said, 'Anna . . .' stopped, turned to Harper and said, 'You oughta get her out of here.'

'I've suggested that. She says she's staying; so I'm staying.'

'That's stupid,' Norden said. She leaned forward and pointed through the windshield. 'See the place with the moon in the window? Let's go in there.'

The Gibbous Moon was run by a pair of gentle aging hippies who knew Norden; the place smelled of steamed vegetables, olive oil and coffee. The counterman called Norden by name; they found a booth, ordered coffee.

'Dick Harnett was the producer of legitimate TV shows back in the sixties, but he was a sex freak and he started making some porno when that was hip, back around the *Deep Throat* days,' Norden said. 'Then feminism came in and porno wasn't hip anymore and nobody legit would touch him. He was scratching around for a while, but then video came along, and you know, he knew how to do that. And he saw what was going to happen. He was one of the first big time video-porn distributors.'

'So he's rich.'

'No, no, after a while, it got so every college kid in L.A. was making a porno film with his girlfriend . . . amateur tapes. The bottom's sort of fallen out of the market. I get the impression that most of those guys are on hard times.'

'He's got this Bunny Films . . .'

'Yeah, pretending he has something to do with *Playboy*. He's had a dozen companies, probably. He's getting old, now – he's still a freak, though, that's the word.'

'A sleaze-dog,' Anna said.

Norden blew gently on her coffee, then nodded: 'Yeah. And the thing is, there's always been violence around his films. He sorts of gets off on the idea of sex by force. Maybe . . . I don't know.'

'Maybe what?' Harper asked. 'You think he might be the guy?'

'He's not young,' Anna said to Harper.

'White hair?' Harper asked.

Norden nodded: 'Big white hair. From way back – his first company was called Silver Fox Films.'

'How do you know all this? From Lutheran Social Services?' Harper asked.

'I work with hookers – young girls,' Norden said. 'Pull them off the street, try to get them out of the life.'

'Gets in fistfights in biker bars,' Anna said.

'Hey, who doesn't,' Norden said, raising her eyebrows as she looked at Anna.

'Huh.' Harper scratched his chin. 'And you know Harnett.'

'I know who he is – I've talked to him. He used street kids from time to time and I've heard that he's made a couple of videos with really young kids. So he's on my *interest* list.'

'You think he might have hired somebody like Jason?' Anna asked.

'From what you said, he's exactly the kind of guy Harnett would use – somebody who wouldn't cost him too much and does good work. Lot of kids from UCLA have worked for him,' Norden said.

Anna said to Harper, 'We've got to find him.'

Harper shook his head: 'First we've got to get a look at him. I mean, if he's the guy . . . you oughta know him.'

'Never heard the name,' Anna said, shaking her head.

'You did that piece on street kids, you might of bumped into him and not known it,' Norden said.

'That was six months ago,' Anna said. 'This all jumped in the last week.'

Back in the car, Anna called Louis and asked him to get a home address for Harnett. As Anna was talking to Louis, Harper asked Norden, 'How'd you get into this? I mean were you . . . ever personally involved with . . .?' He didn't want to ask her if she'd ever been a hooker.

She was amused: 'No. I went to a Lutheran college in Iowa, and then to Guatemala to work with a mission. I came back and went to law school here in California – Berkeley – and joined Lutheran Social Services as a lawyer. I met some street kids, girls, and decided that I liked the mission work better than the law work. I still do some law . . .'

'And you've still held onto the religious aspect . . . even after seeing all the stuff on the street?'

'Oh, absolutely,' Norden said, nodding, her face serious. 'I accept Jesus Christ as my savior, and I believe that he will return soon and judge us and lead those who deserve it to eternal life.'

Harper checked the mirror again, and decided she wasn't joking.

Then Anna hung up the portable and said, 'Louis can't find a home address. There're five Richard Harnetts with unlisted phones in the two counties and they're scattered all over the place.'

'We've still got his office address,' Harper said. 'Let's take a look.' And over his shoulder, he said to Norden, 'Can we drop you somewhere?'

'Heck no. I wouldn't miss this for anything.'

On the way to Burbank, Harper made a quick turn down an alley, accelerated, and Anna said, 'What?' as they whipped past the backs of a row of small stores.

'Just checking,' Harper said, watching his mirror. 'We know he was tracking us.'

They came out of the alley, crossed a street, and went right back into the continuation of the alley. At the end, Harper took a left onto a deserted residential street, then a quick right. 'All right,' he said.

Bunny Films was on the second floor of a shabby fifties concrete-and-brick low-rise office building, with a narrow parking lot wrapped around the building. There was one car in the lot, but it carried an air of abandonment. No lights showed in the building.

'Come back tomorrow,' Harper said.

'Let's not rush off,' Anna said. 'Pull around behind the building. I want to check that door.'

'Felonies are a Bad Thing,' Harper said. 'I'm sure counselor Norden would agree.'

'I just want to look at the door,' Anna said. 'Maybe somebody's around, they'd let us in.'

'Ah, man,' Harper said, but when Anna asked, 'Who

climbed over that fence and got shot at, who broke into that house, who . . .' he said, 'Okay, okay,' and pulled around back and into a parking space with a 'Reserved for Building Tenant' sign. Norden and Anna got out, and Norden said, 'Got shot at?' while Harper waited in the car, engine running.

'We've had a couple of problems,' Anna said. The door was locked: they could see the steel tongue between the door and the frame. 'Not very far in there,' Norden said, stooping to peer at the lock. 'It's sort of tilted up. I bet if you stuck a screwdriver or a tire iron in there, you could pry the door right open.'

'Back in a minute,' Anna said. At the car, she said, 'Hey, Jake, pop the trunk for a minute.'

'Why?'

'I want to look at your golf shoes. Pop the trunk.'

'Damn it, Anna . . .' But he popped the trunk, and the tool kit was there, in the trunk lid, just as she remembered from the last time she'd been in the trunk, a few seconds before she'd been attacked in the parking lot. She turned the hand screw on the tool-box cover, the cover dropped open. She selected a screwdriver, closed the trunk and walked back to the door.

'What do you think?' she asked Norden.

Norden cast a quick look around. A stream of cars was passing on the street, a half-dozen teenagers were lounging around a picnic table at a Foster's Freeze a hundred feet down the street. Norden said, 'Don't make any big moves and do it quick.'

Anna struck the end of the screwdriver in the gap between the door and the frame, put her weight against it, and when the tongue pulled out of the lock, Norden jerked the door open.

'Talk about irresponsible,' Norden said, looking at the door. 'I'm surprised the junkies haven't carried off the furniture.'

'Probably scared to,' Harper said. He'd killed the engine, and walked up behind them. 'We're right out in the open, probably nine people calling the cops right now.'

'Door was open,' Norden said.

'Yeah, right. Screwdriver marks all over it, and we've still got the screwdriver.' Harper pulled the door tight against the frame, took the screwdriver from Anna, pried the frame and door apart again, and popped the lock tongue back into place. 'When I was in uniform, we'd rattle doors, but we'd never try to get inside if the doors were locked,' he said.

No Bunny Films was listed on the directory, but they found a Harnett Enterprises on a row of painted steel mailboxes next to the front entrance. The number indicated an office on the second floor. They skipped the small elevator and climbed a dark, smoke-scented stairway, found a light switch for the second floor and followed a narrow hallway to the end. The office had only a number, but no other identification. An empty name-plate holder was screwed to the wall next to the door.

'Well, shit,' Harper said. 'Maybe he moved.'

'Maybe he just doesn't want people to know where he is,' Anna said. 'If this is his office, there's gotta be something inside with his home address.'

Harper looked up and down the hall, shook his head, put his back against the wall opposite the door, his foot next to the doorknob, and pushed. The lock ripped out of the door, and they were in.

'If the cops come, we're busted,' he said, flipping on the lights. 'Let's make it quick. And for Christ's sake, don't touch anything with your fingertips if you can help it.'

Harnett's office was one large room with a desk in the center, filing cabinets around the edge and a small sofa and easy chair combination on a faded Persian carpet in front of the only window. The window looked over the parking lot, and from there over a fence into a residential back yard. Something in the back yard may have interested Harnett, because a pair of 10 x 50 binoculars sat on the windowsill.

A door led off to the right. It was unlocked, and when Anna pulled it open, she found a closet with a raincoat, a box of shirts, a suit in a plastic wrapper, several rolls of Christmas gift-wrapping paper, a shoe-shine kit in a cardboard box, and two empty suitcases.

The main surface of his L-shaped desk was a heap of business paper – envelopes, faxes, trade magazines, clippings – that flowed across, and in and out of two in and out boxes. The short leg of the L held a Gateway P5-90 tower computer and a Vivitron monitor, with cables to a Hewlett-Packard laser printer. A short butcher-block table held a Panasonic fax machine and a Canon copier. A large-screen TV sat in a wooden cabinet in the corner, and the lights of two different videotape players glowed from beneath it. The desk telephone had five buttons.

'Busy guy,' Anna said. A cup on his desk held a spray of yellow Dixon pencils like a bouquet, and Anna took them out and handed them to Harper and Norden. 'Move stuff with these.'

Anna and Harper used the pencils to probe the paper on the desk, and go through the Rolodex, while Norden explored the file cabinets. At one point, she said, 'Hmm,' looked around, found a box with a half-dozen reams of laser paper still in it, dumped the paper on the floor and carried the box to the file.

'What're you doing?' Harper asked.

'All kinds of correspondence,' Norden said, dumping paper into the box. 'Interesting stuff. I might be able to use it . . .'

Anna said, 'Look at this.' She'd gone back to the closet as Harper continued working through the desk with the pencils, and pulled out the two suitcases. They were empty, but they both had trip labels on them. 'Home addresses,' she said. 'Even phone numbers.'

As Anna copied the address, Norden opened a file cabinet full of videotapes, and another one stacked with skin magazines and a few old reels of 16mm film. 'Look at all this shit,' Norden said. 'Think of how many women are in this.'

'Let's go,' Anna said. 'We got what we need.'

'Been here too long,' Harper said.

'I'm taking the Rolodex, too,' Norden said. 'What a jerk.' She threw the Rolodex into the box full of correspondence and followed Harper to the door. Anna stopped, then turned around.

'C'mon,' Harper said.

'One minute.'

Anna went back, picked up a sheet of paper from the laser printer, went to the cabinet full of videotapes and started dumping piles of them on the floor. Then she chose a tape with one of the more elaborate labels, stuck it into the tape player, used Harnett's remote controls to turn on the TV and the player.

'What're you doing?'

'Shhh . . .'

The tape started with a woman – a porn consumer's idea of a classy businesswoman, in a suit, with long, shoulder-length hair, and a skirt that ended a quarter-inch below her hips – approaching the stoop of a New York brownstone. From the look of it, the plot would be thin. Anna fast-forwarded for ten seconds or so, getting the woman on her knees, giving head to a man with what appeared to be a hair transplant on his chest.

'All right,' she said. 'Just checking.' She ran the tape back to the start, let it run, and said, 'Let's go – and leave the lights on and the door open. And let's leave the door open downstairs.'

'What was that all about?' Harper asked, when they were back in the car.

'Well, we wanted a look at Harnett,' Anna said. 'Now we'll get a look.'

She punched a number into her cell phone and said, 'I want to report a burglary in progress, in Burbank, yes, right now . . .'

When she finished, she hung up and said, 'Okay, so now the cops'll come. They'll find the break-in, and the tape going, so they'll stay a while.'

'And now we call Harnett,' Harper said.

'Exactly.'

'Better let me,' Harper said. 'If he's the guy, he'll know your voice.'

Harnett answered on the third ring, sounding sleepy. Harper said, 'Mr Harnett, this is James T. Peterson with the cleaning company. Mr Harnett, there's been a big break-in at your office, we called the police, but I think you better get up here.'

Harnett arrived in a year-old Buick, the back end of the car making a T-shirt frowny face at them as it bounced over the curb into the parking lot. Norden said, 'Here we go.'

A cop was standing by a squad car, talking on a radio. When Harnett got out of his car, the cop held a hand up to slow him down.

Anna, Harper and Norden were sitting on a concrete picnic table at the Foster's Freeze down the street, licking chocolate-dipped soft vanilla cones. Harnett caught Anna halfway through a lick and she almost choked: 'I know him, I've seen him,' she said, excited. Harnett's white hair stood up in a mane, as though he'd been running his hands through it; he was a heavy-set man with a rounded chin that once might have been square, wearing rumpled khaki chinos and a nylon windbreaker. 'That club on Sunset, the topless Polynesian one where they had the harp player who was shot by her girlfriend . . .'

'Yeah, the LoBall,' Norden said. 'It's closed.'

'Yeah, but we were there to look at the shooting. He did

an interview with somebody else, and I grabbed him and we did a couple of minutes. He was pretty good. He wouldn't give us his name, that's why it didn't ring a bell. I remember him saying he'd rather not give his name. I thought he might have done TV . . .'

'White hair,' said Harper.

'Yeah, but he's kind of fat. That guy in the parking lot – he was soft, but he wasn't fat, exactly . . .'

The cop slammed his car door and led Harnett into the building and out of sight.

'How long ago?'

Anna looked at Norden: 'Must've been, what, a year? Since the shooting?'

Norden nodded: 'About that. The guys who ran the place were always in trouble with the cops, and the shooting was the last straw. I think they were open for a couple more months, and then they were out. There's another place there now.'

Anna said: 'Well. When he comes out, I'm gonna let him see me. See how he reacts.'

Harper frowned: 'If he's the guy, he's nuts.'

'But there're cops all over the place. What's he gonna do?'

The phone rang in her pocket, and she fumbled it out. 'And if he's the guy, it'll freak him out. He'll show us something.'

She pushed the button on the phone and a woman's voice squeaked, 'Anna Batory?'

'Yes?'

'I'm dying.'

'What?' She looked at the phone. 'Who is this?'

'China Lake.' The voice seemed distant, weak. 'I'm dying.'

'What . . .' She was sputtering, and Harper and Norden were looking at her curiously.

Then a man's voice, rougher, familiar: 'She's dying, Anna. And it's your fault.'

Anna closed her eyes and squeezed the phone. 'No – no.'

Harper, alarmed, said, 'What?'

'It's him . . .'

Chapter 21

'Listen to her.' The man's voice was like a snake's, a hiss of pleasure.

Jake had bolted from the car, was running down the street toward the cop car at Harnett's building.

Then the woman in Anna's ear: 'Anna, he stabbed me,' and, less certainly, 'It doesn't hurt much, but I can't move . . .'

'Where are you?'

'She's around, that's where,' the man said. 'I saw you to-night. What are you doing – are you looking for me? If you're looking for me, I'll tell you what, that's not a good idea. I'll cut the top off your goddamn head off and eat your brains.'

The voice was right: the voice was the man in the parking lot, the man who'd shot Creek. Anna listened so hard it hurt, listened for anything in the background that might help her, other voices. Nothing but the hiss of the phone.

'Anna, are you there?'

'I'm here,' she said.

'You're not very talkative.'

'I *am* looking for you, you asshole; and this better be a rotten joke . . .'

261

'Or what?' He laughed. 'What're you going to do?'

'I'll kill you,' Anna said.

'Oh, you'll kill me? You hear that, China? She's going to kill me. Here, you wanna talk?'

China's voice was a whisper. 'I can't see; I'm getting really cold.

'Let her go,' Anna screamed. 'Let her go.'

'No. She's gonna die,' the man said casually. 'You know why? Because I needed a woman, especially after what you did the other night. You cut the shit out of me, Anna. I'm all fucked up.' And just off the phone, 'You're gonna die, aren't you China? Look at the blood already.' And back to the phone: 'She's dying; it's draining right out of her. I cut her legs. It's really purple, the blood, you'd think it'd be redder.'

'You fucker,' Anna shouted, and without thinking, she threw the phone like a baseball, and it bounced across the blacktop, shedding its battery, flipping and bouncing along. Norden said, 'What, Anna, what'd he say . . .?'

But Anna was already running after the phone. She scooped it up, and the battery, jammed the battery back in, said, 'Hello?' Pushed the send button, said, 'Hello, hello, oh, Jesus . . .'

Nobody there. She stood there with the phone in her hand, looked at Norden, then turned around to look down the street at Harnett's building. A cop hurried out of the building, followed by Harper. As they scrambled to the cop car, Harper turned to look toward her. Anna spread her hands, a gesture that said, *Gone*.

'Can't be right,' Anna moaned. She was kneeling on the

front seat of the BMW while Harper cranked it back down toward Sunset. Wyatt would meet them, way out of his jurisdiction, bringing along a couple of L.A. homicide cops. BJ's was still open, people in black climbing the stairs toward the party room. Anna tore through the main floor, peering at tables; eyes followed as she checked each one, and a bartender said, 'Hey . . .' and finally she caught a waitress and asked, 'Have you seen China Lake?'

'If she's here, she's probably back in one of the bathrooms, that's where she usually is,' the woman smirked.

Anna burst into the women's restroom, and two women standing by the counter spun to look at her, one still with a touch of powder cocaine at her nose. 'Christ . . .' One of the stalls was closed, and Anna banged on the door, 'China, is that you?'

'No, go away,' a woman's voice, shrill, not China.

Anna went back out, saw Harper striding toward her, Norden in his wake. She went on down the hall and pushed into the men's room. A guy was standing at a urinal and Anna said, 'Have you seen China Lake?'

The guy tried to shrug, then said, 'What's that?'

'Damn it . . .' She went back into the hall and Harper caught her and said, 'Nothing?'

'No.'

'She's not upstairs,' Harper said. He put both hands on his head, trying to think, and a bouncer came up behind him and said, 'You guys got a problem?'

'Yeah,' Anna said. 'Have you seen China Lake? Or seen her with anybody?'

'What's the problem?'

'We think a fruitcake grabbed her. She could be in serious trouble,' Harper said. He was using his cop voice, and the bouncer said, 'You know, she was here an hour ago. I think I saw her going out, she was alone. Let's go ask Larry.'

He led them back through the club, to the front, and the stairs leading up to the party room. The doorman at the top looked down, and the bouncer yelled, 'Hey, Larry, you seen China?'

'She left.'

'Did she leave with anyone? You see anyone?'

'She was by herself, far as I know.'

Anna asked, 'Did you see a guy in here with a bandage on his face? Right by his eye? Or maybe a big bruise?'

He shook his head: 'Nobody here like that.'

'You think you could have missed it?'

'No way. Thing like that, a guy's probably a troublemaker. We keep our eye out for troublemakers.'

The outside door opened behind them, and Wyatt came through, followed by two men in suits. The bouncer spotted them and said, 'Shit,' and looked up the stairs at Larry and made a quick throat-cutting sign. Larry stepped out of sight.

'She's not here,' Wyatt asked, coming up.

Anna shook her head: 'No. She's gone.'

'Could be a joke,' Harper said. 'Louis wouldn't . . .'

Anna looked at him as though he were crazy, and said, 'No, Louis wouldn't. Jesus, Jake, this is the guy.'

'You're sure?' Wyatt asked.

'I'm sure: I knew the voice,' Anna said.

'Had you heard it before – other than at the parking lot, when he jumped you?' Wyatt asked.

Anna held her hands to her temples, as Harper had: so hard to think, so little time. Or no time at all. 'I think . . . I don't know, I'm getting confused. But when he was talking to me in the parking lot, God, it seemed familiar. Not like everyday familiar, but I knew the voice.'

'Face to face, or on the phone?' asked one of the L.A. cops.

The phone? She hadn't thought of that.

'God, I don't know. I talk to a hundred people every night, running around . . . I don't know.'

Harper chipped in: 'The guy on the door didn't see anyone with a bite on his face. Says he would have seen it.'

'All right,' Wyatt said. He seemed weary, almost too tired to deal with it. 'Let's see if anybody here saw China leave with someone. We got a couple of cars coming.'

'That's all?' Anna asked. 'That's all we can do?'

'Can you think of anything else?' Wyatt asked.

'I'm outa here.' She stepped toward the door, but Wyatt caught her arm.

'Look, we finally got something going on this – we're pulling together a multi-department task force to track this guy,' he said. 'We're gonna need you. We need to set you up where we can watch you.'

'I think it's too late for that,' Anna said. 'He turned some kind of corner with that phone call. He's gotta know you'll be all over him now.'

'We still need to talk with you.'

'I'll call you; I'd really appreciate it if you'd tell me if you shake anything out of these people,' she said, gesturing up the stairs. 'And China: if you hear anything . . .'

Wyatt looked at Harper. 'Jake, can you control her a little? She's gonna wind up dead.'

Jake said, 'I'll try.'

'You wouldn't hold anything back on us?'

Jake shook his head: 'No. We're not playing games: we just want somebody to get him. I don't think there's anything. Well, we thought for a while that he might be a little older, white-haired, but that's gone up in smoke. Anna thinks he's young.'

Wyatt turned to Anna, whose eyes seemed to have unfocused, staring at a spot on the other side of Wyatt's face. Wyatt said, 'Anna? Anna?'

Her eyes snapped back and a small, uncertain smile crinkled her face. 'Yeah. I heard you. He's young, I'm sure of it. Forget white hair. That was a wild-goose chase.' And to Jake: 'Let's go.'

Jake's eyebrows went up, but he nodded and said to Wyatt, 'Talk to you tomorrow.'

Norden was waiting out on the sidewalk: she didn't like cops, and now she was leaning against a fire hydrant, smoking, watching the light bars on the cop cars.

'We all done?' she asked.

'Yeah, for tonight,' Anna said.

'Drop me at my place; I want to get Harnett's files out of the car,' Norden said.

They dropped her at an apartment off La Brea, waited until she was inside, then Jake turned to Anna and said, 'What was that about the white-haired guy and the wild-goose chase? Harnett was a pretty hot possibility an hour ago. He might not be the killer, but he's involved somewhere.'

Anna shook her head and said, 'Aw, he might have known Jason or something, just a coincidence, but he's not the white-haired man. I know who the white-haired man is.'

Jake did a comic double-take: 'Yeah? Well, speak up.'

'It's Wyatt.'

'What?' He grinned, expecting a punchline.

'Yeah, an older guy with white hair. You were talking about it and I was looking at him, and all of a sudden, I realized it *was* him. We were thinking the white-haired guy was after Creek or me, but really – it was Wyatt checking up on Pam Glass, and what was happening with her and Creek, and he didn't want us to know it. That's why he took off. He's hung up on Pam, and he didn't want Pam to know he was hanging around.'

Harper thought it over for a few seconds, then sighed: 'Are you positive?'

'Ninety-nine percent. Next time we see Wyatt, take a good look at him. He's the guy.'

Harper nodded. 'All right. Christ, we commit a felony, we break into somebody's office and fuck him up and he's an innocent bystander.'

'Not especially innocent,' Anna said. 'But we do have a few felonies behind us.'

Harper said, 'Yeah, we do. And if we're not very careful, they're gonna start catching up with us.' He fed the car into a U-turn, and started back toward the hills.

Anna sat up that night; took her gun out of her pocket and spun the cylinder, dumped the shells, dry-fired it at the TV, when the TV was on. Reloaded, looked at it. Waited, for something, not knowing what.

Jake sat up with her for an hour or two, then went to bed. 'You've got to get some sleep,' he said.

'How?'

He looked at her, shrugged. 'If you decide to go out, wake me up. I want to come along. If he's identified me, he could know we're out here. So we've got to take it easy.'

'Okay.'

He pointed a finger at her: 'I swear to God, if you leave without waking me up, I'll kick your ass.'

The dawn came slowly, first a false lightening, then a darkness again, then the real dawn, a great, unhappy light, like an old piece of newsprint being pushed over the mountains to the east.

Anna was sitting in an easy chair, maybe asleep, the gun in her lap, when Jake came out and called her: 'Anna?'

Her eyes either opened, or were already open – she didn't know, it didn't seem like her mind had ever stopped. 'Yeah?'

'Jesus, did you get any sleep at all?'

'I don't know,' she said. She felt wooden. She pushed herself out of the chair, went out to the kitchen, with Harper trailing behind. 'Coffee?'

'I'm gonna try to get a couple more hours. Why don't you come in and lay down?'

'Jake, jeez.'

'Give me ten minutes to put you to sleep. Just come on in . . .'

She followed him back to the bedroom, pulled off her

shirt and jeans and bra, pulled on one of his T-shirts and lay down. He snuggled behind her, said, 'Close your eyes.'

'Jake . . .'

'Just close them, okay? Ten minutes.'

She could feel his arm around her waist, the tops of his thighs on the bottom of hers. She opened her eyes briefly, with difficulty, to look at the clock, and saw the glint of the gun on the nightstand; and closed her eyes again.

The phone woke her.

She startled upright, felt Jake's arm come off her, looked at the clock: She'd been down for four hours. Her mouth tasted like old features taken off a tar road.

Jake was saying, 'Yah . . . Aw, man, where . . . all right.'

When he hung up, she rolled over on her back and looked at him, caught his eyes trying to look away. 'China?'

'Yeah. She's dead. They found her body out in Glendale. That was Wyatt, and . . .'

'What?'

'She's pretty cut up.'

Anna jumped out of bed: 'Let's get over there.'

'Anna.'

'I need to see this,' she insisted.

'Why?' he asked, exasperated.

'Because. So get dressed.' Because she was storing it up. Because she was holding on to these crimes, all these insults, squeezing them into herself.

She drove: Jake was so reluctant that she finally got the keys and climbed into the front seat, and he caught up and piled into the passenger side, and she took them over the hills and east into Glendale. On the way, she called Wyatt, got switched around, and was finally left with a promise that he'd call her. He did, five minutes later:

'Where are you?'

'On the way.'

'I don't think you should.'

'I can identify her,' Anna said. 'I saw her twelve hours ago. Are you there?' she asked.

'On the way.'

'See you there.' And she rang off, before he could object.

'There', was a cluster of vehicles with light bars, a half-dozen men looking down a highway embankment: something she saw every night, now harsher in the light of day.

Wyatt hadn't arrived yet – she didn't recognize any of the cops at the scene. They waved her on down the road, but she stopped, and when the cop came up, she said, 'We're supposed to meet Detective Wyatt here, from Santa Monica. He's on the task force: I talked to China last night, the woman you think is down there. He wanted me to see if I could identify her.'

'Okay . . . just pull up to the head of the line.'

She drove up past the last car and turned to Harper: 'Are you coming?' she asked.

'Yeah. You better leave the gun in the car, though. They'll spot it and take it away from you.'

'Good thought.' She took the gun out of her jacket pocket and pushed it under the front seat. 'Let's go.'

China was halfway down the embankment, wrapped in the

dress she'd been wearing the night before. She'd landed on her face, apparently, but the gravel on the embankment hadn't done any real damage. It'd cut, but there was no blood to run; the cuts looked like scratches in beeswax.

Anna and Harper dropped carefully down the embankment, escorted by a young uniformed cop who watched their faces as they went down, down past the foot with a sock – what used to be called an anklet – and the foot without one, with the thighs impolitely apart, unguarded by underwear, the trails of dark pubic hair, down to the face that had bitten into the gravel . . .

'Yeah,' Anna said, and Harper said, 'Goddammit.' Anna said to the young cop, 'That's China Lake. She's an actress. Was.'

'Do you know next of kin?' the young cop asked.

'No, but . . . I could find out.'

'Anything you could get, we'd appreciate.'

'Yeah.' She never looked back at the body, but she held the image of China's face to her heart. Squeezing it. Filing the memories with the hate.

'Do you want to wait for Wyatt?' Harper asked, as they got back to the top of the embankment.

'What for?' Anna asked bitterly. 'The guy couldn't find his butt with both hands and a searchlight?'

'Not fair,' Harper said, as he followed Anna back to the car.

'Fuck fair,' she said.

'All right, princess. So now what?'

'We gotta go back to my place, so I can get my car. I

don't want you ferrying me all over the place.'

'Anna, I'm happy to . . .'

'I know, I know, but I want my car,' she said. And she added, 'I'm sorry, Jake. But China . . .'

The midday traffic wasn't too bad, and they made it back to Anna's in a half hour. She backed the Toyota out of the garage, as Harper waited in the street, then followed him out, up the San Diego, over the hills to his house. Whey they got there, she said, 'You know, I forgot something . . . I'm gonna go away for a while.'

'I better come with you.'

'Nope. I'm doing this on my own – don't worry, I'll be okay.' She took in his face, softened, and said, 'Listen, I just want to drive around a while, by myself, and get my head straight. And see Creek at the hospital. I'll be careful. I've got this. She patted the pistol in her pocket.

'Goddammit, Anna, you *better* be careful.'

He took her shoulders and kissed her, insistently; she let herself relax into the kiss, held it for a moment, then pushed him away. 'Hold that thought,' she said, 'I'll be back.'

He came out to watch her go, and just before she did, she ran the window down and said, 'He might have tracked us out here – so be careful yourself.'

'It's all private property, and people are pretty insistent about that. He'd have a hard time sneaking in, during the day, anyway,' Harper said. 'But I'll watch.'

Anna went back out the way she came, watching the rearview mirror. She had cars behind her, from time to time, but nothing that looked consistent. She continued back into town, to her house, went in, gathered a few clothes, stuck them in a leather satchel and carried the satchel out to the car.

'Anna, what's happening?' A voice from the sky, and she looked up.

'Hobie?'

'Come on up; we're having margaritas.'

'Aw, I'm on my way to see Creek.'

'How is he?' She could just see the top half of Hobie's moon face past the shingles on a dormer.

'Better, I guess. They said he had to sit still for a few days, but one of these days he'll be up.'

'That's great . . .'

'Listen, this jerk, this killer, the cops think he might be tracking me. If you or Jim see anyone around, take down some tag numbers, huh? I'm carrying my cell phone all the time, you've got the number . . .'

'Give it to me again.'

She gave him the number, and started out again, down the one-way street that took her out of the canal district, and out to the hospital. Watched the rearview mirror. Nothing that seemed furtive, nothing that seemed consistent. But Anna read thriller novels, and thought she could probably trail somebody all over L.A. without being spotted. You stay ten cars back, with traffic the way it was, and you'd never be spotted.

Of course, once he saw which way she was going, he might figure that she was heading for the hospital. There wasn't much on-street parking, he'd figure her for the ramp.

She worked it out: and when the hospital came up, she turned in at the ramp, found a place on the third floor.

Put her pistol in her main pocket, her trigger finger wrapped around the front of the trigger guard so she wouldn't accidentally fire it. Checked the mirrors, got out and walked self-consciously to the hospital entrance.

She saw no one who seemed out of place, who seemed to be watching, who seemed at all interested in her.

Except Creek. When she walked into his room, Creek was on his feet, like a bear in a dressing gown, trailing plastic lines that went to a saline bottle hung from a three-wheeled pole. Pam Glass sat in a chair by the window, knitting.

Creek turned as Anna came in, and grinned, and she said, 'My God, what are you doing out of bed?' and looked at Glass for an answer.

'I'm getting better,' Creek said, but his voice was a croak, and his face still seemed gray.

'The doctor told him to,' Glass said, answering Anna.

'They're sure that's okay?' Anna asked Glass.

'They think it's great,' Glass said. 'As long as he doesn't overdo it.'

'"Overdo" is his middle name,' Anna said.

They discussed it for another fifteen seconds, Anna and Glass talking to each other, checking Creek like he was a defective car, until Creek said, 'Hey, am I the village idiot or something?'

'You're not that responsible,' Anna said. Then she stood on her tiptoes and kissed him on the cheek. 'Jeez, I'm glad to see you up.'

'Where's Harper?' Creek asked. 'He's supposed to be watching you.'

'I had to get away for a little while – I'm being careful,' Anna said. To Glass: 'Have you heard the latest?'

Glass nodded: 'The actress. Brutal. They added a half-dozen guys to the task force, and there's gonna be some news about it.'

Anna recoiled: 'I won't come into it, will I?'

Glass grinned. 'Can't stand the heat, huh? You know how it is . . . a couple of days, and something'll leak.'

'Yeah . . . jeez.' Anna pulled at her lip, staring at Creek. 'You: get back into bed.'

'Why? I feel okay.'

'''Cause I want to take Pam away for a few minutes, and I don't want you dropping dead while we're gone.'

'You'd rather have me laying dead in bed?'

'Yeah, as a matter of fact. Then it wouldn't be my fault for not telling you to lay down.'

Creek shook his head, not following the logic, but sat on the bed, and finally pulled his legs up.

'Stay there,' Glass said.

'Arf, arf,' Creek said. 'Like the family dog. Stay, Fido.'

In the hall, Glass said, smiling but intent, 'I've been wanting to talk to you.'

'About Creek.'

'Yes. Right now, if you crooked your finger, he'd come running. I want to know if you're going to crook.'

Anna shook her head. 'I'm not sure you're right about that – but anyway, Creek and I . . . I don't know. We went past that point. Or I did. And I think he did, but maybe he hasn't figured it out yet.'

'Why didn't . . . you know.'

'He came along at the wrong time, and by the time I was, you know, ready for something . . . it was too late. We'd been sort of . . . brotherly-sisterly for too long.'

'He never tried to . . .' They were both fumbling for words, as though they were creating a special Creek vocabulary, '. . . develop anything?'

'Not directly. Creek looks like a bear, and he's been to jail, and the Marines, and all that – but he's sensitive. He usually knows what I'm thinking before I do, and if you guys last, he'll get that way with you.'

'He already is, a little.'

Anna nodded, grinned and poked Glass on the arm: 'He's a good deal.'

Glass blew hair out of her face and her shoulders drooped, as if her blood pressure had just dropped fifty points. And she said, 'You needed something from me?'

'I just needed to talk to you about your partner.'

'Huh?'

'I think he's the guy we saw up here, that we chased. I think he was trying to check on you.'

The other woman's eyes defocused for a few seconds, then she nodded briskly and said, 'Yeah. Damn.'

'So . . .'

'I'll talk to him,' Glass said. Then she grinned ruefully and said, 'Men really do come from another planet, you know?'

* * *

Anna was ready when she went back into the parking garage: but nothing happened. Nothing. The garage was so silent that no television movie in history could have resisted the moment: the killer and Anna would be there, toe to toe, and Anna would kill him.

Or something.

She was barely prepared for nothing at all.

In the car, she went back to her house, parked nose-in to the garage, left the engine running. Hobie called down, 'Offer's still open,' and she yelled, 'Thanks, Hobie, but I'm out of here.'

She sat in the house for a moment, then walked through the kitchen and checked the lock on the canal-side door, and then went back through the house and out, locked the front and drove back out.

She thought this way: If the killer was watching her, he wouldn't watch from within the canal area. The road through the district was one-way, and narrow, and nobody could wait on it without being noticed. He'd watch either the entrance or the exit, and pick her up coming or going.

All right. Let him pick her up.

She touched the gun in her pocket.

When she told him on the phone that she was going to kill him, it wasn't idle chatter. If she could get him in the right place, she'd do it.

But she'd have to handle it carefully.

She liked Jake a lot, liked everything about him – or, at least, thought she could straighten out the parts of him that weren't quite right. A snip here, a tuck there, and he'd be presentable. But she liked his looks, his attitude, the way he lived.

But she didn't quite understand, deep in her heart, why he hadn't killed the dealer in the hotel. She would have.

So if she was going to stir this killer out of his muck . . . Jake couldn't know.

Chapter 22

Harper was sitting in a lawn chair in front of his house, a hardcover book by his heel, in an attitude of *waiting*. He pushed himself out of the chair when Anna pulled up, and sauntered around the car.

'Long time,' he said. 'Did you get your head straight?'

'About some things,' she said. She stood on her tiptoes, gave him a peck on the lips, feeling guilty for not telling him that she was trolling for the killer. More guilty – this was odd – because he smelled kind of good. She said, 'Creek's walking around.'

'Excellent.' Harper, nice guy, seemed genuinely pleased. 'Listen, I've had a few thoughts.'

'Let's go around back. I've been itching to fire the gun again.'

His eyebrows went up: 'Your violent streak is showing.'

She grinned at him: 'I've just been carrying it everywhere, and . . . I don't know, I've just got the urge to pull the trigger.'

Harper got the earmuffs and a couple of Coke cans and they walked side by side out to the gully. 'We didn't spend enough time with Catwell, Jason's friend at Kinko's,' he said. 'I figured out this much: either it's a coincidence that this killer shows up the day after Jason is killed, or . . .'

He waited for her to fill in the blank, but she couldn't think of anything. 'Or what?'

'Or,' he said, 'it's not. A coincidence.'

'Gosh. You're just like Einstein.'

He held up a finger, his face serious: 'Listen. I don't think it's a coincidence. Maybe it is – I've got some ideas about that, too – but I don't think so. So let's take them one at a time.'

'Go ahead.'

'If it's not a coincidence, then the killer fixed on you between the time you picked up Jason, and the time Jason ran off.'

'Okay.' She was amused by his lawyerly dissection.

'In that time, you only did two things,' he said. 'You went to the animal rights raid and you went to where Jacob was. So you probably picked up the guy at one of those places. We've assumed it was with Jacob, because of the drugs. We were probably wrong.'

Anna frowned, took the pistol out of her jacket pocket, flicked out the cylinder, spun it once, looking at the little undimpled primers. 'We talked to two guys, really, at the animal rights raid,' she said, snapping the cylinder shut. 'One of them was wearing a mask, but he had this voice. I was thinking, maybe someday he could go on TV. Jesus, this guy – it could be him! I mean, he was a little strange, his attitude, I didn't pay much attention because we run into lots of strange people . . .'

'All right,' Harper said. 'Where do we look him up?'

'I don't know – Jason was the contact. But I could find out.'

Harper was absently juggling the empty Coke cans: 'Okay. But before we get too enthusiastic . . . you said there were two guys at the animal rights raid.'

'Yeah,' she nodded, thinking about it. 'The other one, he was just a kid, kind of wimpy.'

Harper found a dirt ledge for the cans, and set them up. 'I saw him on TV – you mean the kid who tried to fight them off.'

'Not a violent type, like me,' Anna said. 'He was crying about getting a bloody nose.'

'Doesn't sound like our guy,' Harper agreed. He pointed at her plastic muffs: 'Pull down your earmuffs, you're too young to lose your hearing.'

Harper stuck his fingers in his ears, and Anna pulled down the earmuffs and pointed the gun at one of the cans. Then a thought struck her and she pulled the muffs back and said, 'I just thought of something else.'

'Yeah?' He took his fingers out of his ears.

'Creek noticed that there was only one guy on the raid, all the rest were women. And they were, I don't know, kind of *busty*. Creek said it looked like a harem.'

'So maybe the guy's a freak.'

'God . . .' She pulled the muffs down again, and Harper stuck his fingers back in his ears and Anna pointed the pistol at the first can, jerked the trigger. She missed by two feet.

'Settle down,' she said aloud. She relaxed, brought the pistol up, fired again and the can flipped up the dirt wall, and clattered back down again, a neat hole punched in the center of the white C-for-Coke. Anna pulled the muffs up and said,' I just thought of something else: He had this pig and it knocked him down . . .'

'I saw that,' Harper said. 'He must've been humiliated.'

'Yeah.' She pulled the muffs back down, emptied the gun. She hit the cans twice more, and the rest of the shots were bunched around them.

'You ain't going to the Olympics,' Harper said, as she shucked the empty shells out. 'But they'd all hit between the nipples.'

'That's all I need,' she said, reloading. She stopped with a shell still in the palm of her hand and said, 'You said if it wasn't a coincidence, all of this starting – you said you had some ideas about that, too.'

'One thing at a time,' Harper said.

She pushed the last shell home. 'Let's go find this guy.'

Louis found him, running down names on the letterhead press release.

'His name is Steven Judge. He and two or three more of them live at what they call the Full Heart Sanctuary Ranch, and it's not far from where you are,' Louis said. 'It's up in Ventura, just on the other side of the Santa Susanas.'

'Half an hour,' Harper said, when Anna told him. He glanced at his watch: 'We've got time.'

The countryside of Southern California was rarely empty, not this close to L.A. and the coast, but the Full Heart Ranch was on a gravel road up a washed-out dirt canyon, about as isolated a place as could be found. The sign at the entrance to the canyon was neat and businesslike, a metal plaque that said, 'Full Heart Ranch', and below that, in smaller letters, 'Animal Sanctuary'. A hundred feet up the trail was another sign, this one resembling the signs in national forests, yellow burnt-in letters on brown-painted boards: 'Welcome. Please register at the ranch house. Do not leave your car before registering – some of our animals are sensitive to the scent of humans.'

'Probably got tigers out there,' Harper said. 'And when they say "humans", they mean, "meat".'

'Probably,' Anna said.

The canyon was a tangle of brush, with an occasional glimpse of trails leading through it; they crossed a low ridge on the way up, and saw the ranch house just below them, in a bowl. A half-dozen outbuildings surrounded the main house, and three cars faced the front of it.

'Pretty nice spread,' Harper said.

'The way this kid looked, the way he acted – he might have some money,' Anna said.

'You think he owns the place?'

Anna shrugged: 'He was the boss that night.'

They parked the car, stepped out, and looked around: They could hear an odd goatlike sound, and they both stepped off to the right to look past the house. A tall, fuzzy-headed animal looked at them over the top of a high board fence, pursed its lips, made the noise again.

'A camel?'

'A llama,' Anna said.

A door banged, and a woman in jeans, a Western shirt and cowboy boots came out onto the ranch house porch.

She looked like a ranch woman, in her early forties, with wide shoulders, a round, moon face, deeply tanned with a scattering of freckles. Her sandy hair was pulled back in a ponytail. 'Can I help you?'

'Yeah, hi,' Anna said. 'We were just looking at your llama. Where'd you get him?'

'We . . . found him,' the woman said, pleasantly. 'He was rather badly abused, or, rather, neglected. The former owner had ideas about breeding llamas. When it didn't work out, he just turned him out and left him in the desert. He would've died, if one of our members hadn't found him.'

'Terrific,' Anna said cheerfully. Harper followed her as she walked up on the porch. 'My name is Anna Batory, and this is my friend Jake Harper. We filmed the raid at the UCLA medical center and Steve mentioned the possibility of doing another piece. Is he around?'

The woman shook her head and said, 'Steven,' and then said, 'I'm sorry you missed him, but he should have told you that he wouldn't be around, He won't be back for another two weeks.'

'Where is he?' Anna asked. 'Can I call him?'

'Sure – or, I think so. He's up in Oregon, at the Cut Canyon Ranch. He went up there the day after the raid, to help organize it. And probably run the river a few times.'

'Cut Canyon?'

'Yes, it's a new ranch that some people are putting together up there. They just got a phone . . . c'mon, I'll get a number. I'm Nancy Daly, by the way, I'm the ranch fore-woman.'

Harper said, 'How do. Like the boots.'

'Genuine vinyl,' the woman said smiling at him.

They followed her inside, where another woman was working at a computer; the other woman turned and smiled briefly, then went back to her work. Daly said, 'Steve has got that square chin and all those teeth. Somehow, it makes him seem a little more organized than he really is.' She was shuffling through the papers on her desk: 'I don't know, I don't seem to have it. God, I've got to do something about this desk.'

'Think it'd be on directory assistance?' Ann asked.

'Should be,' Daly said.

'No problem,' Anna said. She took her cell phone out of her pocket, but the woman shook her head. 'We're too far out. You can use ours. The area code, I don't know, it's probably in the phone book.'

'It's five-oh-three,' Anna said. 'I've got friends up there, they run a pottery.'

She dialed directory assistance, asked for a new listing for Cut Canyon Ranch, got the number, and punched it in.

'Cut Canyon.' Another woman.

'Is Steve Judge there?'

'Yes, somewhere. Can I tell him who's calling?'

'My name's Anna Batory.'

'Hang on. I'll put you on hold. I've got to go find him.'

'Okay,' Anna said.

Harper asked Daly, 'Does Steve . . . own this place, or what?'

'Oh, no,' Daly said. 'His parents provided some seed money. Steve is active with the group, but he avoids bureaucratic entanglements, so to speak. He's a little . . .' She looked at the other woman. 'What is he, Laurie?'

Laurie never looked away from the screen. 'Hippie,' she said.

'Ah . . .'

At that moment, Judge came on the phone: 'Yeah, Steve Judge.'

The voice wasn't the killer's – higher than she remembered, not squeaky, but nasal, rather than full. Anna looked at Harper and shook her head, as she said, 'This is Anna Batory. I stopped by the ranch to see if we might put together another piece on this animal thing.'

'Oh!' Judge said. Then: 'You know, I wasn't too happy about the way the raid thing came out, I think it made me look foolish, with the pig and all.'

'Well – that happens. The stations cut the tape the way they want. We didn't have anything to do with that,' Anna said.

'Okay . . . I guess I'm willing to give it another shot,' Judge said. 'We're just finishing things up here, I was going to head back tonight. When do you want to get together?'

'Couple days, next week,' Anna said, now in no rush.

But Judge rambled on, eager to make another movie. 'The neatest things we've got right now is a vet who's made a specialty out of fixing bird wings,' he said. 'We're gonna start rehabilitating raptors, you know, hawks, eagles. You can't just fix them up and let them go. You have to rehab the wings; people shoot these poor birds . . .'

She let him go, throwing in a couple of questions about the raid, until she was sure it was really him. When she was sure, she looked at Harper and shook her head.

* * *

'Damn it, I thought he was a possibility,' Anna said, as they went down the road from the ranch. The afternoon was sliding into the evening.

'Might still be – could be something tricky going on.'

'I suppose,' Anna said. But she yawned and shook her head. The morning – when she crunched down that highway cut and looked at China Lake – seemed a lifetime back. She yawned and said, 'Let's go see Creek.'

'Fuckin' vinyl cowboy boots,' Harper said. 'You show me a woman who wears vinyl cowboy boots and I'll show you a woman whose . . .' He trailed off, glanced at Anna, and then concentrated on the road ahead.

'Whose what?' Anna demanded.

'Never mind,' Harper said.

Anna took the phone out of her pocket and tried it; still out of range. 'Wait'll we get over the hill,' Harper suggested. 'Two minutes.'

Two minutes, and they were back in range: She had a message waiting, but called Louis and asked him to locate the other kid at the animal raid. Then she punched in the message, and got Wyatt's voice.

'We've got a proposition for you,' he said. 'Call me.'

'Wyatt,' she said to Harper. 'He's got a proposition.'

Wyatt was in the office: 'Things are gonna get out of control pretty soon,' he said, his voice tinny in the little phone. 'We haven't had an O.J. case or anything else for the media assholes.'

'Excuse me?' Anna said.

'. . . Uh, sorry. Anyway, this whole thing is gonna leak, two days, three days, maximum,' he said. 'So one of the

287

task force guys came up with a proposition: We've got a couple of undercover guys who are pretty good with video cameras, they do a lot of surveillance. So you check one of these guys out, and then you go out on the street with him. He could fill in for your friend, Creek. And we put a net around you.'

'Huh. Not bad. Let me talk to Jake about it.'

'There'd be a chance we could spot the guy,' Wyatt said. 'We'd have an undercover video van covering you and even if nothing happens, we could analyze every face in every crowd, every place you go. If he's tracking you, we could spot him.'

'Let me talk to Jake.'

'Okay, but we want to go tonight – four hours from now.'

Harper was adamant: 'No! No fuckin' way. They're so desperate they're willing to turn you into a bull's-eye.'

'When you were working homicide, did you ever use a civilian as a decoy?'

'Only once or twice and it didn't do any good,' Harper said. 'And the situations were really limited, we weren't out roaming around trying to find a psycho.'

'Did you have a relationship with either of those women? Were they women?'

'Yeah, they were women, and of course not, I didn't mess with people in investigations.'

'So you used them,' Anna said. 'Do you think your change in attitude might have something to do with the fact that we're working on a relationship?'

She was so silky with the question that Harper glanced at

her and said: 'Shut up.' And a moment later, 'You're stupid.'

Anna laughed, and said, 'I hope Creek's awake.'

Creek was awake, eating a bowl of raspberry Jell-O and arguing with Pam Glass, who looked more tired than Creek. When Anna and Harper walked in, Glass said, 'God, am I glad to see you. This nitwit is talking about going home in the morning.'

Creek was sitting up in bed, still plugged into the saline drip. He tried to look well. 'I'm feeling a hell of a lot better,' he said, in an unnaturally chipper voice.

'What do the doctors say?' Harper asked.

'If he keeps improving, maybe three days,' Glass said. 'That's the minimum. He's talking about how his insurance runs out. I offered to help him, but he won't take help.'

Creek looked embarrassed and Anna put a hand on her hip and said, 'I bought the insurance, Creek. It ain't runnin' out.'

'So, I thought it might run out.'

Glass's eyes narrowed: 'You were lying to me.'

'That's what I thought,' Creek mumbled.

Glass dropped in a chair. 'I don't even know why I hang around this place,' she said wearily.

'Jeez, Pam, take it easy . . .' Now Creek was worried.

Glass looked at Anna and said, 'Anything?'

'You pal Wyatt wants her to be a target in some stupid decoy operation,' Harper said.

'Decoy?' Now she was interested. 'How would it work?'

Anna explained, and Glass nodded: 'Could work.'

'That's bullshit,' said Creek. He looked at Harper. 'You can't go along with this.'

'Of course not. I already told her how stupid it is . . .'

Anna was looking at Glass. 'You think it could work?'

The other woman nodded. 'Those guys are good. I'd go for it.'

Now it was Creek's turn to be angry: 'Pam, goddammit, you don't know what you're doing. This guy's a psycho.'

'If we thought he was going to shoot her with a sniper rifle, then I'd be against it,' Glass said. 'But he seems to want to get his hands on her. These guys who'll be with her – they're tough guys. He won't take Anna away from them.'

Anna told creek and Glass about the abortive trip to the Full Heart Ranch, and her talk with Steve Judge.

'I hadn't thought of that guy, but now that you bring him up – there's something about him. I think he needs a closer look,' Creek said.

'He's in Oregon,' Anna said.

'That could be some bullshit they pulled,' Creek said.

'I don't think so,' she said. Anna looked at Harper, remembering their conversation while they were shooting.

'You said you had a couple ideas. One of them is the other kid . . . but what's the one you didn't want to talk about? The coincidence?'

Harper shrugged. 'Not much, really,' he said. Then, 'Could I have a little talk with Creek? Alone?'

Anna looked from Harper to Creek and said, 'What's this about?'

Creek shrugged, looking curiously at Harper, and Harper

said, 'If I wanted you to know, I'd just go ahead and ask – so if you don't mind, go talk to Pam. In the hall.'

Anna and Glass let Harper ease them through the door, and shut the door behind himself. 'They don't even know each other,' Anna said.

Two minutes later, the door opened. Harper looked out, and said, 'You better come back in.'

Anna and Glass filed back in, and Creek smiled at Anna, tentatively, the smile flickering like a bad fluorescent bulb.

'What?' Anna demanded.

'Jake, uh, brought something up. He didn't want to talk to you about it unless I thought there was something to talk about.'

'So?'

'So – there might be.'

'So? What is it?'

Creek looked at Harper, shrugged, looked back at Anna and said, 'Clark.'

'Nope, nope, no way, no way,' Anna said. She waved her arms like a home plate umpire calling a runner safe. 'It wouldn't, it's not, Clark wouldn't . . .'

'Probably not,' Creek said. 'But Clark is strange. You know that yourself: I've never met anyone as driven as he was. Every time you two guys got into trouble, it was because he was freaking out with work. Who knows what happened to him since you last saw him – he might've cracked.'

'Not Clark,' Anna said stubbornly.

'Yeah? You've heard his voice,' Creek said. 'Are you sure

it wasn't Clark's? You say it's familiar . . .'

She opened her mouth to say no, it wasn't Clark's – but then she thought, *maybe* it is. The voice was a middle baritone, and Clark's was close to that; and she hadn't heard Clark's voice for years. She closed her eyes, listened to Clark talk. The same?

She opened; her eyes. 'No,' she said. 'It's not the same.'

'Bullshit,' said Creek, because Creek could read her mind. 'You don't know.'

Anna was furious with Creek for talking about Clark. He didn't understand what Clark had been going through when the trouble started: the stress, the politics of the music business, and where they could push an ambitious person, especially when that person was young, confused, exhausted.

And then she thought to herself, *Really? Is that really what you think about Clark*? She'd never really gotten over their relationship, even admitted it to herself. Not because she couldn't, but because of the indefinite way it had ended, '*I love you but . . .*'

Jake came out of the kitchen, carrying a plate of toast and jelly. They were at Anna's house, Anna changing into her work clothes. 'You don't go wandering off through the crowd – Creek said you ran all the way up and down through that hotel when Jacob died, I don't want you getting away from the escorts.'

'Yeah, yeah,' she said, distracted. He put the plate down and caught her around the waist and said, 'Hey. Listen to me. We'll work out this Clark business later – but for now, we gotta keep your ass alive.' He squeezed her butt, but she wiggled away.

'Are you still pissed?' Harper asked.

'Oh, I'm not pissed. Wait a minute: yeah, I am pissed, at Creek.'

'Creek is trying to take care of you,' Harper said. He pushed the plate toward her, and she took a piece of jelly toast.

'I was thinking – I was hoping – that I'd never have to deal with the Clark thing,' Anna said to him. 'Maybe it'd just fade away. It sorta was, but . . . I don't know. Maybe it wasn't.'

'Are you still in love with him?'

'No, I don't think so. But I *was* in love with him. And there was never any end-point; I couldn't ever say, "Well, that's over with, now I can do something else." I needed an end-point.'

'We haven't known each other very long, but I never would have seen you this way,' Harper said, his face intently serious. 'I would've thought that when you broke off with somebody, that'd be it: and you'd never think about him again.'

'Oh, no,' she said, as serious as he. 'With a real relationship, I'd think about it forever. I'll think about you forever, no matter what happens.'

'Really?'

'Really,' she said. 'Forever.'

Louis showed up a half hour later, leading a ratty-looking, dark-haired man, unshaven with a heavy shock of black hair that fell down over his oval face. He wore a green army field jacket from the sixties, with a faded name tag that said Ward.

'Jimmy Coughlin,' he said, shaking Anna's hand and peering at Harper. 'You're Jake Harper.'

'Yeah,' Harper said. He reached out and touched the name tag on Coughlin's jacket. 'Who's Ward?'

'Fuck if I know,' Coughlin said cheerfully. He looked around the living room. 'We ready?'

'You know what you're doing?' Anna asked.

'Sure, no problem,' he said. 'I used to pretend I was a news guy and shoot riots and raids and shit.'

'Let me get my jacket,' Anna said.

Coughlin drove, not fast, but expertly, using all three rearview mirrors. There were three tracking cars, he said, one in front and two behind. Louis sat in the back, in his regular chair, monitoring the radios; when Anna looked out the passenger side window, she could almost pretend that this past week hadn't happened.

'Which way?' Coughlin asked.

'Let's sort of loaf up the PCH, and then catch Sunset where it comes down, and go back east,' Anna said. 'Play it by ear.'

Coughlin nodded, took a small hand radio out of his pocket, and relayed the route to the tracking cars.

'You do this much?' Anna asked.

'Not exactly like this, but, you know – like this,' he said. 'Dopers, mostly?'

'Little of this, little of that' he said. 'Some dope. Doing a little more vice lately, been backing up some of the gang guys.

'You like it?' Anna asked.

'Sure, it's fun,' he said, and she had to smile: he was a cheerful guy, despite his ratlike exterior. Then: 'I couldn't help noticing that you're carrying a gun.'

'Yup.' She nodded.

'You got a permit?' he asked.

'Are you kidding?'

'Maybe you should give it to me – the gun,' he said.

'Maybe not,' Anna said.

'I could take it,' he suggested.

'Cop takes gun from woman stalked by serial killer who brutally murdered movie actress.' She looked over her shoulder at Louis. 'Could we get that on the air?'

'Are you kidding?' Louis said. 'I could sell it everywhere. But it'd sound better if we said, "Cop takes gun from woman stalked by serial killer who brutally murdered movie actress, while gangs run wild with assault rifles in South-Central".'

'That *is* an improvement,' Anna said.

'It'd do okay,' Louis said. 'But if you could get him to rough you up a little bit, we'd get more than we got for the jumper.'

'How about it?' Anna said, turning back to Coughlin and batting her eyes. 'Do you carry a club or a sap or anything? Could you push me around a little? I mean, I kind of . . . like it.'

Louis said, 'Cop takes gun from beautiful woman stalked by serial killer who brutally murdered glamorous, drug-abusing "90210" actress, abuses her with baton, while gangs run wild with assault rifles in South-Central – and she likes it.'

Coughlin hunched over the steering wheel and shook his head sadly. 'Christ, this could be a long night,' he said.

Chapter 23

They took the Pacific Coast Highway north as far as Sunset, Sunset back east. They narrowly missed hitting a Mercedes Benz 500E that came rocketing out of a Beverly Hills side street and crossed Sunrise without slowing. 'Rich junkies,' Coughlin muttered. 'Eat that speed and can't handle it.'

'Fire back in Bel Air,' Louis said. He had his headphones on.

'Any good?' Anna asked, turning to look at him. He'd belted himself into his office chair.

'Doesn't sound like much,' Louis said, as he punched numbers into a scanner. 'But I think I've heard the name. Jimmy James Jones?'

'I don't know' Anna said. 'It rings a bell.'

'Preacher,' Coughlin said. 'He used to have a TV show.'

Anna nodded. 'That's right, good.' To Louis: 'Anything about women, or people hurt?'

'Nope. Mostly smoke. Jimmy James Jones called in the report himself and he's still in the house.'

Coughlin glanced at her expectantly, but Anna said, 'Keep going.'

* * *

'How do you decide?' Coughlin asked, after a while. Sunrise rolled along outside the windows, a shabbier section near Hollywood, a few men and women strolling along the streets, cars playing games along the curbs. 'How do you know what to go to?'

'Magic,' Anna said.

'I'm serious,' he said. He jabbed at the brake. A woman with a shopping cart looked for a moment as though she might lurch into the street.

'So am I,' Anna said. 'I don't know how to decide. You just go on the sound of it.'

'Like what?'

'Like the fire: that could be something. If Jimmy James Jones was just a little more famous – not much more, just a little bit – we'd go over. If there were people hurt, we'd think about it. But the thing is, all the local stations are so sensitive to anything with a celebrity, that they've probably got their trucks rolling right now. So even if it turned out to be good, we might not sell much, because everybody would have it. Louis only mentioned it because we're close enough that we could probably get there first.'

'First isn't always enough,' Coughlin said.

'No,' Anna said, shaking her head. 'Sometimes it's enough – but not always. When the story is minor, then it's absolutely necessary. Or if the story has one crucial moment, then you've got to be there for that moment. Like we shot this kid a week ago, the kid who fell off the building . . .'

'Harper's kid.'

'Yeah. We didn't know Jake then . . . anyway, it's not

really much of a story, but the event was spectacular. It's something nobody ever sees – we were just there by accident. There was no way for anybody else to make up for our film. They had to have it. With the Jimmy James Jones fire story, all they need is a shot of some fire trucks and hoses, and a comment from Jones. You can be really late and get all that.'

Coughlin nodded. 'So how do you know *where* to go? When nothing's going on?'

'I fish. Get a feeling. Some nights just have a quiet feeling in one place, so you decide to go somewhere else. Like, I think we ought to check up the valley tonight. We haven't been there in a while.'

'Up the Hollywood?'

'Yeah, the Hollywood to Mission Hills, back on the San Diego, maybe jump off at Ventura if anything's going on . . .'

They were coming up on Mission Hills when Louis blurted, 'Okay, we got a holdup at a Starbucks and a guy's down, where are we? Have we crossed Mission yet?'

'Two minutes to Mission,' Anna said.

'Get off, go east,' Louis said. He was punching numbers into the laptop. 'Okay, three blocks east, right side, we should see it, they got one guy down and one of the clerks threw a pot of boiling coffee on the holdup guy, he's still in the street, he might be blind, he's still armed, cops on the way . . .'

'Could be good,' Anna said to Coughlin, 'but we gotta hurry.'

'I am hurrying,' he said. 'I'm doing seventy.'

'I mean *hurry*,' Anna said. She took the pistol out of her pocket, popped the lock box with the Nagra, took the tape recorder out and put the gun in the box and relocked it. When she turned back, they were hurtling down an off-ramp toward a stoplight and she stretched out over the dashboard, looking to the left, and said, 'Nothing coming, nothing coming, forget the light, go . . .'

Coughlin took it sedately through the curve and Anna said, 'Damn it, you gotta *drive*.'

'Jesus,' Coughlin said, but he floored it and the truck took off.

Three blocks ahead, there were people in the street: 'That's gotta be it,' she said.

Louis was fumbling with the main camera, and said to Coughlin, 'All right, the camera's all set. Just pull the trigger.'

'Yeah, yeah.'

Louis reached over the seat and put the headset over the top of Coughlin's head. 'Pull it down over your ears.'

'Right there – pull right up on that curb,' Anna shouted. 'Put two wheels up, get up there.'

'Fuckin' people are nuts,' Coughlin said, but he put two wheels on the curb, stood on the brake, and Anna was out the door.

A man was lying on the street with his hands on his face, moaning, bleeding from the face, a revolver on the sidewalk ten feet away. A tough-looking teenager in a letter jacket was standing over him. Sirens began screaming in. Coughlin was out with the camera, but not moving fast enough. Anna screamed at him on the headset: 'This way, move! Move! Run, for Christ's sake.'

Coughlin broke into a trot, the camera bouncing on his

shoulder, and Anna pointed at the man on the street, and the teenager. 'What happened? What happened? Tell the camera what happened.'

'Guy come running out of the store and ran right into that door and cracked his head open,' the teenager told Coughlin's camera. 'He had the gun and people were inside yelling to get out of the way, he shot somebody, so I kicked the gun over there and he tried to get up and I set him down again.'

Anna allowed a second's space as Coughlin panned from the man on the street to the teenager and back, and Anna said, 'What's your name? Where do you come from? What were you doing here?'

As the teenager started talking again, she ran inside the store. Another man was on the floor, and a half-dozen Starbucks counterpeople were gathered around him. She said, 'Coughlin, get in here, right now. Get the scene on the floor. Hurry, goddammit, the cops are almost here.'

The cops *were* there. Coughlin trotted into the store and began walking sideways, working around the group on the floor, and one of the counterwomen stood up and pointed a finger at him and said, 'Get out of here, that's not allowed, that's not allowed.'

Anna shouted at the woman, 'Look at the guy, he's bleeding, help him,' and the woman looked back down, and then grabbed a napkin holder and dropped onto her knees and pulled out a four-inch loaf of napkins and handed it to another woman who was apparently trying to staunch a wound. Coughlin was looking past the camera and Anna shouted, 'Keep running for Christ's sake . . .'

Three cops hurried in the door. One spotted the camera

and waved it away, and Coughlin took it down again. Anna said, 'Okay, come this way, come toward me, toward the side door.' As they went, she asked the crowd of coffee-drinkers, 'Did anyone see this? Any witnesses?'

Two or three nodded, and she said, 'We'd like to get statements outside, if anyone has time.'

'Will this be in the newspaper tomorrow?' somebody asked.

'Maybe TV,' Anna said.

A paramedic truck arrived as they did the interviews, and Coughlin moved away again to catch the wounded man being carried out. The shooter with the burned face was cuffed and put in another ambulance, and then there was nothing but a crowd of gawkers and the flashing lights on the cop car.

'This way, back to the truck,' Anna told Coughlin. 'Hurry.'

'I'm running my ass off,' he snarled.

She shook her head: 'Still not moving fast enough,' she said.

Coughlin caught up with her halfway to the truck, pulled the headset off and said, 'What's the rush?'

'Cops might give us a hard time, especially if the Starbucks people complain. Might want to look at the tape: we gotta get out of here before they start thinking about it.'

He nodded, and hurried along with her. Louis took the camera and Coughlin jumped into the driver's seat. 'Kind of a rush,' he said, starting the truck.

'Yeah, but you gotta move,' Anna said. 'You were way too slow.'

'Hey, I'm a beginner,' he said. He took the truck out into

the street, as Louis popped the tape out of the camera. 'I did all right for a beginner.'

She shrugged, then smiled. 'Yeah, I guess. For a guy who doesn't know the rules. But next time, rules number one and two: drive fast, then run.'

'Yes, ma'am.' He laughed, a little giddy. Then: 'How come nobody else showed up? No competition?'

Anna shrugged: ''Cause this didn't amount to anything. The victim wasn't even killed – though getting the shooter was a little different. I hope you shot the gun on the street.'

'Yeah, yeah . . .'

'Anyway, there's no way this would make the papers, much less TV news, just on what happened. Routine hold-up shooting. We might have a couple of good images, so maybe it'll make it – not because it means anything, but because the images are good.'

'I hope I got some,' Coughlin said nervously, looking over his shoulder at Louis. 'I just kept pulling the trigger.'

'You did okay,' Louis said from the back of the truck. He had the tape up on a monitor. 'It's not great, but it's usable.'

Anna watched as Louis rolled through it, then turned to Coughlin. 'A couple of things: You move too fast from one subject to the next. You show the guy on the ground, the shooter, and the gun, but only for a couple of seconds each time. You have to dwell on them for a moment. Remember, we can always cut, but we can't get more. Same with the wounded guy inside. You gotta stay on him: he's the interest, and the women working on him. But mostly the wounded guy.'

'I was thinking I should help,' Coughlin said.

'No,' Anna said. 'You can't think that way if you ride with us. You're *making* the movie, not acting in it. You're an eye.'

'That's cold,' Coughlin said.

'That's the way it is,' said Anna.

A couple of minutes later, Coughlin took the radio out of his pocket, pushed the transmit button and asked, 'Anything?'

He listened, then said to Anna, 'Nothing.'

Anna got out her phone and started dialling TV stations.

Two kids, motorheads from a valley technical school, were chasing each other down the Ventura, when one lost it and rolled his rebuilt Charger off the freeway and down an embankment. They started that way, but when Anna got an exact location from Louis, she called it off. 'If we get up there, we're trapped in traffic,' she said. 'Not worth the time.'

'The kid's dead,' Coughlin said.

'Yeah, but we can't get in and out, and that's the main thing,' Anna said.

A chase started on the Santa Monica, the highway patrol running after a Porsche 928. Anna pointed them down the San Diego as Louis monitored the chase.

'He's probably gonna have to make a decision when he gets to the San Diego,' she said. 'Either north or south. If he comes this way, we might have a shot. A nine twenty-eight means there's some money. Could be a movie tie-in . . .'

But the Porsche went straight on, dropped onto the PCH and suddenly pulled over and gave it up.

Nothing.

* * *

Later on, they headed for a truck fire, broke off before they got there. Arrived too late at a shooting incident, found nobody hurt and cops everywhere. Coughlin checked again, and the trailing cars had not spotted anyone tracking them.

'Waste of time,' Anna said, pulling on her lower lip. 'We're wasting time.'

'Got to be a little patient,' Coughlin said.

Very late, they were rolling south on Sepulveda, looking for any movement at all, when Louis said, 'Body found.'

'Where?'

'Mmm . . . it's over a fence. Must be pretty high, because they can see it but they can't get to it. No address yet.'

'Okay.' Coughlin was concentrating on the driving, Louis worked the radios, and Anna let her mind drift. All evening, she'd felt herself drifting away from the immediacy of the truck; out of it.

The problem was Clark. Were they done? Certainly. Or probably. But all those years ago, when they were working their music together, she playing it, Clark composing; when they were going to concerts together, and clubs, toying with rock 'n roll; when Clark was putting together the 'Jump Rope Concerto', the first work to bring him notice; in the years they were doing that, she had woven a mental web around them, a cocoon to hold them – and when suddenly it began to come apart, she'd never dealt with it. She'd fantasized, instead, of pulling all the strands back together.

And now she thought, this perfect house she'd built in Venice, with all the homely touches from the Midwest: was this a nest for Clark? Is that where the energy had come from? Because he'd like it. No – he'd love it. She'd been obsessive about it, all the small touches, the quilts, the rag carpets on the wooden floors, the folk art, the pottery.

Was that what she'd been doing? Building for a man who'd engineered a break that had hurt her worse than anything since the death of her mother?

'Bellagio,' Louis said.

Anna, frowned, missing it. 'What?'

'The body was found off Bellagio.'

'Over a fence?' she asked, sitting up.

'Yeah.'

'Get an address,' she snapped. To Coughlin: 'If it's over a fence, it could be the Bel Air Country Club. Get up on the freeway, let's go . . .'

The body was on the golf course, but so were the cops, and they couldn't get close. Coughlin edged the truck up to a cop car and the cop said, 'Get the fuck out of here.'

'Hey, I'm just trying . . .'

'Didn't you hear me, dummy? Get the fuck out of here,' the cop said. He was young, with a pale, Nordic face, untouched by any apparent emotion other than irritation.

'All right, but I gotta go up there to turn around.'

'Hey! You ain't coming through here,' the cop said. 'Just back it up.'

'I can't back it up.'

'Back the fuckin' truck up or I'll have your ass out here on the street, wise-guy.'

Coughlin backed the truck up, muttering under his breath, Anna and Louis watched in amusement, and when they finally got turned, Louis said, 'Fuckin' pigs.'

Coughlin looked up into the mirror and said, 'I shoulda kicked his ass.'

'They would have thumped you like a tub of apple juice,' Anna said.

Coughlin continued on down the street, paused at the corner, snarled, 'Little fuckin' Nazi rat.' And then: 'You gotta put up with this all the time?'

'All the time,' Anna said. 'The cops see the dish on the roof, and it's open season.'

'You cause us a lot of trouble,' Coughlin said.

'No, we don't,' Anna said. 'You cause yourself a lot of trouble. Like your little Nazi back there. He could have been polite; instead, he treats us like dirt. So . . . why should we be nice?'

'Shit.' Coughlin put the truck into a driveway, backed up, turned around.

Anna said, 'What're you doing?'

'Going back.'

Louis and Anna sat in silence as Coughlin took the truck back up the road, then slowed as he came to the cop car blocking access to the body. The young cop saw them coming, put his hands on his hips, shook his head and then jabbed a finger at the curb. Coughlin pulled over and rolled the window down.

'Are you deaf or stupid?' the cop asked, looking up at Coughlin.

Coughlin stuck an ID card out the window. 'I'm a sergeant

with the Los Angeles Police Department, working an undercover detail, is what I am. And what I feel like doing is coming out there and kicking your ass up around your neck, you little prick,' he said. 'But I can't because I'd be breakin' cover. So what I'm gonna do instead, is, I'm gonna call my buddy down in personnel and see if we can fuck with your records. See if we need anybody directing traffic around sewer projects about sixteen hours a day . . .'

He went on for a while, while the young cop opened and shut his mouth like a dying fish. Then Coughlin threw the truck into reverse, backed into a drive, and headed out again.

'Feel better?' Anna asked.

'Much.' Then: 'First time I've ever done anything like that.'

'You oughta do it more often,' Anna said. 'Good for everybody's souls.'

She'd liked him before. Now she liked him better. After a while, she said. 'You might be able to make a living at this.'

'Yeah?'

'Maybe. You got the first part of the attitude.'

But that was it for the night. The following cars waited at both ends of Dell, watching cars, and for people on foot; Coughlin walked her down to her house, where a light showed in the window. Harper came to the door.

'Anything?'

'Nothing,' Coughlin said.

'All quiet here,' Harper said.

Anna said, 'It was absolutely flat. No feeling of anything. I think the guy has backed off.'

'No. He's fixed on you. He can't help himself. He's hanging around, but he knows we're here, too. He'll try to figure something out.'

'Nobody'll get in or out of here,' Coughlin said. 'We've got vans at both ends, night vision gear, the whole works.'

'Just gotta wait,' Harper said.

When Coughlin was gone, Harper asked, 'Do you want something to eat?'

'I usually have soup, or something light,' Anna said. 'Something to get the buzz off.'

'Got chicken noodle soup in the kitchen,' he said. 'Go wash your face; I'll get it.'

They sat at the table, eating the soup and soda crackers, and she talked about the night with Coughlin; and as they talked, she felt looser and easier, and suddenly was enjoying herself. The time of the early morning, coming down, had always been one of her favorites; sharing it suddenly seemed to make it even better.

Then Harper said, seriously, 'I'm not very romantic.'

That had nothing to do with the night. She said, cautiously, 'What?'

'I don't know how to talk about this – I didn't know how to talk about it with my wife, but I . . .' He seemed embarrassed. 'I sort of . . . hunger for you.'

'We could probably think of a way to take the edge off,' she said, lightly, instinctively deflecting him.

'I'm not talking about sex; or I am, but not only sex,' he said. He looked around the kitchen. 'I'm just, right now, eating soup, having the best time I've had in fifteen years. And I just don't want it to stop.'

'That's pretty romantic,' she said. He flushed, and then she did, sitting with the soup, and then Harper said, 'Eat your soup.'

'I am.'

'Well, hurry.'

Before she went to sleep, Harper a weighty lump on the other side of the bed, Anna was suddenly suffused with a sense of sadness and fear: she'd missed this, but she was also afraid of it. Afraid that it would end; afraid that it wouldn't end. Afraid that she could lose control.

Harper got up in the morning. Anna made a few noises at him as he crept out of the bedroom, then went back to sleep. The phone rang just after one, and she crawled across the bed to pick it up.

Creek. 'How'd it go last night?'

'Okay,' she said. 'You don't have to hurry and heal up anymore. This cop is a great cameraman.' There was a second of silence and she said, 'Jesus, Creek, that was a joke.'

'Pretty fuckin' funny,' he said.

'God, you get shot a little and people start having to be sensitive around you . . . what're you doing?'

Another second of silence. 'I was thinking about Clark again. And if you say he's not the guy, then I believe you ninety-nine percent: I'm serious. But since we've got people being killed, you've gotta check the other one percent.'

'I'm not talking to the cops about Clark,' she said.

'I understand that,' he said. 'You've got to get Harper to check – Pam will help. She's got a badge, Harper's a lawyer, they could find out all kinds of stuff. And it'd all be in the family that way.'

She thought about it for a few seconds, then said, 'He didn't do it.'

'I believe you,' he said. 'But.'

'I'll talk to Jake,' she said.

Harper was on the tiny strip of canal-side lawn with a golf club, making slow-motion swings. Anna looked out over the sink, saw him, and when he turned, waved, and he twirled the club like a baton and headed for the door.

'Morning,' he said. 'Or good afternoon.'

'Want to run?' she asked.

'Love to, but I'd probably have a heart attack,' he said.

'Well, I'm gonna go down to the beach and run.'

'No, you're not,' he said.

'I am, too.'

'No.' He shook his head. 'If I've got to run you down – and I could – and carry you back to the house, I will. You're not going to run on the beach. I couldn't keep up with you, and that's something he may have been watching you do. If you want to run someplace else, I'll take you there.'

She put her hands on her hips: 'Now you're messing with me.'

'Damn right,' he said. 'What do you want for breakfast?'

She ran on the beach, but not on Venice Beach. Harper drove her to Santa Monica, parked on the bluff across from an art deco hotel, and they walked down an access stairway, across the highway, and onto the beach a few hundred yards

311

from where Jason had been found.

'I didn't see any cops following,' Anna said.

'That's good,' Harper said. 'But they're there.'

She ran most of a mile north, turned, ran back past him to the pier, then back. The beach was nearly empty, and Harper could see her all the way; and she could see everyone around her.

'Not the same,' she said, when she got back. She was barely breathing hard. 'I felt like I was wearing a leash.'

'Gonna have to do for a while,' he said. He mussed her hair, kissed her on the lips, and put her in the car. The feeling of being on a leash had been unpleasant; the feeling of being squired about was not. 'We're not trying to run your life,' Harper said. 'We're just taking care for a few more days.'

'Did you think about Clark?' she asked. She'd told him about Creek's phone call.

'I'll talk to Pam – there are a few checks we could get done right away, through the cops, without talking to Wyatt. See if he had any problems with the police back east. I can get credit reports, see if I can find a guy to look around Harvard.'

'That'll take forever.'

'Not with computers – we'll have most of the paper in an hour or two,' he said. 'Getting a guy to look around Harvard – we could hear something tomorrow, if I can find the right guy.'

'I don't want him to know about it,' Anna said.

'He won't feel a thing,' Harper said.

'Still . . . Ah, God.'

'Up to you.'

On the way back, she decided: 'Go ahead with the calls on Clark – but you know what? I want to see him. Let's see if we can find him.'

'Today? We oughta get some paper on him first.'

'So you said it'd take a couple of hours; so do it. We'll go look at him tonight.'

'What about going out with Coughlin?'

'I'm thinking about putting him off. He's a good guy, but I don't think it's gonna work . . .'

'Wyatt seems to . . .'

'Maybe Wyatt's not thinking about him as much as I am,' Anna said. 'If you put yourself in his shoes, why would he follow me on the job? There're cops everywhere I go. There are two guys with me everywhere I go. I'd more expect him to try my place, or your place. Follow us when we're alone, like at the driving range.'

'Or at the beach, this morning.'

'Except that we've got escorts,' she said. 'Unless . . .'

'Unless what?'

'Unless he's lost interest. I just can't understand this thing, why he'd be so interested in me.'

Harper looked at her. 'You don't understand because your mind isn't fucked, and his is. Maybe he's still got enough control to lay back, just long enough to loosen you up, and get you thinking that you can go out on your own again. And when you do, he'll be there.'

'Yeah?' The thought scared her, but the fear wasn't blinding.

Because when he found her – she'd have found *him*.

Chapter 24

Anna called Wyatt to tell him that she wouldn't be going out with Coughlin that night. Wyatt wasn't in, but she left a voice-mail, and added that she'd be at the hospital visiting Creek. Pam Glass was already at the hospital, and Anna called to ask her about an FBI check on Clark.

'I could do it in a few minutes, from here; I'd need his full name and date of birth,' she said.

Anna gave her the information. 'Get it as quick as you can. I'm coming down to see Creek.'

'I'll have it by the time you get here,' Glass said. 'We have a new room, by the way.'

Anna took the new room number, and when she got off the line, Harper said, 'Do you think you'll be okay on your own? You've got the escort out there.'

'I'll be fine,' she said. 'Where're you going?'

'I've gotta make it down to the office, sign some paychecks. Make some calls back to Boston.'

'Remember . . .'

'Yeah. I'll go easy.'

Anna never saw her shadow on the way to the hospital. She

315

knew they were there, because she'd called to tell them she was leaving. Which car they were, or van or truck, she could never decide. Inside the hospital ramp, she saw no one: but she kept her hand on the pistol in her jacket pocket as she walked to the entrance.

'Paranoid,' she thought, as she went through the doors.

Creek was outside the new room, walking down the corridor in a flimsy white hospital gown. Anna caught him just outside his room and put her hand through the slit in the back of the gown and squeezed his butt. Creek jumped, then limped into the hospital room, while Anna followed, laughing.

'Goddamn sexual harassment from the boss,' Creek told Glass, who was reading the style section of the *L.A. Times.* 'And I'm hurt.'

'Be brave,' Glass said.

'Like he'd never grabbed a butt,' Anna said.

'I do it in a spirit of tenderness and multiculturalism,' Creek said indignantly.

Anna, watching him in amusement, suspected that he was actually offended. She momentarily considered an apology, then decided that he'd have to live with it. No apologies.

Creek sputtered, 'I'd never just sneak up on . . .' and then his eyes went past Anna, and she turned.

Wyatt, wearing his raincoat, stepped into the room. 'Hello.'

'Hey . . .'

'I came to see if I can change your mind,' he said to Anna. His eyes drifted toward Glass, who was sitting on a chair next to Creek's bed, her bare feet curled beneath her, looking frankly domestic.

'I don't think so.'

Wyatt brought his eyes back to Anna, and they squared off.

'I can't order you to go, because you're a civilian,' Wyatt said, grimly patient. 'But the shit is gonna hit the fan pretty soon, when the media get this. When the word about China Lake gets out, they're liable to drive this guy out of sight. We've gotta work everything we can, while we can.'

'It's not working,' Anna said flatly. 'If he comes after me, it won't be on the job.'

'He doesn't have to come after you,' Wyatt insisted. 'All he has to do is cruise you. And if we keep you out of sight, except when you're working – he's gonna cruise you. He's gonna want to see you. We ran a dozen cars last night.'

'And got nothing,' Anna said.

'But he'll come.'

They went on for a few more minutes. Wyatt pressing, Anna resisting, until Glass said, 'If you saw me in the truck . . . I could be Anna.'

Anna and Wyatt both turned toward her, and she uncurled her legs and stood up. 'We're about the same size and weight, and our hair color's the same,' she said. 'I could get a pair of wire rims at Woolworth's and take the lenses out. I'm not doing anything now, except listening to Creek pissing and moaning.'

Anna looked at her, then at Wyatt, then back at Glass, tilted her head. 'If you're willing, that's a possibility.'

Wyatt was sceptical, but finally agreed: 'If that's the only way we can do it. Damn it, though. What're you gonna do, Anna?'

Anna smiled, just a turn of the lips: Jake and I have been trying to spend a little time together, in peace and quiet.'

'Oh.' Wyatt nodded. Behind him, Creek rolled his eyes.

When Wyatt had gone to call the task force leader, Anna asked Glass, 'What'd you get on Clark?'

Glass shook her head: 'Nothing. He had his driver's license suspended for three speeding tickets in three months. That's it.'

'Yeah, I knew it,' Anna said. 'He's out of it.'

'He's not out of it,' Creek insisted.

'Creek . . .'

'Let's see what Jake gets,' Creek said.

They talked for a few more minutes, then Wyatt returned: 'It's all set, but Pam has gotta get to your place without being noticed.'

'I'll drive her,' Anna said. 'She can leave her car here in the hospital ramp.'

'All right. Coughlin will be there at nine.' He looked at Glass. 'You be careful.'

Glass kissed Creek good-bye, and she and Anna left together, Glass carrying the remnants of the newspaper. Anna caught their reflection in the elevator doors as they waited: side by side, with the slight blurring in the stainless steel, they could have been mistaken for each other. Glass was perhaps an inch taller, Anna had just slightly wider shoulders. Both had short, efficient haircuts.

So what if the guy came for her, and they took him down, and she wasn't even there to see it? Anna touched the gun in her jacket pocket, then shook her head. No. They wouldn't take him that way.

'I'd hate to deal with this guy one on one,' Glass was saying. 'Most guys, you can manipulate. But you get a guy like this . . . have you ever gotten tangled up with a guy who's nuts?'

'No.' They got in the elevator and pushed a button.

'When I was on the street, we got a call about a guy in a halfway house: he'd done some time on some sex offenses, mostly exhibitionism, most of it aimed at little girls,' Glass said. 'Anyway, he was drunk, out on the street, flashing everybody who came by. When we got there, we couldn't find him. He'd walked off. He wasn't supposed to be dangerous or anything, so me and my partner split up, trying to find him. I walked down to this ice cream shop and stopped to ask some people at a bus stop, and he came out of the shop behind me and saw the uniform and freaked out and came up behind me and wrapped his arms around me and picked me up off the ground and started squeezing.'

'Jeez.'

'Yeah. He was huge. Strong. I felt like an egg, I felt like he could crush me. I couldn't move my arms, I just kept trying to talk to him, but he was nuts: he had a mind like a little mean kid having a temper tantrum. I couldn't get him to put me down, and the more I struggled, the tighter he squeezed until I couldn't breathe.'

'How'd you get loose?'

'My partner came along, called for backup and started whacking the guy with his baton. But the guy kept turning in circles and squeezing me, and then the backup arrived and the three guys got us all down on the ground and pried his arms off. I was black and blue . . . my ribs looked like the American flag, where his arms were. Great big stripes.'

The elevator door opened and Anna said, 'It's a weird thing, men and muscles. It's like they think about it all the time.'

'What makes me mad is that some wimpy little jerk who never lifts anything heavier than a fork can whack me around because he'd got fifty pounds on me and he's twice as strong, and he's not even trying. It's all hormones.'

'Yeah, but . . . that's why God made us smarter,' Anna said.

'That's true,' Glass conceded.

Glass lay in the back seat of Anna's car, reading the comics, as Anna drove back home. Harper's BMW was squeezed into a tight space in front of the house, and Anna had to maneuvre the car to get it into the garage. They went inside, and found Harper at the kitchen table, eating a bowl of Golden Crisp with milk.

'What?' he asked.

Anna gave him a quick rundown, and he looked at Glass. 'Put on the right clothes, at night . . . it'll work. Keep moving, though.'

'Anything at all on Clark?'

'Mmm,' Harper said. He quickly finished the cereal and carried the bowl to the sink. 'Just a little thing.'

'He won't find out . . .'

'No, no. I've got a friend in a law firm there, they've got a researcher on staff. She walked over and talked around the music department. She said she was checking on a mortgage history.'

'So what'd she find?' Anna asked impatiently. 'The little thing.'

'There's a rumor of a sexual harassment complaint made by a graduate student – a woman graduate student – in a composition seminar. Apparently nothing was ever filed, no legal action, but there was . . . something.'

'Just a rumor,' Anna said dismissively.

'No. There was something,' Harper said. 'We can't really find out what, unless we ask more directly. And he'd most likely hear about it.'

Anna shook her head. 'Then don't.'

Glass glanced at Harper, then said, 'Anna, this is a little more important than your feelings. Or his. Remember China Lake . . .'

'I remember China Lake. But Clark didn't do it.'

'One of his students has a recital tonight; he'll be there. Eight o'clock at Schoenberg Hall,' Harper said.

'Yeah?' Anna's eyebrow went up.

'We could pick him up after the recital,' Harper said, his voice casual. 'Find out what he does with his evenings.'

'And we'd have time to stop by Kinko's first, and talk to Catwell again,' Anna said.

'We could do that,' Harper said.

Coughlin would pick Glass up at the regular night-crew starting time, ten o'clock. If they left any earlier, they thought the stalker would miss them.

Glass said, 'When we go out tonight, if we don't find anybody tailing us, we'll probably cruise just long enough to seem legitimate, then come back here, like I was picking up something. Then go back out again. Give him another chance to pick us up. If we still don't get anything, we'll be back around midnight.'

'So you're gonna lay low until then?' Harper asked.

'I gotta get some sleep,' Glass said. She yawned: 'Watching Creek is tiring.'

'Keep the doors locked,' Harper said. 'The guy's been here at least twice.'

Anna snuck out to Harper's car after dark, and curled up on the back seat, out of sight.

'I don't have much faith in this Catwell thing,' Harper said over the seat.

'We just have to keep talking,' Anna said. 'The cops keep saying that I know the guy. Sooner or later, I'll pick him out. I probably should have already.'

Bob Catwell was not at Kinko's.

An unconsciously beautiful young blonde woman told them that Catwell had 'rented a room in some frat house up on the hill. Down in the basement, you have to walk around the side on this gravel tracklike thing, and you see this door. Like, his room used to be the coal bin or something.'

She drew a sketch on a piece of copy paper, and Anna thanked her and they headed out.

'Do you think she knows how beautiful she is?' Harper asked on the way to the car.

'Somewhere down in her brain she knows that she gets special treatment,' Anna said. 'Unless she's particularly stupid, and she didn't seem to be.'

The frat house was built on the side of a hill, with a narrow, rutted drive leading around back. Harper found a parking place and they walked back, and down the drive. Eight or nine feet of old poured-concrete foundation was exposed along the back side. The only window was boarded over with a sheet of plywood, but they could see light through a hairline crack at one edge. And at the door, they could smell the burning dope.

'You could get high standing outside,' Harper said.

He turned the knob and pushed: the door unexpectedly popped open, and he stepped through, Anna at his elbow. Catwell was sprawled on a battered green sofa in front of a seventies color television, watching 'Ren and Stimpy' reruns. He sat up, scared, when they burst in, dropped the joint he was smoking, recognized them, then scrambled to get the joint out of the couch. 'What the fuck do you want? Did you . . . get the fuck out of here . . .'

'Gotta talk,' Anna said, stepping around Harper. Catwell finally found the joint and then stood there, looking at it, not sure what to do with it. 'Give me that,' Anna said.

He handed it to her, and she took a hit, exhaled and handed it back: 'Now we're all criminals together, huh? So relax, and we gotta talk.'

Catwell, uncertain, hit on the joint himself, a last time, then pinched it out.

'Like a doper's bowling alley in here,' Harper said, waving at a layer of smoke that hung two-thirds of the way to the ceiling.

'You don't like it, get lost,' Catwell said.

'Both of you, shut up,' Anna said. To Catwell: 'Listen, we need to talk again. We need to know more about what Jason was doing. Not who he bought the dope from, just in general.'

'That guy still chasing you?' Catwell's eyes were glassy, and his speech a little slow, but he seemed to be tracking.

'He killed another woman,' Anna said.

'Where're the fucking cops?' Catwell asked. 'Out chasing hippies?'

'They're looking,' Anna said. 'We need to know who Jason was talking to, anything you know, especially the night before he died. Did you see him that night?'

'No, I didn't. I knew he was going out with you, though. He'd been talking about setting the whole thing up, the raid,' Catwell said. He dropped on the couch again, looked at the dead joint in his hand. 'You know, I miss that dickhead. I keep thinking I oughta go see him about something, but then I remember, he's gone.'

'I know how it is,' Harper said soberly.

'You knew he was setting up raid coverage,' Anna said. 'You know who he was talking to about it?'

'Just those guys over there,' Catwell said. 'The animal guy and that other surfer asshole.'

'We know the animal guy,' Anna said. 'He's up in Oregon. Who's the surfer?'

'You know, you had him on TV. The pig guy, the guy knocked down by the pig. I must've seen it fifty times,' Catwell said, gesturing at the television.

Anna was confused. 'Wait a minute – he was the animal guy, right? Steve?'

Now Catwell was confused: 'No, no, the other guy. He was setting it up with the animal guy, the guy who took care of the animals.'

Harper and Anna looked at each other, then Anna got down on her knees so she could look Catwell squarely in the face. 'You're telling me that the whole thing was set up – both sides? That the animal rights raiders and the kid inside the building were all set up by Jason?'

'Sure.' Catwell nodded, then looked from Anna to Harper and back with just a touch of amusement. 'I thought you knew that. The whole thing was like a fuckin' movie. The guy in the building is the guy who left the door unlocked so the animal people could get in.'

Anna said, 'Shit,' and stood up.

Catwell continued: 'I don't know if the raider people knew who left the door open, 'cause Jase was being pretty quiet about the whole thing. I just knew because we were dopin' buddies. But he sort of went over and told the surfer asshole about the animal up there, and the labs, and told them he could get them in. Then he fixed it for the guy inside to leave the door open, and for that guy to fight with them. It looked pretty real on TV – they were pretty rough, so maybe the raider guys didn't know.'

'Why do you keep calling the surfer guy an asshole?' Harper asked.

Catwell shrugged. 'You know, he's one of those fuckin' blond short-hair oh-wow surf's-up pussy-hounds with big fuckin' white teeth and never had to work in his whole fuckin' life . . .' He looked at the dead joint again. 'How come guys like him don't get killed?'

Anna shrugged: 'Way of the world. But what about the other kid, the one who took care of the animals. What about him?'

'I don't know. He's in theater, or something.'

'Theater? I thought he was some kind of science geek.'

Catwell shook his head: 'Theater, is what Jason said.'

They talked for a few more minutes, but Catwell had nothing more. He lit up again as they were leaving, and Harper said, 'You oughta lock the door.'

'I will,' Catwell said, in the squeaky top-of-the-mouth speech of a man holding his breath. 'Soon as I can afford a lock.'

Outside, on the driveway, Anna said, 'The whole thing was a setup. Christ, I'd hate to have that get around.'

'Screw you with the TV people?'

'I don't know – I mean, it was good tape, so they'd probably use it anyway. But it sorta makes us look like chumps.'

'What do you think about this kid?'

'. . . Who set us up? I don't know: I talked to him for a couple of minutes, came onto him a little bit, you know, just to cheer him up,' Anna said. They were walking up the hill toward the street. They could hear rock music from one of the frat houses, and a man laughing. 'God, he seemed real. He didn't seem like . . . he seemed like a nerd, is what I'm saying. Not like somebody who'd be out trying to physically intimidate people.'

'You said this guy was strong, but kind of soft.'

She nodded: 'Yeah. I just don't see him as being strong. But I don't know: *he could be.* I mean, he completely sucked me in. And if he's really in theater, he probably is in some kind of shape.' She thought about it, then said,' Let's run him down. Find out.'

'What about Clark?' Harper asked.

'What time is it?' She couldn't see her watch in the dark.

'Time to go, if we're gonna catch him,' Harper said. 'We oughta be there now.'

Anna took the cell phone out of her jacket. 'It's not Clark . . . And now that this kid has come up, I think we should concentrate on him. I'll talk to Louis, see if he can track the kid down.'

'How long will it take?'

'I don't know, but Louis can usually find people. He's got all the phone directories and he can get into utility records. The utilities have just about *everybody* . . .'

'Except maybe some students and illegals.' They came to the end of the driveway. 'So why don't we go catch Clark, while Louis looks for the kid.'

She nodded, reluctantly. It only made sense. 'All right.' she said. 'Where's the car?'

Harper pointed the key down the street and pushed a button, and the car flashed its parking lights at them. 'What's his name?' Harper asked, as they walked toward it. 'The kid?'

Anna shrugged: 'I don't remember. The names never stick for more than a day or two.'

'Strange business, Batory.'

'Strange times, Harper.'

Chapter 25

The two-faced man was dressed in a light Lycra full-length windsurfer's suit, pitch-black from the neckline to the black Nike gym shoes. With a nylon stocking over his head, he was a shadow.

He moved slowly, carefully, letting his body feel the way through the dark. He had a bum bag wrapped around his ribs, a rope wrapped around his waist, and the pistol under his arm.

Moving like a snake, sliding the last few inches toward the unsuspecting mouse . . .

Anna's house showed a light in a side window, but it was the kind of too-dim light that people left when they were gone – a light in a hallway, somewhere. Not a reading light or a TV light or a work light; a waiting light.

He closed on the back porch. He'd been there before, but this time, she wasn't home. There was no one inside to hear him . . . unless the cops had set something up. Unlikely, but possible, and the possibility added to the intensity of the approach.

He sat in the shadow of the porch for five minutes,

listening. And he heard voices, coming down from above, with a little music that he couldn't place. Old music, the kind you hear late at night when you're driving out in the desert. People on a porch, he thought, in the next house. He measured the unexcited voices, then slowly, carefully unhooked the bum bag, unzipped it, took out the screwdriver and the roll of duct tape.

He knew from the last time where the lock was. He planned to break out the glass again, but more carefully. He'd hold the pieces in place with the tape, rather than letting them fall inside.

But when he got to his knees on the porch, he found a piece of plywood covering the window. He tested it with the screwdriver. The plywood moved. Huh. More pressure – and when he pried hard enough, he could feel the wood give.

He dropped the duct tape and worked the screwdriver around the perimeter of the plywood plug. After a minute, the top and left edges were free. He worked on the bottom edge, then pushed his hand through the slot and it opened like a little door.

He stopped to listen again, then reached inside. He had to stretch, to go in all the way to his shoulder, but the deadbolt was there and he flipped the handle; the door opened easily.

Inside, he listened again, then pressed the plywood window plug roughly into place. He used the penlight to navigate across the kitchen, followed the light down the hall, around the little office, then up the stairs to the bedroom.

The bedroom smelled of her: her perfume, or just her body.

He listened, then probed the bedroom. Went through the chest of drawers, through the closets, looked at photographs in a grass basket, dug through a trunk, through a jewelry box; smelled her perfume, dabbed some of it on his throat.

Stretched out on her bed; turned his face into her pillow.

Hated her; but still loved her, too, he thought.

He was still there, on the bed, when she got back.

Felt a finger of panic: then remembered the closet.

Crept into it, made himself small, in the back, with the shoes, behind the hanging lengths of the hippie dresses.

Took the gun out, placed the long, cool length of it against his face.

Heard voices: she was with a man. The bodyguard.

He'd wait until he was gone, and take her.

End her.

And if the bodyguard stayed?

He worked it out: Take the bodyguard first. No warning, just step up and do it.

Then her.

He tried to control his breathing, but found it difficult.

Hate/sex/death/darkness. The odor of Chanel. The silken feel of her dresses on his face . . .

He waited.

Chapter 26

Louis found the kid's name – Charles McKinley. An address was listed in the university directory, but when Louis called it, the phone had been disconnected.

'Student,' Louis said to Anna.

'We need an address,' Anna said. When she got off the phone, she said to Harper, 'We've got to go after this kid. This little stunt he pulled . . . there's something in here. A couple of different personalities, or something.'

'It won't hurt to take a look at Clark while we're waiting,' Harper said. 'If Louis says the kid's not in the directory, then it'll take a while to find him.'

Anna shook her head, but said, 'I guess.' Harper made sense, but the gloom was on her. She dreaded the idea of spying on Clark.

Harper pulled away from the curb and headed down the hill, into the campus, silent, knowing that she was working through it. She stared out the window at the passing landscape and wondered why the idea of surveillance worried her so much.

She turned the question in her mind until she arrived at the nexus: *If we get back together, I'll have to tell him. And*

*if I tell him, I'll be admitting that I thought he might be
this killer. But only if we get back together, and we won't.
But if we do . . .*

The thoughts tumbled over each other, always running
into the paradox: *we won't, but if we do . . .*

A barefoot man in a ragged winter coat, the kind people
wore in Minnesota, stood on the corner by the Shell station
and held up a cardboard sign hand-lettered with Magic
Marker: *will work for drugs.* He laughed crazily, drunkenly
– or maybe somebody had dropped some acid on him – at
the passing cars. Harper guided the BMW past him,
wordlessly, glancing at Anna from time to time.

'That's where the trouble started,' Anna said, looking at
the gas station as they went by.

'What?'

'That's where we picked up the woman who took us into
the animal rights thing . . . we were right down there at the
medical center.'

'Maybe the kid's up there, McKinley,' Harper suggested.
'You want to run in? We've still got a little time.'

She thought about it for a second. Anything seemed
preferable to looking for Clark: 'Sure.'

'I'll wait – take the gun,' Harper said.

Anna ran up to the front of the building while Harper idled
at the curb. The building was locked, but she could see a
security guard inside. She banged on the door, and the guard
got up, reluctantly, and walked toward her, cracked the door.

'Can I help you?'

'I'm trying to find Charles McKinley. He works up in the
animal labs.'

'He's not here tonight,' the guard said, talking through the crack. 'He's been off since last week.'

''Cause of the animal rights thing?'

'Yup. He's been all over the TV. He was on the "Today" show, even.'

'Great,' Anna nodded. 'Does anybody know where he lives?'

'I couldn't tell you if I did know,' the guard said. 'But I don't, anyway.'

'Got a phone number?'

'I don't think so . . . I could look, I guess.'

'Thanks, I'd appreciate it.'

The guard pulled the door closed and went back to his desk, rummaged around for a while, and came back, shaking his head. 'Nothing there. Best thing to do is call tomorrow morning. Somebody might know. But – he's a student.'

'Nothing?' Harper asked.

'He's not there.'

They drove the next two blocks in silence, dumped the car in a parking garage and walked toward the music building.

'I hate this,' Anna said. She felt like she was plodding through paste.

'Where's he most likely to come out?'

She thought about it, and again got caught in the memories: playing with Clark, exploring the building, playing every instrument they could find. They spent several nights in the place, even made love on a library table, when neither one of them would back off the dare.

'Right out the front,' she said, reluctantly. 'He used to always try to park in the Number Two parking structure, it's just down the block.'

'So let's find a place to sit,' Harper said. He was being stubborn about it. He could have offered to break it off, to concentrate on the kid. He could have accepted Anna's argument that she knew Clark well enough to vouch for him. But instead, Harper moved her along, pulling her into it.

Schoenberg Hall was a low white building on the south side of a grassy sunken square called Dickson Plaza. Anna found a spot on the steps on the north side of the plaza, where they could see the main entrance to the building. She said, 'I wish I had that joint.'

'That'd keep you sharp,' Harper said, dropping down beside her.

'I don't need sharp.' She looked at her watch. 'Should be ending.'

Ten minutes went by. Then the door opened, and a woman walked out. A minute later, a couple. Another minute, and a stream of people pushed out of the building, chatting and laughing as they headed down the walk.

'Lot of people. Must've been pretty good,' Anna said. 'No Clark?'

'If it's really his student, they're probably hanging around until everyone leaves, talking about it.'

'Is that fun? A good time?'

She let the question hang for a second, then said, 'Mostly. It can be pretty terrible. But even when it's terrible, it's kind of fun. You know, people mess up. If they're your friends, you pretend it was nothing. If they're your enemies, you tell

336

everybody that you feel sorry for them, and you still think it's possible that they can recover. Stab them in the back.'

'Did you ever mess up?'

'Sure. Everyone does. But if you do it with confidence, keep on counting, you can get away with it. You can get away with a lot, when you're playing alone or with a good group. That's part of the fun, too. A secret that nobody knows except the players.'

'Never played music,' Harper said. 'Can't even whistle.'

'Everybody can whistle,' Anna said. She whistled the first few notes of 'Yankee Doodle'.

'Nope. Can't do that. I can make a noise, but . . .'

She touched his sleeve: 'There he is. That's Clark.'

Clark was walking with a woman who was carrying a cello case, and Anna said, half-joking, but her voice fierce, 'Oh, Christ, a cello.'

'What?' Harper asked. He was whispering, though Clark and the woman were seventy-five yards away.

'Cello players are supposed to be, you know, sexy. All those hours with a big vibrating instrument between their knees.'

'Hmm.'

'Yeah, it's gotta be bullshit.'

'Why?'

'I don't know.'

The other couple walked past, still seventy-five or eighty yards away, and Harper said, 'Walk behind me – he'll recognize your walk if he sees you.' Anna looked after Clark, and realized that she would recognize him from the back, anywhere, just by the walk. How had Harper known that?

'Okay.'

They followed Clark and the woman around the end of the building, and Anna said, 'They're headed for Structure Two.'

'You sure?'

'There's nothing else over there, unless they're walking somewhere. I can't see them walking far with that cello.'

'Run and get the car,' Harper said, tossing her the keys. 'I'll meet you outside the structure. And run – and keep the goddamn gun handy.'

Anna grabbed the keys and turned and ran before he finished the sentence. The parking structure they'd used was four hundred yards away, and took her a couple of minutes to reach, but since it was further from the music building, she didn't have to contend with other people getting out of the recital.

She ran up the stairs to the second level, where they'd parked. Stopped and listened. Heard a car somewhere in the structure. She ran toward the car, popping the car door with the automatic key.

As she came up to the car door, she was seized with the fantasy that somebody was looming behind her: she saw nothing at all, but she climbed frantically into the car and hit the electric lock button. The locks snapped down, and she twisted, looking out the windows . . . nothing. Nobody. Her heart was beating so hard she thought she could hear it, but a minute later, she paid the parking fee and was on her way, no other cars in sight.

Harper was waiting at the other structure. He flagged her

down, and she stopped and crawled into the passenger seat as he got in on the driver's side.

'What?' she asked.

'Woman's got a Dodge van. They talked for a couple of more minutes, then he headed up to the next floor. The van just got out a minute ago.'

She didn't want to ask, but did anyway: 'Did he kiss her goodnight?'

'No.' Harper didn't smile at the question, just shook his head. 'Christ, you're hung up on this guy. And I shoulda said yes.'

'I don't know what I am; I think I might be goofy,' Anna said. Then: 'When I saw him the first time, at the gas station, he had a Volvo station wagon.'

'You remember?'

'Yeah, because . . . it's about what I'd have expected.'

As she said it, a dark-blue Volvo wagon nosed out of the structure, then turned left and drove past them.

'Here we go . . .'

Clark led them down to Wilshire, and then to Santa Monica, right on Santa Monica toward the Pacific.

'He lives the other way,' Harper said.

'Mmm.'

Clark was in a hurry, slicing in and out of traffic. Harper let him get several cars ahead.

'If he sees us running like he is, he'll watch us,' Harper said. 'I hope he doesn't just bust a light, or we'll be stuck.'

They stayed with him all the way into Santa Monica, into another parking structure. Harper got in line behind him for a parking ticket, as Anna slumped in the passenger seat, then followed him up the structure, continuing on when Clark found a space.

Harper took two more turns, then pulled in.

'Stay behind me again, until we know where he is,' Harper said.

'How far are we?'

'Other side of the structure, half a floor lower,' Harper said. 'He may already be going down the stairs.'

They ran to the stairs, and Harper eased the door open. They heard a door bang, and Harper said, 'Shit, we'll have to take a chance. Come on.'

'No. I'll wait here – you call me.'

Harper nodded and ran down the stairs, opened the door, then called up, 'He's out here, hurry . . .'

Anna ran down to him, and followed through the door, and suddenly found themselves in Santa Monica Place, a three-story shopping center, in a crowd of people.

'He's a hundred feet up there,' Harper said. Anna stepped half out from behind him, saw Clark's head and shoulders. His hair *was* thinning, she thought. But he moved well, like he'd been taking care of himself. He was wearing a tan linen jacket and jeans.

Harper said, 'Come on. We've got to stay close or we'll lose him.'

'Oh, Jesus, Jake . . .' She clutched at his arm. 'God, he can't see me.'

'If he does, you're with me, on a date,' Harper said. 'One of those things.'

'Aw . . .'

But she went down past the rows of shops to an escalator, and watched as Clark headed down.

'Go slow,' Anna said. They waited until Clark was off at the bottom.

'Stand behind me,' Harper said. 'He's headed for the food court . . .'

Anna, peeking out from behind Harper's shoulders, saw Clark disappear around a corner, into the food court. 'Let's go,' Harper said, and he started walking down the escalator, hopped off at the bottom, and hurried to the last spot they'd seen Clark; Anna dodged along behind, trying to stay in his shadow. When they turned the corner, Clark was gone.

'Where'd he go?' Jake asked quietly.

Anna scanned the crowd: 'I don't know.'

Harper led her to one side: 'He was right here . . . look for the jacket.'

No jacket.

'Christ . . .' Harper turned around. 'Where in the hell did he go?'

They couldn't find him. He had absolutely vanished.

Finally, Anna said, 'Let's get out of here. I don't want him popping up in my face. That'd screw us.'

Harper nodded: 'All right.' And, 'Do you think he spotted us?'

'I don't think so. He seemed to be in a big hurry.'

'So where the hell did he go? Into one of the concession stands?'

'I don't know. I just hope he wasn't watching us – I hope he didn't see us. I knew we shouldn't have done this.'

Harper stopped her: 'Anna, we should do *everything*. Every tiny possibility. We oughta give Clark's name to the cops, and let them check him out.'

'No.' End of story.

Clark's car was still where he'd left it. 'We could wait,' Harper said, glancing at his watch. 'The shopping center closes in ten minutes. There's a space we could watch from.'

Anna, once reluctant, was now curious: where'd he gone? She didn't want to watch him, only to know. He'd walked into the shopping center and disappeared. Maybe he'd gotten inside and started jogging down toward the end, or pulled off his jacket and they'd missed him in scanning the crowd . . . Maybe he'd spotted them, and was hiding, because he didn't want to meet her face to face.

'Let's wait – for a while. I'll call Louis.'

They waited for more than an hour, slumped in the car, talking in a desultory way. Louis still hadn't found anything on McKinley.

After an hour, Harper called an end to it: 'It's after ten. Let's go on back to your place, see if anything turned up.'

'All right. But, goddammit, Jake, we're stuck.'

Chapter 27

The lights were on in the living room, and Anna called, 'Pam? Hello?'

But Glass had gone.

'Got the house all to ourselves, my little potato dumpling,' Harper said, snagging her around the waist.

Anna twisted in his hands, to face him, said, 'Potato dumpling my ass,' and he said, 'No, definitely not your ass,' and she stood on her tiptoes to kiss him.

But now Harper was looking past her, toward the kitchen, and he said, 'What's that? In the kitchen.'

His voice carried a chill, and Anna turned again, and looked toward the kitchen. She didn't see anything until he said, 'On the floor.' A stain spread across the floor, as though somebody had spilled hot grape jam and left it to coagulate.

Anna caught Harper's chill, and pulled away and stepped toward the kitchen. 'Careful,' he said, catching her, and she felt in her jacket pocket for the gun. They moved to the edge of the kitchen, and Anna reached inside and flipped on the light.

The stain was the size of a large human hand; liquid, purple.

'Blood,' Harper said. 'Don't go in. We might need crime scene.'

'Oh, Jesus, look at the window.' Harper looked at the window by the door. The plywood plug had been forced in, and only partly pushed back in place. 'He's got her,' Anna said. She grabbed Harper's jacket sleeve: 'He's got her, Jake. He thought she was me.'

'Gotta call Wyatt, and gimme the gun,' Harper grunted. Harper started going through the house, opening doors, checking everything, Anna trailing behind. As they went, Anna ran through the phone's memory, found Wyatt's home number, pushed the call button. Wyatt answered, sleepily: 'What?'

'This is Anna: have you seen Pam?'

Wyatt was instantly alert, picking up the vibration in her voice: 'No. What happened?'

'We came home, expecting to meet her here, but she wasn't here. But it looks like somebody broke in through the back, and there's blood on the kitchen floor.'

'Oh, Jesus Christ, you stay right there. Stay there!'

And he was gone.

Anna punched in Creek's number at the hospital. Creek was awake, but hadn't seen Pam: 'What's happening, Anna?'

Anna explained, and Creek groaned, 'Goddammit, I can't move, I'm wired in here, I'm gonna get . . .'

'No,' Anna shouted. 'You stay there. Maybe she'll turn up. We gotta have somebody there . . . that's where she'll come.'

Two minutes later, a minivan screeched to a stop outside,

and five seconds after that, a second one. Two plainclothes cops climbed out of each, milled for a second, then started for the door. Harper and Anna met them on the front porch: 'You're sure it's blood?' the first man asked.

'Pretty sure,' Harper said.

'She left here a half hour ago, ten minutes after they got back,' the cop said. He looked at Anna. 'She was driving your car, we figured it was all right – actually, we thought it was you.'

Another cop was kneeling in the kitchen. He sniffed the stain on the floor, and looked back at them: 'It's blood.'

'And there's the window,' Anna said. She'd gone to the garage door, opened it. The garage was empty.

'Maybe she's okay, maybe she went out for something,' Anna said; but she didn't believe it. She simply wanted someone else to believe.

Harper looked at her and shook his head.

'He didn't get in here,' one of the other cops said, defensively. 'We watched every goddamned car that came in here, and the only one that turned down the street was that Korean guy.'

'He didn't come in a car,' Anna said. 'He took my car, and there's no other car out here. He snuck in.'

'How? We were watching people on the street; and how in the hell are you gonna sneak around in this place? All the houses are jammed asshole-to-elbow and everybody's nervous about burglars and there's no place to sneak from.'

They were still arguing when Wyatt arrived. He was wearing suit pants and a jacket over a striped pajama shirt, and carried a rumpled dress shirt and tie in his fist.

He listened for two minutes, then said to Anna, 'I thought about this on the way over. It's gotta be somebody on the inside. Somebody here in Venice, probably on your street.'

'Inside?'

'Gotta be,' he said. He ticked off the points: 'He killed a guy who claimed to be having a romance with you. Okay: that could come from simply following you around. But then he came here, and he just vanished. Then he went after your friend Creek, right down the street, and he got away again.'

'He went into his house,' Harper said.

Wyatt nodded. 'That would explain a lot,' Harper said.

Anna was thinking furiously: God knows there were enough strange and troubled people in Venice; that was almost a qualification to owning a home there. But who?

'So you mean the whole thing was a coincidence?' Harper asked. 'That because it happened on the night my son died, and everything else . . . the animal raid and everything . . . we just made it up?'

Wyatt nodded. 'It's possible – or maybe he was following her that night, and something he saw set him off.'

Harper said, 'So have your guys check the logs and find out who came out of here after Anna . . .'

They worked through it, but Anna kept hearing Harper's word, 'coincidence'. None of it felt like coincidence: the flow of her life had turned the night of Jason's death. That felt like the beginning of something. To think that it had all started before then – maybe long before then, in the mind of one of her neighbors – just didn't fit. Didn't feel right.

She stood up and said to Harper, 'I'm gonna run next door and talk to Hobie and Jim. They're up on the roof half the time, maybe they saw something . . . In fact, with everybody here, I bet they're out on the roof now.'

She went out the back door, looked up: 'Hobie? Jim? You guys up there?'

A second later, Hobie's voice floated down: 'What's going on?'

'Trouble. Can you come down?'

'Be right there – out the back door.'

Anna met them in the dark space between their two houses, explained what had happened. Jim whistled and said, 'I heard the garage door go up and down, but that was about it.'

Hobie said, 'I didn't even hear that.'

'I think you were making popcorn,' Jim said.

'I'm sorry, Anna. Jesus, I hope the guy doesn't do anything nuts.'

Anna turned back to the house. As she walked along the canal, just before she got to the steps on the back stoop, she unconsciously lifted her foot over a heavy formed-concrete flowerpot. She'd cracked her foot on it thirty times, had always sworn to move it someday . . . and suddenly realized it was gone. Nothing there.

People were fucking with her house . . .

And Anna's phone rang. She took it out of her pocket and was about to click it on, then stopped, looked at Harper: 'It's him. He wants me to hear her die.'

'Don't answer,' Harper said, urgently. He turned to Wyatt and said, 'Are you still set up on her phone?'

'Yeah.'

'You gotta get this one,' Anna said. 'I think he's calling

like he called with China Lake. Maybe . . .'

'Jesus.' They stared at the phone until the tone stopped.

Wyatt began setting up a neighborhood search, and at the same time, sealing the area off. Harper took Anna aside and said, 'We gotta tell them about Clark.'

'Not yet. Let's find the kid. Jake, it can't be Clark.'

'That sounds like wishful thinking . . . where'd he go tonight? Why'd he disappear?'

'We don't know that he did. We probably just missed him. Wyatt thinks we've made most of this up – just put stuff together and come up with fantasy. That's what we've done with Clark.'

'I still think . . .'

'Let's concentrate on McKinley. Please.' She was begging him.

'We don't even know where he is, Anna,' Harper said in exasperation.

Anna held up a hand. 'Got an idea,' she said. 'I should have thought of this before.'

She took the phone out and scrolled through to the Witch, and pushed the button. The Witch answered on the first ring.

'This is Anna,' Anna said.

'What'ya got?'

'A question. You know that kid that got in the fight with the animal activists? Nosebleed and all?'

'Yeah. But talk faster, I'm on a deadline.'

'You had him on a couple of talk shows.'

'Shit, he was on "Today", what do you mean, a couple talk shows . . .'

'All right, all right, but the day after the raid, you shot extra stuff on him. I need his address, where he lives, and a phone number.'

'Anna, I don't have any time . . .'

'I need the fuckin' numbers,' Anna shouted.

'Hey . . .'

'Listen,' Anna said, urgently now, quieter. 'Get somebody to dig the address and numbers up, and I'll give you a lead on a story that's better than the jumper. A freebie. And believe me, if you knew what it was, you'd kill your mother for it. I'm not joking: I'll feed it to you in the next couple of days.'

After a moment of silence: 'Anything to do with China Lake?'

Anna hesitated, then said, 'Everything to do with China Lake, and she's just the start.'

The Witch screeched, 'This kid is in the China Lake killing?'

'No, no, for Christ's sake, he didn't have anything to do with it, that's a different story. But I've got an inside thing on China Lake – a serial killer thing,' Anna said. 'If you get McKinley's address or phone number back to me, I'll tip you the other story.'

'So what's happening with McKinley?' the Witch asked suspiciously.

'He's fucking with me,' Anna said. 'The miserable little shit. I'm gonna crucify him.'

'That sounds promising,' the Witch said. 'I'll have somebody look around.'

'Right now,' Anna said. 'This is serious. I'm calling a couple more stations. The first one who gives me the address and phone number, I'll give them the China Lake story.'

'You know, you can be a major pain in the ass.'

'Yeah, but a fairly cheap pain, considering what I deliver. So call me back.'

'Hold on, just hold on . . . I'm gonna put the phone down, I'll be right back.'

Anna held on. Harper said, 'What?'

'Maybe something,' Anna said.

The Witch was back: 'You got a pencil?'

Wyatt, nearing panic, was sealing Venice.

Anna, with McKinley's phone number, and Louis tracking the address, told him they were going to look for a kid they'd interviewed the night of Jason's murder.

'You've got to stay in touch,' Wyatt said anxiously. 'We'll call you if we need you: If you get one ring, then one ring, then one ring on your phone, you know, fifteen seconds apart, answer the third one.'

'Okay,' Anna said, and they were gone.

McKinley lived in a bleak cinder-block apartment in Culver City. The parking lot was beginning to break up, with weeds growing through it in patches. Harper parked in a handicapped spot and they took an exterior walkway up; the concrete corners in the stairwell smelled of urine. The walkway had steel railings, and wheelless bike frames were chained to the railings in front of half the doors.

'Students,' Anna said.

'It was three-thirty-seven?' Harper asked.

'Yeah . . .'

The door faced a narrow inner-courtyard, with a half-dozen concrete picnic tables scattered down its length. A half-dozen student-age men sat at one of the tables, smoking, listening to music on a boom box, talking in Spanish.

McKinley's room was dark, the door locked.

'Can't kick it,' Harper said quietly. 'Too many people, too much noise.'

'Let's see if we can find a manager,' Anna said.

The manager had a first-floor apartment facing the parking lot. A dark-eyed woman answered the door, spoke to them in a language that Anna thought might be Farsi, then waved her hands in a gesture that said, 'Wait', went back into the apartment and shouted something. Returning to the door, she made a 'come in' gesture, pointed to the back and said another word. 'I think she means somebody's in the bathroom,' Harper said.

The woman smiled and pointed a finger up: 'Bat-room . . . yes.'

Anna nodded, looked around – and spotted the key board behind the open door. The woman was walking toward the back of the apartment again, and Anna said to Harper, 'Block me out – I'm gonna see if I can grab a key.'

'What?'

'There's a key board behind the door.'

Harper stepped sideways, and Anna pushed the door closed a few inches. Behind it, she could see the room numbers under wire pegs, most with keys hanging from them. Then a toilet flushed in the back, and the woman called something out to them.

Harper said, 'Thank you, thank you,' and Anna, still eclipsed by his body, pushed the door another few inches.

The 337 peg held two keys.

'Can I try for it?' She muttered.

'She's looking right at us,' Harper said, turning to her. 'Hold on . . .'

Harper walked toward the woman, talking. 'We wanted to talk to one of your renters.'

The woman said something else, jabbing her finger at the back. Anna watched, and as Harper got close to her, with the woman looking up at him, he stepped cleanly between them and Anna lifted the key.

Dropped it. Stepped on it. Stood with her hands crossed in front of her as Harper and the woman stood jabbering at each other. Then a man's voice said, 'Hello,' and both Harper and the woman turned toward the back. Anna stooped and picked the key up, and put it in her jacket pocket. She stepped away from the door and the key board.

Harper told the manager that he and Anna were friends of McKinley's from UCLA, but weren't sure they had the right apartment complex.

'Yes, yes, he is here. Apartment three-thirty-seven,' the manager said, bobbing his head. 'He has been much on the television, yes? You see him on the television? He's a hero, yes?'

Anna, smiling. Bobbing her head: 'Yes, a hero . . .'

Outside.

'Get the key?'

'Got it.'

'Hope they don't notice.'

'We'd have to be pretty unlucky – some of the apartments have two or three keys, some don't have any.'

'Hope the key works.'

'Hope we don't find a body.'

'Don't even think it.'

The key worked. They stepped inside, and Anna flipped on the lights. 'Hello? Charles? Chuck?' They were in the living room with a TV set, a love seat, an unmatched easy chair with a missing leg replaced by a paperback novel. An adjoining kitchen dining area was off to the right, and another door went to the left. Anna stepped quickly over to the door: A bedroom. A knot of sheets on a futon, but no blankets. The place smelled of Cool Ranch Doritos.

'Let's get through it quick,' Anna said. 'You look for a Rolodex or address book or anything . . . I'll just see what he's got.'

'Got a phone number,' Harper said a minute later. 'It's on a refrigerator magnet. I think he uses it.'

'Okay. We can get it to Louis . . .'

Anna had instinctively gone to the bedroom. McKinley didn't have a chest of drawers, and had built a group of shelves with bricks and unpainted pine boards. T-shirts, underwear and jeans were stacked on the shelves; a small closet held a couple of jackets, some oxford cloth shirts, two pairs of athletic shoes, one pair of worn-out loafers and dust-bunnies the size of softballs.

The futon was on a frame: she picked up the head end of it, looked underneath. A shoebox. She pulled the shoebox out, opened the lid, and found a half-dozen videotapes, all commercial, all pornographic.

'What?' Harper asked, sticking his head in the door.

'Porno,' Anna said. 'A couple of bondage tapes. That might indicate a fantasy thing with capturing people.'

'Yeah, well, probably a hundred thousand guys have bondage tapes. And not all the tapes are bondage.'

'All right. But something to keep in mind.' She put the box back.

Harper said, 'I hate going through a guy's stuff like this. I'd hate to have somebody do it to me.'

'You have a box of porno tapes?'

'No. But I've got letters and pictures of old friends . . . Nothing that I wouldn't show anyone, but I wouldn't want somebody just trashing through it.'

'Interesting, though,' Anna said. 'Get to see what people are really like.'

'Probably why you're good at your job,' Harper said. He headed back to the kitchen and a moment later, said, 'He's got an answering machine.'

Anna had found nothing at all: 'Run it back.'

The messages were all routine, most of them were from the same woman. The last one, time-stamped at six o'clock that evening, was male: 'Molly said bring some Diet Pepsi, that's all the Lees ever drink.'

'Find a Molly?' Anna asked.

'There's an address book . . .' Harper walked to the kitchen counter, picked up a plastic address book with a bank advertisement on the cover. He found a Molly on the first page, with a phone number. He checked, and it was the same phone number as the one on the refrigerator magnet.

'Let's go look,' Anna said.

'What're we gonna do if we find him?' Harper asked. 'We already lost the first guy we tried to follow . . .'

'Screw it: We don't have any time. Let's brace him. I'll know the voice.'

Louis turned the phone number into a name and address, and the address was a small apartment three blocks from the university.

'Upscale,' Harper said.

The apartment had inner and outer doors, the inner doors locked, but a row of mailboxes showed one 'M. O'Neill' on the second floor. Anna picked up the house phone and buzzed the apartment. A woman answered, and Anna said, 'Is this Molly?'

'Yes?'

'My name is Anna Batory. I'm looking for Charles McKinley, and I was hoping he might he here.'

'Just a minute . . .'

McKinley came down, surprised to see her. Pushed open the inner door so they could go inside. 'How'd you find me?'

His voice was a baritone, without the gravel of the voice on the phone. But the gravel, Anna thought, could be the product of sexual excitement, or aggression.

'We've got a really serious problem,' Anna said.

The kid didn't hear her; instead, he babbled on, his hands jumping around, awkwardly, nerdlike. 'God, you can't believe the TV shows I've been on,' he said. His fair skin was going pink with excitement. 'I had a couple of agents calling me . . .'

'Shut up, Charles,' Anna snapped.

He stopped. 'What?'

'No more bullshit. We know you set up the whole show with Jason and the animal rights people, that the whole thing was a fake.'

McKinley seemed to pull inside himself, and the nerd positively disappeared. 'Shoot,' he said. Then he shrugged and grinned at her, and said, 'Good run while it lasted.'

Harper was off to one side, and Anna glanced at him. He shook his head, a quick one-sided horizontal move, but she read in the shake what she was thinking: *Not this guy.*

'You know Jason's dead?'

'What?' He was startled, and again, it seemed real enough.

'What are you studying?' Anna asked suddenly. 'Are you in theater, or something like that?'

'Yeah,' he said. 'That's how I met Jason. What happened to him? Christ, I was supposed to call him but I couldn't ever get him.'

'Because he was already dead,' Anna said. 'Murdered. The same night as the raid. We thought you might know something about it.'

'What?' He looked quickly at Harper. 'You can't . . . are you the police?'

'The cops'll be coming around,' Harper said. 'But the guy who did the killing is stalking Anna, here. We're trying to get a name: and your name came up.'

'My name? How'd my name come up?'

'Because whoever is stalking Anna probably picked her

out that night – and the only thing she did that night was the raid, and a . . . suicide.'

'And I didn't talk to anyone at the suicide,' Anna said.

'Well, I'm not doing it – I mean, I've been in New York.'

'New York?'

'Yeah. I was on the "Today" show. I didn't get back until this morning. That's what we're doing tonight, we're celebrating.'

'Celebrating what?'

'Well, you know . . .' he gestured, meaning, *I'm a hero*. 'They've had all these animal rights people on, and all these other weirdos, and so now they decided to get me on. I've been on like six shows . . . He was murdered? How was he murdered . . . ?'

'Listen, your friend Molly . . . Can you buzz her, ask her to come down? How many people are up there?'

'Six. No, seven.'

'Ask them to come down.'

McKinley went to the mailbox, pushed the call button, and Molly answered.

'Uh, Molly, could you and the guys come down here? Something's come up. Yeah, we'll tell you when you get down. Right now . . .'

Anna was thinking furiously: 'How'd you set us up? Whose idea was it?'

McKinley shrugged: 'Jason's, I guess. I'd seen him around, and mentioned I'd gotten a job feeding the animals up there at night. And he already knew Steve Judge with the animal rights group. I mentioned feeding the animals, and like, the next day, he was back with this idea.'

'So it was you and Steve and Jason,' Anna said.

'And Sarah.'

'Sarah?'

'Yeah. You know, the Bee. She was the brains of the group; Steve was basically the jock who carried shit around for them.'

McKinley had a few more details about the raid: 'If you think somebody was stalking you, you oughta look at that guard, everybody calls him Speedy. He's a goofy sucker.'

'The guard at the medical center?'

'Yeah, the one with the crew cut. He's some kind of Nazi.'

Anna shook her head: 'Didn't even see him.'

A stairway door popped open, and a woman with deep blue hair stepped into the lobby; six more people, three women, three men, all in their early twenties, trailed behind.

'What's going on?' the blue-haired woman asked.

'Charles can tell you,' Anna said. 'We have a very serious situation: a woman's been kidnapped, and all we need to know is if Charles has been here for a while. Since eight o'clock, say.'

They all looked from Charles to Anna, then back to Charles, and then all simultaneously nodded.

'Since seven,' blue-hair said. 'Since ten after seven, I remember, I was putting the roast in . . .'

'Let's go,' Anna said to Harper.

Outside, Anna said, 'We're running out of time. I don't know why he hasn't called back. He'll be calling. Let's find the Bee. Maybe she can tell us . . .'

She was frantic: wanted to scream, she wanted to run somewhere, do something.

'Anna, this is just like when I was chasing shadows on Jacob. We're finding people, but not the guy. We've got to stop running long enough to *think*. And when I think about it, I think Wyatt might be right.'

'He's in my neighborhood?'

'Something like that; that's a possibility. He keeps coming to your house, fuckin' with you.'

'Fucking with my house,' Anna said. She looked at her watch: He'd had Pam for at least a couple of hours now.

'The other thing is . . .'

'Clark.'

'Yeah, that's the other thing,' he said.

Chapter 28

Clark's apartment was in Westwood, six blocks from the music building. Halfway there, Anna said, urgently, 'We've got no time for this, no time.'

'We should have made time,' Harper said. They were halfway to Clark's apartment complex. 'And what else can we do? I mean, we could still call Wyatt, and have the cops do it.'

'No.'

Anna fell back in her seat, looked out the window: If the cops got close to Clark, they'd tear him apart. Because Clark was odd – he was a composer of classical music, probably the least likely job in America. And he actually made money at it. And he had attitudes that had driven even his friends crazy: arrogant, conceited, charming, angry.

Not violent. Not that she'd ever seen. When he got angry, he got sullen, a cool, withdrawing anger, not a hot, plate-throwing tantrum. He'd never tear her house up.

On the other hand, her house wasn't really torn up. Just the broken window. And the guy had to break a window, if he wanted to get in the house. The destruction wasn't wanton . . .

Except for the pot. What had he done with that pot?

Anna shook her head, pushed her glasses back up her nose: she was losing it. She was five minutes from a confrontation she dreaded as much as anything she could think of, and she was worried about a flowerpot.

'Jake.' She grabbed his arm. 'Jake: we gotta go back to my place. Now.'

Exasperated. 'Anna, we're two minutes away . . .'

'Jake, forget it, we gotta go back.'

'Why?'

'Something happened to my flowerpot.'

The pot had been there earlier in the day. She didn't remember seeing it, but she would have missed it. It was simply part of the landscape.

Harper trailed Anna through the house, past the crime-scene cops. Wyatt was on the telephone, said something, then put a hand over the receiver: 'Find him?'

'Yeah. It's not him,' Anna said. 'Anything here?'

Wyatt shook his head and returned to the phone.

At the back door, Anna flipped on the porch light, and went out to look at the spot where the pot had been. 'It's too big to carry anyplace,' she said. 'It probably weighs fifty pounds.'

'I can't see anything,' Harper said, scuffing around in the grass.

'I'll get a flashlight,' Anna said. She went inside, got a flashlight out of a kitchen drawer and went back out.

The depression where the pot had stood was a clear ring of raw dirt in the grass going down to the canal. And two feet toward the canal, a lump of dirt that had probably been inside the pot.

Anna pointed the light over the sea wall, into the murky canal water. The stuff looked like it might have come out of a radiator, a funny green, with gray depths to it. But down there in the water, was . . . something. Something that bobbed . . . up and down, up and down. Something with a round end. A head?

She stepped back, shivered, turned and went up on the porch: 'Hey, you guys,' she yelled. 'You better come out here.'

She thought of Pam in the water, anchored by the pot; swallowed. Please don't let it be. Please.

One of the crime-scene cops came to the door. 'What?'

Anna pointed the light into the water. 'There's something that shouldn't be here . . . we can't tell what it is.'

The cop walked out on the porch, followed by a second one, and then Wyatt, jostling past them.

Anna said, 'Somebody moved a big flowerpot, and maybe put it over the side. I . . .'

Wyatt looked into the water: 'Oh, Christ,' he said, softly.

The first cop looked down into the water, then dropped face down onto the seawall, reached into the water. Couldn't quite touch whatever it is.

'I'll have to get in,' he said. 'I'll wreck my suit.'

'Put in for it,' Wyatt said.

'Fuck it.' The cop peeled off his jacket, shirt and pants, put his shoes back on, and slipped over the side in his underwear. 'Cold,' he said.

Then he reached down into the murk, and just as quickly pulled his hand back.

'What is it?' Anna said. She could barely breathe.

'Not a body,' he said. 'I don't know.'

Wyatt exhaled, glanced at Anna. Below, the cop reached carefully through the water again, then said, 'Plastic,' and lifted.

The thing came out of the water, and Anna said, 'Kayak. We were looking at the end of a kayak.'

Harper: 'A goddamned kayak. That's how he got in and out.'

Wyatt: 'Shit. He's not from here.'

'But somebody must have seen him putting it in, up by . . .'

And Anna looked at Harper and said, 'Steve Judge.'

'What?'

She grabbed him by the shirt, both hands, her face six inches from his: 'Remember, out at the ranch? The woman, what's her name? Daly? She said Steve Judge was up in Oregon running rivers.'

'But he was in Oregon,' Harper said.

'What's this?' Wyatt asked.

Anna took a minute to explain, and Wyatt said, 'Gotta check it.'

'He lives in Pasadena,' Anna said. 'We've got an address.'

She found an address in her book, pulled the page and handed it to Wyatt.

'Long shot,' Wyatt muttered, as he hurried back into the house.

Another car arrived out front, and as they moved back inside, Anna called information, got the number for the Full Heart Ranch, dialed it. No answer. Dialed again. Still nothing.

'If Steve's the guy, we oughta go out to the ranch,' Anna told Harper.

'Let the cops do it,' Harper said. 'And it's really a long shot.'

'What, send a deputy who doesn't know what's going on? He'd get lost out there, at night. The cops can surround his house in Pasadena, no problem, but if Steve's the guy, and he's up at the ranch, he'd see them coming a million miles away,' Anna said. 'We know the road. We can go out there and park by the gate and walk in.'

'Anna, that's crazy.'

'Well, what're we gonna do?' she shouted at him. 'He's got Pam. He's gonna kill her. We can't just hang around here with two hundred cops. He's not gonna be here, whoever he is.'

Harper looked at her, and the cops working in the house, and all the lights and cars, and said, 'I'll need a gun. We can stop at my place. It's on the way.'

They took the San Diego over the hill, moving fast. Anna said, 'The name of the ranch in Oregon. Was it Cut River Canyon?'

'Don't remember. That sounds good.'

Anna punched in the information number for Oregon, got an operator: 'I don't show a Cut River Canyon, but I show a Cut Canyon . . .'

'That's it.' Anna muttered the number to herself as she redialed. The phone rang eight times, Anna muttering, 'C'mon, c'mon,' and on the ninth ring, was answered by an irritated woman, who snapped: 'Hello?'

'Yes. My name is Anna Batory, from Los Angeles. I talked to someone at the Cut Canyon Ranch who connected me to a man named Steven Judge. Are you the woman who connected me?'

'Yes. Do you know what time it is? Steven isn't here ...'

Anna interrupted: 'Ma'am, somebody in Los Angeles has murdered at least three people in the last week and now has kidnapped a woman. And this is somehow tied to me. The police say he is stalking me. Mr Judge's name has come up a couple of times in the course of the investigation, but if he was really up at Cut Canyon when I called, then he can't have anything to do with it.'

There was a long hesitation, and then the woman asked, 'Are you with the police?'

'I can have the office in charge of the L.A. County serial-murder task force call you in five minutes, if you have something to say,' Anna said.

Another pause. 'And this isn't a joke. We didn't receive anything like this information . . . before.'

'You mean from Mr Judge?'

'Yes, from Steve. The stalking, I mean, he suggested it might be somewhat the other way around, that's why we . . .'

'Ma'am, I'm going to have Lieutenant Wyatt from the Santa Monica police department – he's the head of the task force for this series of crimes – I'm going to have him call you in the next five minutes. Please tell him everything you know.'

'How do I know this isn't some kind of, of, arrangement? That he's a policeman?'

'If you would like, you could call the Santa Monica Police Department on your own. I'll give you the area code, you can get the number from information – and they will transfer you to Lieutenant Wyatt.'

'Oh, God. Okay, I'll call Santa Monica.'

'Wait five minutes,' Anna said. 'I've got to tell Lieutenant Wyatt that you'll be calling.'

Anna gave the woman the area code for Santa Monica, rang off, said to Harper, 'I think he's the one, all right, Steve Judge,' and punched in the Santa Monica police department number. A woman answered, and Anna told her that she needed to speak to Wyatt immediately, and spent a minute filling the woman in. She rang off again and Harper said, 'I've got a bad feeling about this.'

She said, 'Jake, I know you do. But he's probably in Pasadena, anyway. This is just something that we can cover better than the cops could. If the cops even decide to go up to the ranch, it'll take them three or four hours to get a SWAT team over there . . . trying to talk to Ventura, trying to figure out where it is and how to get there. They'll have to get maps and all that stuff . . . There's no way Pam'll get out alive: he's nuts, he's itching to kill her. There's no way they'll even find him, until it's too late. And if he gets out, where's the evidence that he was even there?'

'There'd be some prints in your car, his behavior . . .'

'But that won't get Pam out.'

The phone rang in her lap and she picked it up, ready to switch it on, already hearing Wyatt's voice, when Harper swatted it out of her hand. 'No, no,' he said urgently. 'What if it's him?'

But there was no second ring. Then five seconds later, it rang again. She didn't wait for the third time, but said, 'Hello?'

Wyatt said, 'You were supposed to wait for the third ring.'

'No time,' Anna said.

'What's happening? Where are you?'

'We're running up to Ventura to check on something . . . just in case,' Anna said. 'Listen, a woman's going to call you from a place called Cut Canyon Ranch, up in Oregon.'

She explained the circumstances, and Wyatt said, 'You think they did something weird with the call?'

'It's not weird, if you're wired right,' Anna said. 'You just push a button. No big deal. But if they were faking it, then there's a lot better chance that he's the guy.'

'All right, I'll talk to her.'

'Are you heading for Pasadena?'

'We're on the way, but we're still getting people together.'

'Good luck. And gimme your number.'

Wyatt dictated a number; Anna rang off and said to Harper, 'Still getting people together. Damn, damn, damn, there's no time for that.'

Anna sat in the car while Harper ran inside his house. He was back a minute later, carrying a short rifle, fumbling with a box of shells. 'Gimme,' Anna said. 'You drive, I'll load.'

'You know how?'

'I can figure it out.'

'Just feed them in the bottom, there's a release just in front of the trigger guard.'

'Think it's enough gun?' Anna asked, looking at the magazine mechanism.

'It's an old Ruger forty-four,' Harper said. 'It'll do the job.'

They slewed out the end of his driveway, Jake driving with both hands as Anna fed the short fat shells into the rifle. The rifle was short, with a smooth walnut stock: comfortable. And then the phone rang. Once, twice, three times: not Wyatt.

Anna passed it to Jake, who listened, said, 'She's not here . . . Yeah, but she just left it in the car. Who is this? Well, probably about a half hour, I'm on my way to pick her up. Okay. Message from Pam. Do you have a number? Okay. Yeah, half an hour, you know, give or take.'

He rang off, looked at Anna and nodded: 'Message from Pam.'

'That was him.'

'Yeah. No number.'

'Shoot.'

'Call Wyatt, tell him, see if they got a record of it.'

Anna nodded, but asked, 'How long to the ranch, do you think?'

He glanced at the car clock, then said, 'Half an hour, maybe.'

'Got to be a few minutes faster than that,' Anna said.

He nodded, and Anna took the phone to call Wyatt. But as she was about to punch in the number, it rang again. 'Give it to me,' Harper said. Anna handed it to him.

'Hello? Hello?' He shook his head, clicked off, handed it back. 'Check up call,' he said. 'He was calling to see if the phone was busy. To see if we turned right around to call somebody.'

'No dummy,' Anna said.

'Crazy as a loon, but not stupid,' Harper said.

'Drive faster,' Anna said. She sat with the gun upright, the butt of the little gun resting on the seat between her thighs, looking out the window.

'Most likely a wild-goose chase,' Harper said.

'Most likely,' she said.

She waited another minute, then tapped Wyatt's phone number in. 'Yeah?'

'We just got a call from the guy, within the last minute or so, if you're doing a trace.'

'Nothing's working, but I'll check,' he said. 'The woman from Oregon called: you were set up. He was somewhere down here when you called for him.'

'All right. We're building a picture, and he fits,' Anna said.

'Better'n that. I just talked . . . Jesus watch out . . .' Wyatt broke away, speaking to somebody else. 'Just missed a goddamn truck by about an inch,' he said, talking to Anna again. 'Listen, a woman named Daly called about three minutes after the Oregon woman, wanted to know what was going on. She said you screwed them on that animal rights protest, and you might be out to frame Judge for some reason.'

'Bullshit.'

'Yeah, I know. Anyway, I asked her when she'd last seen him, and she said she saw him this morning. And I asked if he showed any signs of injury from a fight.'

'His cheek,' Anna said, remembering the fight in the parking lot.

'Exactly,' Wyatt said. 'She said there was something wrong with his cheek and she looked at it and he got mad – she said there was a bruise covered with makeup. He told her he'd been bitten by a cat that he supposedly was trying to pick up.'

'Goddamn, he's the guy,' Anna said.

'He looks good: and we're getting some people together up in Ventura, heading out to that ranch. We'll be ready in a couple of hours.'

'Right,' Anna said. She pulled her face back from the phone, and started rubbing her hand across the mouthpiece. 'We're on the way there, now. If you don't get something from Pasadena . . .'

'Anna, you're breaking up.'

'Can't hear you,' Anna said, blocking most of what she said with her fingers. 'Can't . . .'

She punched the 'end' button: she would not be told at this point to wait for a few hours.

'What?' Harper asked.

'He's the guy,' Anna said.

'But he might not be at the ranch.'

'Oh, he's there,' Anna said. 'He's there, all right. I can smell him.'

She bared her teeth, and Harper stared at her for a second, then jerked his eyes back to the dark road. Anna felt like she did on those nights when she and the crew were really operating, when everything was turning in their favor: like the night of the raid, and Jacob's leap. She was on, and she could feel the attraction of the ranch.

The ranch was pulling her in.

Chapter 29

The night was so deep that it seemed like a piece of black velvet had been folded over the car; the only relief came from the dark-walled tunnel carved out by the BMW's high beams.

Anna punched Louis' number into the phone, at the same time saying, 'I'd like to talk to Daly. I wonder if she knows where Judge is?'

'She would have told Wyatt,' Harper said.

Louis' number got no response at all: now they *were* out of range.

'I thought those fuckin' towers were everywhere. They're building one on the hill over my house,' Harper said.

'Not everywhere,' Anna said. Harper slowed at a gravel intersection, and they peered up at a road sign. 'Right,' Anna said. 'Two miles.'

Harper didn't hesitate at the ranch gate. He passed it by, still climbing the gravel road, over a rise, down the side of a canyon, up the rise on the other side, around a turn.

He pulled over against the mountainside, killed the engine. 'Five tenths of a mile,' he said. 'Five- or six-minute jog.'

'Let's go,' Anna said, popping her door.

'There's a flash in the glove box,' he said. His voice was tight, edgy. 'Better get it. Give me the rifle.'

Anna handed him the Ruger and found the flash, a black aluminium cylinder about the length and diameter of a fat man's cigar.

On the road, Anna found she could cup her fist around the flash, and project a needle-thin beam of light, enough to keep them on the gravel. As their eyes adjusted, moonlight began to show. Anna turned, looking for the moon, and finally, below a break in the hillside, found it lurking in the trees above them, a quarter-crescent.

'There'll be more light up on top,' she whispered, as they jogged.

Harper grunted, then put up a hand, touching her chest. 'Coming up,' he said. Anna slowed, felt the slope of the road easing beneath her feet. The drive had started up from a short flat stretch; they should be close.

'There,' she said. The galvanized gate was a gray shadow in the darker brush around it. 'Let me check it.'

She shined the needle of light on the post side of the gate, sliding down the metal joint between the hinges. Nothing.

'All right?' Harper asked.

'Just a minute.' She checked the opening side, and found the contact: 'No, it's alarmed,' she said. Harper came up, squatted, looked at the light. Anna aimed it at the patch of ceramic insulator set in the post. 'We've got one like it on the farm,' she whispered. 'There's a magnet in the gate and a needle in the post. When you move the gate, the needle goes with the magnet and hits a contact, and that sets off the buzzer inside.'

'Can't even climb over?'

'Nope. That'll push the gate down. Let's look at the fence.'

The barbed-wire fence showed a single strand of electric wire running along the top. 'Bottom should be okay,' Anna said. 'Let's find a low spot, where we can squeeze under.'

They found a spot fifty feet down the road, the desert brush ripping at their jackets as they slid under the wire. Anna stood, pulling pieces of dead brush from her hair.

'You okay?' Harper whispered.

'Yeah. Let's go.'

They jogged the first couple of hundred feet up the hill, but Harper was enough out of shape that he caught her arm and told her to slow down. Impatiently, she walked ahead of him, urging him along.

The hill seemed to go on forever, gently sinuous, always climbing. After ten minutes, they topped the first rise and saw the orange glow of a yard light. Harper caught her arm and said, 'Stop for a minute. We've got to talk.'

They squatted beside the road, looking slightly down at the ranch yard. The house was ahead and to the right, with an open yard further to the right. A light showed in what they knew was the office window, along with the blue glow of a computer monitor or television. Another light showed behind that, but from the same window, adding a slightly warmer glow. There was no movement in the window with the light: and the light had the stillness of an empty room.

To the far left of the house, they could just see the hulk of the barn; between the barn and the house, two buildings – a garage, Anna thought, and what must once have been a machine shed.

A hundred yards behind the house were two long gray-white structures, almost too far out to recognize; but Anna thought that they must once have been chicken coops. Directly behind the house, a hundred feet back, the beginning of the corral complex.

As Anna squatted by the road, picking out the main features of the ranch, she could smell the broken brush beside the road, and the dirt beneath their feet: like Wisconsin on a dry summer's night, but with the special peppery pungency of the desert.

'Don't see your car,' Harper said. 'Maybe he ditched it in town. Wherever he unloaded the kayak.'

'But then he'd have to transfer Pam.'

'Yeah . . . unless he killed her at your place, and left her in the car.'

Harper said it thoughtlessly, but the image of Pam curled in the trunk of the Toyota struck Anna with a vivid force, and she groaned, a soft exhalation.

'What?'

'God, if she's dead . . .'

'Let's cross behind the barn, check the out-buildings,' Harper whispered. 'That'll give us cover coming up to the house.'

'All right.'

They slid to the left, staying close to the underbrush as they moved into the opening around the house. Once away from the driveway, the land opened up into sparse pasture, dotted with clumps of brush. Anna used little squirts of light to guide them past the house to the barn, around the barn to the back, and then, crouching, with Harper's rifle hovering over her head, into the barn itself.

The barn was empty, but redolent with the odor of horse manure and hay. They checked the ground floor, found a range of horse-keeping equipment and stacks of feed supplement on a line of pallets.

'All right,' Harper said. 'Machine shed.'

They went out the back of the barn again, around the side, crept across a short open space to the machine shed, knelt by a window, listening. After a minute, Anna put her head up, peeked through the window. Could see nothing at all. Squeezed the flash, caught a quick glimpse of red.

'I think it's there, the car,' she breathed in Harper's ear. 'Something red in there.'

'Jesus . . .'

They slid to the front corner of the shed. Like the garage, the shed was old, probably pre-World War II, and the sliding doors hung from rusty overhead tracks. Harper reached around the corner and gave one of the doors a shove, and it moved a few inches. He pushed again, and got another foot.

'We can get in. Move slow, stay low,' he said. He went around the corner, and Anna followed, watching the window in the house. When she was inside the garage, Harper slowly pushed the garage door back in place.

Anna turned, wrapped her fist around the head of the flashlight, and turned it on: the beam caught the fender of her Toyota, played down the side. 'That's it,' she said. 'That's mine.' She played the beam across the back, onto the plates: 'Yeah, that's mine,' she said.

'Kill the light.'

Anna killed the light and they both moved toward the

car. Harper touched a window, opened the passenger door, slowly, carefully, felt in front and in the back. Nothing.

'Can you pop the trunk?'

'Yeah. We'll have to go around.'

Anna scuttled around the car, felt up the door to the window. The window was down three or four inches, enough to get her arm through the gap. She stretched into the car, trying to reach the dome light.

'What're you doing?' Harper whispered.

'If you open this door an inch, the light comes on,' Anna said. 'I'm trying to shut it off.'

She fumbled with the switch, said, 'I think that's it,' and tried the door. No light. The trunk-opener lever was just in front of the seat, and she pulled it, heard the trunk pop, and crawled behind the car. Harper was pushing the trunk lid up, and Anna shone the flash into it.

The trunk was empty, but Harper ran his fingers the width of it once, twice, then stopped, pressed, and lifted his fingers toward Anna. They were black in the light. He pulled them back, sniffed, and he said, 'Blood. Not much. So she probably was alive when he took her out of here.'

'How do you know?'

'Why take her out if she's dead?'

Anna nodded, and crawled toward a window facing the house. 'So he's here. Now what?'

'I was afraid . . . What's that?'

Anna looked to the right, saw the splash of light off the brush beside the house.

'Car coming up the hill,' she said. Anna heard the slide of the rifle as Harper jacked a shell into the chamber. She fumbled the pistol from her pocket as the lights grew brighter on the trees.

Ten seconds later, a pickup pulled into the yard, and a woman hopped out and stormed toward the porch. They could see her face when she first opened the truck door, and her figure as she hurried under the yard light to the porch.

'That's Daly,' Harper said.

'Jeez, do you think she knows?' Anna asked.

'She looks mad about something.' The woman fumbled at the door, unlocking it, then pushed inside and flicked on a light. She slammed the door behind her, but before she did, they heard her shout, 'Steve?'

'Wonder what happened?' Harper asked.

'I don't know, but if he's still in the house, and we want to move up, this is the time. If he's in there, it sounds like he'll have his hands full,' Anna said.

They crawled back out through the garage door, circled back around the barn, into the darkness of the brush, and came up behind the house, near the corrals. An animal made a spitting sound as they passed: 'What the hell was that?' Harper whispered.

'I don't know; I hope it doesn't bite.'

They stopped at the side of the corral, and looked across the intervening fifty feet at the house.

'Gonna have to decide something,' Harper said.

'Whatever's in the corral. Probably the llama. I don't think they're dangerous,' Anna said. 'I'm gonna roll through there and work my way up to the gate. 'If I don't see anything, I'm gonna make a run across the yard – you get ready with the rifle.'

'Maybe I oughta make the run.'

'No. You've got the rifle, I've just got this thing,' Anna said, holding up the pistol. 'At fifty feet I might not be able to hit the house.'

As she said it, she slipped under the lowest rail of the corral. Whatever was in the corral stayed at the back. She could here it stomping nervously, maybe the Llama, maybe a pony, as she moved to the gate.

Taking a breath, she glanced back at the spot where she'd left Jake, and stuck one leg through the gate.

BAAAAAZZZZZZZZ . . .

The buzzer sounded like the end of the world, as loud as a jet plane, fifteen feet overhead.

In a half-second, she knew exactly what had happened: the gate was alarmed, just like the gate at the bottom of the hill. A light beam or movement sensor was probably buried in the gatepost, out beyond the gate itself, so an animal inside the corral couldn't set it off – but she'd put her leg right through it.

She'd been so occupied with the thought of closing on the house that she hadn't thought to look. And she didn't stop to think when the buzzer went. Instead, she scrambled sideways, across the corral, to the far corner, holding tight to the pistol.

The buzzing went on for three or four seconds, and then, just as abruptly, stopped. For another twenty seconds, nothing moved inside the house, and Anna, watching the back door, began to relax.

'Anna?' Jake's stage whisper cut through the dead silence. She turned her head to answer when the back door banged open, and what looked like a drunk staggered onto the back porch, twisting, turning in the dim light.

'Anna?' The voice. She knew it this time. 'Anna, I know you're out there.'

Anna, straining toward the turning figure, finally made it out; not one person, but two. A man with his arm around a woman's neck, the woman struggling against him; and when her struggles became too violent, he would lever her off the ground until she stopped.

'Anna . . .' Judge was screaming her name. Anna said nothing. Maybe he'd decide that an animal had set off the alarm. Maybe he'd come out where they could get at him: but at the moment, the woman's body blocked any possibility of a shot.

'Are you out there? I know you're out there.' The struggle on the porch started again, and Anna lifted the pistol and aimed it, took it down again: no way.

'Anna . . .' He was bawling into the night. Then: 'You think I'm fucking around? Think again, huh? Think again, Anna.'

He moved back toward the door, reached inside, and clicked on a yellow porch light.

'I know you're out there. You like to make movies? Make a movie of this.'

He suddenly kicked the struggling woman's legs from beneath her and she went down. At the same moment, he let go of his grip on her neck. She landed on one thigh and her hand, twisted, head down: the man pointed his hand at her head and there was a sudden crack, and an arrow of flame, and the woman flattened.

Shot in the head.

Anna, not thinking, only reacting, thrust her pistol at the door and fired, and a half-second later Jake opened up: but the man was already back through the door. Anna, though, was rolling under the bottom bar of the corral, on her feet, running at the porch, firing a second time at the dark rectangle of the open door. In the back of her head she could hear Jake screaming, 'Anna! Anna! No, Anna!'

But at the same instant, she was through the door. To her left, the back of the man, turning to look at her just as he went through an internal doorway.

Steve Judge, but strangely different than the animal rights raider she remembered: he seemed older, thinner, harsher, wilder, with a long black pistol in one hand . . . But he was reeling away from the gunfire, and in the half-second he was visible to Anna, she managed to get the gun down and fire another shot, wildly, but in his direction. He screamed, then a second later, fired back, the bullet burying itself in the wall to Anna's left.

Belatedly, she went down, now holding the pistol out in front of her. And from behind, Harper was suddenly there with the rifle. He knelt beside her, and she saw that he was feeding fresh shells into the magazine.

'He's through there,' Anna said, in a harsh whisper. 'He's running. Let's take him.'

'For Christ's sake, rush him in a dark house? He'd take both of us.'

'We gotta . . .'

'No. What we gotta do, is look at the woman on the porch.'

Anna turned her head: 'Jeez – I thought she was dead. He shot her in the head.'

'I didn't have time to look, but lots of times, people don't die.'

'Keep the gun on the door,' Anna said. 'I'll go look.'

'Is he still inside?'

'I didn't hear the front door go. I think so.'

Harper braced the rifle against the wall as Anna slithered toward the door. Just before she got to the doorstep, Judge screamed from the front: 'Anna. I'm gonna cut your friend's belly open. You wanna hear it?'

Anna stopped, glanced at Harper.

Harper shrugged, got halfway to his feet and whispered, 'Yell something at him. A threat, anything.'

Anna screamed, 'You motherfucker, if you hurt Pam, I'll cut your balls off. I promise, I'll cut your balls.'

As she screamed, Harper pushed to his feet, did a quick tiptoe across the door, hesitated just an instant at the far door where Anna had last seen Judge. He looked back, then burst through the door, out of sight: Anna was four steps behind him, but the dark room ahead was suddenly lit by a half dozen muzzle blasts, the crashing of furniture, Harper screaming, another shot, and the banging of the front door.

Then Anna was through into the dark chaos of the office, pushing the gun in front of her, moving . . . and stumbling over a body.

'Christ . . .' Harper.

'You hurt?'

'Yeah, I'm shot in the hip,' he groaned. 'Not bad, but it hurts like a sonofabitch.'

'Where is he? Outside?'

'Yeah, I heard the door. He's gone.'

'How about Pam?'

'I don't know. I don't know if he had her.'

'I believed him.'

'Well, if he had her, he didn't take her with him, because he went out of here in a hurry. Christ, we were six feet apart, I just couldn't get the gun around.'

There was light coming into the room from the back, from the room they'd just rushed through. Anna said, 'Move around into the light, stay behind the desk, I gotta look and see how bad it is.'

And at that moment, someone groaned from the other side of the room. The groan was hurt enough, harsh enough, that the hair stood up on Anna's.

Harper whispered, 'Pam.'

Anna groped in her pocket, and found the flashlight had stayed with her through the wild scramble across the yard and into the house. She wrapped her fist around it, and shot the needle of light across the room. She passed over Glass's body the first time, then wondered about the shadow in the corner, and came back to it.

Yes. A body, not a shadow. Anna left Harper, creeping across the office carpet, got to Glass, rolled her. Couldn't see; put her head close to the other woman's ear and said, 'Pam – this is Anna. How bad are you?'

Glass muttered something unintelligible. Anna looked around, trying to think what to do. Had to get her to some light. Finally, afraid that she might be hurting her worse, she tugged and pulled Glass across the carpet. Glass remained inert, sometimes mumbling to herself.

'How bad?' Harper whispered.

'I don't know. We need light.'

'Pull that desk around . . .'

Anna managed to move one of the desks enough to provide cover from the only window that Judge could see through: and turned on a light.

Pam Glass had been terribly beaten: her nose was broken, her teeth were broken, one cheekbone was wrong, her lips were twice as big as they should be, and the color of fresh liver.

'Aw, Jesus,' Anna said. But she could do nothing about it. 'Let me look at your hip,' she said to Harper. Harper rolled, showed her a bullet hole passing through his jeans in his thigh just below his butt. There was no exit wound.

'Not much blood,' she whispered.

'Yeah, I don't think it's too bad, but Jesus, my leg just doesn't want to work,' he said.

'I'm gonna go look at Daly. Can you cover me?' And for just a tiny sliver of a second she thought how odd it was to be using the language of television cop shows: cover me. What did she know about cover? 'I'll go out on the porch.'

'Yeah. Turn off the light, first. And we gotta try the phones.'

'Daly first.'

Anna hit the light, waited for a second, then went through the door on her stomach while Harper sat in the door, scanning the dark, ready to fire at any sign of a muzzle blast.

But the woman was dead: Anna knew it the moment that she touched her. She was already going cold, and had the peculiar stillness of those who'd gone on. But she grabbed the woman's shirt, and pulled her back through the door.

'Alive?' Harper whispered, as they pulled back.

'No. I don't think so.'

Anna slumped against a wall, and Harper touched the woman. 'No, she's gone.'

'Let's get back to Pam.'

'Let's get the phone . . .'

Glass's breath was short, harsh, irregular. As Anna knelt over her, she blew a blood bubble, which burst on her blood-crusted lips. Anna said, 'She's in trouble, Jake. We've got to get her to a hospital.'

Harper was already crawling across the office. He groped on top of the desk, found a phone, pulled it down, listened, said 'Shit.'

'What?'

'Dead. He must've pulled wires somewhere. Probably outside the house.'

'We've got to get her out of here,' Anna said urgently. 'We can't wait. Jake – I think she's dying.'

Chapter 30

They sat for a moment, huddled over Glass, watching her breathe. Thinking. Anna asked, finally, 'Can you walk?'

'I don't know.' Harper looked around, found a blind spot where he couldn't be seen, pushed himself up on the wall, tested the leg and nearly collapsed.

'Maybe – but not very far. I could hop pretty fast.'

'Forget it,' Anna said. Then: 'Here's what we do. We've got to get him talking to us. Anything. Just get him talking. Then we'll know about where he is, which side of the house. Then I'll sneak out the other side, with your car keys. Once I'm away from the house, in the dark, he'll never find me. And he doesn't know where your car is. Once I'm in the car, I'll come crashing up here – I'll get as close to the back porch as I can without wrecking it. That's five feet you'll have to cross. Can you carry Pam that far?'

'Anna . . .' He was staring at her, unhappy. 'Anna, I can carry her, but, Jesus, that's crazy.'

'Can you think of anything else?'

He looked down at the linoleum, thinking. A few seconds later he said, 'If we can figure out where the phone goes out, and where he is, if they're different, I might be able to patch the wires.'

'Do you know anything about telephones?'

'No, but if he's just cut the wires . . .'

'I don't know if you can just put them back together,' Anna said. 'Even if we find out where he is, and you can get out, he could move. If you're just lying out there on the ground, messing with wires . . . you'd be dead. If I run, it doesn't matter what he does once I'm out of here: he can't catch me.'

'Christ.' He ran his hand through his hair, moved, groaned.

'And if we mess with the wires, and the phones still don't work, we'll have lost the time – and we don't have any time.' She touched Pam, looking across her at Harper.

Harper broke his eyes away for a moment, then shook his head, grinned, put his hand on top of her head and mussed her hair. 'Don't worry about wrecking the car,' he said. 'Fuck the car. Put it right on the porch.'

'Okay.'

'Let me get my back against the wall with Pam. If he tries to come in, I'll light the motherfucker up.'

Anna nodded, grinned back at him, squeezed his good leg: 'It's the only way. Let's see if we can get him talking.'

Anna started, crawling to a window on the back of the house, knocking it out with a chair. The shattering of the glass should attract his attention, if he was still out there. She sat on her heels like a dog baying at the moon, and shouted: 'Steve. What do you want? What do you want?'

Nothing.

Jake had moved to the hallway between the back room and the office. He called softly, 'Nothing here.'

'Steve,' Anna shouted. 'Where are you? What do you want? Are you still there?'

The voice, not far away: 'I'm still here.'

And a second later, a shot: not the pistol any more, a loud *crack*, and plaster flew from the wall overhead.

'Shit,' Harper yelped. 'He's got a rifle. A big one.'

'Always gotta be killing something around here, putting them out of their misery,' the voice shouted.

He was over toward the garage, or maybe the barn, Anna thought.

'What do you want?'

'I want you dead,' the voice answered. 'But I want to mess with you for a while.'

Another shot, this time into the office.

Anna crawled past Harper, who said, 'We've gotta get better protection. Sooner of later, he'll think about shooting lower, onto the floor, and then we're in trouble. Those goddamn slugs are going halfway through the house. Maybe all the way.'

Anna said, 'Okay,' and crawled into the office. The desks were wooden. Not much help. There was another door off to the left, and she went that way.

'What do you think now, about messing with my head? What do you think now?' Judge screamed, still from the direction of the garage.

'We weren't messing with you,' Harper shouted back. 'How were we messing with you?'

'You're always messing with me, all of you,' Judge screamed back.

Anna crawled through the door and found herself in the bathroom – and in the corner was a cast-iron bathtub, just what you might hope for in an old ranch house. She crawled back through the office.

'Jake – there's a big old iron tub in the bathroom.'

'That'd help,' Harper said. 'Let's see if we can move her.'

Judge was still screaming at them: 'All the time, all my life, you fuckers. Let's see what you think about it now I've got the big gun.'

'What the hell is he talking about?' Harper panted. He trailed his leg behind him as they moved Glass across the office floor and into the bathroom, wincing every time he had to pull his leg forward.

'I don't know,' Anna said. 'He's nuts.'

'Let me do this,' Harper said. He was on one knee beside Glass, and picked her up, gently, and lifted her over the side of the tub. She opened one eye and said, 'Car?'

'She's awake,' Harper grunted.

'We're trying to get you out of here,' Anna said.

She crawled to the door and shouted at Judge: 'The cops are coming. If you get out of here now, maybe you've got a chance.'

'If the cops were coming, they would have been here,' Judge screamed back. 'If I take you down, I walk. I'll drag you out in the desert somewhere, with a shovel.'

Anna turned away, said to Harper, 'I'm going, out the side of the back room,' and Harper said, 'Goddamn, Anna . . .'

Anna: 'Yell something at him.'

Harper pushed himself up from behind the bathtub and as Anna crawled down the hall to the back room, shouted, 'Shut the fuck up, you fuckin' moron.'

Crack. A slug pounded through the side wall of the back room, but much lower this time. Anna was sprayed with splinters of lath and plaster. The bullet missed by three feet.

'Anna?'

'Yeah, I'm okay.'

The windows on the side of the back room were double-hung, with slide latches. She turned the latch on the first one, struggled to lift the window, got it up. There was a screen on the outside, with hooks inside. She unhooked it, and pushed it open.

Harper was shouting: 'The women are both still alive in here. If you stop now, you'll just go to treatment.'

Crack.

Something wooden exploded in the office. 'Is he in the same place?' Anna called back to Harper.

'I think so . . . came from the same direction.'

'I'm gone.'

Anna boosted herself over the window ledge and dropped to the ground. There was a stretch of open yard in front of her, before she got into the brush. She took a breath, and sprinted across it, keeping the house between her and the spot they thought Judge might be. She passed a bush, slowed, turned, dropped to her belly.

Light poured from the house and she could hear Harper

yelling, but could not make out what he was saying. And she heard Judge shouting back from the other side.

She had the gun and she thought: 'If I take him now . . .'

But if she tried and lost, she'd be dead, and so would Harper and Glass. She moved back a bit into the brush, turned on the flashlight and let the needle of light lead her toward the driveway. The moon was higher now and if she didn't look straight at it, she could see that lighter strip that marked the rut coming up from the road.

She turned off the flashlight: better to let her eyes adjust. A minute passed, and another, as she patiently moved toward the track. She couldn't afford to blunder into a tree, or twist an ankle.

Then Judge spoke: 'Hey.'

Close by; the hair rose on her neck. He was not within an arm's length, but within fifty feet, she thought. She couldn't hear him breathing, but she could hear the snap of twigs beneath his feet. He said it again, 'Hey.'

The gun was in her jacket pocket. She slumped onto the ground, eased her jacket up over her face. In the dark, with her dark hair, if she could keep her face covered, she'd be nearly invisible. She used to play war with her brothers, running around the house on a summer's night with guns made out of splintered boards. If you were dressed right, you could hide in a radish patch.

No radishes up here . . .

Then a thump, and the sound of a man's feet pounding on the hard earth, running, sprinting, but just a few feet. Again, close by – to the right? Twenty feet? Did the shadow move? She pointed the pistol at the shadow. The shadow was gray, man-shaped. Was it moving? It seemed to be moving toward her . . .

'HEY ANNA.' Not the shadow. Judge screamed at the house, and now he was off to her left, coming up on the window she'd crawled through. Would he step into the yard? How long a shot would it be? And she thought, *Time*.

But if she could take him out.

She pivoted in her spot, waiting. Then *crack*, and she saw the muzzle flash from the rifle. Seventy-five feet away, back in the brush. Judge was apparently moving around the house.

If she moved on him, while he was sitting still, he'd hear her: there was too much dry brush. She bit her lip, thinking, then turned down the road. The ground was rising beneath her, and she felt vulnerable, slinking along. Was he right there, behind her? Then the road began to fall. She stopped, drew back into the brush, and looked back toward the farmhouse. Nothing moving, nothing . . .

Crack . . .

She didn't see the flash, but it sounded as though it came from the back, the way Judge had been going. Anna started down the slope in a hurry, and when the yard light dropped out of sight, she turned the flashlight on again, gave it full play out in front, and ran down the hill.

Never in her life had her legs seemed shorter, the distances longer. Twice she thought she saw the gate ahead, and passed the spot with no gate in sight. The third time, it was the gate. What about the alarm? No help for it. She'd have to trip it to get the car in anyway. To save time, she pulled the gate open as she went through, then turned and ran up the dark road toward the car.

She was breathing hard when she got to it, fumbled for the key, found it, pushed the unlock button when she was still fifty feet downhill. The taillights blinked and the interior lights came on, and a few seconds later, she was cranking the engine over.

Lights on going back up the hill? Yes. The lights might push Judge back, might confuse him, get him running. They wouldn't have long . . .

She swung through the gate, and started up the dark lane, scanning the sides of the road. Had to keep moving fast: if he was planning to ambush her along the way, he might be only five feet from the car when she passed.

She kept her foot down and the car bounded up the ruts, throwing her around in the seat: no seat belt, she might not have time to get it off. At the top of the rise, she hit the high beams, caught the ranch house full in her headlights. No sign of Judge, nothing moving except herself in the car. And the car was moving fast – too fast. She skidded around the side of the ranch, straightened it out, spotted the back porch . . . hammered the car right to the edge of the porch, flicked open the door . . .

'JAKE!' she screamed. 'JAKE!'

Nobody there. She leaned out the door to scream again, and saved herself:

Crack . . .

And the passenger side window exploded, showering her with splinters of glass.

Crack . . .

The back window went out. The gunfire was coming from out in the darkness, back toward the buildings she thought might have been chicken houses.

She jammed the car into park and threw herself across the porch, through the door into the house.

Crawled frantically to the bathroom.

Harper was there, groaning, bleeding: 'Hit me,' he moaned, 'Got me from the side.' And he looked at her. 'Ah, Jesus, what happened to you, you're bleeding . . .'

Anna half-rose to look in the mirror: she had several small cuts on her face, apparently from the window glass. As soon as she saw them, they started to burn. But they weren't bad, she thought. She dropped back down to Harper.

'Let me see where you're hit, let me see.'

He rolled to show her; the slug had hit him in the pelvic bone, and angled down to come out the inside of his thigh. A purple stream of blood flowed from the lower part of the wound, which he'd partially stopped with a sock.

'Lord . . .' Anna dug into her coat, found the Hermès scarf she kept stuffed in the inside pocket, flipped it into a coil and bound the sock to the wound.

'Fuckin' killin' me,' Harper said.

Crack . . .

Apparent miss.

'We got to find some way out,' Anna said frantically. 'The car is right outside the door, but he's shooting it to pieces.'

'I don't know if I could make it out anyway,' Harper moaned. 'Do you think you could run for it? I can probably hold him off a while longer, he just got me with a lucky shot. If you could run to someplace where the phone would work . . .'

'God!' Anna, trying to think. She looked over the rim of the tub at Glass, who now had both eyes open. Glass recognized her, tried to speak, her broken lips working, but nothing came out.

Crack. Another miss. How do you miss a house?

'Let me go look at the car,' she said to Harper, and she scrambled back out into the hallway, through the back room. The car was still there, engine running.

Crack . . .

Missed again; she frowned, wondering what he was doing. He wasn't shooting at the car. She looked back toward the room where Harper was hidden, decided. She'd have to go. If he could hold them off for ten minutes, like he said, she might be able to get back.

She decided, and scrambled back to tell Harper.

Crack – and the house lights went, all at once.

'Coming for ya now, Anna,' the voice screamed.

'Come on in,' Anna shouted back. 'The cops will be here in five minutes, and then we're gonna kill you. You hear that? In five minutes, you're gonna die. Think about it, Stevie – five minutes, no more Steve. Just a piece of trash they're gonna throw in a hole, and nobody'll care. Not even your parents . . . Your parents'll be embarrassed to be related to you . . .'

Crack . . .

'That's right, piss him off,' Harper said, and she could hear the grin in his voice.

And that pissed her off. She was bleeding herself, she had the blood of two people dying on her hands, and one of those persons was trying to laugh.

'Goddamn you, Jake,' she hissed.

'What?'

'Keep your mouth shut. No matter what you hear, keep your mouth shut, and stay here. Don't move. Don't come to help me. Okay? Number two: You shoot the next thing that comes through the bathroom door. If I decide to come through, I'll tell you. Otherwise, just shoot it down.'

'What're you going to do?'

'I'm gonna kill this sonofabitch.'

'How?'

'I don't know,' she said, her voice deadly. 'But I'm going to.'

She moved out of the bathroom into the office, groping her way in the dark. She could hear the car engine running in the background – and then suddenly, it stopped.

And the voice: 'I killed the guy, didn't I?'

'Get the fuck away from here,' Anna screamed. 'Get away from me.'

He wasn't coming in – he was staying outside, and the next time he spoke, his voice came through a window in the back.

'I don't see anybody. I don't see anyone.' Then from another window, maybe the bathroom window: 'Where is everybody? Everybody else dead?'

Anna pushed further into the office room, found shelter behind a desk. Couldn't see much: when it came to it, she thought, it might be whoever saw the other person first. Fifty-fifty.

But he *knew* the place, and she didn't.

And now he was around in front. 'Hey Anna, come on out.'

'Get away from here,' she screamed. 'The cops are coming.'

'You were trying to run away from me, weren't you? You went down and got the car and you were all gonna run out of here, but something happened. And I know what it was. I hit the guy. I killed him. He's dead, isn't he? This is a thirty-ought-six, makes a big hole.'

His voice was working around to the side, now coming through a shot-out window behind her.

She needed a set: a movie set. And a scene . . .

'I'm coming in, Anna. I'm coming in. Bet you can't guess where . . .'

She moved to a corner of the room, pulled her knees up to her chin. She called softly, 'Jake, can you hear me? Jake, can you hear me? Are you there?'

'He's not there,' the voice said. 'Jake's dead. He's a dead motherfucker, Anna.'

'What do you want from me? What do you want? Tell me,' she screamed.

'All I wanted was the goddamn time of day, but you couldn't even give me the time of day. You'd fuck all those other people, but you wouldn't even talk to me. And you were like, you were perfect. You and me would've been perfect, but you wouldn't even talk.'

'I didn't even know you,' Anna shouted.

His voice came from a different window, pitched lower. 'I wanted to talk at the raid: you saw me at the raid, I was leading the raid, but you wouldn't even talk to me then.'

Pause: then the voice from another window.

'You saw me lead it, you wouldn't even talk to the leader. *I set the whole fucking thing up* after that night at the club when I first saw you, so you could judge me in action, and you wouldn't even talk. You just made fun of me with that pig. Which is dead, by the way. I cut that pig's throat, God, it bled, it bled about a gallon . . .'

He was circling the house, speaking from one window, then the next, then skipping a window.

From the back, now: 'I was really disappointed,' he said. 'And then at that golf place? When I'd set everything up, just you and me? And you did it again, you humiliated me – you *humiliated* me. What made you think you could get away with that? And now you're going to pay, Anna. Just like that pig.'

Anna whispered harshly, 'Jake, you gotta help me. Jake, I lost my glasses. Jake, I can't see . . . where's the gun? Jake?'

She heard him coming. She took her glasses off and put them in her pocket, and the world around her went soft. She pulled her knees up tight to her face, hunched her shoulders, pulled herself further back into the darkest corner of the room.

Heard his footfalls.

'Go away,' she cried. 'Just go away . . . haven't you done enough?'

'No.'

Now he was inside. Close. But she still couldn't see him. She tried to pull back even further, pull her knees higher. 'Go away,' she moaned, 'Please, just let me alone.'

'Look at me, Anna. I've got a gun.'

'I can't see,' she cried, 'I can't see anything, my glasses . . .'

A brilliant light cut across her face, just for an instant, and was gone.

'Aw. Little girl can't see?'

'Go away . . .'

He was coming in now, like a rat to a cheese. She was holding her breath, waiting for a blow, the wait unbearable . . .

'Here I am, Anna.' He was right there, on his hands and knees, only six feet away. She could see his face in a fuzzy way, the blond hair, the square chin, the eyes a little too close together.

He had the pistol in one hand, the muzzle pointing roughly toward her face. The butt of the rifle was on the floor, and he was leaning on it. 'We're gonna have some fun. We could have had some fun for a long time, if you'd come away from your bodyguard in that parking lot, but you had to do this.'

The tip of the barrel touched one cheek, which seemed to be turning black.

'Do what?' she whimpered.

'Fuckin' bite me,' he said. He moved closer, his hand still at the cheek. 'So it's payback time, Anna. Steve is gonna have lots of fun . . .'

Close enough: 'Have fun with this,' Anna said. And the way she said it startled him. She could see well enough to identify the flinch, the sudden clutching fear, and then she opened her knees.

The pistol was there, of course, between her thighs, and

pointing at the middle of his throat.

He had just enough time to say, 'Don't.'

Anna shot him.

And sat for three full seconds in dazed, blinded silence, Steve Judge slumped in front of her. He hadn't jerked back, or been thrown back: he'd simply gone straight down. She fumbled her glasses out of her pocket, pushed them back on her nose, tried to stand up.

'Jake?' she called weakly.

'Anna?' He was close. She took the flash from her pocket and shined it back toward the bathroom. Harper was propped in the doorway, the rifle in his hand, a long trail of blood behind him, his face as pale as parchment.

'I killed him,' Anna said.

At that moment, Judge stood up.

His eyes were crazy and half of his neck seemed to be missing. But he had one hand clasped to the wound and he pushed up and pivoted toward her, his eyes crazy, his mouth open, the white teeth straining at her.

Anna stepped back, thrust the pistol out, and fired into his chest from six inches: one, two, three, and Judge went down again. Harper, behind her, was shouting, 'No more, Anna,' but Anna stepped over Judge and fired two more shots into his head.

This time he didn't move.

'Asshole,' Anna snarled. She was still pulling the trigger, the clicks echoing in the suddenly silent shambles.

Anna carried Pam to Harper's car, brushed glass fragments

off the seat and put her down. Harper was too heavy: he crawled, dazed, to the porch, and Anna turned the half-wrecked vehicle around until she could get him in the passenger side and wedge the door closed. Something was wrong with the door, but it seemed to hold.

Her scalp was bleeding badly; every time she put her right hand to her ear, it came away with a palm full of blood. She pointed the car down the drive, and took it out as easily as she could.

They'd come in and out the same way each time, and that was the way she knew: there might have been a faster way to get an ambulance out to them, but she didn't have time to look.

She tried the phone after five minutes. No connection. She tried again at seven or eight minutes, without luck. At ten minutes, she got 911.

'My God, everybody's shot,' she babbled as she guided the car to the side of the road. She knew about where she was, gave enough direction that an ambulance could find them.

She called Wyatt, told him.

He was still shouting questions when she dropped the phone.

Chapter 31

Anna Batory was waiting at the dock when they came in on the *Lost Dog*, Creek and Glass with another couple, a pair of gay and ferociously competitive endodontists.

Creek cut the outboard when they were fifty feet from the berth, reached over the side, released the transom lock and pulled the motor out of the water. The boat's momentum carried it gracefully on, and then Creek pushed the tiller over and it turned, slowed, slowed more, and Glass stepped over the rail onto the finger pier, dropped the bow line over a cleat and snubbed the boat off.

Anna stood up, brushed off her butt. 'How'd it go?'

Glass was bubbling: 'It was amazing. These things, there was a boat, I mean . . .'

'Spit it out,' Creek laughed.

'Some of those boats were as big as locomotives. And they were this close,' Glass said, spreading her hands a foot apart. 'One guy got hit in a turn, and he called this other guy an asshole, and they're gonna fight when they get back.'

The beating barely showed on her anymore: when she'd gone into the hospital, the doctors were afraid that her brain had been permanently damaged. As it was, she'd been almost herself in a week, and out of the hospital in two. At four weeks, the bruising had faded, and the cuts were healed. She looked like somebody had scrubbed parts of her face with a Brillo pad, and her nose wasn't as straight as it once had been, but she no longer looked like she might die.

She still had headaches, though: the doctors said they might continue for a while. Maybe a long while. On the other hand, they might stop. Any day now. Or something like that.

Creek, a month later, was almost as good as new; was beginning to talk about the whole episode as a myth that might have happened to someone else. As a good story, to be embroidered upon, on slow nights in the truck.

Anna was the only one who still hurt.

The cuts on her face had all been minor. The cut in her scalp had been deeper, and had done something to the hair follicles: a thin, knife-edge line of hair was growing out white. The doctors said it would probably never be black again; but it might. Or something.

But her main problem was Harper.

After she'd shot Judge, she'd turned, and in the light of Judge's flash, had seen Harper crawling toward her, trying to help her. Answering her cries for help. When it had turned out that Anna had been mouse-trapping Judge – when she'd emptied the pistol into Judge's head – something had changed.

He loved her, he said, but he wasn't coming around. She could feel him avoiding her. She pushed, tried to talk: and only once got him going, after a two-martini dinner, and he talked about her face when she'd fired the last shots into Judge.

Anna realized that she frightened him. She didn't want to, but she did.

The endodontists helped clean up the boat, and said good-bye.

'Are we going for beer?' Anna asked Glass.

'God, I hope so. My throat is full of dust.'

'When's he gonna let you drive?' Anna asked.

'Mmm, I've got no definite commitment, but I'm thinking to myself, probably in the beer can races, next week.'

Behind her, Creek rolled his eyes, and Glass said, 'Creek.'

'What?'

'I felt your eyes rolling.'

'Aw, Jesus Christ,' Creek said.

They went down the street to a diner, and found another two dozen racers around the bar and in the dining room. Anna ordered a cheeseburger and a Diet Coke, Creek and Glass got beers. After a while, Creek and Anna began talking about the next night: they would be back on the street in twenty-four hours.

'What we gotta start doing is, we gotta start looking for more feature stuff. There's no good reason we couldn't set up a feature every day just to get the cameras rolling,' Creek said.

'Oh, bullshit, Creek, you know that half the time we can't sell . . .'

''Cause we haven't been concentrating on the angles. You gotta have the right angle on this kind of thing . . .'

'I think somebody's calling me,' Glass said after a while.

She picked up her second beer and headed for another table of boat racers, was greeted with a chorus of Heys.

'She gets along with them,' Anna said, watching her.

'Because she's a macho freak,' Creek said. 'You oughta see her out there on the foredeck. She's like a machine with the pole, going end-for-end, she never loses track . . . She's gonna be a good spinnaker guy.'

'What does she think about your gay endodontist pals?'

'Ah, she was sort of suspicious; you know, she's sort of a 'phobe. But those guys are so fuckin' mean that she couldn't help liking them.'

Creek laughed, and looked so basically happy that Anna laughed with him and said, 'God, Creek, you're gonna start checking out strollers, next thing.'

'Nah,' he said, looking after Glass. Then he turned back to Anna and dropped his voice: 'What's with Jake?'

'Aw, man.' Anna said. The smile died on her face. No tears, but her chin trembled, and she pushed her glasses up her nose. 'It's just . . . God, I don't know.'

'You still in love with him?'

'I don't even know if I ever was,' she said. 'I could have been, I think. But we never had a chance.'

'Aw, he'll straighten out.' He took a pull at his Corona, but his eyes never left Anna's.

She shook her head: 'You know what, Creek? He's not coming back. He's just not.'

'I'm sorry, Anna.'

'Man, there's only been two guys in my whole life that I ever felt quite like that about,' she said. She tried a smile. 'At least I know I can still feel like that about a guy.'

'Mmm.' Creek looked away, out the window, at the marina, and the forest of masts, waiting for the sea.

Later that night, with Glass asleep in his bed, Creek sat in his cluttered living room reading *Sherlock Holmes and the Red Demon*. He turned the last page, sighed, put the book down and his feet up. Thought about a beer, rejected the thought. Finally got a sweatshirt, let himself out, quietly, not to disturb Glass.

He took his Ford pickup out of the Marina, caught the San Diego for a couple of stops, exited on Wilshire, loafed down past UCLA.

The apartment complex was just past Westwood, one of the glittering glass towers on the south side of the street. The night crew knew most of the bigger complexes – rich people died in them on a regular basis. But even if he hadn't known where it was through the night crew, he would have gone directly to it anyway: he'd cruise the place a dozen times in the past week, unable to make himself stop.

This time he did stop, walked across the parking structure in the crisp night air.

Apartment 976. The place had double doors, and just inside, a row of brass mailboxes. He found 976. Looked at it for a long ten seconds, shook his head, pressed the buzzer.

Five seconds later, a man's voice, baritone, not unlike Judge's voice.

'Who is it?'

'My name's Creek,' he said. 'Is this Clark?'

'Yes?'

'I've come to see you about a woman,' Creek said.

Strait

Kit Craig

When urbane, attractive Will Strait comes to teach at Evard College, the close-knit community of the isolated university campus welcomes him with open arms. But Clair Sailor, whose husband Nick was responsible for employing Strait, senses something wrong. As her friends desert her, as her children are ostracized and a series of increasingly frightening accidents begins to plague her family, Clair is convinced Strait is to blame.

The more she learns of Strait, and the secret he hides behind his all-too-perfect facade of family and career, the more Clair is sure that the man her husband invited into their lives is intent on destroying them. But can Clair convince anyone else of what is happening? Before it's too late?

0 7472 4937 7

HEADLINE
FEATURE

Watch Me

A. J. Holt

FBI agent Jay Fletcher's life is her work, and she knows her work, using her computer genius to bring to justice some of America's most brutal murderers, can save lives. Her special project, C-BIX, a programme that can flush potential serial killers out of innocent databases, is about to reap rich rewards for her agency, yet somehow Jay isn't the heroine she should be. For C-BIX is swift, effective and, at the moment, illegal . . .

Sidelined to a fire-investigation unit in Santa Fe, Jay cannot bear to walk away from C-BIX. And when she gets wind of a local serial killer, she can't resist trying to track him down. It is then that Jay stumbles on the haul of her career – an Internet network of serial killers hidden behind a computer role-playing game. One by one, Jay begins to hunt down the network's members, dispensing her own brand of swift justice, whilst the monstrous leader of the group, the Iceman, remains a single step ahead of her.

Eventually, pursued by her own desperate demons from the past, Jay Fletcher must come face to face with a terrible truth: you set a thief to catch a thief, and to catch a serial killer she's become the very thing she abhors . . .

0 7472 4933 4

A selection of bestsellers from Headline

STRAIT	Kit Craig	£5.99 ☐
DON'T TALK TO STRANGERS	Bethany Campbell	£5.99 ☐
HARVEST	Tess Gerritsen	£5.99 ☐
SORTED	Jeff Gulvin	£5.99 ☐
INHERITANCE	Keith Baker	£5.99 ☐
PRAYERS FOR THE DEAD	Faye Kellerman	£5.99 ☐
UNDONE	Michael Kimball	£5.99 ☐
THE VIG	John Lescroart	£5.99 ☐
ACQUIRED MOTIVE	Sarah Lovett	£5.99 ☐
THE JUDGE	Steve Martini	£5.99 ☐
BODY BLOW	Dianne Pugh	£5.99 ☐
BLOOD RELATIONS	Barbara Parker	£5.99 ☐

All Headline books are available at your local bookshop or newsagent, or can be ordered direct from the publisher. Just tick the titles you want and fill in the form below. Prices and availability subject to change without notice.

Headline Book Publishing, Cash Sales Department, Bookpoint, 39 Milton Park, Abingdon, OXON, OX14 4TD, UK. If you have a credit card you may order by telephone – 01235 400400.

Please enclose a cheque or postal order made payable to Bookpoint Ltd to the value of the cover price and allow the following for postage and packing:

UK & BFPO: £1.00 for the first book, 50p for the second book and 30p for each additional book ordered up to a maximum charge of £3.00.

OVERSEAS & EIRE: £2.00 for the first book, £1.00 for the second book and 50p for each additional book.

Name ....

Address ....

....

....

If you would prefer to pay by credit card, please complete:
Please debit my Visa/Access/Diner's Card/American Express (delete as applicable) card no:

Signature .... Expiry Date ....